George Manville Fenn

In Honour's Cause

George Manville Fenn

In Honour's Cause

ISBN/EAN: 9783337186227

Printed in Europe, USA, Canada, Australia, Japan

Cover: Foto ©Andreas Hilbeck / pixelio.de

More available books at **www.hansebooks.com**

CONTENTS.

IN HONOUR'S CAUSE.

CHAPTER I.

TWO YOUNG COURTIERS.

" HA—ha—ha—ha !"

A regular ringing, hearty, merry laugh—just such an outburst of mirth as a strong, healthy boy of sixteen, in the full, bright, happy time of youth, and without a trouble on his mind, can give vent to when he sees something that thoroughly tickles his fancy.

Just at the same time the heavy London clouds which had been hanging all the morning over the Park opened a little to show the blue sky, and a broad ray of sunshine struck in through the anteroom window and lit up the gloomy, handsome chamber.

Between them—the laugh and the sunshine—they completely transformed the place, as the lad who laughed threw himself into a chair, and then jumped up again in a hurry to make sure that he had not snapped in two the sword he wore in awkward fashion behind him.

The lad's companion, who seemed to be about a couple of years older, faced round suddenly from the other end of the room, glanced sharply at one of the doors, and then said hurriedly :

" I say, you mustn't laugh like that here."

"It isn't broken," said he who had helped to make the solemn place look more cheerful.

"What, your sword? Lucky for you. I told you to take care how you carried it. Easy enough when you are used to one."

The speaker laid his left hand lightly on the hilt of his own, pressed it down a little, and stood in a stiff, deportment-taught attitude, as if asking the other to study him as a model.

"But you mustn't burst out into guffaws like that in the Palace."

"Seems as if you mustn't do anything you like here," said the younger lad. "Wish I was back at Winchester."

"Pooh, schoolboy! I shall have enough to do before I make anything of you."

"You never will. I'm sick of it already: no games, no runs down by the river or over the fields; nothing to do but dress up in these things, and stand like an image all day. I feel just like a pet monkey in a cage."

"And look it," said the other contemptuously.

"What!" said the boy, flushing up to the temples, as he took a step toward the speaker, and with flashing eyes looked him up and down. "Well, if you come to that, so do you, with your broad skirts, saltbox pockets, lace, and tied-up hair. See what thin legs you've got too!"

"You insolent—— No, I didn't mean that;" and an angry look gave place to a smile. "Lay your feathers down, Master Frank Gowan, and don't draw your skewer; that's high treason in the King's Palace. You mustn't laugh here when you're on duty. If there's any fighting to be done, they call in the guard; and if any one wants to quarrel, he must go somewhere else."

"I don't want to quarrel," said the boy, rather sulkily.

"You did a moment ago, for all your hackles were sticking up like a gamecock's."

"Well, I don't now, Drew," said the boy, smiling

frankly; "but the place is all so stiff and formal and dull, and I can't help wanting to be back in the country. I used to think one was tied down there at the school, but that was free liberty to this."

"Oh, you young barbarian! School and the country! Right enough for boys."

"Well, we're boys."

The other coughed slightly, took a measured pace or two right and left, and gave a furtive glance at his handsome, effeminate face and slight form in the glass. Then he said, rather haughtily:

"You are, of course; but I should have thought that you might have begun to look upon me as a man."

"Oh, I will, if you like," said the other, smiling,—"a very young one, though. Of course you're ever so much older than I am. But there, I'm going to try and like it; and I like you, Forbes, for being so good to me. I'm not such a fool as not to know that I'm a sort of un-licked cub, and you will go on telling me what I ought to do and what I oughtn't. I can play games as well as most fellows my age; but all this stiff, starchy court etiquette sickens me."

"Yes," said his companion, with a look of disgust on his face; "miserable, clumsy Dutch etiquette. As different from the grand, graceful style of the old *régime* and of St. Germains as chalk is from cheese."

"I say," said the younger of the pair merrily, after imitating his companion's glances at the doors, "you must not talk like that here."

"Talk like what?" said the elder haughtily.

"Calling things Dutch, and about St. Germains. I say, isn't that high treason?"

"Pooh!—Well, yes, I suppose you're right. Your turn now. But we won't quarrel, Franky."

"Then, don't call me that," said the boy sharply; "Frank, if you like. I did begin calling you Drew. It's shorter and better than Andrew. I say, I am ever so much obliged to you."

"Don't mention it. I promised Sir Robert I would look after you."

"Yes, my father told me."

"And I like Lady Gowan. She's as nice as she is handsome. My mother was something like her."

"Then she must have been one of the dearest, sweetest, and best ladies that ever lived," cried the boy warmly.

"Thank ye, Frank," said the youth, smiling and laying his arm in rather an affected manner upon the speaker's shoulder, as he crossed his legs and again posed himself with his left hand upon his sword hilt. But there was no affectation in the tone of the thanks expressed; in fact, there was a peculiar quiver in his voice and a slight huskiness of which he was self-conscious, and he hurriedly continued :

"Oh yes, I like you. I did at first ; you seemed so fresh and daisy-like amongst all this heavy Dutch formality. I'll tell you everything ; and if you can't have the country, I'll see that you do have some fun. We'll go out together, and you must see my father. He's a fine, dashing officer ; he ought to have had a good command given him. I say, Frank, he's great friends with Sir Robert."

"Is he ? My father never said so."

"Mine did ; but—er—I think there are reasons just now why they don't want it to be known. You see your father's in the King's Guards."

"Yes."

"Well, and mine isn't. He is not very fond of the House of Brunswick."

"I say, mind what you are saying."

"Of course. I shouldn't say it to any one else. But, I say, what made you burst out into that roar of laughter about nothing ?"

"It wasn't about nothing," said Frank, with a mirthful look in his eyes.

"What was it then? See anything out of the window?"

"Oh no; it was in this room."

"Well, what was it?"

"Oh, never mind."

"Here, I thought we were going to be great friends."

"Of course."

"Then friends must confide in one another. Why don't you speak?"

"I don't want to offend you."

"Come, out with it."

"Well, I was laughing at you."

"Why?"

"To see you admiring yourself in the glass there."

Andrew Forbes made an angry gesture, but laughed it off.

"Well, the Prince's pages are expected to look well," he said.

"You always look well without. But I wish you wouldn't do that sort of thing; it makes you seem so girlish."

There was another angry gesture.

"I can't help my looks."

"There, now, you're put out again."

"No, not a bit," said the youth hastily. "I say, though, you don't think much of the King, do you?"

"Oh yes," said Frank thoughtfully; "of course."

"Why?"

"Why? Well, because he's the King, of course. Don't you?"

"No! I don't think anything of him. He's only a poor German prince, brought over by the Whigs. I always feel ready to laugh in his face."

"I say," cried Frank, looking at his companion in horror, "do you know what you are saying?"

"Oh yes; and I don't think a great deal of the Prince. My father got me here; but I don't feel in my place, and I'm not going to sacrifice myself, even if I am one of the pages. I believe in the Stuarts, and I always shall."

"This is more treasonable than what you said before."

"Well, it's the truth."

"Perhaps it is. I say, you're a head taller than I am."

"Yes, I know that."

"But you don't seem to know that if you talk like that you'll soon be the same height."

"What, you think my principles will keep me standing still, while yours make you grow tall ? "

"No. I think if it gets known you'll grow short all in a moment."

"They'll chop my head off? Pooh! I'm not afraid. You won't blab."

"But you've no business to be here."

"Oh yes, I have. Plenty think as I do. You will one of these days."

"Never! What, go against the King !"

"This German usurper you mean. Oh, you'll come over to our side."

"What, with my father in the King's Guards, and my mother one of the Princess's ladies of the bed-chamber ! Nice thing for a man to have a son who turned traitor."

"What a red-hot Whig you are, Frank! You're too young and too fresh to London and the court to understand these things. He's King because a few Whigs brought him over here. If you were to go about London, you'd find every one nearly on the other side."

"I don't believe it."

"Come for a few walks with me, and I'll take you where you can hear people talking about it."

"I don't want to hear people talk treason, and I can't get away."

"Oh yes, you can; I'll manage it. Don't you want to go out?"

"Yes; but not to hear people talk as you say. They must be only the scum who say such things."

"Better be the scum which rises than the dregs which sink to the bottom. Come, I know you'd like a run."

"I'll go with you in the evening, and try and catch some of the fish in that lake."

"What, the King's carp! Ha—ha! You want old Bigwig to give you five pounds."

"Old Bigwig—who's he?"

"You know; the King."

"Sh!"

"Pooh! no one can hear."

"But what do you mean about the five pounds?"

"Didn't you hear? They say he wrote to some one in Hanover saying that he could not understand the English, for when he came to the Palace they told him it was his, and when he looked out of the window he saw a park with a long canal in it, and they told him that was his too. Then next day the ranger sent him a big brace of carp out of it, and when they told him he was to behave like a prince and give the messenger five guineas, he was astonished. Oh, he isn't a bit like a king."

"I say, do be quiet. I don't want you to get into trouble."

"Of course you don't," said the lad merrily. "But you mustn't think of going fishing now. Hark! there are the Guards."

He hurried to the window, through which the trampling of horses and jingling of spurs could be heard, and directly after the leaders of a long line of horse came along between the rows of trees, the men gay in their scarlet and gold, their accoutrements glittering in the sunshine.

"Look well, don't they?" said Andrew Forbes. "They

ought to have given my father a command like that. If he had a few regiments of horse, and as many of foot, he'd soon make things different for old England."

"I say, do be quiet, Drew. You'll be getting in trouble, I know you will. Why can't you let things rest."

"Because I'm a Royalist."

"No, you're not; you're a Jacobite. I say, why do they call them Jacobites? What Jacob is it who leads them?"

"And you just fresh from Winchester! Where's your Latin?"

"Oh, I see," cried the boy : "Jacobus—James."

"That's right; you may go up. I wish I was an officer in the Guards."

"Behave yourself then, and some day the Prince may get you a commission."

"Not he. Perhaps I shall have one without. Well, you'll go with me this evening?"

"Oh, I don't know."

"That means you would if you could. Well, I'll manage it. And I'll soon show you what the people in London think about the King."

"Sh! some one coming."

The two lads darted from the window as one of the doors was thrown open, and an attendant made an announcement which resulted in the pages going to the other end to open the farther door and draw back to allow the Prince and Princess with a little following of ladies to pass through, one of the last of the group turning to smile at Frank Gowan and kiss her hand.

The boy turned to his companion, looking flushed and proud as the door was closed after the retiring party.

"How handsome the Princess looked!" he said.

"Hush!" said Forbes. "Pretty well. Not half so nice as your mother; you ought to be proud of her, Frank."

"I am," said the boy.

"But what a pity!"

"What's a pity?"

"That she should be in the Princess's train."

"A pity! Why the Princess makes her quite a friend."

"More pity still. Well, we shall be off duty soon, and then I'll get leave for us to go."

"I don't think I want to now."

"Well I do, and you'd better come and take care of me, or perhaps I shall get into a scrape."

"No, you will not. You only talk as you do to banter me."

"Think so?" said Andrew, with a peculiar smile. "Well, we shall see. But you'll come?"

"Yes," said Frank readily, "to keep you from getting into a scrape."

CHAPTER II.

THE water in the canal looked ruddy golden in the light glowing in the west, as the two pages passed through the courtyard along beneath the arches, where the soldiers on guard saluted them, and reached the long mall planted with trees.

"Halt! One can breathe here," said Frank, with his eyes brightening. "Come along; let's have a run."

"Quiet, quiet! What a wild young colt you are! This isn't the country."

"No; but it looks like a good makeshift!" cried Frank.

"Who's disloyal now? Nice way to speak of his Majesty's Park! I say, you're short enough as it is."

"No, I'm not. I'm a very fair height for my age. It's you who are too long."

"Never mind that; but it's my turn to talk. Suppose you get cut shorter for saying disloyal things under the window of the Palace."

"Stuff! Rubbish!"

"Is it? They give it to the people they call rebels pretty hard for as trifling things," said Andrew, flushing a little. "They flogged three soldiers to death the other day for wearing oak apples in their caps."

"What? Why did they wear oak apples in their caps?"

"Because it was King Charles's day; and they've fined

and imprisoned and hung people for all kinds of what they call rebellious practices."

"Then you'd better be careful, Master Drew," said Frank merrily. "I say, my legs feel as if they were full of pins and needles, with standing about so much doing nothing. It's glorious out here. Come along ; I'll race you to the end of this row of trees."

"With the people who may be at the windows watching us ! Where's your dignity ? "

"Have none. They wouldn't know it was us. We're not dressed up now, and we look like any one else."

"I hope not," said Andrew, drawing himself up.

Frank laughed, and his companion looked nettled.

"It is nothing to laugh at. Do you suppose I want to be taken for one of the mob ? "

"Of course I don't. But, I say, look. I saw a fish rise with a regular flop. That must be a carp. They are fond of leaping out of the water with a splash. I say, this isn't a lake, is it ? Looks like a river."

"Oh, I don't know—yes, I do. Some one said it's part of a stream that comes down from out beyond Tyburn way, where they hang the people."

"Ugh ! Horrid ! But look here, the water seems beautifully clear. Let's get up to-morrow morning and have a bathe. I'll swim you across there and back."

"Tchah ! I say, Frank, what a little savage you are ! "

"Didn't know there was anything savage in being fond of swimming."

"Well, I did. A man isn't a fish."

"No," said Frank, laughing ; "he's flesh."

"You know, now you belong to the Prince's household, and live in the King's Palace, you must forget all these boyish follies."

"Oh dear ! " sighed Frank.

"We've got to support the dignity of the establishment as gentlemen in the Prince's train. It wants it badly enough, with all these sausage-eating Vans and Vons and Herrs. We must do it while things are in this state for the sake of old England."

"I wish I had never come here," said Frank dismally. "No, I don't," he added cheerfully. "I am close to my mother, and I see father sometimes. I say, didn't he look well at the head of his company yesterday?"

"Splendid!" cried Andrew warmly. "Here, cheer up, young one; you'll soon get to like it; and one of these days we'll both be marching at the heads of our companies."

"Think so?" cried Frank eagerly.

"I'm sure of it. Of course I like our uniform, and thousands of fellows would give their ears to be pages at the Palace; but you don't suppose I mean to keep on being a sort of lapdog in the anteroom. No. Wait a bit. There'll be grand times by-and-by. We must be like the rest of the best people, looking forward to the turn of the tide."

Frank glanced quickly at the tall, handsome lad at his side, and quickened his pace and lengthened his stride to keep up with him, for he had drawn himself up and held his head back as if influenced by thoughts beyond the present. But he slackened down directly.

"No need to make ourselves hot," he said. "You'd like to run, you little savage; but it won't do now. Let the mob do that. Look! that's Lord Ronald's carriage. Quick! do as I do."

He doffed his hat to the occupant of the clumsy vehicle, Frank following his example; and they were responded to by a handsome, portly man with a bow and smile.

"I say," said Frank, "how stupid a man looks in a great wig like that."

"Bah! It is ridiculous. Pretty fashion these Dutchmen have brought in."

" Dutchmen ! What Dutchmen ? "

"Oh, never mind, innocence," said Andrew, with a half laugh. "Just think of how handsome the gentlemen of the Stuart time looked in their doublets, buff boots, long natural hair, and lace. This fashion is disgusting. Here's old Granthill coming now," he continued, as the trampling of horses made him glance back. "Don't turn round; don't see him."

"Very well," said Frank with a laugh; "but whoever he is, I don't suppose he'll mind whether I bow or not."

"Whoever he is!" cried Andrew contemptuously. "I say, don't you know that he is one of the King's Ministers ? "

"No," said Frank thoughtfully. "Oh yes, I do; I remember now. Of course. But I've never thought about these things. He's the gentleman, isn't he, that they say is unpopular ? "

"Well, you are partly right. He is unpopular; but I don't look upon him as a gentleman. Hark ! hear that ? " he shouted excitedly, as he looked eagerly toward where the first carriage had passed round the curve ahead of him on its way toward Westminster.

"Yes, there's something to see. I know; it must be the soldiers. Come along; I want to see them."

"No, it isn't the soldiers; it's the people cheering Lord Ronald on his way to the Parliament House. They like him. Every one does. He knows my father, and yours too. He knows me. Didn't you see him smile ? I'll introduce you to him first time there's a levee."

"No, I say, don't," said Frank, flushing. "He'd laugh at me."

"So do I now. But this won't do, Frank ; you mustn't be so modest."

The second carriage which had passed them rolled on round the curve in the track of the first and disappeared, Frank noticing that many of the promenaders turned

their heads to look after it.   Then his attention was taken
up by his companion's words.

"Look here," he cried; "I want to show you Fleet
Street."

"Fleet Street," said Frank,—"Fleet Street: Isn't that
where Temple Bar is?"

"Well done, countryman! Quite right."

"Then I don't want to see it."

"Why?" said Andrew, turning to him in surprise at
the change which had come over his companion, who
spoke in a sharp, decided way.

"Because I read about the two traitors' heads being
stuck up there on Temple Bar, and it seems so horrible
and barbarous."

"So it is, Frank," whispered Andrew, grasping his
companion's arm. "It's horrible and cowardly. It's
brutal; and—and—I can't find words bad enough for the
act of insulting the dead bodies of brave men after they've
executed them. But never mind; it will be different some
day. There, I always knew I should like you, young one.
You've got the right stuff in you for making a brave, true
gentleman; and—and I hope I have."

"I'm sure you have," cried Frank warmly.

"Then we will not pass under the old city gate, with its
horrible, grinning heads: but I must take you to Fleet
Street; so we'll go to Westminster Stairs and have a boat
—it will be nice on the river."

"Yes, glorious on an evening like this," cried Frank
excitedly; "and, I say, we can go round by Queen Anne
Street."

"What for? It's out of the way."

"Well, only along by the Park side; I want to look up
at our windows."

"But your mother's at the Palace."

"Father might be at home; he often sits at one of the
windows looking over the Park."

"Come along then," cried Andrew mockingly; "the good little boy shall be taken where he can see his father and mother, and—hark! listen! hear that?" he cried excitedly.

"Yes. What can it be?"

"The people hooting and yelling at Granthill. They're mobbing his carriage. Run, run! I must see that."

Andrew Forbes trotted off, forgetting all his dignity as one of the Princess's pages, and heedless now in his excitement of what any of the well-dressed promenaders might think; while, laughing to himself the while, Frank kept step with him, running easily and looking quite cool when the tall, overgrown lad at his side, who was unused to outdoor exercise, dropped into a walk panting heavily.

"Too late!" he said, in a tone of vexation. "There the carriage goes, through Storey's Gate. Look at the crowd after it. They'll hoot him till the soldiers stop them. Come along, Frank; we shall see a fight, and perhaps some one will be killed."

CHAPTER III.

THE excitement of his companion was now communicated to Frank Gowan, and as fast as they could walk they hurried on toward the gate at the corner of the Park, passing knot after knot of people talking about the scene which had taken place. But the boy did not forget to look eagerly in the direction of the row of goodly houses standing back behind the trees, and facing on to the Park, before they turned out through the gate and found themselves in the tail of the crowd hurrying on toward Palace Yard.

The crowd grew more dense till they reached the end of the street with the open space in front, where it was impossible to go farther.

"Let's try and get round," whispered Andrew. "Do you hear? They're fighting!"

Being young and active, they soon managed to get round to where they anticipated obtaining a view of the proceedings; but there was nothing to see but a surging crowd, for the most part well dressed, but leavened by the mob, and this was broken up from time to time by the passing of carriages whose horses were forced to walk.

"Oh, if we could only get close up!" said Andrew impatiently. "Hark at the shouting and yelling. They are fighting with the soldiers now."

"No, no, not yet, youngster," said a well-dressed man

close by them; "it's only men's canes and fists. The Whigs are getting the worst of it; so you two boys had better go while your heads are whole."

"What do you mean?"

"Oh, I know a Whig when I see one, my lad."

"Do you mean that as an insult, sir?" said Andrew haughtily.

"No," said the gentleman, smiling; "only as a bit of advice."

"Because if you did——" said Andrew, laying his hand upon his sword.

"You would send your friends to me, boy, and then I should not fight. Nonsense, my lad. There, off with your friend while your shoes are good, and don't raise your voice, or some one will find out that you are from the Palace. Then the news would run like wild fire, and you ought to know by this time what a cowardly London mob will do. They nearly tore Sir Marland Granthill out of his carriage just now. There, if I am not on your side, I speak as a friend."

Before Andrew could make any retort, and just as Frank was tugging at his arm to get him away, they were separated from the stranger by a rush in the crowd, which forced them up into a doorway, from whose step they saw, one after the other, no less than six men borne along insensible and bleeding from wounds upon the head, while their clothes were nearly torn from their backs.

Then the shouting and yelling began to subside, and the two lads were forced to go with the stream, till an opportunity came for them to dive down a side street and reach the river stairs, where they took a wherry and were rowed east.

"I should like to know who that man was," said Andrew, after a long silence, during which they went gliding along with the falling tide.

"He spoke very well," said Frank,

" Yes; but he took me for a Whig," said the youth indignantly.

" But, I say, what was it all about ? "

" Oh, you'll soon learn that," replied Andrew.

" Is there often fighting like this going on in the streets ? "

" Every day somewhere."

" But why ? " said Frank anxiously.

" Surely you know ! Because the Whigs have brought in a king that the people do not like. There, don't talk about it any more now. I want to sit still and think."

Frank respected his companion's silence, and thankful at having escaped from the heat and pressure of the crowd, he sat gazing at the moving panorama on either side, enjoying the novelty of his position.

His musings upon what he saw were interrupted by his companion, who repeated his former words suddenly in a low, thoughtful voice, but one full of annoyance, as if the words were rankling in his memory.

" He took me for a Whig."

Then, catching sight of his companion's eyes watching him wonderingly :

" What say ? " he cried. " Did you speak ? "

" No; you did."

" No, I said nothing."

Frank smiled.

" Yes, you said again that the man in the crowd took you for a Whig."

" Did I? Well, I was thinking aloud then."

" Where to, sir ? " asked the waterman, as he sent the boat gliding along past the gardens of the Temple, " London Bridge ? "

" No; Blackfriars."

A few minutes later they landed at the stairs, and, apparently quite at home in the place, Andrew led his companion in and out among the gloomy-looking streets

and lanes of the old Alsatian district, and out into the con-
tinuation of what might very well be called High Street,
London.

" Here we are," he said, as he directed their steps toward one of the narrow courts which ran north from the
main thoroughfare ; but upon reaching the end, where a
knot of excitable-looking men were talking loudly upon
some subject which evidently interested them deeply, one
of the loudest speakers suddenly ceased his harangue and
directed the attention of his companions to the two lads.
The result was that all faced round and stared at them
offensively, bringing the colour into Andrew's cheeks and
making Frank feel uncomfortable.

" Let's go straight on," said the former ; and drawing
himself up, he walked straight toward the group, which
extended right across the rough pavement and into the
road, so that any one who wanted to pass along would be
compelled to make a circuit by stepping down first into the
dirty gutter.

" Keep close to me ; don't give way," whispered Andrew ;
and he kept on right in the face of the staring little crowd,
till he was brought to a standstill, not a man offering to
budge.

" Will you allow us to pass ? " said Andrew haughtily.

" Plenty o' room in the road," shouted the man who had
been speaking.   " Aren't you going up the court ? "

" I do not choose to go into the muddy road, sir,
because you and your party take upon yourselves to block
up the public way," retorted Andrew, giving the man so
fierce a look that for a moment or two he was somewhat
. abashed, and his companions, influenced by the stronger
will of one who was in the right, began to make way for
the well-dressed pair.

But the first man found his tongue directly.

" Here, clear the road ! " he cried banteringly.   " Make
way, you dirty blackguards, for my lords.   Lie down, some

of you, and let 'em walk over you. Lost your way, my lords? Why didn't you come in your carriages, with horse soldiers before and behind? But it's no use to-day; the Lord Mayor's gone out to dinner with his wife."

A roar of coarse laughter followed this sally, which increased as another man shouted in imitation of military commands:

"Heads up; draw skewers; right forward; ma-rr-rr-ch!"

"Scum!" said Andrew contemptuously, as they left the little crowd behind.

"Is the city always like this?" said Frank, whose face now was as red as his companion's.

"Yes, now," said Andrew bitterly. "That's a specimen of a Whig mob."

"Nonsense!" cried Frank, rather warmly; "don't be so prejudiced. How can you tell that they are Whigs?"

"By the way in which they jumped at a chance to insult gentlemen. Horse soldiers indeed! Draw swords! Oh! I should like to be at the head of a troop, to give the order and chase the dirty ruffians out of the street, and make my men thrash them with the flats of their blades till they went down on their knees in the mud and howled for mercy."

"What a furious fire-eater you are, Drew," cried Frank, recovering his equanimity. "We ought to have stepped out into the road."

"For a set of jeering ruffians like that!" cried Andrew. "No. They hate to see a gentleman go by. London is getting disgraceful now."

"Never mind. There, I've seen enough of it. Let's get down to the river again, and take a boat; it's much pleasanter than being in this noisy, crowded place."

"Not yet. We've a better right here than a mob like that. It would be running away."

"Why, how would they know?" said Frank merrily.

"I should know, and feel as if I had disgraced

myself," replied Andrew haughtily. "Besides, I wanted to see a gentleman."

"What, up that court?" said Frank, looking curiously at his companion.

"Yes, a gentleman up that court. There are plenty of gentlemen, and noblemen, too, driven nowadays to live in worse places than that, and hide about in holes and corners."

"Oh, I say, don't be so cross because a lot of idlers would not make way."

"It isn't that," said the youth. "It half maddens me sometimes."

"Then don't think about it. You are always talking about politics. I don't understand much about them, but it seems to me that if people obey the laws they can live happily enough."

"Poor Frank!" said Andrew mockingly. "But never mind. You have got everything to learn. This way."

The boy was thinking that he did not want to learn "everything" if the studies were to make him as irritable and peppery as his companion, when the imperative order to turn came upon him by surprise, and he followed Andrew, who had suddenly turned into a narrower court than the one for which he had first made, and out of the roaring street into comparative silence.

"Where are you going?"

"This way. We can get round by the back. I want to see my friend."

The court was only a few feet wide, and the occupants of the opposing houses could easily have carried on a conversation from the open windows; but these occupants seemed to be too busy, for in the glimpses he obtained as they passed, Frank caught sight of workmen in paper caps and dirty white aprons, and boys hurrying to and fro carrying packets of paper.

But he had not much opportunity for noticing what

business was being carried on, for they soon reached the
end of the court, where a fresh group of men were
standing listening to a speaker holding forth from an open
window, and the lad fully expected a similar scene to that
which had taken place in the main street.

But people made way here, and Andrew, apparently
quite at home, turned to the left along a very dirty lane,
plunged into another court, and in and out two or three
times in silence, along what seemed to the boy fresh from
quaint old Winchester a perfect maze.

" I say, Drew," he said at last, "you must have been
here before."

"I? Oh yes! I know London pretty well. Now
down here."

He plunged sharply now round a corner and into the
wide court he had at first made for, but now from its
northern end. So quick and sudden was the movement
made that the two lads, before they could realise the fact,
found themselves in another crowd, which filled this court
from end to end. The people composing it were principally
of the rough class they had seen grouped at the lower part,
but fully half were workmen in their shirt sleeves, many
of them with faces blackened by their occupation, while
a smaller portion was well dressed, and kept on moving
about and talking earnestly to the people around.

" Too late," said Andrew, half to himself.

" Yes ; we shall have to go round and reach the street
farther along," said Frank quietly. " We don't want to
push through there."

" But it's here I want to see my friend."

" Does he live in this place ? "

" No ; but he is sure to be there—in that house."

The lad nodded at a goodly sized mansion about half-way
down the court; and even from where they stood they
could make out that the place was crowded, and that
something exciting was going on, the crowd in the court

outside being evidently listeners, trying to catch what was said within, the murmurs of which reached the two lads' ears.

All at once there was a loud outburst of cheering, shouting, and clapping of hands, as if at the conclusion of a speech; and this was responded to by a roar of yells, hoots, and derisive cries from the court.

"Oh! too late—too late," muttered Andrew. "Silence, you miserable crew!"

But where heard his words passed unnoticed, those around evidently taking them as being addressed to the people in the great tavern.

"Let's get away—quickly, while we can," said Frank, with his lips close to his companion's ear; but the lad shook him off angrily, and then uttered a cry of rage, for at that moment there was a loud crash and splintering of glass, the mob in the court, evidently under the direction of the well-dressed men, hurling stones, decayed vegetables, and rubbish of all kinds in at the windows of the tavern.

This was responded to by shouts of defiance and a rain of pots, glasses, and pails of water; and even the pails themselves were hurled down upon the heads of the people in the court, while a long oaken settle which came clattering down fell crosswise, the end coming within a few inches of a man's head.

"Oh, do let's go!" Frank very naturally said, gripping Andrew's arm hard.

But the lad seemed to have suddenly gone crazy with excitement, shouting and gesticulating with the rest, directing his words, which sounded like menaces, at the people crowding at the window of the house.

At this the mob cheered, and, as if in answer to his orders, made a rush for the door, surging in, armed for the most part with sticks, and as if to carry the place by assault.

" I can't go and leave him," thought Frank ; and directly after—as he looked up the court toward the end by which they had entered, and down from which they had been borne until they were nearly opposite the house—"if I wanted to," he muttered, as he saw how they were wedged in and swayed here and there by the crowd.

The noise increased, the crowd beginning to cheer loudly, as crowds will when excited by the chance to commit mischief, and Frank remained ignorant of the reasons which impelled them on, as he watched the exciting scene. The sound of blows, yells of defiance, and the angry, increasing roar of those contending within the house, set his heart beating wildly. For a few minutes, when he found himself shut in by the people around, a feeling of dread came over him, mingled with despair at his helplessness, and he would have given anything to be able to escape from his position ; but as he saw man after man come stumbling out bruised and bleeding, and heard the cries of rage uttered by those who hemmed him in, the feeling of fear gave place to indignation, and this was soon followed by an angry desire to help those who, amidst the cheers of their fellows, pressed forward to take the place of those who were beaten back.

It was at this moment that he saw two well-dressed men waving swords above their heads, and, white now with rage, Andrew turned to him.

" The cowards—the dogs !" he whispered. " Frank lad, you will be man enough to help ? "

" Yes, yes," panted the boy huskily, with a sensation akin to that which he had felt when hurt in his last school fight, when, reckless from pain, he had dashed at a tyrannical fellow-pupil who was planting blow after blow upon him almost as he pleased.

" Draw your sword then, and follow me."

Frank made a struggle to wrench himself free, but it was in vain.

" I can't!" he panted. " My arms are pinned down to my side."

"So are mine," groaned Andrew. "I can hardly breathe."

A furious yell of rage arose from fifty throats, and the two lads saw the attacking party come tumbling one over the other out of the tavern, driven back by the defenders, who charged bravely out after them, armed with stick and sword ; and almost before the two lads could realise their position they found themselves being carried along in the human stream well out of reach of the blows being showered down by the rallying party from the house, who literally drove their enemies before them, at first step by step, striking back in their own defence, rendered desperate by their position, then giving up and seeking refuge in flight, when with a rush their companions gave way more and more in front.

For a few minutes the heat and pressure were suffocating, and as Frank and his companion were twisted round and borne backward, the former felt a peculiar sensation of giddy faintness, the walls swam round, the shouting sounded distant, and he was only half-conscious when, in company with those around, he was shot out of the narrow entrance of the court ; and then the terrible pressure ceased.

CHAPTER IV.

FRANK'S EYES BEGIN TO OPEN.

EVERYTHING else seemed to the boy to cease at the same time, till he became conscious of feeling cold and wet, and heard a voice speaking:

"And him quite a boy too. I wonder what his mother would say.—Here, drink this, my dear; and don't you never go amongst the crazy, quarrelsome wretches again. I don't know what we're coming to with their fighting in the streets. It isn't safe to go out, that it isn't. Drink it all, my dear; you'll feel better then. I always feel faint myself if I get in a crowd."

Frank had heard every word, with a peculiar dreamy feeling that he ought to listen and know who the boy was so addressed. Then he became conscious that it was he who was drinking from a mug of water held to his lips; and, opening his eyes, he looked up into a pleasant, homely face bending over him in an open doorway, upon whose step he was sitting, half leaning against the doorpost, half against the woman who was kneeling at his side.

"Ah, that's better," said the woman. "Now you take my advice; you go straight home. You're not a man yet, and don't want to mix yourself up with people fighting about who ought to be king. Just as if it matters to such as us. As I often tell my husband, he'd a deal better attend to getting his living, and not go listening to people argifying whether it's to be the king on the other side of the water or on this. I say, give me peace and—— You feel better, don't you?"

"Yes, thank you," said Frank, making an effort to rise; but the moment he tried the ground seemed to heave up beneath him.

"You're not quite right yet, my dear; sit still a little longer. And you too with a sword by your side, just as if you wanted to fight. I call it shocking, that I do."

"But I am much better," said Frank, ignoring the woman's remarks. "I can walk now. But did you see my friend?"

"Your friend? Was it one of those rough-looking fellows who came running down with you between 'em, and half a dozen more hunting them, and they pushed you in here and ran on?"

"Oh no. My friend is a—— Ah! there he is. Drew! Drew!"

Looking white and strange, Andrew Forbes was coming hurriedly down the narrow lane, when he heard his name pronounced, and looking round he caught sight of his companion, and hurried to his side.

"Oh, here you are!" he panted. "I've been looking for you everywhere. I was afraid they had taken you to the watch-house. I couldn't keep by you; I was regularly dragged away."

"Were you hurt?" cried Frank excitedly.

"Felt as if my ribs were all crushed in. But what about you?"

"I suppose I turned faint," said Frank. "I didn't know anything till I found myself here, and this lady giving me water."

"Oh, I'm not a lady, my dear," said the woman, smiling, —"only a laundress as does for some of the gentlemen in the Temple. There now, you both go home; for I can see that you don't belong to this part of the town. I dare say, if the truth was known, he brought you here."

Frank was silent, but he glanced up at Andrew, who was carefully rearranging his dress and brushing his cocked hat.

"I thought as much," said the woman. "He's bigger, and he ought to have known better than to get into such a shameful disturbance.—What's that?—Lor' bless me, no, my dear! Why should I take a mark for a mug of cold water? Put it in your pocket, my dear; you'll want it to buy cakes and apples. I don't want to be paid for doing a Christian act."

"Then thank you very much," said Frank warmly, offering his hand.

"Oh! if you will," said the woman, "I don't mind. It isn't the first time I've shook hands with a gentleman."

The woman turned, smiling with pleasure, as if to repeat the performance with Andrew Forbes; but as she caught sight of his frowning countenance her hand fell to her side, and she dropped the youth a formal curtsey.

"Thank you for helping my friend," he said.

"You're quite welkum, young man," said the woman tartly. "And if you'll take my advice, you won't bring him into these parts again, where they're doing nothing else but swash-buckling from morning to night. The broken heads I've seen this year is quite awful, and——"

Andrew Forbes did not wait to hear the rest, but passed his arm through that of Frank, and walked with him swiftly down the narrow lane toward the waterside.

"You're not much hurt, are you?"

"Oh no. It was the heat and being squeezed so."

"Don't say you were frightened, lad!" cried Andrew.

"I was at first; but when I saw the people being knocked about so, I felt as if I wanted to help."

"That's right. You've got the right stuff in you. But wasn't it glorious?"

"Glorious?"

"Yes!" cried Andrew excitedly. "It was brave and

gallant to a degree. The cowardly brutes were three times as many as the others."

"Oh no; the other side was the stronger, and they ought to have whipped."

"Nonsense! You don't know what you are talking about," said Andrew warmly. "The miserable brutes were five or six times as strong, and the brave fellows drove them like a flock of sheep right out of the court, and scattered them in the street like chaff. Oh, it made up for everything!"

Frank put his hand to his head.

"I don't quite understand it," he said. "My head feels swimming and queer yet. I thought the people in the house were the weaker—I mean those who dashed out shouting, 'Down with the Dutchmen!'"

"Of course," cried Andrew; "that's what I'm saying. It was very horrible to be situated as we were."

"Yes, horrible," said Frank quietly.

"Not able to so much as draw one's sword."

"Too much squeezed together."

"Yes," said Andrew, with his face flushed warmly. "I did cry out and shout to them to come on; but one was so helpless and mixed-up-like that people could hardly tell which side they belonged to."

"No," said Frank drily; "it was hard."

He looked meaningly at his companion as he spoke; but Andrew's eyes were gazing straight before him, and he was seeing right into the future.

"Did you see your friend you wanted to speak to?" said Frank, as they reached the river-side.

"See him? Yes, fighting like a hero; but I couldn't get near him. Never mind; another time will do. I little thought I should come to the city to-day to see such a victory. It all shows how things are working."

"Going to ride back by boat?" said Frank, as if to change the conversation.

"Oh yes; we can't go along Fleet Street and the Strand. The streets will be full of constables, and soldiers out too I dare say. They're busy making arrests I know; and if we were to go along there, as likely as not there'd be some spy or one of the beaten side ready to point us out as having been in it."

They reached the stairs, took their place in a wherry, and as they leaned back and the waterman tugged at his oars, against tide now, Frank said thoughtfully:

"I say, what would have happened if somebody had pointed us out?"

"We should have been locked up of course, and been taken before the magistrate to-morrow. Then it would all have come out about our being there, and—ha—ha—ha!— the Prince would have had vacancies for two more pages. —I shouldn't have cared."

"I should," said Frank quickly, as he saw in imagination the pained faces of father and mother.

"Well, of course, so should I. Don't take any notice of what I said. Besides, we can be so useful as we are."

"How?" said Frank thoughtfully. "It always seems to me that we are but a couple of ornaments, and of no use at all."

"Ah! wait," said Andrew quietly. Then, as if feeling that he had been in his excitement letting his tongue run far too fast, he turned to his companion, and said gently:

"You are the son of a gallant officer and a beautiful lady, and I know you would not say a word that would injure a friend."

"I hope not," said Frank, rather huskily.

"I'm sure you would not, or I should not have spoken out as I have. But don't take any notice; you see, a man can't help talking politics at a time like this. Well, when will you come to the city again?"

"Never, if I can help it," said Frank shortly; and that

night in bed he lay sleepless for hours, thinking of his companion's words, and grasping pretty clearly that King George I. had a personage in his palace who was utterly unworthy of trust.

"And it's such a pity," said the boy, with a sigh. "I like Andrew Forbes, though he is a bit conceited and a dandy; but it seems as if I ought to speak to somebody about what I know. My father—my mother? There is no one else I should like to trust with such a secret. But he has left it to my honour, and I feel pulled both ways. What ought I to do?"

He fell asleep at last with that question unanswered, and when he awoke the next morning the thought repeated itself with stronger force than before, "Why, he must be at heart a traitor to the King!" and once more in dire perplexity Frank Gowan asked himself that question, "What shall I do?"

CHAPTER V.

THE OFFICER OF THE GUARDS.

IT would not take much guessing to arrive at the course taken by Frank Gowan. He cudgelled his brains well, being in a kind of mental balance, which one day went down in favour of making a clean breast of all he knew to his mother; the next day up went that side, for he felt quite indignant with himself.

Here, he argued, was he, Frank Gowan, freshly appointed one of the Prince's pages, a most honourable position for a youth of his years, and with splendid prospects before him, cut off from his old school friendships, and enjoying a new one with a handsome, well-born lad, whom, in spite of many little failings at which he laughed, he thoroughly admired for his dash, courage, and knowledge of the world embraced by the court. This lad had completely taken him under his wing, made him proud by the preference he showed for his companionship, and ready to display his warm admiration for his new friend by making him the confidant of his secret desires; and what was he, the trusted friend, about to do? Play traitor, and betray his confidence. But, then, was not Andrew Forbes seeking to play traitor to the King?

"That's only talk and vanity," said the boy to himself. "He has done nothing traitorous; but if I go and talk to any one, I shall have done something—something cruelly treacherous, which must end in the poor fellow being sent away from the court in disgrace, perhaps to a severe punishment."

He turned cold at the thought.

"They hang or behead people for high treason," he thought; "and suppose Drew were to be punished like that, how should I feel afterward? I should never forgive myself. Besides, how could I go and worry my mother about such a business as this? It is not women's work, and it would only make her unhappy."

But he felt that he might go to his father, and confide the matter to him, asking him on his honour not to do anything likely to injure Drew.

But he could not go and confide in his father, who was generally with his regiment, and they only met on rare occasions. By chance he caught sight of him on duty at the Palace with the guard, but he could not speak to him then. At other times he was at his barrack quarters, and rarely at his town house across the Park in Queen Anne Street. This place was generally only occupied by the servants, Lady Gowan having apartments in the Palace.

Hence Frank felt that it would be very difficult to see his father and confide in him, and he grew more at ease in consequence. It was the way out of a difficulty most dear to many of us—to wit, letting things drift to settle themselves.

And so matters went on for some days. Frank had been constantly in company with Andrew Forbes, and his admiration for the handsome lad grew into a hearty friendship, which was as warmly returned.

"He can't help knowing he is good-looking," thought Frank, "and that makes him a bit conceited; but it will soon wear off. I shall joke him out of it. And he knows so much. He is so manly. He makes me feel like an awkward schoolboy beside him."

Frank knitted his brow a little over these thoughts, but he brightened up with a laugh directly.

"I think I could startle him, though," he said half aloud, "if I had him down at Winchester."

It was one bright morning at the Palace, where he was standing at the anteroom window just after the regular morning military display, and he had hardly thought this when a couple of hands were passed over his eyes, and he was held fast.

"I know who it is," he said, "though you don't think it. It's you, Drew."

"How did you know?" said that individual merrily.

"Because you have hands like a girl's, and no lady here would have done it."

"Bah! hands like a girl's indeed! I shall have to lick you into a better shape, bear. You grow too insolent."

"Very well; why don't you begin?" said Frank merrily.

"Because I don't choose. Look here, young one; I want you to come out with me for a bit this afternoon."

"No, thank you," replied the boy, shaking his head. "I don't want to go and see mad politicians quarrel and fight in the city, and get nearly squeezed to death."

"Who wants you to? It's only to go for a walk."

"That was going for a walk."

"Afraid of getting your long hair taken out of curl?" said Andrew banteringly.

"No; that would curl up again; but I don't want to have my clothes torn off my back."

"You won't get them torn off this afternoon. I want you to come in the Park there, down by the water-side. You'll like that, savage."

"Yes, of course. Can we fish?"

"No, that wouldn't do; but I tell you what: you can take some bread with you and feed the ducks."

"Take some bread with me and feed the ducks!" cried the boy contemptuously.

"Well, that's what I'm going to do. Then you won't come?"

"Yes, I will, Drew, if I can get away. Of course I will. Oh, mother, you there?"

Lady Gowan had just entered the room, and came up toward the window, smiling, and looking proud, happy, and almost too young to be the mother of the stout, manly-looking boy who hurried to meet her; and court etiquette did not hinder a loving exchange of kisses. She shook hands directly after with Andrew Forbes.

"I am afraid that you two find it very dull here sometimes," she said.

"Well, yes, Lady Gowan," said the youth, "I often do. I'm not like Frank here, with his friends at court."

"But I have so few opportunities for seeing him, Mr. Forbes. After a few weeks, though, I shall be at home yonder, and then you must come and spend as much time there as you can with Frank."

Andrew bowed and smiled, and said something about being glad.

"Frank dear," said Lady Gowan, "I have had a letter from your father this morning, and I have written an answer. He wants to see you for a little while. He is at home for a couple of days. You can take the note across."

"Yes," cried Frank, flushing with pleasure; but the next moment he turned to Andrew with an apologetic look.

"What is the matter?" said Lady Gowan. "Am I interrupting some plans?"

"Oh, nothing, nothing, Lady Gowan," said Andrew, warmly.

"I was going out with Drew, mother; but we can go another time. He will not mind."

"But it was only this afternoon."

"Oh!" cried Lady Gowan, "he will be back in an

hour or so. I am glad that you were going out, my boy;
it will make a little change for you. And I am very glad,
Mr. Forbes, that he has found so kind a companion."

Andrew played the courtier to such perfection, that as
soon as she had passed out of the room with her son Lady
Gowan laughed merrily.

"In confidence, Frank," she said, "and not to hurt
Mr. Forbes's feelings, do not imitate his little bits of
courtly etiquette. They partake too much of the dancing-
master. I like to see my boy natural and manly. There,
quick to your father, with my dear love, and tell him I am
longing for his leave, when we can have, I hope, a couple
of months in Hampshire."

"Hah!" ejaculated Frank, as he hurried across the
Park; "a couple of months in Hampshire. I wonder how
long it will be?"

Ten minutes later he was going up two steps at a time
to the room affected by his father in the spacious house
in Queen Anne Street, where, as soon as he threw open
the door, he caught sight of the lightly built but vigorous
and active-looking officer in scarlet, seated at the window
overlooking the Park, deep in a formidable-looking letter.

"Ah, Frank, my dear boy," he cried, hurriedly thrusting the letter into his breast, "this is good. What, an
answer already? You lucky young dog, to have the best
woman in the world for a mother. Bless her!" he cried,
kissing the letter and placing it with the other; "I'll read
that when you are gone. Not come to stay, I suppose?"

"No, father," cried the boy, whose eyes flashed with
excitement as they took in every portion of the officer in
turn. "I've only come to bring the note; mother said
you wished to see me."

"Of course, my boy, so as to have a few words. I just
catch a glimpse of you now and then, but it's only a nod."

"And I do often long so to come to you," cried Frank,
with his arm upon his father's shoulder.

"That's right, boy," said Sir Robert, smiling and taking his hands; "but it wouldn't do for the captain of the guard to be hugging his boy before everybody, eh? We men must be men, and do all that sort of thing with a nod or a look. As long as we understand each other, my boy, that's enough, eh?"

"Yes, father, of course."

"But bravo, Frank; you're growing and putting on muscle. By George, yes! Arms are getting hard, and—— good——fine depth of chest for your age. Don't, because you are the Prince's page, grow into a dandy maccaroni milk-sop, all scent, silk, long curls, and pomatum. I want you to grow into a man, fit for a soldier to fight for his king."

"And that's what I want to do, father," said the lad proudly.

"Of course you do; and so you will. You are altering wonderfully, boy. Why, hallo! I say," cried the captain, with mock seriousness, as he held his son sidewise and gazed at his profile against the light.

"What's the matter, father?" cried Frank, startled.

"Keep your head still, sir; I want to look. Yes, it's a fact—very young and tender, but there it is; it's coming up fast. Why, Frank boy, you'll soon have to shave."

"What nonsense!" cried the boy, reddening partly at being laughed at, but quite as much with satisfaction.

"It's no nonsense, you young dog. There's your moustache coming, and no mistake. Why, if I had a magnifying-glass, I could see it quite plainly."

"I say, father, don't; I can't stop long, and—and—that teases one."

"Then I won't banter you, boy," cried Sir Robert, clapping him heartily on the shoulder; "but, I say, you know: it's too bad of you, sir. I don't like it."

"What is, father? What have I done?"

"Oh, I suppose you can't help it; but it's too bad of

you to grow so fast, and make your mother look an old woman."

"That she doesn't, father," cried the boy. "Why, she's the youngest-looking and most beautiful lady at court."

"So she is, my boy—so she is. Heaven bless her!"

"And as for you, father, you talk about looking old, and about me growing big and manly; I shall never grow into such a fine, handsome officer as you."

"Why, you wicked, parasitical, young court flatterer!" cried Sir Robert; "you're getting spoiled and sycophantish already."

"I'm not, father!" cried the boy, flushing; "it's quite true, every word of it. Everybody says what a noble-looking couple you are."

"Do they, my boy?" said the father more gently, and there was a trace of emotion in his tone. "But there's not much couple in it, living apart like this. Ah, well, we have our duty to do, and mine is cut out for me. But never mind the looks, Frank, my boy, and the gay uniform; it's the man I want you to grow into. But all the same, sir, nature is nature. Look there."

"What, at grandfather's portrait?"

"Yes, boy. You will not need to have yours painted, and I have not had mine taken for the same reason. Is it like me?"

"Yes, father. If you were dressed the same, it would be exactly like you."

"In twenty years' time it will do for you."

Frank laughed.

"But I say yes, sir," cried Sir Robert. "Why, in sixteen years' time, if I could have stood still, we two would be as much alike as a couple of peas. But in sixteen years perhaps I shall be in my grave."

"Father!"

"Well, I'm a soldier, my boy; and soldiers have to run risks more than other men."

" Oh, but you won't; you're too big and brave."

" Ha—ha—ha ! Flattering again. Why, Frank, I sometimes think I'm a coward."

"You! A coward! I should like to hear any one say so."

" A good many will perhaps, boy. But there, never
mind that ; and perhaps after all you had better not
follow my profession."

" What ! not be a soldier ! "

" Yes.   Do you really wish to be ? "

" Why of course, father ; I don't want to be a palace
lapdog all my life."

" Bravo, Frank ! well said !" cried the father heartily.
" Well, you come of a military family, and I dare say I can
get you a commission when the beard really does grow so
that it can be seen without an optic glass."

" Oh, I say, father, you're beginning to tease again.
I say, do get up and walk across the room."

" Eh ?   What for ? "

" I want to look at you."

Sir Robert smiled and shook his head.   Then, slowly
rising, he drew himself up in military fashion, and
marched slowly across the room and back, with his broad-
skirted scarlet and gold uniform coat, white breeches, and
high boots, and hand resting upon his sword hilt, and
looking the beau ideal of an officer of the King's Guards.

" There, have I been weak enough, Frank ?" he said,
stopping in front of his son, and laying his hands affectionately upon his shoulders. "All show, my boy. When
you've worn it as long as I have, you will think as little of
it ; but it is quite natural for it to attract a boy like you.
But now sit down and tell me a little about how you spend
your time.   I find that you have quite taken up with
Andrew Forbes. His father promised me that the lad
should try and be companionable to you. Forbes is an
old friend of mine still, though he is in disgrace at court.
How do you get on with Andrew?   Like him ?"

"Oh, very much, father."

"Well, don't like him too much, my boy. Lads of your age are rather too ready to make idols of showy fellows a year or two older, and look up to them and imitate them, when too often the idol is not of such good stuff as the worshipper. So you like him?"

"Yes, father."

"Kind and helpful to you?"

"Oh, very."

"Well, what is it?"

"What is what, father?"

"That cloudy look on your face. Why, Frank, I've looked at you so often that I can read it quite plainly. Why, you've been quarrelling with Andrew Forbes!"

"Oh no, father; we're the best of friends."

"Then what is it, Frank? You are keeping something back."

Sir Robert spoke almost sternly, and the son shrank from gazing in the fine, bold, questioning eyes.

"I knew it," said Sir Robert. "What is it, boy? Speak out."

It was the firm officer talking now, and Frank felt his breath come shorter as his heart increased the speed of its pulsations.

"Well, sir, I am waiting. Why don't you answer?"

"I can't, father."

"Can't? I thought my boy always trusted his father, as he trusts his son. There, out with it, Frank. The old saying, my lad, The truth may be blamed, but can never be shamed. What is it—some scrape? There, let's have it, and get it over. Always come to me, my boy. We are none of us perfect, so let there be no false shame. If you have done wrong, come to me and tell me like a man. If it means punishment, that will not be one hundredth part as painful to you as keeping it back and forfeiting my confidence in my dear wife's boy."

"Oh, I would come. I have wanted to come to you about this, but I felt that I could not."

"Why?"

"Because it would be dishonourable.'

"Perhaps that is only your opinion, Frank. Would it not be better for me to give you my opinion?"

The boy hesitated for a moment. Then quickly:

"I gave my word, father."

"To whom?"

"Andrew Forbes."

"Not to speak of whatever it is?"

"Yes, father."

Sir Robert Gowan sat looking stern and silent for a few moments as if thinking deeply.

"Frank boy," he said at last. "I am a man of some experience; you are a mere boy fresh from a country school, and now holding a post which may expose you to many temptations. I, then, as your father, whose desire is to watch over you and help you to grow into a brave and good man, hold that it would not be dishonourable for you to confide in me in every way. It can be no dishonour for you to trust me."

"Then I will tell you, father;" and the boy hastily laid bare his breast, telling of his adventures with Andrew Forbes, and how great a source of anxiety they had proved to be.

"Hah!" said Sir Robert, after sitting with knitted brows looking curiously at his son and hearing him to the end. "Well, I am very glad that you have spoken, my boy, and I think it will be right for you to stand your ground, and be ready to laugh at Master Andrew and his political associations. It is what people call disloyal and treasonable on one side; on the other, it is considered noble and right. But you need not trouble your head about that. Andrew Forbes is after all a mere boy, very enthusiastic, and led away perhaps by thoughts of the

Prince living in exile instead of sitting on the throne of England. But you don't want to touch politics for the next ten years. It would be better for many if they never touched them at all. There, I am glad you have told me."

"So am I now, father. But you will not speak about it all, so as to get Drew in disgrace?"

"I give you my word I will not, Frank. Oh, nonsense! It is froth—fluff; a chivalrous boy's fancy and sympathy for one he thinks is oppressed. No, Frank, no words of mine will do Drew Forbes any harm; but as for you—— "

"Yes, father."

"Do all you can to help him and hold him back. It would be a pity for him to suffer through being rash. They might treat it all as a boy's nonsense—— No, it would mean disgrace. Keep him from it if you can."

"I, father! He is so much older than I am, and I looked up to him."

"Proof of what I said, Frank," cried Sir Robert, clapping his son upon the shoulder. "He is a bright, showy lad; but you carry more ballast than he. Brag's a good dog, you know, but Holdfast's a better. Now, then, I think you ought to be going back. Good-bye, my boy. I look to you to be your mother's protector more and more. Perhaps in the future I may be absent. But you must go now, for I have an important letter to write. My dear love to your mother, and come to me again whenever you have a chance."

Sir Robert went down to the garden door with his son, and let him out that way into the Park.

"Mind," he said at parting. "Keep away from political mobs."

"I will," said Frank to himself, as he turned back. "Well, it will be all right going with Drew this afternoon, as it is only to feed the ducks."

CHAPTER VI.

FRANK FEEDS THE DUCKS.

SOMETHING very nearly akin to a guilty feeling troubled Frank upon meeting his fellow-page that afternoon; but his father's promise, in conjunction with his words respecting Andrew's actions being merely those of an enthusiastic boy, helped to modify the trouble he felt, and in a few minutes it passed off. For Andrew began by asking how his friend's father was, and praising him.

"I always liked your father, Frank," he said; "but he's far too good for where he is. Well, we're off duty till the evening. Ready for our run?"

"Oh yes, I'm ready," said Frank, laughing; "but you won't run unless somebody's carriage is being mobbed. You could go fast enough then."

"Well, of course I can run if I like. Come along."

"Where's the bread?" asked Frank.

"Bread? What bread? Are you hungry already?"

"No, no; the bread you talked about."

"The bread I talked about? What nonsense! I never said anything about bread that I can remember."

"Well, you said we were going to feed the ducks."

"Oh—h—h!" ejaculated Andrew; and he then burst into a hearty fit of laughter. "Of course: so I did. I didn't think of it. Well, perhaps we had better take some. Ring the bell, and ask one of the footmen to bring you some."

Frank thought it strange that his companion, after proposing that they should go and feed the ducks, had forgotten all about the bread.   However, he said no more, but rang, and asked the servant to get him a couple of slices.

The man stared, but withdrew, and came back directly.

"I beg your pardon, sir," he said; "but did you wish me to bring the bread here?"

"Certainly.   Be quick, please.   We are waiting to go out."

The man withdrew for the second time, and the lads waited chatting together till Andrew grew impatient.

"Ring again," he cried.   "Have they sent to have a loaf baked?   It's getting late.   Let's start.   Never mind the bread."

"Oh, let's have it now it's ordered.   How are we to feed the ducks without?"

"Throw them some stones," said Andrew mockingly. "Come along.   We'll look at other people feeding them— if there are any.   Look here; it's twenty minutes by that clock since you gave the order."

At that moment another footman opened the door, and held it back for one of his fellows to enter bearing a tray covered with a cloth, on which were a loaf, a butter-dish, knives, plates, glasses, and a decanter of water.

"Oh, what nonsense!" cried Andrew impatiently. "There, cut a slice, Frank, put it in your pocket, and come along, or we shall be late."

"I did not know that ducks had particular hours for being fed," thought the boy, as he cut into the loaf, and then hacked off two slices instead of one, the two men-servants standing respectfully back and looking on, both being too well trained to smile, as Frank thrust one slice into his pocket and offered the other to Andrew.

"Oh, I don't want it," he said impatiently.

"Better take it," cried Frank.   "I shan't give you any of mine."

Andrew hesitated for a moment, and then snatched a

handkerchief from his pocket, wrapped the slice in it, and thrust the handkerchief back.

"Perhaps I had better take one too," he said aloud; and then to his companion as they went out : "Makes one look so ridiculous and childish before the servants. They'll go chattering about it all over the place."

"Let them," said Frank coolly. "I don't see anything to be ashamed of."

"No," said Andrew, with something like a sneer, "you don't ; but you will some day. There, let's make haste."

It did not strike the lad that his companion's manner was peculiar, only that he felt it to be rather an undignified proceeding ; but he said nothing, and accommodating his stride to Andrew's long one, they crossed the courtyard, went out into the Park, and came in sight of the water glittering in the sun.

"There's a good place," said Frank. "Plenty of ducks close in."

"Oh, there's a better place round on the other side," said Andrew hastily. "Let's go there."

"Anywhere you like," said Frank, "so long as we're out here on the fresh grass again. What a treat it is to be among the green trees !"

"Much better than the country, eh ?"

"Oh no; but it does very well. I say, I wish we might fish."

"Oh, we'll go fishing some day. Walk faster; we're late."

"Fast as you like. What do you say to a run? You can run, you say, when you like."

"Oh no, we needn't run ; only walk fast."

"Or the ducks will be impatient," said Frank, laughing.

"Yes, or the ducks may be impatient," said Andrew to himself, as he led on toward the end of the ornamental water nearest to where Buckingham Palace now stands, and bore off to the left ; and when some distance back along the farther shore of the lake and nearly opposite to St. James's Palace, he said suddenly:

"Look, Frank, there is some one beforehand;" and he pointed to where a gentleman stood by the edge of the water shooting bits of biscuit with his thumb and finger some distance out, apparently for the sake of seeing the ducks race after them, some aiding themselves with their wings, and then paddling back for more.

The two lads walked up to where the gentleman was standing, and as he heard them approach he turned quickly, and Frank saw that he was a pale, slight, thin-faced, youngish-looking man who might be forty.

"Ah, Andrew," he said, "you here; how are you? You have not come to feed the ducks?"

"Oh yes, I have," said Andrew, giving the stranger a peculiar look; "and I've brought a friend with me. Let me introduce him. Mr. Frank Gowan, Captain Sir Robert Gowan's son, and my fellow-servant with his Royal Highness. Frank, this happens to be a friend of mine—Mr. George Selby."

"I am very glad to meet any friend of Andrew Forbes," said the stranger, raising his hat with a most formal bow. "I know Sir Robert slightly."

As he replaced his hat and smiled pleasantly to the salute Frank gave in return, he took a biscuit from his pocket, and began to break it in very small pieces, when, apparently without any idea of its looking childish, Andrew took out his piece of bread, and after a moment's hesitation Frank did the same, the ducks in his Majesty's "canal," as he termed it, benefiting largely by the result.

"Any news?" said Andrew, after this had been going on for some minutes, and as he spoke he turned his head and looked fixedly at Mr. Selby.

"No, nothing whatever; everything is as dull as can be," was the reply, and the fixed look was returned.

There seemed to be nothing in these words of an exciting nature, and Frank was intent upon a race between two green-headed drakes for a piece of crust which he had jerked out to a considerable distance; but all the same Andrew Forbes drew a deep breath, and his face flushed up. Then he glanced sharply at Frank, and looked relieved to find how his attention was diverted.

"Er—er—it is strange what a little news there is stirring nowadays," he said, huskily.

"Yes, very, is it not?" replied their new companion; "but I should have thought that you gentlemen, living as you do in the very centre of London life, would have had plenty to amuse you."

"Oh no," said Andrew, with a forced laugh. "Ours is a terrible humdrum life at the Palace, so bad that Gowan there is always wanting to go out into the country to find sport, and as he cannot and I cannot, we are glad to come out here and feed the ducks."

"Well," said the stranger gravely, jerking out a fresh piece of biscuit, "it is a nice, calm, and agreeable diversion. I like to come here for the purpose on Wednesday and Friday afternoons about this time. It is harmless, Forbes."

"Very," said the youth, with another glance at Frank; but he was breaking a piece of crust for another throw, and another meaning look passed between the two, Forbes seeming to question the stranger with his eyes, and to receive for answer an almost imperceptible nod.

"Yes, I like feeding the ducks," said Selby. "One acquires a good deal of natural history knowledge thereby, and also enjoys the pleasure of making new and pleasant friends."

This was directed at Frank, who felt uncomfortable, and made another bow, it being the proper thing to do, as his new acquaintance—he did not mentally call him friend— dropped a piece of biscuit, to be seized by a very fat duck, which had found racing a failure, and succeeded best by coming out of the water, to snap up the fragments which dropped at the distributors' feet.

As the piece of biscuit fell, the stranger formally and in a very French fashion raised his cocked hat again.

" And so you find the court life dull, Mr. Gowan," he said.

"Yes," said the boy, colouring. " You see, I have not long left Winchester and my school friends. Miss the ga——sports; but Andrew Forbes has been very friendly to me," he added heartily.

" Of course you feel dull coming among strangers; but never fear, Mr. Gowan, you will have many and valuable friends I hope, your humble servant among the number. It must be dull, though, at this court. Now at Saint——"

" That's my last piece of bread, Selby," said Andrew hastily. " Give me a bit of biscuit."

" Certainly, if I have one left," was the smiling reply, with another almost imperceptible nod. " Yes, here is the last. Of course you must find it dull, and we have not seen you lately at the club, my dear fellow. By the way, why not bring Mr. Gowan with you next time?"

" Oh, he would hardly care to come. He does not care for politics, eh, Frank?"

" I don't understand them," said the boy quietly.

"You soon will now you are resident in town, Mr. Gowan; and I hope you will favour us by accompanying your friend Forbes. Only a little gathering of gentlemen, young, clever, and I hope enthusiastic. You will come?"

" I—that is——"

"Say yes, Frank, and don't be so precious modest. He will bring up a bit of country now and then. But he is fast growing into a man of town."

"What nonsense, Drew!" cried the boy quickly.

"Yes, what nonsense!" said the new acquaintance,

smiling. "Believe me, Mr. Gowan, we do not talk of town at our little social club. I shall look forward to seeing you there as my guest. What do you say to Monday?"

"I say yes for both of us," said Andrew quickly.

"I am very glad. There, my last biscuit has gone, so till Monday evening I will say good-bye—*au revoir.*"

"Stick to the English, Selby," said Andrew sharply. "French is not fashionable at St. James's."

"You are quite right, my dear Forbes. Good-bye, Mr. Gowan. It is a pleasure to shake your father's son by the hand. Till Monday then, my dear Forbes;" and with a more courtly bow than ever, the gentleman stalked slowly away, with one hand raising a laced handkerchief to his face, the other resting upon his sword hilt.

"Glad we met him," said Andrew quickly, and he looked unusually excited. "One of the best of men. You will like him, Frank."

"But you should not have been so ready to accept a stranger's invitation for me."

"Pooh! he isn't a stranger. He'll be grateful to you for going. Big family the Selbys, and he'll be very rich some day. Wonderful how fond he is, though, of feeding the ducks."

"Yes, he seems to be," said Frank; and he accompanied his companion as the latter strolled on now along the bank after finishing the distribution of bread to the feathered fowl by sending nearly a whole biscuit skimming and making ducks and drakes on the surface of the water; but the living ducks and drakes soon ended that performance and followed the pair in vain. For Andrew Forbes had suddenly become very thoughtful; while his companion also had his fit of musing, which ended in his saying to himself:

"I wish I was as clever as they are. It almost seemed as if they meant something more than they said. It comes from living in London I suppose, and perhaps some day I shall get to be as sharp and quick as they are.   Perhaps, though, it is all nonsense, and they meant nothing.   But I wish Drew had not said we'd go.   I'm not a man, and what do I want at a club?   I don't know anything that they'd want to know, living as I do shut up in the Palace."

But there Frank Gowan was wrong, for what went on at St. James's Palace in the early days of the eighteenth century was of a great deal of interest to some people outside, and he never forgot the feeding of the ducks.

CHAPTER VII.

HOW FRANK GOWAN GREW ONE YEAR OLDER IN ONE DAY.

"I SEEM to have so many things to worry me," thought Frank. "Any one would think that in a place like this without lessons or studies there would be no unpleasantries; but as soon as I've got the better of one, another comes to worry me."

This was in consequence of the invitation for the following Monday. His mind was pretty well at ease about his confidential talk with his father; but he was nervous and uncomfortable about the visit to the club, and several times over he was on the point of getting leave to go across to Sir Robert to ask his opinion as to whether he ought to go.

"I can't go and bother my mother about such a thing as that," he mused. "I ought to be old enough now to be able to decide which is right and which is wrong. Drew thinks and talks like a man, while it seems to me that I'm almost a child compared to him.

"Well, let's try. Ought I to go, or ought I not? There can't be any harm to me in going. There may be some friends of Drew's whom I shan't like; but if there are I needn't go again. It's childish, when I want to become more manly, to shrink from going into society, like a great girl.—I'll go. If there's any harm in it, the harm is likely to be to Drew, and—yes, of course; I could save him from getting into trouble.

"Then I ought to go," he said to himself decisively, and

he felt at ease, troubling himself little more about the matter, but going through his extremely easy duties of waiting in the anteroom, bearing letters and messages from one part of the Palace to the other, and generally looking courtly as a royal page.

Then the Monday came, with Andrew Forbes in the highest of spirits, and ready to chat about the country, his friend's life at Winchester, and to make plans for running down to see them when his father and mother went out of town.

"I don't believe you'd like it if you did come," said Frank.

"Oh yes, I should.   Why not?"

"Because you'd find some of the lanes muddy, and the edges of the roads full of brambles.   You wouldn't care to see the birds and squirrels and hedgehogs, nor the fish in the river, nor the rabbits and hares."

"Why, those are all things that I am dying to see in their natural places.   I wish you would not think I am such a maccaroni.   Why, after the way in which you have gone on about the country, isn't it natural that I should want to see more of it?"

He kept on in this strain to such an extent that, instead of convincing his companion, he overdid it, and set him wondering.

"I don't understand him a bit," he said to himself; "and I wish he wouldn't keep on calling me my dear fellow and slapping me on the back.   I never saw him so wild and excitable before."

The lad's musings were interrupted to his great disgust by Andrew coming behind him with the very act and words which had annoyed him.   For he started and turned angrily upon receiving a sounding slap between the shoulders.

"Why, Frank, my dear fellow," cried Andrew, "what ails you?   Hallo! eyes flashing lightning and brow heavy with thunder.   Has the gentle, shepherd-like swain from the country got a temper of his own ? "

" Of course I have," cried the boy angrily.   " Why don't you let it lie quiet, and not wake it up by doing that ! "

" Is the temper like a surly dog, then ? " cried Andrew, laughing mockingly.   " Will it bite ? "

" Yes, if you tease it too much," snapped out Frank.

" Oh, horrible !   You alarm me ! " cried Andrew, bounding away in mock dread.

" Don't be a fool ! " cried Frank angrily ; and the tone and gesture which accompanied the request sobered Andrew in a moment, though his eyes looked his surprise that the boy whom he patronised with something very much like contempt could be roused up into showing so much strength of mind.

" What's the matter, Frank boy ? " he said quietly ; " eaten something that hasn't agreed with you ? "

" No," said the boy sharply.   " I haven't eaten it—I can't swallow it."

" Eh ?   What do you mean ?   What is it ? "

" You," said Frank shortly.

" Oh ! " said Andrew, raising his eyebrows a little and staring at him hard ; " and pray how is it you can't swallow me ? "

" Because you will keep going on in this wild, stupid way, and treating me as if I were some stupid boy whom you meant to make your butt."

" What, to-day ? "

" Yes, and yesterday, and the day before that, and last week, and—and ever since I've been here."

" Then why didn't you tell me of it if I did, like a gentleman should, and not call me a fool ? "

" I didn't ; I said don't be a fool."

" Same thing.   You insulted me."

" Well, you've insulted me dozens of times."

"And amongst gentlemen, sir," continued Andrew haughtily, and ignoring the other's words, "these things mean a meeting. Gentlemen don't wear swords for nothing. They have their honour to defend. Do you understand?"

"Oh yes, I understand," said Frank warmly. "I haven't been behind the trees in the big field at Winchester a dozen times perhaps without knowing what that means."

"Pish!" said Andrew contemptuously; "schoolboys' squabbles settled with fists. Black eyes, bruised knuckles, and cut lips."

"Well, schoolboys don't wear swords," cried Frank, who was by no means quelled. "I learned fencing, and I dare say I could use mine properly. I've fenced with my father in the holidays many a time."

"Then I shall send a friend to you, sir," said Andrew fiercely.

"You mean an enemy," said Frank grimly.

"A friend, sir—a friend," said Andrew haughtily; "and you can name your own."

"No, I can't, and I shouldn't make such a fool of myself," cried Frank defiantly.

"You are very free, sir, with your fools," cried Andrew. "Such language as this is not fitted for the anteroom in the Palace."

"I suppose I may call myself a fool if I like."

"When you are alone, sir, if you think proper, but not in my presence. Perhaps you will have the goodness to name your friend now; it will save time and trouble."

Frank looked at his companion sharply.

"Then you mean to fight?"

"Yes, sir, I mean to chastise this insolence."

"They wouldn't let us cross swords within the Palace grounds."

"Pooh! No paltry excuses and evasions, sir," cried Andrew, in whose thin cheeks a couple of red spots appeared. "Of course we could not hold a meeting here. But there is the Park. I see, though. Big words, and now the dog that was going to bite is putting his tail between his legs, and is ready to run away."

"Is he?" said Frank sharply, and a curiously stubborn look came into his face. "Don't you be too sure of that. But, anyhow, I'm not going to cross swords with you in real earnest."

"I thought so. You are afraid that I should pink you."

"Who's afraid?"

"Bah!" cried Andrew contemptuously. "You are."

"Oh, am I?" growled Frank. "Look here; I'm sure my father wouldn't like me to fight you with swords, whether you pinked me as you call it, or I wounded you."

"Pish! Frank Gowan, you are a poltroon."

"Perhaps so; but look here, Andrew Forbes, you've often made me want to hit you when you've been so bounceable and patronising. Now, we were going to see your friend to-night——"

"We are going to see my friend to-night, sir. Even if gentlemen have an affair, they keep their words."

"If they can, and are fit to show themselves. I'm not going to that place with you this evening, though I had got leave to go out. You can go afterwards if you like; but if you'll come anywhere you like, where we shan't be stopped, I'll try and show you, big as you are, that I'm not a coward."

"Very well. I dare say we can find a place. But your sword is shorter than mine. You must wear my other one."

"Rubbish! I'm not going to fight with swords!" cried Frank.

"What! you mean pistols?"

"I mean fists."

"Pah ! like schoolboys or people in the mob."

"I shan't fight with anything else," said Frank stubbornly.

"You shall, sir.   Now, then, name your friend."

"'*Frank Gowan, you are a poltroon.*'" [p. 61.

"Can't ; he wouldn't go. He's such a hot, peppery fellow too."

"Then he is as big a coward as you are."

"Look here," said Frank, almost in a whisper.   "I don't know so much as you do about what we ought to do here, but I suppose it means a lot of trouble; and if it does I can't help it, but if you call me a coward again I'll hit you straight in the face."

"Coward then!" cried Andrew, in a sharp whisper. "Now hit me, if you dare."

As he spoke he drew himself up to his full height, threw out his chest, and folded his arms behind him.

Quick as thought Frank doubled his fist, and as he drew back his arm raised his firm white knuckles to a level with his shoulder, and then reason checked him, and he stood looking darkly into his fellow-page's eyes.

"I knew it," cried the latter—"a coward; and your friend is worse than you, or you wouldn't have chosen him."

"Oh! don't you abuse him," said Frank, with his face brightening; and his eyes shone with the mirth which had suddenly taken the place of his anger.

"What! do you dare to mock me?" cried Andrew.

"No; only it seemed so comic. You know, I've only had one friend since I've been here. How could I ask you?"

For a few moments Andrew stood gazing at him, as if hardly knowing how to parry this verbal thrust, and then the look which had accompanied it did its work.

"I say," he said, in an altered tone, "this is very absurd."

"Yes, isn't it?" said Frank. "I never thought we two were going to have such a row."

"But you called me a fool."

"Didn't! But you did call me a coward. Ha—ha! and yourself too. But, I say, Drew, you don't think I'm a coward, do you?"

Andrew made no reply.

"Because I don't think I am," continued Frank. "I always hated to have to fight down yonder. And as soon as we began I always felt afraid of hurting the boy I

fought with ; but directly he hit out and hurt me I forgot
everything, and I used to go on hammering away till
I dropped, and had to give in because he was too much
for me, and I hadn't strength to go on hammering any
more. But somehow," he added thoughtfully, and with
simple sincerity in his tones, "I never even then felt as if
I was beaten, though of course I was."

"But you used to beat sometimes?" said Andrew
quietly.

"Oh yes, often ; I generally used to win. I've got
such a hard head and such bony knuckles. But, I say,
you don't think I should be afraid to fight, do you?"

"I'm sure you wouldn't be," cried Andrew, with
animation, "and—and, there I beg your pardon for treating
you as I have and for calling you a coward. It was a lie,
Frank, and—will you shake hands?"

There was a rapid movement, and this time the boy's
fist flew out, but opened as it went and grasped the thin
white hand extended toward him.

"I say, don't please ; you hurt," said Andrew, screwing
up his face.

"Oh, I beg your pardon," cried the boy. "I didn't
mean to grip so hard. I say, though, is it as the officers
say to the soldiers?"

"What do you mean?" said Andrew wonderingly.

"As you were?"

"Of course. I'm sure our fathers never quarrelled and
fought, and I swear we never will."

"That's right," cried Frank.

"And I never felt as if I liked you half so much as I do
now. Why, Frank, old fellow, you seem as if you had
suddenly grown a year older since we began to quarrel."

"Do I?" said the boy, laughing. "I am glad. No,
I don't think I am. But, I say, we mustn't quarrel often
then, for I shall grow old too soon."

"I said we'd never quarrel again," said Andrew

seriously; "and somehow you are really a good deal older than I have thought. But, I say, we must go and meet Mr. Selby to-night."

"Oh yes, of course; and I shall always stand by and stop you in case you turn peppery to any one else, and stop you from fighting him."

"If it was in a right cause you would not."

"I shouldn't?"

"No; I believe you would help me, and be ready to draw on my behalf."

Frank turned to the speaker with a thoughtful, far-off look in his eyes, as if he were gazing along the vista of the future at something happening far away.

"I hope that will never come," he said quietly, "for when I used to fight with my fists, as I said, I always forgot what I was about. How would it be if I held a drawn sword?"

"You would use it as a gentleman, a soldier, and a man of honour should," said Andrew warmly. ·

"Should I?" said Frank sadly.

"Yes, I am sure you would."

CHAPTER VIII.

THE TRAITORS' HEADS.

"WHERE is Mr. Selby's club?" asked Frank, as they started that afternoon to keep their appointment.

"You be patient, and I'll show you," replied Andrew.

"But we are not going by water, are we?"

"To be sure we are. It's the pleasantest way, and we avoid the crowded streets. I am to introduce you, so I must be guide."

This silenced Frank, who sank back in his seat when they stepped into a wherry without hearing the order given to the waterman; and once more his attention was taken up by the busy river scene, which so engrossed his thoughts that he started in surprise on finding that they were approaching the stairs where they had landed upon their last visit, but he made no remark aloud.

"I did not know it was in the city," he said, however, to himself; and when they landed, and Andrew began to make his way toward Fleet Street, his suspicion was aroused.

"Is the club anywhere near that court where there was the fight?" he said suddenly.

"Eh? Oh yes, very near! This is the part of London where all the wits, beaux, and clever men meet for conversation. You learn more in one night listening than you do in a month's reading. You'll like it, I promise you."

Frank was silent, and in spite of his companion's promise felt a little doubtful.

"Have you known Mr. Selby very long?" he asked.

"Depends upon what you call long."

"Do you like him?"

"Oh yes, he's a splendid fellow. So are his friends splendid fellows. You'll like them too. Thorough gentlemen. Most of them of good birth."

Frank was silent again; but he was becoming very observant now, as he noticed that, though they were going by a different way, they were tending toward the scene of their adventure, and the fight rose vividly before his imagination. But all was perfectly quiet and orderly around. There were plenty of people about, but all apparently engaged in business matters, though all disposed to turn and look after the well-dressed youths, who seemed foreign to their surroundings.

It was a relief to Frank to find that there were no signs of an idling crowd, and he was congratulating himself upon that fact when, after increasing his pace as if annoyed at being noticed, Andrew said sharply:

"Walk a bit faster. How the oafs do stare!"

"Why, Drew!" cried Frank, suddenly checking himself, as his companion, who had led him to the spot from the opposite side, suddenly turned into the court where they had been wedged in the crowd.

"What is it?" said his companion impatiently. "Come along, quick!"

"But this is the place where they were fighting."

"Of course; I know it is. What of it? They're not fighting now."

As he spoke he was glancing rapidly up and down the court, and with his arm well through that of Frank he urged him on toward the door of the large house.

Frank was annoyed at having, as he felt, been deceived as to their destination, and ready to hang back. But he

felt that it would seem cowardly, and that Andrew's
silence had been from a feeling that if he had said where
they were coming he would have met with a refusal, while
the next moment the boy found himself in the passage of
the house.

A burly man, in a big snuff-coloured coat, confronted
them, arranging a very curly wig as he came, but smiled,
bowed, and drew back to allow the visitors to pass; and
with a supercilious nod Andrew led on, apparently quite
familiar with the place, and turned up a broad, well-worn
staircase, quite half of whose balusters were perfectly new
and unpainted, evidently replacing those broken out for
weapons during the fight.

The sight of these and their suggestions did not increase Frank's desire to be there, but he went on up.

"For this time only," he said to himself; "but I'm not
going to let him cheat me again."

A buzz of voices issued from a partly opened door on
the first floor, and Andrew walked straight in without
hesitation, Frank finding himself in the presence of about
twenty gentlemen, standing at one end of a long room,
along whose sides were arranged small tables laid for
dinner.

The conversation stopped on the instant, and every eye
was turned toward the new-comers, who doffed their hats
with the customary formal bows, when, to the great relief
of Frank, one gentleman detached himself from the group
and came to meet them.

"How are you, Mr. Selby?" said Andrew loudly.

"The happier for seeing you keep your engagement,"
said their friend the feeder of ducks, smiling. "Mr.
Gowan, I am delighted to find my prayer has not been
vain. Let me introduce you to our friends here of the
club. We look upon this as a home, where we are all
perfectly at our ease; and we wish our visitors—our
neophytes—to feel the same. Gentlemen, let me intro-

duce my guest, Mr. Frank Gowan. I think some of you have heard his father's—Sir Robert Gowan's—name."

There was a warm murmur of assent, and to a man the party assembled pressed forward to bid the visitors welcome. So pleasantly warm was the reception given to him, and so genuine the efforts made to set him at his ease, that the lad's feeling of diffidence and confusion soon began to pass away, and with it the feeling of uneasiness; for the boy felt that these gentlemen could not have been of the party engaged in the riot, and he had nearly persuaded himself that, as this was evidently a public tavern, quite another class of people had occupied the room on his previous visit to the place, only he could not make this explanation fit with Andrew's excitement and desire to join in the fight.

But he had little time for thought. His bland and pleasant-spoken host took up too much of his attention, chatting fluently about the most matter-of-fact occurrences, political business being entirely excluded, and cleverly drawing the lads out in turn to talk about themselves and their aspirations, so ably, indeed, that before the agreeable little dinner served to these three at a table close to the window was half over, Frank found that he was relating some of his country life and school adventures to his host, and that the gentlemen at the tables on either side were listening.

The knowledge that he was being overheard acted as an extinguisher to the light of the boy's oratory, and he stopped short.

"Well?" said his host, with a pleasant smile; while Andrew leaned back, apparently quite satisfied with the impression his companion was making. "Pray go on. You drew the great trout close to the river-bank. Don't say you lost it after all."

"Oh no, I caught it," said Frank, colouring; "but I am talking too much."

"My dear boy," said Mr. Selby, "believe me, your fresh, young experiences are delightful to us weary men of the town. Cannot you feel how they revive our recollections of our own boyish days? There, pray don't think we are tired of anecdotes like this. Forbes here used to be fond of the country; but he has grown such a lover of town life and the court that he hardly mentions it now."

He went on playfully bantering Andrew, till quite a little passage of give-and-take ensued, which made Frank think of what a strange mixture of clever, vain boy and thoughtful man his fellow-page seemed to be, while his own heart sank as he began to make comparisons, and he felt how thoroughly young he seemed to be amongst the clever men by whom he was surrounded.

But all the time his ears were active, and he listened for remarks that would endorse his suspicions of the principles of the members. Still, not a word reached him save such as strengthened Andrew's assurance that Mr. Selby was one of a party of clever men who liked to meet for social intercourse. The fight must have been with other people who occupied the room, he thought, and in all probability had nothing to do with this club at all.

The evening passed rapidly away, and before Frank realised that it was near the time when they ought to be back at St. James's Mr. Selby turned to him.

"We are early birds here," he said; "so pray excuse what I am about to say, and believe that I am delighted to have made your acquaintance, one which is the beginning, I feel, of a life friendship. Gentlemen," he said, rising, "it is time to part till our next meeting. Hands round, please, and then adieu."

He turned to Frank, and held out his hand with a smile.

"Our little parting ceremony," he said.

The boy involuntarily held out his, ready to say good-bye ; but it was clasped warmly by Selby in his left and retained, while Andrew with a quick, eager look took his other.

Frank stared, for the rest, who had increased by degrees to nearly forty, all joined hands till they had formed a ring facing inward.

What did it mean ? For a moment the boy felt ready to snatch his hands away ; but as he thought of so doing, he felt the clasp on either side grow firmer, and in a clear, low voice their host said :

" Across the water."

" Across the water," was echoed in a low, deep murmur by every one but Frank.

Then hand ceased to clasp hand, people began to leave, and Mr. Selby went quickly to the other end of the room.

" All over," said Andrew, in a quick whisper. " Now then off, or we shall get into trouble for being late."

" Yes, let's go," said Frank, in a bewildered way ; and he went downstairs with his companion, and out into the cool, pleasant night air of the street.

" We shall have to walk," said Andrew, " so step out."

Frank obeyed in silence, and nothing more was said till, without thinking of where they were, they saw Temple Bar before them.

" What did they mean by that ? " said Frank suddenly.

" By what ? "

" Joining hands together and saying ' Across the water.' "

" Oh, nothing. A way of saying good-bye if you live in Surrey."

" Don't treat me as if I were a child," cried Frank passionately. " I'm sure it meant more than that."

" Well, suppose it does, what then ? "

" What then ? Why, you have been tricking and deceiving me. Just too as it seemed that we were going to be the best of friends."

"Nonsense! We are the best of friends, tied more tightly than ever to stand by each other to the end."

"Then there is something in all this?"

"Of course there is. You knew there was when we agreed to come."

"I did not!" cried Frank indignantly; "or if I thought that there might be, I felt that it was only a little foolish enthusiasm on your part, and that Mr. Selby was only a casual friend."

"Oh no; he is one of my best friends."

"Drew, I shall never forgive you. It was mean and cruel to take me there in ignorance of what these men were."

"Very nice gentlemanly fellows, and you looked as if you enjoyed their society."

"I see it all clearly enough now," continued Frank excitedly, and without heeding; "they are Jacobites."

"Not the only ones in London, if they are."

"And 'Across the water' means that man—the Pretender."

"Hush! Don't call people names," said Andrew, in a warning whisper. "You never know who is next you in the street."

"I don't care who hears me. It is the truth."

"Don't you be peppery now. Why, you were all amiability till we came away."

"Because I could not think that there was anything in it. I could not believe you would play me such a trick."

"All things are fair in love and war," said Andrew.

"It is a base piece of deception, and I'll never trust you again."

"Oh yes, you will, always. You'll like them more and more every time you go."

"I go there again? Never!"

"Oh yes, you will, often, because we all like you, and you are just the boy to grow into the man we want. I had no sooner mentioned your name to Mr. Selby than he said, 'Yes, he must join us, of course.'"

"Join you? Why, you are a band of conspirators."

"Silence, I tell you! That man in front heard you and turned his head."

"I don't care."

"Then I must make you. Look here, Frank, whatever we are, you are the same."

"I!" cried the boy in horror.

"Of course. This is twice you have come to our club, and there is not a man there to-night who does not look upon you as our new brother."

"Then they must be undeceived."

"Impossible! You have joined hands with us, and breathed our prayer for him across the water."

"I did not; I never opened my lips."

"You seemed to; anyhow, you clasped hands with us, and that is enough."

"I refuse to have any dealings with your club, and for your sake as well as mine I shall acquaint my father with everything that has taken place."

"That would not matter," said Andrew coolly. "But you will not. I introduced you to Mr. Selby, who had come on purpose to see you."

"Then that feeding ducks was a design?"

"Of course it was; the spies and the guard might interfere with a stranger hanging about at the water-side, but they can have nothing to say to a man feeding the ducks."

"Oh, what base treachery and deception! But I will not be tricked like this. It was the act of a traitor."

"It was the act of a friend to save you in the troubles that are to come."

"I don't care what you say. I will clear myself from even a suspicion of being an enemy of the King."

"You are a friend of *the* King," said Andrew, tightening

his hold of his companion's arm; "and you cannot draw back now."

"I can, and will. Why can I not? Who is to prevent me?"

"Every man you saw there to-night—every man of the thousand who was not there. Frank boy, ours is a great and just cause, and the sentence on the man who has joined us and then turns traitor——"

"I have not joined."

"You have, and I am your voucher. You are one of us now."

"And if I go back, what then?" cried Frank contemptuously.

"The sentence is death."

"Bah! nonsense! But let me tell you this, that the sentence really is death for him who, being the King's servant, turns traitor. Who stands worse to-night, you or I?—Oh!" ejaculated the boy quickly, and with a sharp ring of horror in his tones; "look there!"

The moon was shining brightly now, full upon the grim-ooking old city gateway, and Frank Gowan stood where he had stopped short, as if paralysed by the sight before him.

"Yes, I know," said Andrew coolly, as he looked up; "I have seen them before. Traitors' heads."

CHAPTER IX.

FRANK HAS A BAD NIGHT.

"I WISH I had a better head," sighed Frank, as he lay in bed that night; "it seems to get thicker and thicker, and as if every time I tried to think out what is the best thing to do it got everything in a knot."

He turned over, and lay hot and uncomfortable for a few minutes, and then perhaps for the hundredth time he turned over again, found his pillow comfortless, and jumped up into a sitting position, to punch and bang it about for some minutes, before returning it to its place, lying down, and finding it as bad as ever.

"It's of no use," he groaned; "I shall never get a wink of sleep to-night. I wish I could get up and dress, and go for a walk out there in the cool by the side of the water; but as soon as I got outside I should be challenged by the guard. I don't know the password, and I should be arrested and marched off to the guardroom. Even if I could get down there by the canal, I should feel no better, for I should be thinking of nothing else but feeding the ducks."

This thought made him twist and writhe in the bed to such an extent that the clothes refused to submit to the rough treatment, and glided off to seek peace and quietness upon the floor. The pleasant coolness was gratifying for a few minutes; but the boy's love of order put an end to his lying uncovered, and he sprang out of bed, dragged the truant clothing back, remade his bed extremely badly, and once more lay down.

The occupation relieved him for a while, and he began to hope that he would go to sleep; but the very fact of his endeavouring to lose consciousness made him more wakeful, and he lay with wide-open eyes, going over the events of the evening, till he got into a passion with Andrew Forbes, with Mr. George Selby, and most of all with himself.

"How could I be such an idiot as to go? I ought to have known better. I might have been sure, after what I had seen, that there was something wrong. But then," he groaned, "I did fancy something was wrong, and I went to try and keep Drew out of mischief. Oh, what an unlucky fellow I am!

"It's of no use," was his next thought. "I shall never do any good here, only keep on getting into trouble. Why, if this were to be known, it would bring disgrace on my father and mother, and they would have to leave court— father would perhaps lose his commission."

He sprang up again in horror at the very thought of this, drew up his knees, and passed his arms round them, to sit for long enough packed up with his chin upon his knees somewhat after the fashion of a Peruvian mummy.

"It's horrible," he groaned to himself—"horrible, that's what it is. And this is being what mother calls a good son. They'll be nice and proud of me when they know.

"Ah—h—h—h! There goes that wretched old clock over the gateway again! It can't be five minutes since it chimed before. It seems to have been chiming ever since I came to bed. What time is it, I wonder? Bah! three-quarters past. Three-quarters past what? Oh dear, how thirsty I am! and I've had three glasses of water since I came to bed. Going to feed the ducks! Oh, I wish I'd said I'd go out and fight with Drew, and pinked him as he calls it. He wouldn't have been able to lead me into this scrape. But more likely he would have pinked me. Well, and a precious good thing too. It would have been all right, and I couldn't then have gone.

"Phew! how hot it is. My skin seems to prickle and tingle, as if somebody had been playing tricks with the bed; and all this time I believe that miserable dandy Drew is snoring away, and not troubling a bit. There, if it isn't chiming again! It can't be a quarter of an hour since I heard it last. Ting, tang. Last quarter. Well, go on; four quarters, and then strike, and I shall know what time it is. What! A quarter past? Well, a quarter past what? Oh, that clock's wrong. It chimed three-quarters just now. It can't have chimed the four quarters since, and struck the hour; it's impossible. I'm sure it must be wrong."

He threw himself down again in despair, feeling as if sleep were farther off than ever.

"Oh dear!" he moaned; "Drew told me I seemed a year older after that row. I feel another year older since then; and if it goes on like this, I shall be like an old man by morning. But there, I'm not going to give up in this cowardly way. I'll show Master Drew that I'm not such a boy as he thinks for. It's all nonsense! Just because I went and dined there with him and his friend, and was then led into standing up with them and joining hands, I'm to be considered as having joined them, and become a Jacobite! Why, it's childish; and as to his threats of what they would do if I ran back, I don't care, I won't believe it. I'm not such a baby. Death indeed! I've only just begun to live.

"Ugh! it was very ugly, very shocking to see those heads stuck up there over Temple Bar; and yet Drew took it as coolly as could be. Why, it was he who ought to have been frightened, not I. And I'm not frightened—I won't be frightened. I won't say anything; but I'm not going there again. No, I won't speak—unless they do threaten me. Then I must tell all. But only wait till morning, and I'll have it out with Master Drew. Not quite so much of a schoolboy as he thinks me.

"There'll be no sleep for me to-night," he said at last, in a resigned way. "Well, it's perhaps so much the better. I have been able to think out what I mean to do, and now I'll just try and arrange what I shall say to Drew in the morning ; and, after that, I'll get up and dress, and have a long read. I do wonder, though, what time it is."

He then lay wondering and waiting for the clock to chime again, but he did not hear it chime its next quarter, for now that he had made up his mind not to go to sleep, sleep came to him with one of those sudden seizures which drop us in an instant into the oblivion which gives rest and refreshment to the wearied body and brain.

Then, all at once, as he lay with his eyes closed, he did hear it plainly.

"Ah, at last !" he cried,—"first quarter, second quarter, third quarter, fourth quarter. Now, then, I shall know what time it is."

The clock struck, and he counted—nine.

Then he listened for more, opened his eyes, and stared in amazement at the light streaming through the shuttered windows, and leaped out of bed.

"Why," he cried, "it's breakfast-time ! I must have been asleep after all."

Then he stood looking back into yesterday, for the evening's proceedings came to him with a flash.

"A Jacobite !" he said aloud; "and those heads upon the top of the gate !"

CHAPTER X.

IT was a bright morning; but now it seemed to Frank Gowan that the world had suddenly turned back. Andrew Forbes met him in the most friendly way after breakfast. He was almost affectionate in his greeting.

"Didn't dream about the traitors' heads on Temple Bar, did you?"

"No," said Frank coldly. "I lay awake and thought about them."

"Ugh!" ejaculated Andrew, with a shudder. "What gruesome things to take to bed with you. I didn't; I was so tired that I went off directly and slept like a top."

Frank looked at him in disgust.

"Hallo! what's the matter?" cried his fellow-page. "Not well?"

"I was wondering whether you had any conscience."

"I say, hark at the serious old man!" cried Andrew merrily. "Whatever made you ask that?"

"Because it seemed impossible you could have one, to treat it all so lightly after taking me there last night."

"I don't see how you can call it that. You were invited, and you went with me."

"That's a contemptible piece of shuffling," cried Frank.

Andrew flushed up and frowned.

"Pooh!" he said, laughing it off. "You are tired and cross this morning. What a fellow you are for wanting to quarrel! But we can't do that, now we're brethren."

"No, we are not," said Frank hotly. "I'll have nothing to do with the miserable business."

"Colt kicking on first feeling his harness," said Andrew merrily. "Never mind, Frank; you'll soon get used to it."

"Never."

"And it's a grand harness to wear. I say, what's the good of making a fuss about it? You'll thank me one of these days."

"Then you have no conscience," cried Frank sternly.

"Why, Frank, old boy, you make me feel quite young beside you. What a serious old man you've grown into! But if you will have it out about conscience," he continued warmly, after a glance at each of the doors opening out of the room in which they were, "I'll tell you this: my conscience would not let me, any more than would the consciences of thousands more, settle down to being ruled over by a German prince, invited here by a party of scheming politicians, to the exclusion of the rightful heir to the throne. What do you say to that?"

"Only this," said Frank: "that you and I have nothing to do with such things as who ought to be king or who ought not. We're the Prince's servants, and we are bound to do our duty to him and his father. If we go on as you propose, we become conspirators and traitors."

"Oh, I say, what a sermon; what a lot about nothing! People don't study these things in war and politics. I'm for the simple right or wrong of things. I say it's wrong for King George I. to be on the throne, so I shall not stick at trifles in fighting for the right."

"Well, if you talk like that in a place where they say that walls have ears, you'll soon save me the trouble and pain of speaking."

"There was no one to hear but you, and you're safe," said Andrew, laughing. "Brothers don't betray brothers, for one thing; and you know what I told you last night.

If you were to betray us, your life would not be safe for a day."

" Pish ! "

"Oh, you take it that way, do you ? You think you are safe because you are here in the Palace, surrounded by guards. Now, I'll tell you something that you don't know. You believe that I am the only one here who is ready to throw up his hat and draw his sword for the King."

"Yes, and I'm right."

"Only ignorant, Frank, my boy. Now listen. We Jacobites have people everywhere ready to strike when the time comes. Here in this Palace we have ladies and gentlemen forced to keep silence for the present, but who will be in ecstasies as soon as they know the good news Mr. Selby gave me last night. Why, the King's and Prince's households contain some of our staunchest people ; and if you like to go lower, there are plenty of us even among the Royal Guards. Now, what do you say to that ? "

" It can't be true."

" Very well ; I shan't quarrel with your ignorance. But look here, Frank ; take my advice : Don't you do anything foolish, for so sure as you betray any secret you possess there will be hundreds of hands against you—yes, boy as you are, and unimportant as you think yourself. If you breathe a word, it is not merely against me, but against the safety of scores here ; and to save themselves one or the other will send his sword through you at the first opportunity, wipe it, put it back in its sheath, and walk away. No one would be the wiser, and poor Frank Gowan, of whom his mother and father are so proud, would lie dead, while I should have lost the friend for whom I care more than for any one I ever met."

"You don't ; it isn't true," cried Frank. " If it were, you would not have led me into this scrape."

"Yes, I should. I tell you that you will thank me some day."

"For making me a traitor ?"

"Nonsense! Who can be a traitor who fights for his rightful king ? There, let's leave it now. You have been brought into the right way, and you are ready to fight against it because you don't see the truth yet; but it will all come out, and—very soon."

"What ?" cried Frank, for there was a meaning look to accompany the latter words.

"I'm not going to repeat what I said; but you will soon see."

"Then I must speak out at once. I shrank from it for fear of troubling my mother; but now you force me to."

"Don't, Frank. I shouldn't like to see you hurt."

"Whether I'm hurt or whether I'm not is nothing to you."

"Yes, it is. I have told you why. I couldn't bear to see you struck down."

"I don't believe that I should be."

"I do, and I don't want you to risk it, for one thing. For the other, I don't want to be arrested, and to have my head chopped off, for you couldn't speak without getting me into trouble."

Frank stared at him with his purpose beginning to waver.

"I might get off easily, being what they would call a mere boy. But I don't know; perhaps they would think that, as I was in a particular position in the Palace, they ought to make an example of me."

He laughed lightly as he threw himself into a seat by the window.

"I've no one to care about me except the dad, and a little more trouble wouldn't hurt him very much. Perhaps he'd be proud because I died for the King. I say, would you like to know why I am such a steady follower of him across the water ? "

Frank didn't speak, but his eyes said yes.

" Because I found how my poor father was wrong-treated. He's free, but he's little better than a prisoner. He's looked upon as a traitor, and I'm kept here principally as a sort of hostage to make him keep quiet. That's it, and they'll shorten me for certain if they find anything out. Poor old dad, though ; I dare say he'll be sorry, for he likes me in his way."

The trampling of horses was heard in the distance, and Andrew turned sharply.

" Here they come again. How bright and gay they look this morning ! Ah ! I should have liked to live and be an officer in a regiment like that, ready to fight for my king ; but I suppose I am not to be tall enough," he added, with a mocking laugh. " Wonder whether they'll stick my head on Temple Bar. Now, Frank, here's your chance ; come and shout to the nearest officer—'Stop and arrest a traitor !' Well, why don't you? He will hear you if you holloa well."

Frank made no reply.

" Oh," cried Andrew, " you are letting your chance go by. Well, perhaps it's better, and it will give me time to send a message to warn the dear old dad. No, that wouldn't do, because he would at once settle that it was your doing, and then—well, I should have signed your death-warrant, Franky. It would be all over with us both, and pretty soon. You first, though, for our people wouldn't stop for a trial. I say : feel afraid ? Somehow I don't. Perhaps that will come later on. Sure to, I suppose ; for it must be very horrible to have to die when one is so young, and with so many things to do. Going ? "

" Yes," said Frank gravely, as he turned away.

" Good-bye, then. Perhaps we shan't see each other again."

A peculiar thrill ran through Frank, and his heart gave one great throb. But he did not turn round. He went out of the room, to go somewhere to be alone—to try to think quietly out what he ought to do, and to solve the problem which would have been a hard one for a much older head, though at that moment it seemed to the boy as if he had suddenly grown very old, and that the present was separated from his happy boyish days by a tremendous space.

CHAPTER XI.

ANOTHER INVITATION.

SEVERAL days passed, and at each fresh meeting Andrew Forbes looked at his fellow-page inquiringly, as if asking whether he had spoken out yet; but the lad's manner was sufficient to show that he had not, though Frank was very cool and distant when they were alone.

Then Andrew began to banter his companion.

"Head's all right yet," he said one morning, laughing; and he gave it a slow twirl round like a ball in a socket. "Feels a bit loose sometimes; not at all a pleasant sensation. You're all right still, I see. Felt a bit nervous about you, though, once or twice."

Frank frowned slightly; but Andrew went on.

"I noticed one of us trying the point of his sword; and twice over after dark I saw men watching this window, and that made me think that you must have spoken, especially as I saw Lady—well, never mind names—examining something she had drawn out of the bosom of her dress. She slipped it back as soon as she saw me, but I feel certain that it was a sort of bodkin or stiletto. 'That's meant for poor Frank,' I said to myself; for, you know, in history women have often done work of that kind. But, there, you don't seem to have any holes in you; so I suppose you are all right for the present."

"How can you joke about so serious a matter?" cried Frank.

" Because I want to put an end to this miserable pique between us," cried Andrew warmly. " It's absurd, and I hate it. I thought we were to be always friends. I can't bear it, Frank, for I do like you."

" It was your doing," said the lad coldly.

" No. It was the wretched state our country is in that did it all."

" You always get the better of me in arguments," said Frank, " so I am not going to fight with you in that way. But I know I am right."

" And I know that I am right," cried Andrew.

" I shall not, as I said before, try to argue with you. We could never agree."

" No; it wants some one else to judge between us, and I'll tell you who's the man."

" I don't see how we can speak about our troubles."

" No need to," said Andrew. " He'll know all about it. Let's leave it to old Father Time. He proves all things. But, I say, Frank, don't be obstinate. There's a meeting of the friends the day after to-morrow. You'll come with me if we can get away ? "

" I shall do all I can to stop you from going ! " cried Frank.

" By betraying me ? "

" No ; I can't do that. I promised to be your friend ; and though it may be my duty, I couldn't do such a treacherous thing."

" As if I didn't know," said Andrew, laying his arm on the lad's shoulder. " Do you think I would have been so open if I had not been sure of you ? There, you will come ? "

" Never again."

" Never's a long time, Frank. Come."

" Once more, no ! "

" To take care of me, and keep me from being too rash."

"I can't betray you and your friends," said Frank sadly; "but I can do all that is possible to save you from a great danger."

"And so can I you. I'm right."

"No; I am right."

"You think so now; but I know you will come round. In the meantime, thank you, Frank. I knew, I say, that you would be staunch; but I'll tell you this: a word now from you would mean the breaking up of that party in the city, and, unless I could warn them in time, the seizure and perhaps death of many friends, and amongst them of one whom I love. I told him everything about you, and of our friendship, and it was he who bade me to bring you out in the Park there, so that he might see you first, and judge for himself whether he should like you to join us."

"You mean Mr. George Selby?"

"Yes, I mean Mr. George Selby," said Andrew, with a peculiar smile and emphasis on his words. "It was a very risky thing for him to come here close to the Palace with so many spies about; but throwing biscuits to the ducks was throwing dust in the people's eyes as well."

"Yes. I felt that it was a trick," said Frank sadly.

"Obliged to stoop to tricks now, my lad. Well, he was delighted with you, and told me how glad he was for me to have such a friend. He says you must be of us, Frank, so that in the good times ahead you may be one of the friends of the rightful king. You'll like Mr. George Selby."

"I hate him," said Frank warmly, "for leading you astray, and for trying to lead me in the same evil way."

"Tchut! Some one coming."

The "some one" proved to be the Prince with a train of gentlemen, nearly all of whom were Germans, and they passed through the anteroom on their way out.

"See that tall, light-haired fellow?" said Andrew, as soon as they were alone again.

"The German baron?"

"Yes, the one in uniform."

"Yes.   He's the Baron Steinberg, a colonel in the Hanoverian Guards."

"That's the man.   He came over on Saturday.   Well, I hate him."

"Why?   Because he's a German?"

"Pooh!   I shouldn't hate a man because he was a foreigner.   I hate him because he's an overbearing bully, who looks down on everything English.   He quite insulted me yesterday, and I nearly drew upon him.   But I didn't."

"What did he do?"

"Put his hand upon my shoulder, and pushed me aside.   'Out of the way, booby!' he said in German. A rude boor!"

"Oh, it was his rough way, perhaps.   You mustn't take any notice of that."

"Mustn't I?" exclaimed Andrew.   "We shall see. That isn't all.   I hate him for another thing."

"You're a queer fellow, Drew.   I think you divide the world into two sets—those you hate and those you love."

"And a good division too.   But these German fellows want teaching a lesson, and somebody will be teaching it if they don't mend.   Oh! I hate that fellow, and so ought you to."

"Why?   Because he is a German?"

"Not for that.   I'll tell you.   I didn't see you yesterday, or I'd have told you then.   You were in the big reception-room?"

"When my father was on duty with his company of the Guards?"

"Yes, and your mother was in the Princess's train."

"Yes, and I didn't get one chance to speak to her."

"Well, that fellow did; he spoke to her twice, and I saw him staring at her insolently nearly all the time the Princess and her ladies were there."

"Well?"

"That is all," said Andrew shortly. "They'll be at her drawing-room this afternoon, and if I were you I should go and stop near Lady Gowan as much as I could."

"I should like to," said Frank, looking at his friend wonderingly; "but of course I can't go where I like."

A few minutes later one of the servants brought in a note and handed it to Frank, who opened it eagerly.

"No answer," he said to the man; and then he turned to his companion. "Read," he said. "From my father."

"'Come and dine at the mess this evening, and bring Andrew Forbes,'" read the lad, and he flushed with pleasure.

"Of course you will not come," said Frank mockingly. "You could not be comfortable with such a loyal party."

"With such a host as Captain Sir Robert Gowan!" cried Andrew. "Oh yes, I could. I like him." He smiled rather meaningly, and then the conversation turned upon the treat to come, both lads being enthusiastic about everything connected with the military.

This was broken into by the same servant entering with another note.

"My turn now, Frank," said Andrew merrily; "but who's going to write to me?"

To his annoyance, as he turned to take the note, the man handed it to Frank and left the antechamber.

"Well, you seem to be somebody," cried Andrew, who now looked nettled.

"From my mother," said Frank, after glancing through the missive.

"Lucky you; mother and father both here. My poor

father nowhere, hiding about like a thief. Talk about friends at court ! "

" It does seem hard for you," said Frank. " See what she says."

" H'm ! 'So sorry not to be able to speak to you yesterday. Come to my rooms for an hour before the reception this afternoon. I long to see you, my dear boy.' "

Andrew handed back the letter with a sigh.

" Lucky you, Frank. I say, don't repeat what I said about yesterday."

" Of course not."

" That's right. Men talk about things when they are alone which would frighten ladies. She might get thinking that I should get up a quarrel with that Steinberg."

" I'm sure my mother wouldn't think anything of the sort," said Frank, smiling at his friend's conceit.

" Oh, I don't know," said Andrew importantly. " Yes I do, though. It was a rather stupid remark. But I wish I were you, Frank," he continued, with a genuine unspoiled boyish light coming into his eyes, which looked wistful and longing. " Perhaps, if I had a mother and father here in the court, I should be as loyal as you are."

" Of course you would be. Well, they like you. You're coming to dine with my father to-night, and I wish I could take you with me to see my mother early this afternoon."

" Do you—do you really, Frank ? " cried the lad eagerly.

" Of course I do ; you know I always say what I mean."

" Then thank you," cried the lad warmly ; " that's almost as good as going."

" I'll ask her to invite you next time. Hallo ! where are you off to ? "

" Only to my room for a bit."

" What for ? Anything the matter ? "

"Matter? Pish! Well, yes. I'm thinking I'd better be off, for fear, instead of my converting you, you'll be taking advantage of my weakness, offering me a share in Sir Robert and Lady Gowan for a bribe, and converting me."

"I wish I could," said Frank to himself, as his companion hurried out of the room. "Why not? Suppose I were to take my mother into my confidence, and ask her to try and win him away from what is sure to end in a great trouble!"

CHAPTER XII

THE TROUBLE GROWS.

FRANK was thinking in this strain when he went to his mother's rooms in the Palace soon after, and her maid showed him at once to where she was sitting reading, having dressed for the Princess's reception in good time, so as to be free to receive her son.

"Oh!" ejaculated the maid, as she was just about to leave the room; and there was a look of dismay in her countenance.

"What is it?" cried Lady Gowan, turning sharply with her son clasped in her arms.

"Your dress, my lady—the lace. It will be crushed flat."

"Oh," said Lady Gowan, with a merry laugh, "never mind that. Come in an hour and set all straight again."

"Yes, my lady," said the maid; and mother and son were left alone.

"As if we cared for satins and laces, Frank darling, at a time like this. My own dear boy," she whispered, as she kissed him again and again, holding his face between her white hands and gazing at him proudly. "There, I'm crushing your curls."

"Go on," said Frank; "crush away. You can brush them for me before I go—like you used to when I was home for the holidays."

"In the dear old times, Frank darling," cried Lady

Gowan, "when we did not have to look at each other from a distance. But never mind; we shall soon go down into the country for a month or two, away from this weary, formal court, and then we'll have a happy time."

Frank gazed proudly at his mother again and again during that little happy interview, which seemed all sunshine as he looked back upon it from among the clouds of the troubles which so soon came; and he thought how young and girlish and beautiful she appeared. "The most beautiful lady at the court," he told himself, "as well as the sweetest and the best."

Time after time the words he wished to speak rose to his lips, for the longing to make her his confidante over the Jacobite difficulty was intense. But somehow at the critical moments he either shrank from fear of causing her trouble and anxiety, or else felt that he ought not to run the risk of bringing Andrew into trouble after what had passed. He knew that Lady Gowan would not injure the mistaken lad; but still there was the risk of danger following. Besides, he had to some extent confided in his father, and would probably say more; so that if it was right that Lady Gowan should know, his father would speak.

She gave him very little chance for making confidences till just at the end of the hour she had set apart for him, when the maid appeared to repair the disorder which she alone could see, but was dismissed at once.

"Another ten minutes by the clock, and then Mr. Frank will be going."

The maid withdrew.

"Oh, how time flies, my darling!" said the lady. "And I had so many more things to say to you, so much advice to give to my dearest boy. But I am proud to have you here, Frank. Your father's so much away from me, that it is nice to feel that I have my big, brave son to protect me."

Frank coloured, and thought of his companion's words.

"It reconciles me more to being here, my boy," she continued; "for you see it means your advancement as well. But these are very anxious, troublous times for both your father and me. And you are going to dine with him at the mess this evening. Well, you are very young, and I want to keep you still a boy; but, heigh-ho! you are growing fast, and will soon be a man. So be careful and grow into the brave, honourable, loyal gentleman I wish you to be."

"I will try so hard," he said eagerly; and once more he longed to speak out, but she gave him no time, though at the last moment he would hardly have spoken. As it was, he stood feeling as if he were very guilty while she held his hand.

"Of course, my dear," she said, "you are too young to have taken any interest in the political troubles of the time; but I want you to understand that it's the happiest thing for England to be as it is, and I want you as you grow older to be very careful not to be led away by discontented men who may want to plunge the country into war by bringing forward another whom they wish to make king."

"Mother!" began Frank excitedly.

"Don't interrupt me, dear. In a few minutes you must go. Whatever feelings your father and I may at one time have had, we are now fixed in our determination to support those who are ncw our rulers. The Prince has been very kind to us, and the Princess has become my dearest friend. I believe she loves me, Frank, and I want her to find that my boy will prove one of her truest and best followers. I want you to grow up to be either a great soldier or statesman."

"I shall be a soldier like my father," said Frank proudly.

"We shall see, Frank," said Lady Gowan, smiling. "You are too young yet to decide. Wait a little—bide a wee, as they say in the north country. Now you must go; but you will promise me to be careful and avoid all who might try to lead you away. Think that your course is marked out for you—the way to become a true, loyal gentleman."

"I promise, mother," said the lad firmly.

"Of course you do, my boy," said Lady Gowan proudly. "There, kiss me and go. I have to play butterfly in the court sunshine for a while; but how glad shall I be to get away from it all to our dear old country home."

"And so shall I, mother," cried Frank, with his eyes sparkling.

"For a holiday, Frank. Life is not to be all play, my boy; and recollect that play comes the sweeter after good work done. There, I had you here for a pleasant chat, and I have done nothing but give you lessons on being loyal to your king; but we are separated so much, I have so few opportunities for talking to you, that I am obliged to give you a little serious advice."

"Go on talking to me like that, mother," said the boy, clinging to her. "I like to hear you."

"And you always will, won't you, Frank?"

"Of course," he said proudly.

"One word Frank, dear, and then you must go. Do you know why I have spoken like this? No, I will not make a question of it, but tell you at once. Andrew Forbes"—Frank started and changed colour—"is your very close companion, and with all his vanity and little weaknesses, he is still a gallant lad and a gentleman. Poor boy! he is very strangely placed here at the court, an attendant on the Prince and Princess, while his father is known to be a staunch adherent of the Pretender —a Jacobite. He was your father's closest friend, and I knew his poor wife—Andrew's mother—well. It was very sad her dying so young, and leaving her motherless boy to the tender mercies of a hard world just when dissensions

led his father to take the other side. The Princess knows
everything about him, and it was at my request that he
was placed here, where I could try and watch over him.
Now, naturally enough, Andrew has leanings toward his
father's side; but he must be taught to grow more and
more staunch to the King, and I want you, who are his
closest companion, to carefully avoid letting him influence
you, while you try hard to wean him from every folly, so
that, though he is older in some things, he may learn the
right way from my calm, grave, steady boy."

"But, mother——"

"Yes," she said, smiling; "I can guess what you are
about to say. Go, dearest. No : not another word.—Yes,
I am ready now."

This to her maid, who was standing in the doorway,
looking very severe ; and Frank was hurried out to return
to his own quarters.

CHAPTER XIII.

A VERY BAD DINNER.

"AND I could have told her so easily then," thought Frank, as he went away feeling proud and pleased, and yet more troubled than ever. "Wean Andrew from his ideas? I wonder whether I could. Of course I shall try hard; and if I succeeded, what a thing to have done! I'm not going to think which side is right or wrong. We're the King's servants, and have nothing to do with such matters. Drew has been trying to get me over to their side. Now I'm going to make him come to ours, in spite of all the Mr. George Selbys in London."

That afternoon the Princess's reception-rooms were crowded by a brilliant assemblage of court ladies and gentlemen, many of whom were in uniform; and there was plenty to take the attention of a lad fresh from the country, without troubling himself about political matters. He saw his father, but not to speak to. The latter gave him a quick look and a nod, though, which the boy interpreted to mean, "Don't forget this evening."

"Just as if I am likely to," thought Frank, as he gazed proudly after the handsome, manly-looking officer. He had a glimpse or two of his mother, who was in close attendance upon the Princess, and with a natural feeling of pride the lad thought to himself that his father and mother were the most royal-looking couple there.

At last he found himself close to Andrew Forbes, who

eagerly joined him, their duties having till now kept them separate.

"Isn't it horrible?" said Andrew, with a look of disgust in his flushed face.

"Horrible! I thought it the grandest sight I have ever seen. What do you mean by horrible?"

"This guttural chattering of the people. Why, you can hardly hear an English word spoken. It's all double Dutch, till I feel as if my teeth were set on edge."

"Nonsense! Good chance to learn German."

"I'd rather learn Hottentot. Look too what a lot of fat, muffin-faced women there are, and stupid, smoky, sour-krout-eating men. To my mind there are only two people worth looking at, and they are your father and mother."

Frank, who had felt irritated at his companion's persistent carping, began to glow, for he felt that his companion's words were genuine.

"Yes, they do look well, don't they?"

"Splendid. I do like your mother, Frank."

"Well, she likes you."

"H'm. I don't know," said the lad dubiously.

"But I do," said Frank quickly. "She told me so only this afternoon."

"What! Here, tell me what she said."

"That she knew your mother so well, and that it was sad about her dying so young, and that she felt, as I took it, something the same toward you as she did toward me."

"Did—did she talk like that, Frank?" said Andrew, with his lower lip quivering a little.

"Yes; and told me she hoped I should always be a good friend to you, and keep you out of mischief."

"Stuff!" cried Andrew. "I'm sure she did not say that."

"She did," said Frank warmly. "Not in those words, perhaps; but that was what she meant."

Andrew laughed derisively.

"Why, I'm a couple of years nearly older than you."

"So she said; but she spoke as if she thought that I could influence you."

"Bless her!" said Andrew warmly. "I feel as proud of her as you do, Frank, only I'm sorry for her to be here amongst all these miserable German people. Look, there's that stuck-up, conceited Baron Brokenstone, or whatever his name is. A common German adventurer, that's what he is; and yet he's received here at court."

"Well, he's one of the King's Hanoverian generals."

"I should like to meet him under one of our generals," said Andrew. "I consider it an insult for a fellow like that to be speaking to your mother—our mother, Frank, if she talks about me like that. I hate him, and feel as if I should like to go and hit him across the face with my glove."

"What for? Oh, I say, Drew, what a hot-headed fellow you are."

"It isn't my head, Franky; it's my heart. It seems to burn when I see these insolent Dutch officers lording it here, and smiling in their half-contemptuous, half-insulting way at our English ladies. Ugh! I wonder your father doesn't stop it. Look at him yonder, standing as if he were made of stone. I shall tell him what I think to-night."

"You would never be so foolish and insulting," said Frank warmly. "He would be angry."

"No, I suppose I must not," said Andrew gloomily. "He would say it was the impertinence of a boy."

They had to separate directly after, and a few minutes later Frank saw his father crossing the room toward the door. Frank was nearest, and by a quick movement reached it first, and stepped outside so as to get a word or two from him as he came out. But Sir Robert was stopped on his way, and some minutes elapsed before Frank saw the manly, upright figure emerge from the gaily dressed crowd which filled the anteroom, and stride toward him, but evidently without noticing his presence.

"Father," he whispered.

Sir Robert turned upon him a fierce, angry face, his eyes flashing, and lips moving as if he were talking to himself. But the stern looks softened to a smile as he recognised his son, and he spoke hurriedly :

"Don't stop me, my boy; I'm not fit to talk to you now. Oh, absurd!"

"Is anything the matter, father?" said Frank anxiously, as he laid his hand on his father's arm.

"Matter? Oh, nothing, boy. Just a trifle put out. The rooms are very hot. There, I must go. Don't forget to-night, you and young Forbes."

He nodded and strode on, leaving his son wondering; for he had never seen such a look before upon his father's face.

He thought no more of it then, for his attention was taken up by the coming of the Princess with her ladies, the reception being at an end ; while soon after Andrew Forbes joined him, and began questioning him again about Lady Gowan, and what she had said about his dead mother, ending by turning Frank's attention from the emotion he could hardly hide by saying banteringly :

"You'll have to be very strict with me, Frank, or you'll have a great deal of trouble to make me a good boy."

"I shall manage it," said Frank, with a laugh ; and not very long after they were on their way to the Guards' messroom, both trying to appear cool and unconcerned, but each feeling nervous at the idea of dining with the officers.

Sir Robert was there, looking rather flushed and excited, as he stood talking to a brother-officer in the large room set apart for the Guards ; but his face lit up with a pleasant smile as the boys entered, and he greeted them warmly, and introduced them to the officer with him.

"Makes one feel old, Murray," he said, "to have a couple of great fellows like these for sons."

"Sons? I thought that——" began the officer.

"Oh, about this fellow," said Sir Robert merrily. "Oh yes, he's Forbes's boy; but Lady Gowan and I seem to have adopted him like. Sort of step-parents to him—eh, Andrew?"

"I wish I could quite feel that, Sir Robert," said Andrew warmly.

"Well, quite feel it then, my lad," said Sir Robert, clapping him on the shoulder. "It rests with you.— Think Frank here will ever be man enough for a soldier, Murray?"

"Man enough? Of course," said the officer addressed. "We must get them both commissions as soon as they're old enough. Forbes might begin now."

"H'm! Ha!" said Sir Robert, giving the lad a dry look. "Andrew Forbes will have to wait a bit."

Then, seeing the blood come into the lad's face at the remark which meant so much:

"He's going to wait for Frank here.—Well, isn't it nearly dinner-time?—Hungry, boys?"

"Er—no, sir," said Andrew.

"Frank is," said Sir Robert, smiling at his son.

"Can't help it, father," said the boy frankly. "I always am."

"And a capital sign too, my lad," said the officer addressed as Murray. "There's nothing like a fine healthy appetite in a boy. It means making bone and muscle, and growing. Oh yes, he'll be as big as you are, Gowan. Make a finer man, I'll be bound."

"Don't look like it," said Sir Robert merrily; "why, the boy's blushing like a great girl."

The conversation was ended by the entrance of several other officers, who all welcomed the two lads warmly, and seemed pleased to do all they could to set at their ease the son and *protege* of the most popular officer in the regiment.

Captain Murray, his father's friend, was chatting with Frank, when he suddenly said :

" Here are the rest of the guests."

Six German officers entered the room, and Frank started and turned to glance at his father, and then at Andrew, whom he found looking in his direction ; but Sir Robert had advanced with the elderly colonel of the regiment, and Captain Murray rose as well.

"I shall have to play interpreter," he said, smiling. " Come along, and the colonel will introduce you two, or I will. They don't speak any English ; and if you two do not, your father and I are the only men present who know German."

The introductions followed, and feeling very uncomfortable all the while, Frank and his companion were in due course made known to Baron Steinberg, Count Von Baumhof, and to the four other guests, whose names he did not catch ; and then, by the help of Captain Murray and Sir Robert, a difficult conversation was carried on, the German officers assuming a haughty, condescending manner towards the Guardsmen, who were most warm in their welcome.

At the end of a few minutes Captain Murray returned to where the two lads were standing, leaving Sir Robert trying his best to comprehend the visitors, and translating their words to the colonel and his brother-officers.

" Rather an unthankful task," said the captain, smiling. " These Germans treat us as if they had conquered the country, and we were their servants. Never mind ; I suppose it is their nature to."

" Yes," said Andrew warmly ; " they make my blood boil. I know I am only a boy ; but that was no reason why they should insult Frank Gowan here and me with their sneering, contemptuous looks."

"Never mind, my lad. I noticed it. Show them, both of you, that you are English gentlemen, and know how to treat strangers and guests."

"Yes, yes, of course," said Frank hastily.

"They will be more civil after dinner. Ah, and there it is."

For the door was thrown open, one of the servants announced the dinner, and the colonel led off with Baron Steinberg, after saying a few words to Sir Robert, who came directly to his brother-officer.

"The colonel wishes the places to be changed, Murray," he said, "so that you and I can be closer to the head of the table on either side, to do the talking with the visitors. I wish you would take my boy here on your left. Forbes, my lad, you come and sit with me."

Andrew had begun to look a little glum at being set on one side on account of the German officers; but at Sir Robert's last words he brightened up a little, and they followed into the messroom, which was decorated with the regimental colours; the hall looked gay with its fine display of plate, glass, flowers, and fruit, and the band was playing in a room just beyond.

The scene drove away all the little unpleasantry, and the dinner proceeded, with the colonel and his officers doing their best to entertain their guests, but only seeming to succeed with the two pages of honour, to whom everything was, in its novelty, thoroughly delightful. The German officers, though noblemen and gentlemen, gave their hosts a very poor example of good breeding, being all through exceedingly haughty and overbearing, and treating the attempts of Sir Robert and Captain Murray to act as their interpreters to the colonel and the other officers with a contempt that was most galling; and more than once Frank saw his father, who was opposite, bite his lip and look across at Captain Murray, who, after one of these glances, whispered to Frank:

" Your dad's getting nettled, my lad, and I find it very consoling."

"Why?" said Frank, who felt annoyed with himself for enjoying the evening so much.

"Why? Because I was fancying that I must have a very hasty temper for minding what has been taking place. Do you know any German at all?"

"Very little," said Frank quickly.

"What a pity! You could have said something to this stolid gentleman on my right. He seems to think I am a waiter."

" I thought he was very rude several times."

"Well, yes, I suppose we must call it rude. The poor old colonel yonder is in misery; he does hardly anything but wipe his forehead. Does not young Forbes speak German?"

"No, he hates it," said Frank hastily.

"Enough to make him," muttered the captain. "But never mind; you must both come and dine with us another time, when we are all Englishmen present. This is a dreary business; but we must make the best of it."

He turned to say something courteous to the heavy, silent officer on his right, but it was coldly received, and after a few words the German turned to converse with one of his fellow-countrymen, others joined in, and the colonel looked more troubled and chagrined than ever.

The dinner went slowly on; and at last, with the conversation principally carried on by the German guests, who were on more than one occasion almost insolent to their entertainers, the dessert was commenced, several of the officers drawing their chairs closer, and a young ensign, who looked very little older than Frank, whispered to him :

" I heard your father say that you were coming into the army."

" Yes, I hope to," replied the lad.

"Then you set to at once to study German. We shall be having everything German soon."

"Then I shall not join," said Andrew across the table; and the officer on his right laughed.

Sir Robert and Captain Murray were too much occupied now to pay any attention to their young guests, who found the officers below them eager to make up for this, and they began chatting freely, so that this was the pleasantest part of the evening. But at the upper part of the table matters were getting more strained. The colonel and his friends, whom he had placed with the foreign guests, after trying hard all through to make themselves agreeable and to entertain the visitors, had received so many rebuffs that they became cold and silent, while the Germans grew more and more loud in their remarks across the table to each other. Many of these remarks were broad allusions to the country in which they were and its people, and the annoyance he felt was plainly marked on Sir Robert's brow in deeply cut parallel lines.

Ignoring their hosts, the visitors now began to cut jokes about what they had seen, and from a word here and there which, thanks to his mother, Frank was able to grasp, they were growing less and less particular about what they said.

Baron Steinberg had had a great deal to say in a haughtily contemptuous manner, and Frank noticed that whenever he spoke his friends listened to him with a certain amount of deference, as if he were the most important man present. He noted, too, that when the baron was speaking his father looked more and more stern, but whenever it fell to his lot to interpret something said by the colonel he was most studiously courteous to the guest.

Frank had grown interested in an anecdote being related for his and Andrew's benefit by one of the young officers below, and as it was being told very humorously his back was half turned to the upper part of the table, and he was leaning forward so as not to miss a word. At the same time, though, he was half conscious that the baron on the colonel's right was talking loudly, and saying something which greatly amused his compatriots, when all at once Sir Robert Gowan sprang to his feet, and Captain Murray cried across the table to him :

"Gowan! for Heaven's sake take no notice."

Frank's heart began to throb violently, as he saw his father dart a fierce look at his brother-officer, and then take a couple of strides up the side of the table to where the baron sat on the colonel's right.

"Gowan, what is the matter?" cried the colonel. "What has he said?"

"I'll interpret afterwards, sir," said Sir Robert, in a deep, hoarse voice, "when we are alone;" then fiercely to the baron in German: "Take back those words, sir. It is an insult—a lie!"

The baron sprang to his feet, his example being followed by his brother-officers, and, leaning forward, he seemed about to strike, but with a brutally contemptuous laugh he bent down, caught up his glass, and threw it and its contents in Sir Robert's face.

Every one had risen now, and Captain Murray made a rush to reach the other side ; but before he was half-way there, Frank had seen his father dart forward, there was the sound of a heavy blow, and the German baron fell back with his chair, the crash resounding through the room, but only to be drowned by the fierce roar of voices, as the German officers clapped their hands to their swordless sides, and then made a rush to seize Sir Robert.

The colonel could not speak a word of German, but his looks and gestures sufficed as he sprang before them.

"Keep back, gentlemen!" he said; "I am in ignorance of the cause of all this."

"A most gross insult, sir!" cried Captain Murray angrily.

"Silence, sir!" cried the colonel. "These gentlemen were my guests, and whatever was said Captain Sir Robert Gowan has committed an unpardonable breach of social duty. To your quarters, sir, without a word."

"Right, colonel," replied Sir Robert quietly, as he stood pale and stern, returning the vindictive looks of the German guests, who would have attacked him but for the action taken by his brother-officers.

What took place afterward was confused to Frank by the giddy excitement in his brain; but he was conscious of seeing the baron assisted to a chair, and then talking in savage anger to his compatriots, while at the other end of the room there was another knot where the younger officers and Captain Murray were with Sir Robert.

"It was a mad thing to do, Gowan," cried the former.

"Flesh and blood could not bear it, lad," replied Frank's father. "Mad? What would you have done if in the presence of your son those words had been uttered?"

"As you did, old lad," cried Captain Murray, with his face flushing, "and then stamped my heel upon his face."

There was a low murmur of satisfaction from the young officers around.

"Hah!" said Sir Robert, "I thought so." Then with a quiet smile he caught Andrew's and Frank's hands: "So sorry, my dear boys, to have spoiled your evening Go now.—Murray, old lad, see them off, and then come to my quarters."

"Oh, Sir Robert," whispered Andrew, clinging to his hand, and speaking in a low, passionate voice, "I am glad. That did me good."

"What! You understood his words?"

"I? No."

"That's right! Go now, Frank boy. One moment, my lad. You are suddenly called upon to act like a man."

" Yes, father ! What do you want me to do ? "

" Keep silence, my lad. Not a word about this must reach your mother's ears."

" Come, Frank, my lad," said Captain Murray gently. " You are better away from here."

The words seemed to come from a distance, but the lad started and followed the captain outside, where the young officers gathered about him, eager to shake hands and tell him that they were all so glad ; but he hardly heard them, and it was in a strangely confused way that he parted from Captain Murray, who said that he could go no farther, as he wanted to hurry back to Sir Robert.

Then the two lads were alone.

" What does it all mean, Drew ? " cried Frank passionately. " Oh, I must go back. It's cowardly to come away from my father now."

" You can't go to him. He'll be under arrest."

" Arrest ! " cried Frank.

" Yes, for certain. But don't look like that, lad. It's glorious—it's grand."

" But arrest ? He said it was an insult. They can't punish him for that."

" Punishment ? Pooh ! What does that matter ? Every gentleman in the army will shout for him, and the men throw up their caps. Oh, it's grand—it's grand ! And they'll meet, of course ; and Sir Robert must—he shall—he will too. He'll run the miserable German through."

" What ? Fight ! My father fight—with him ? "

" Yes, as sure as we should have done after such a row at school."

" But—with swords ? "

" Officers don't fight with fists."

" Oh ! " cried Frank wildly ; " then that's what he meant when he said that my mother must not know."

CHAPTER XIV.

FRANK GOWAN lay awake for hours that night with his brain in a wild state of excitement. The scene at the dinner, the angry face of his father as he stood defying the baron's friends after striking the German down, the colonel's stern interference, and his orders for Sir Robert to go to his quarters—all troubled him in turn; then there was the idea of his father being under arrest, and the possibility of his receiving some punishment, all repeating themselves in a way which drove back every prospect of sleep, weary as the lad was; while worst of all, there was Andrew Forbes's remark about an encounter to come, and the possible results.

It was too horrible. Suppose Sir Robert should be killed by the fierce-looking baron! Frank turned cold, and the perspiration came in drops upon his temples as he thought of his mother. He sat up in bed, feeling that he ought to go to his father and beg of him to escape anywhere so as to avoid such a terrible fate. But the next minute his thoughts came in a less confusing way, and he knew that he could not at that late hour get to his father's side, and that even if he could his ideas were childish. His father would smile at him, and tell him that they were impossible—that no man of honour could fly so as to avoid facing his difficulties, for it would be a contemptible, cowardly act, impossible for him to commit.

"I know—I know," groaned the boy, as he flung himself down once more. "I couldn't have run away to escape from a fight at school. It would have been impossible. Why didn't I learn German instead of idling about as I have! If I had I should have known what the baron said. What could it have been?"

The hours crept sluggishly by, and sleep still avoided him. Not that he wished to sleep, for he wanted to think; and he thought too much, lying gazing at his window till there was a very faint suggestion of the coming day; when, leaving his bed, he drew the curtain a little on one side, to see that the stars were growing paler, and low down in the east a soft, pearly greyness in the sky just over the black-looking trees of the Park.

It was cold at that early hour, and he shivered and crept back to bed, thinking that his mother in the apartments of the ladies of honour was no doubt sleeping peacefully, in utter ignorance of the terrible time of trouble to come; and then once more he lay down to think, as others have in their time, how weak and helpless he was in his desires to avert the impending calamity.

"No wonder I can't sleep," he muttered; and the next moment he slept. For nature is inexorable when the human frame needs rest, or men would not sleep peacefully in the full knowledge that it must be their last repose on earth.

Five minutes after, his door was softly opened, a figure glided through the gloom to his bedside, and bent over him, like a dimly seen shadow, to catch him by the shoulder.

"Frank! Frank! Here, quick! Wake up!"

The lad sprang back into wakefulness as suddenly as if a trigger had been touched, and all the drowsiness with which he was now charged had been let off.

"Yes; what's the matter? Who's there?"

"Hush! Don't make a noise. Jump up, and dress."

" Drew ? "

" Yes. Be quick ! "

" But what's the matter ? "

" I couldn't sleep, so I got up and dressed, and opened my window to stand looking out at the stars, till just now I heard a door across the courtyard open, and three men in cloaks came out."

" Officers' patrol—going to visit the sentries."

" No ; your father, Captain Murray, and some one else. I think it was the doctor ; he is short and stout."

" Then father's going to escape," said Frank, in an excited whisper.

" Escape ! Bah ! " replied Andrew, in a tone full of disgust. " How could he as a gentleman ? Can't you see what it means ? They're going to a meeting."

" A meeting ? " faltered Frank.

" Oh, how dull you are ! Yes, a meeting ; they're going to fight ! "

Frank, who had leisurely obeyed his companion's command to get up and dress, now began to hurry his clothes on rapidly, while Andrew went on :

" I don't know how they've managed it, because your father was under arrest ; but I suppose the officers felt that there must be a meeting, and they have quietly arranged it with the Germans. Of course it's all on the sly. Make haste."

" Yes. I shan't be a minute. You have warned the guard of course ? "

" Done what ? " said Andrew.

" Given the alarm," panted Frank.

" I say, are you mad, or are you still asleep ? What do you mean ? "

" Mad ! asleep ! Do you think I don't know what I'm saying ? "

" I'm sure you don't."

" Do you think I want my father to be killed ? "

"Do you think your father wants to be branded as a coward? Don't be such a foolish schoolboy. You are among men now. I wish I hadn't come and woke you. They'll be getting it over too before I'm there."

He made a movement toward the door, but Frank seized him by the arm.

"No, no; don't go without me," he whispered imploringly.

"Why not? You'd better go to bed again. You're just like a great girl."

"I must go with you, Drew. I'm afraid I didn't hardly know what I was saying; but it seems so cold-blooded to know that one's own father is going to a fight that may mean death, and not interfere to stop it."

"Interfere to stop it—may mean death! I hope it does to some one," whispered Andrew fiercely. "There, let go; I can't stop any longer."

"You're not going without me. There, I'm ready now."

"But I can't take you to try and interfere. I thought you'd like me to tell you."

"Yes, I do. I must come, and—and I won't say or do anything that isn't right."

"I can't trust you," said Andrew hastily. "It was a mistake to come and tell you. There, let go."

"You are not going without me!" cried Frank, fiercely now; and he grasped his companion's arm so firmly that the lad winced.

"Come on, then," he said; and, with his breath coming thick and short, Frank followed his companion downstairs and out of the door of the old house in the Palace precincts, into the long, low colonnade.

They closed the door softly, and ran together across the courtyard in the dim light, but were challenged directly after by a sentry.

"Hush! Don't stop us," whispered Andrew. "You know who we are—two of the royal pages."

"Can't pass," said the man sternly.

"But we must," said Frank, in an agonised whisper. "Here, take this."

"Can't pass," said the man; "'gainst orders. You must come to the guardroom."

But he took the coin Frank handed to him, and slipped it into his pocket.

"We want to go to the meeting—the fight," whispered Andrew now. "We won't own that you let us go by."

"Swear it," said the man.

"Yes, of course. Honour of gentlemen."

"Well, I dunno," said the man.

"Yes, you do. Which way did they go when they passed the gate?"

"Couldn't see," said the man; "too dark. I thought it was one of them games. My mate yonder 'll know, only he won't let you go by without the password."

"Oh yes, he will," said Andrew excitedly. "Come on."

"Mind, I never see you go by," said the man.

"Of course you didn't," said Andrew; "and I can't see you; it's too dark yet."

They set off running, and the next minute were at the gate opening on to the Park, where another sentry challenged them.

"I'm Mr. Frank Gowan, Captain Sir Robert Gowan's son, and this is Mr. Andrew Forbes, Prince's page."

"Yes, I know you, young gentlemen; but where's the password?"

"Oh, I don't know," said Andrew impatiently. "Don't stop us, or they'll get it over before we're there. Look here; come to our rooms any time to-day, and ask for us. We'll give you a guinea to let us go."

"I dursn't," said the man, in a whisper.

"Which way did they go?" said Frank, trembling now with anxiety.

"Strite acrost under the trees there. They've gone to the bit of a wood down by the water."

"Yes; that's a retired spot," panted Andrew. "Here, let's go on."

"Can't, sir, and I darn't. It's a jewel, aren't it?"

"Yes, a duel."

"Well, I'm not going to be flogged or shot for the sake of a guinea, young gentlemen, and I won't. But if you two makes a roosh by while I go into my sentry-box, it aren't no fault o' mine."

He turned from them, marched to his little upright box, and entered it, while before he could turn the two lads were dashing through the gate, and directly after were beneath the trees.

It was rapidly growing lighter now; but the boys saw nothing of the lovely pearly dawn and the soft wreaths of mist which floated over the water. The birds were beginning to chirp and whistle, and as they ran on blackbird after blackbird started from the low shrubs, uttering the chinking alarm note, and flew onward like a velvet streak on the soft morning glow.

In a minute or so they had reached the water-side, and stopped to listen; but they could hear nothing but the gabbling and quacking of the water-fowl.

"Too late—too late!" groaned Frank. "Which way shall we go?"

"Left," said Andrew shortly. "Sure to go farther away."

They started again, running now on the grass, and as they went on step for step:

"Mayn't have begun yet," panted Andrew. "Sure to take time preparing first.—There, hark!"

For from beneath a clump of trees, a couple of hundred yards in front, there was an indistinct sound which might have meant anything. This the boys attributed to the grinding together of swords, and hurried on.

Before they had gone twenty yards, though, it stopped; and as all remained silent after they had gone on a short distance farther, the pair stopped, too, and listened.

"Going wrong," said Frank despairingly.

"No. Right," whispered Andrew, grasping his companion's arm; for a low voice in amongst the trees gave what sounded like an order, and directly after there was a sharp click as of steel striking against steel, followed by a grating, grinding sound, as of blade passing over blade.

Frank made a rush forward over the wet grass, disengaging his arm as he did so; but Andrew bounded after him, and flung his arms about his shoulders.

"Stop!" he whispered. "You're not going on if you are going to interfere."

"Let go!" said Frank, in a choking voice. "I'm not going to interfere. I am going to try and act like a man."

"Honour?"

"Honour!" and once more they ran on, to reach the trees and thread their way through to where a couple of groups of gentlemen stood in a grassy opening, looking on while two others, stripped to shirt and breeches, were at thrust and parry, as if the world must be rid of one of them before they had done.

As Frank saw that one was his father—slight, well-knit, and agile—and the other—heavy, massively built, and powerful—the Baron Steinberg, the desire was strong to rush between them; but the power was wanting, and he stood as if fixed to the spot, staring with starting eyes at the rapid exchanges made, for each was a good swordsman, well skilled in attack and defence, while the blades, as they grated edge to edge and played here and there, flashed in the morning light ; and as if in utter mockery of the scene, a bird uttered its sweet song to the coming day.

There were moments when, as the German's blade flashed dangerously near Sir Robert's breast, Frank longed to close his eyes, but they were fixed, and with shuddering emotion he followed every movement, feeling a pang as a deadly thrust was delivered, drawing breath again as he saw it parried.

For quite a minute the baron kept up a fierce attack in this, the second encounter since they had begun, but every thrust was turned aside, and at last, as if by one consent, the combatants drew back a step or two with their breasts heaving, and, without taking their eyes off each other, stood carefully re-rolling up their shirt sleeves over their white muscular arms.

And now a low whispering went on among the officers, German and English, who were present, and Andrew said softly in Frank's ear :

"Don't move—don't make a sign. It might unsettle Sir Robert if he knew you were here."

Frank felt that this was true, and with his heart beating as if it would break from his chest he stood watching his father, noting that his breathing was growing more easy, and that he was, though his face was wet with perspiration, less exhausted than his adversary, whose face appeared drawn with hate and rage as he glared at the English captain.

Suddenly Captain Murray broke the silence by saying aloud to the German officers :

"We are of opinion, gentlemen, that only one more encounter, the third, should take place. This should decide."

"Tell them not to interfere," said Steinberg fiercely, but without taking his eyes off his adversary. Then in French, with a very peculiar accent, he cried, "*En garde!*" and stepped forward to cross swords with Sir Robert once more.

The latter advanced at the same moment, and the blades clicked and grated slightly, as their holders stood motionless, ready to attack or defend as the case might be.

For nearly half a minute they stood motionless, eye fixed on eye, each ready to bring to bear his utmost skill, for, from the first the German had fought with a vindictive rage which plainly showed that he was determined to disable, if he did not slay, his adversary; while, enraged as he had been, there was, after some hours of sleep, no such desire on the part of Sir Robert. He desired to wound his enemy, but that was all; and as he at the first engagement realised the German's intentions, he fought cautiously, confining himself principally to defence, save when he was driven, for his own safety, to retaliate.

The seconds and those who had come as friends, at the expense of a breach of discipline and the consequences which might follow, had grasped this from the first; and though he had great faith in his friend's skill, Captain Murray had been longing for an opportunity to interfere and end the encounter. None had presented itself, and the German officers had so coldly refused to listen to any attempt at mediation that there was nothing for it but to let matters take their course.

And now, as the adversaries stood motionless with their blades crossed, Sir Robert's friends felt to a man, as skilled fencers, that the time had arrived for him to take the initiative, press his adversary home, and end the duel by wounding him.

But Sir Robert still stood on his guard, the feeling in his breast being—in spite of the terrible provocation he had received—that he had done wrong in striking his

colonel's guest, and he kept cool and clear-headed, resolved
not to attack.

Then, all at once, by an almost imperceptible movement
of the wrist, the baron made his sword blade play about
his enemy's, laying himself open to attack, to tempt his
adversary to begin.

Twice over he placed himself at so great a disadvantage
that it would have been easy for Sir Robert to have
delivered dangerous thrusts ; but the opportunities were
declined, for the English captain's mind was made up,
and Frank heard an impatient word from Murray's lips,
while Andrew uttered a loud sigh.

Then, quick as lightning, the baron resumed his old
tactics, sending in thrust after thrust with all the skill he
could command.   His blade quivered and bent, and seemed
to lick that of Sir Robert like a lambent tongue of fire ;
and Frank felt ready to choke, as he, with Andrew, unable
to control their excitement, crept nearer and nearer to the
actors in the terrible life drama, till they were close behind
Captain Murray and the other English officers, hearing their
hard breathing and the short, sharp gasps they uttered as
some fierce thrust was made which seemed to have gone
home.

But no : giving way very slightly, in spite of the fashion
in which he was pressed by the German, Sir Robert
turned every thrust aside ; and had he taken advantage of
his opportunities, he could have again and again laid the
baron at his feet, but not in the way he wished, for his
desire now was to inflict such a wound as would merely
place his enemy *hors de combat.*

A murmur now arose amongst the Englishmen, for
the affair was becoming murderous on one side.   But the
German officers looked on stolidly, each with his left hand
resting upon the hilt of his sword, as if ready to resent
any interference with the principals in a deadly way.

There was no hope of combination there to end the

encounter, and once more Captain Murray and his friends waited for Sir Robert to terminate the fight, as they now felt that he could at any time.

For, enraged by the way in which he was being baffled by the superior skill of his adversary, the baron's attack was growing wild as well as fierce; and, savagely determined to end all by a furious onslaught, he made a series of quick feints, letting his point play about Sir Robert's breast, and then, quick as lightning, lunged with such terrible force that Frank uttered a faint cry. His father heard it, and though he parried that thrust, it was so nervously that he was partly off his guard with that which followed, the result being that a red line suddenly sprang into sight from just above his wrist, nearly to his elbow, and from which the blood began to flow.

A cry of "Halt!" came from Captain Murray and his friends, and this was answered by a guttural roar from the baron, while, as the former, as second, stepped forward to beat down the adversaries' swords, the German officers at once drew their weapons, not to support the baron's second, but as a menace.

It was all almost momentary, and while it went on the baron, inspired by the sight of the blood, pressed forward, thrusting rapidly, feeling that the day was his own.

But that strong British arm, though wounded, grasped the hilt of Sir Robert's blade as rigidly as if it were of the same metal; and as the baron lunged for what he intended for his final thrust, he thoroughly achieved his object, but not exactly as he meant. His sword point was within an inch of Sir Robert's side, when a quick beat in octave sent it spinning from his hand, while at the same instant, and before the flying sword had reached the ground, Sir Robert's blade had passed completely through his adversary's body.

The German officers rushed forward, not to assist their fallen leader, but, sword in hand, evidently to avenge his fall, so taking the Englishmen by surprise that, save Sir Robert's second, neither had time to draw.

It would have gone hard with them, but, to the surprise of all, there was a short, sharp order, and an officer and a dozen of the Guards dashed out of the clump of trees which sheltered the duellists, to arrest the whole party for brawling within the Palace precincts.

CHAPTER XV.

THE CONQUEROR.

THE German party blustered, but the officer in command of the Guards had no hesitation in forcing them to submit. They threatened, but the fixed bayonets presented at their breasts, and the disposition shown by the sturdy Englishmen who bore them to use them on the instant that an order was given, ended in a surrender.

As the baron fell, the feeling of horror which attacked Frank passed away, and, handkerchief in hand, he sprang to his father's side, binding it tightly round the wound, and following it up by the application of a scarf from his neck.

"Ah, Frank lad," said Sir Robert, as if it were quite a matter of course that his son should help him ; and he held up his arm, so that the wound could be bound while he spoke to Captain Murray.

"It was an accident," he said excitedly. "I swear that I was only on my defence."

"We saw," said the captain quietly. "He regularly forced himself on your blade."

"How is he, doctor ?" said Sir Robert excitedly.

"Bad," replied the surgeon, who was kneeling beside the fallen man, while his disarmed companions looked fiercely on.

"Don't worry yourself about it, Gowan," said one of Sir Robert's brother-officers ; "the brute fought like a savage, and tried his best to kill you."

"I'd have given ten years of my life sooner than it should have happened.—That will do, boy."

"Bad job, Gowan," said the officer who had arrested them. "The colonel was very wild as soon as he knew that you had broken arrest and come to this meeting, and it will go hard with you, Murray, and you others."

"Oh, we were spectators like the boys here," said one of the officers.

"Yes, it's a bad job," said Captain Murray; "but a man must stand by his friend. Never mind, Gowan, old fellow; if they cashier us, we must offer our swords elsewhere. I say," he continued, turning to the captain of the guard, "you are not going to arrest these boys?"

"The two pages? No; absurd. They found out that there was an affair on, and came to see. Got over the wall, I suppose. I should have done the same. I can't see them. Now, doctor, as soon as you say the word, my men shall carry our German friend on their muskets. How is he?"

"As I said before—bad," replied the surgeon sternly. "Better send two men for a litter. He must be taken carefully."

"Then I'll leave two men with you while I take my prisoners to the guardhouse. Fall in, gentlemen, please. You boys get back to your quarters. Now, messieurs —meinherrs, I mean—you are my prisoners. Vorwarts! March!"

"Aren't you faint, father?" whispered Frank, who took Sir Robert's uninjured arm.

"Only sick, boy—heartsick more than anything. Frank, your mother must know, and if she waits she will get a garbled account. Go to her as soon as you get to the Palace, and tell her everything—the simple truth. I am not hurt much—only a flesh wound, which will soon heal."

" And if she asks me why you fought, father," whispered Frank, " what am I to say ? "

Sir Robert frowned heavily, and turned sharply to gaze in his son's eyes.

"Frank boy," he said, " you are beginning trouble early; but you must try and think and act like a man. When I go, your place is at your mother's side."

" When you go, father ? "

" Yes, I shall have to go, boy. Tell her I fought as a man should for the honour of those I love. Now say no more; I am a bit faint, and I want to think."

The strange procession moved in toward the gates, the German officers talking angrily together, and paying little heed to their fellow-prisoners, save that one of them darted a malignant glance at Sir Robert Gowan, which made Andrew turn upon him sharply with an angry scowl, looking the officer up and down so fiercely that he moved menacingly toward the lad; but the Guardsman at his side raised his arm and stepped between them.

Just then the boys' eyes met, and Frank, who was still supporting his father, gave his friend a grateful look.

When the guardhouse was reached, it was just sunrise, upon as lovely a morning as ever broke ; and it contrasted strangely with the aspect of the men who had been out for so sinister a design.

Frank felt something of the kind as the door was opened to admit his father, one accustomed to command, and now ready to enter as a prisoner ; but he had very little time then for private thought, for the colonel suddenly appeared, and without a glance at Sir Robert said sharply:

" Well ? "

" Too late to stop it, sir," reported the officer in command. " Captain Sir Robert Gowan wounded in the arm."

" Baron Steinberg ? "

"The doctor is with him, sir. A litter is to be sent at once."

"But—surely not——"

"No, not dead, sir; but run through the body."

"Tut, tut, tut!" ejaculated the colonel; and he turned now to Sir Robert with words of reproach on his lips, but the fixed look of pain and despair upon his officer's features disarmed him, and he signed to the prisoner to enter.

"What shall I do now, father?" said Frank. "Let me fetch another doctor."

"Nonsense, boy. Only a flesh wound. Go back to the Park at once; I want to hear what news there is."

"Of the baron, father?"

"Yes; make haste. I must know how he is."

Frank gave a quick, short nod, pressed his father's hand, and hurried out, to find Andrew, whom he had forgotten for the moment, walking up and down in front of a knot of soldiers, looking as fretful as a trapped wolf in a cage.

"They wouldn't let me come in," he said impatiently.

"I only got in because I was supporting my father," said Frank quickly. "Come along; I'm going to see how the baron is. Has the litter gone?"

"No; there are the men coming with it now."

The two lads set off running, Andrew's ill-humour passing off in action, and he chatted quite cheerily as they made for the Park.

"Your father was splendid, Frank!" he cried. "I was proud of him. What a lesson for those haughty sausage-eaters!"

"But it is a terrible business, Drew."

"Stuff! only an affair of honour. Of course it may be serious for your father if the baron dies: but he won't die. Some of his hot blood let out. Do him good, and let all these Hanoverians see what stuff the English have in them. Don't you fidget. Why, every one in the Guards will be delighted. I know I am. Wouldn't have missed that fight for anything."

"You don't ask how my father's wound is."

"No, and he would not want me to. Nasty, shallow cut, that's all. Here we are."

They trotted into the opening where the greensward was all trampled and stamped by the combatants' feet, and found the doctor kneeling by his patient just as they had left him, and the two Grenadiers with grounded arms standing with their hands resting on the muzzles of their pieces.

"Hallo! young men," cried the doctor, rising and step-ping to them. "Is that litter going to be all day?"

"They're bringing it, sir," said Frank; "we ran on first. How is he now?"

Frank looked at the white face before him with its contracted features and ghastly aspect about the pinched-in lips.

"About as bad as he can be, my lad. A man can't have a sharp piece of steel run through his chest without feeling a bit uncomfortable. Lesson for you, my boys. You see what duelling really is. You'll neither of you quarrel and go out after this."

"Why not?" said Andrew sharply. "I should, and so would Frank Gowan, if we were insulted by a foreigner."

"Bah!" cried the doctor testily. "Nice language for a boy like you."

"Please tell me, sir," said Frank anxiously. "Will he get better?"

"Why do you want to know, you young dog?" said the doctor, turning upon him sharply. "No business here at all, either of you."

"My father is so anxious to know. I want to run back and tell him."

"Oh, that's it!" said the doctor gruffly. "No business

to have broken out to fight ; but I suppose I must tell him.
Go back and say that the baron has got a hole in his
chest and another in his back, and his life is trying to slip
out of one of them ; but I've got them stopped, and that
before his life managed to pop out.   Lucky for him that I
was here ; and I'm very glad, tell your father, that it has
turned out as it has, for I stood all through the ugly business, expecting every moment that he would go down
wounded to the death."

"Yes, I'll tell him," said Frank hurriedly.

"Don't rush off like that, boy.   How should you like to
be a surgeon ? "

"Not at all, sir."

"And quite right," said the doctor, taking out his box,
and helping himself to a liberal pinch of snuff.   "Nice
job for a man like me to have to do all I can to save the
life of a savage who did all he could to murder one of my
greatest friends.   There, run back and tell him to make
his mind easy about my lord here.   I won't let him die,
and as soon as I can I'll come and see to his arm."

The boys ran off again, passing the litter directly ; but
when they reached the guardhouse, the sentry refused to
let them pass, and summoned another of the Guards, who
took in a message to the captain who made the arrest.

He came to the door directly, and learned what they
wanted.

"I can't admit you," he said.   "The colonel's orders
have been very strict.   I'll go and set your father's mind
at rest, for of course he'll be glad that he did not kill his
adversary."

The captain nodded in a friendly way, and went
back.

"He can't help himself, Frank," said Andrew.   "Don't
mind about it.   And there won't be any punishment.   The
King and the Prince will storm and shout a bit in Dutch,
and then it will all blow over.   Your father's too great a

favourite with the troops for there to be any bother, and the bigwigs know how pleased every one will be that the Dutchman got the worst of it. I say, look; it's only half-past five now!"

"What: not later than that!" cried Frank in astonishment, for he would have been less surprised if he had heard that it was midday.

"Here they come," whispered Andrew; and, turning quickly, Frank saw the soldiers bearing in the wounded baron, with the doctor by his side, and they waited till they saw the litter borne in to the guardroom, and the door was shut.

"I say, who would have thought of this when we were going over to the messroom yesterday evening? What shall we do now—go back to bed?"

"To bed!" said Frank reproachfully. "No. I have the worst to come."

"What, are you going to challenge one of the Germans? I'll second you."

"Don't be so flippant. There, good-bye for the present."

"Good-bye be hanged! You're in trouble, and I'm going to stick to you like a man."

"Yes, I know you will, Drew; but let me go alone now."

"What for? Where are you going? You're not going to be so stupid as to begin petitioning, and all that sort of nonsense, to get your father off?"

"No," said Frank, with his lower lip quivering; "he'll fight his own battle. I've got a message from him for my mother, and I have to break the news to her."

Andrew Forbes uttered a low, soft whistle, and nodded his head.

"Before she gets some muddled story, not half true. I say, tell her not to be frightened and upset. Sir Robert shan't come to harm Why, we could raise all London if they were to be queer to him.   But take my word for it, they won't be."

Frank hardly heard his last words, for they were now in the calm, retired quadrangle of the Palace, one side of which was devoted to the apartments of the ladies in attendance upon the Queen and Princess, and the lad went straight to the door leading to his mother's rooms, and rang.

CHAPTER XVI.

FRANK HAS A PAINFUL TASK.

FOR the moment Frank Gowan forgot that it was only half-past five, and after waiting a reasonable time he rang again.

But all was still in the court, which lay in the shade, while the great red-brick clock tower was beginning to glow in the sunshine. There were some pigeons on one of the roofs preening their plumes, and a few sparrows chirping here and there, while every window visible from where the boy stood was whitened by the drawn-down blinds.

He rang again and waited, but all was as silent as if the place were uninhabited, and the whistling of wings as half a dozen pigeons suddenly flew down to begin stalking about as if in search of food sounded startling.

"Too soon," thought Frank; and going a little way along, he seated himself upon a dumpy stone post, to wait patiently till such time as the Palace servants were astir.

And there in the silence his thoughts went back to his adventures that morning, and the scene, which seemed to have been enacted days and days ago, came vividly before his eyes, while he thrilled once more with the feeling of mingled horror and excitement, as he seemed to stand again close behind Captain Murray, expecting moment by moment to see his father succumb to the German's savage attack.

There it all was, as clear as if it were still going on, right to the moment when the baron missed his desperate thrust and literally fell upon his adversary's point.

"It was horrid, horrid, horrid," muttered the lad with a shiver; and he tried to divert his mind by thinking of how he should relate just a sufficiency of the encounter to his mother, and no more.

"Yes," he said to himself. "I'll just tell her that they fought, that father was scratched by the baron's sword, and then the baron was badly wounded in return.

"That will do," he said, feeling perfectly satisfied; "I'll tell her just in this way."

But as he came to this determination, doubt began to creep in and ask him whether he could relate the trouble so coolly and easily when his mother's clear eyes were watching him closely and searching for every scrap of truth; and then he began to think it possible that he might fail, and stand before her feeling guilty of keeping a great deal back.

"I know I shall grow confused, and that she will not believe that poor father's arm was only scratched, and she'll think at once that it is a serious wound, and that the baron is dead."

He turned so hot at this that he rose quickly, and walked along all four sides of the quadrangle to cool himself before going to the door once more and giving a sharp ring.

"Are the servants going to lie in bed all day?" he said peevishly. "They ought to be down before this."

But the ring meeting with no response, he sat down again to try and think out what the consequences of the events of the morning would be. Here, however, he found himself confronted by a thick, black veil, which shut out the future. It was easy enough to read the past, but to imagine what was to come was beyond him.

At last, when quite an hour had passed, he grew

impatient, and rang sharply this time, to hear a window opened somewhere at the top of the house; and when he looked up, it was to see a head thrust forth and rapidly withdrawn.

Five minutes or so afterward he heard the shooting of bolts and the rattling down of a chain, the door was opened, and a pretty-looking maidservant, with sleep still in her eyes, confronted him ill-humouredly.

" How late you are!" cried Frank.

" No, sir; please, it's you who are so early. We didn't go to bed till past one."

" Is Lady Gowan up yet ?"

" Lor' bless you, sir, no! Why—oh, I beg your pardon, I'm sure, sir. I didn't know you at first; it's her lady-ship's son, isn't it ?"

" Yes, of course. I want to see her directly."

" But you can't, sir. She won't be down this two hours."

" Go and tell my mother I am here, and that I want to see her on important business."

" Very well, sir; but I know I shall get into trouble for disturbing her," said the maid ill-humouredly. " She was with the Princess till ever so late."

The girl went upstairs, leaving Frank waiting in the narrow passage of the place, and at the end of a few minutes she returned.

" Her ladyship says, sir, you are to come into her little boudoir and wait; she'll dress, and come down in a few minutes."

Frank followed the maid to the little room, and stood waiting, for he could not sit down in his anxiety. He felt hot and cold, and as if he would have given anything to have hurried away, but there was nothing for it but to screw up his courage and face the matter.

" She'll be half an hour yet," he muttered, " and that will give me time to grow cool; then I can talk to her."

He was wrong; for at the end of five minutes there was the rustling of garments, and Lady Gowan entered, in a loose morning gown, looking startled at being woke up by such a message.

"Why, Frank, my darling boy, what is it?" she cried, as the boy shrank from her eyes when she embraced him affectionately. "You are ill! No; in trouble! I can see it in your eyes. Look up at me, my boy, and be in nature what you are by name. You were right to come to me. There, sit down by my side, and let it be always so—boy or man, let me always be your *confidante*, and I will forgive you and advise you if I can."

Frank was silent, but he clung to her, trembling.

"Speak to me, dear," she said, drawing him to her and kissing his forehead; "it cannot be anything very dreadful—only some escapade."

His lips parted, but no words would come, and he shivered at the thought of undeceiving her.

"Come, come, dear," she whispered, "there is no one to hear you but I; and am I not your mother?"

"Yes, but——"

That was all. He could say no more.

"Frank, my boy, why do you hesitate?" she whispered, as she passed her soft, warm hand over his forehead, which was wet and cold. "Come, speak out like a brave lad. A boy of your age should be manly, and if he has done wrong own to it, and be ready to bear the reproof or punishment he has earned. Come, let me help you."

"You help me?" he gasped.

"Yes, I think I can. You dined at the mess last night; your face is flushed and feverish, your head is hot, and your hands wet and cold. Phœbe tells me that in her sleep she heard you ringing at the bell soon after five. Is this so?"

"Yes," he said with his eyes and a quick nod of the head.

"Hah! And am I right in saying that you have had scarcely any or no sleep during the night?"

He nodded again quickly, and felt as if it would be impossible to try and set his mother right.

"Hah! I am angry with you. I feel that I ought to be. There has been some escapade. Your father would have watched over you while he was there. It must have been afterwards—Andrew Forbes and some of the wild young officers. Yes, I see it now; and I never warned you against such a peril, though it is real enough, I fear."

"Oh, mother, mother!" groaned the boy in agony.

"I knew it," she said sternly; "they have led you away to some card- or dice-playing, and you have lost. Now you are fully awake to your folly."

The boy made a brave effort to speak out, but still no words would come.

"Well," said Lady Gowan, taking his hand to hold it firmly between her own.

But he was still silent.

"I am angry, and cruelly disappointed in you, Frank," she said sternly. "But your repentance has been quick, and you have done what is right. There, I will forgive you, on your solemn promise that you will not again sin like this. I will give you the money to pay the miserable debt, and if I have not enough I will get it, even if I have to sell my diamonds."

She looked at him as if expecting now a burst of repentant thanks; but he remained speechless, and a feeling of resentment against him rose in Lady Gowan's breast, as she felt that this was not the return the boy should have made to her gentle reproof, her offer to free him from his difficulty, and her eyes flashed upon him angrily.

"Oh, mother!" he cried, "don't look at me like that."

"I must, Frank," she said, loosing his hand, "you are not meeting me in this matter as you should."

"No, no," he cried, finding his tongue now, and catching her hands in his, as he sank on his knees before her. "Don't shrink from me, though it does seem so cruel of me."

"More cruel, my boy, than you think," she said, as she resigned her hands to him lovingly once more. "Speak out to me, then. It is what I fear?"

"Oh no, no, mother darling," he groaned. "I must speak now. It is far worse than that."

"Worse!" she cried, with a startled look in her eyes. "Some quarrel?"

He bowed his head, partly in assent, partly to escape her piercing look.

"And you are no longer a schoolboy—you wear a sword. Oh, Frank, Frank! you—Andrew Forbes."

He shook his head and bowed it down. Then he raised it firmly and proudly, and met his mother's eyes gazing wildly at him now, as she tried to release her hands, but as he held them tightly, pressed them with her own against her throbbing breast.

"He told me to come to you as a man and break the news."

"He—your father—told you—to break the news. Ah, I see it all. A quarrel—and they have fought—but he bade you come. Then he lives!"

"Yes, yes, mother dear. He is wounded, but very slightly in the arm."

Lady Gowan uttered a low, piteous cry, and sank upon her knees beside her son, with her lips moving quickly for some moments, as he supported her where they knelt together.

"Wounded—dangerously?" she moaned.

"No, no; believe me, mother, slightly in his sword arm. He walked back with me."

"To his quarters?"

"No. He was arrested."

"Ah!" ejaculated Lady Gowan. "Arrested—why?"

Frank hastily explained.

"Oh the horror of these meetings! But this man, your father struck him? But why?"

Frank repeated his father's message, and Lady Gowan looked bewildered.

"I cannot understand," she said. "These German officers are favourites of the King, and the baron must have cruelly insulted your father, or he, who is so brave and strong and gentle, would never have done this. They are proud and overbearing, and I know treat our English officers with contempt. Yes, it must have been from that. When was it?"

"At daybreak."

"Where?"

"Just yonder in the Park."

"And your father took you?" said Lady Gowan, with a look of horror.

"No, no, mother; he did not know I was there till it was just over, and he told me how it was."

"Yes, I see."

"I was horrified and frightened when Drew came and told me. I could not keep away."

"No," she said softly, "of course not. I should have gone myself had I known. But your good, brave father wounded, and the man who insulted him escaped unhurt!"

"No, no, mother; he is——"

"Frank! Not dead?" she cried in horror, for the boy stopped.

"No, no; but very dangerously wounded. The soldiers carried him back on a litter, but the doctor says that he will live."

Once more, while she knelt there, Lady Gowan's lips moved as her eyes closed, and she bent down her head above her son's shoulder.

At last she raised it, and said, firmly:

"We must be brave over this terrible misfortune, Frank dear. But tell me; do I know the worst?"

"Yes, yes, mother; I meant to keep a great deal back, and I can't look in your eyes, and say anything that is not perfectly true."

"And never will, my son," she cried, with a wildly hysterical burst of tears, which she checked in a few moments. "There, your mother is very weak, you see, dear; but I am going to be strong now. Then that explains the sternness of the arrest. Let us look the matter in the face. Your father struck this German nobleman, the guest of the regiment. They fought this morning, and the cause of the trouble is badly hurt. The King and the Prince will be furious. They will look upon it as a mutinous attack upon one of their favourites. Yes, I must see the Princess at once. I will go to her chamber now; so leave me, my boy, and wait. I will write to you, and I must try and get a note to your father. There, go, my own brave boy, and be comforted. The trouble may not be so great after all, for we have a friend who loves us both—the Princess, and she will help me in my sore distress. There, go, my boy; she must have the news from me, as your father contrived that it should come to me. I can go to her chamber at any time, for she has told me again and again that she looks upon me as her dearest friend."

The next minute Frank was crossing the quadrangle on his way back, feeling relieved of much of his burden; but before he reached the quarters occupied by the royal pages, Andrew Forbes stood before him.

"At last!" he said. "I've been waiting here ever since. How does she take it?"

" Bravely," said Frank, with a proud look. " She has just gone in to tell the Princess."

"And she will get Sir Robert out of the scrape if she can. But it won't do, Frank," said Andrew, shaking his head. " She'll be very kind to your mother, but you may as well know the worst. She can't; for his Majesty will have something to say about his baron. Your father might as well have hit the King himself."

CHAPTER XVII

THE KING'S DECREE.

" ANY fresh news ? "

"No. Have you any ? "

"Not much; but I've seen the doctor again this morning."

"You told me yesterday that he said you were not to dare to come to him any more."

"Yesterday! Why, that was four days ago."

"Nonsense! That would have been before the duel."

"I say, Frank, are you going out of your mind ? "

"I don't know," said the boy wearily. "My head's muddled with want of sleep."

"Muddled? I should think it is. Why, it's a week to-day since that glorious fight in the Park."

"Glorious ? "

"Yes. I wish our officers would challenge all the German officers, fight them, and wound them, and send them out of the country."

"Don't talk nonsense. Talk about the doctor. He did tell you not to come any more."

"Yes; he said he wouldn't be bothered by a pack of boys."

"Yes; he said the same to me every time I went."

"Every time! Have you been there much ? "

"About four times a day."

"No wonder he was snappish to me, then."

"I suppose it has been tiresome, and he has called me

all sorts of names, and said I worried his life out; but he always ended by smiling and shaking hands."

"You haven't been this morning of course?"

"Yes, I have."

"Well?"

"He says father's arm is going on well; but the baron is very bad."

"Serve him right."

"But I want him to get well."

"Oh, he'll get well some day. He's such a big, thick fellow, that it's a long wound from front to back, and takes time. Be a lesson to him. I say, how's Lady Gowan?"

"Very miserable and low-spirited."

"Humph!" ejaculated Andrew; and he glanced in a curious, furtive way at his companion. "I say, I thought the Princess was to speak to the King, and get your father pardoned."

"She did speak to him, and the Prince has too."

"Well?"

"We don't know any more yet. I suppose my father is kept under arrest so as to punish him."

"Yes," said Andrew, with a strange hesitation, which took Frank's attention.

"Why did you say 'yes' like that?" he cried, with his dull, listless manner passing off, and a keen, eager look in his eyes.

"Did I say 'yes' like that?"

"You know you did. What is it you are keeping back, Drew?"

"I say, don't talk like that," said Andrew petulantly. "I never saw such a fellow as you are. Here, only the other day you looked up to me in everything, and I tried to teach you how to behave like a young man of the world in courtly society."

"Yes, you did, and I am greatly obliged; but——"

"Seems like it," said Andrew sharply. "Then all at

once you set up your hackles, and show fight like a young
cockerel, and begin bouncing over me—I mean trying to;
and it won't do, young Gowan. I'm your senior."

"Yes, yes, I know," cried Frank angrily; "but this is
all talk, just for the sake of saying something to put me off.
Now speak out; what is it you're keeping back?"

"There you go again, bully Gowan! Here, I say, you
know I'm not going to stand this. You keep your place."

"Don't, don't, Drew, when I'm in such trouble!" cried
Frank appealingly.

"Ah! that's better. Now you've dropped into your
place again, boy."

"You have something fresh—some great trouble—and
you are hiding it from me."

"Well, how can I help it?" said Andrew. "You're bad
enough as it is, and I don't want to make matters worse."

"But that's what you are doing. Why don't you
speak?"

"Because you'll go and tell dear Lady Gowan, and it
will half kill her."

"What!" cried Frank, springing at his companion, and
catching him by the shoulder.

"And I look upon her as if she was my mother as well
as yours, and I'd cut off my hand sooner than hurt her
feelings more."

"I knew there was something fresh," cried Frank excitedly; "and, whatever it is, I must tell her, Drew. I
promised her that I'd be quite open, and keep nothing
from her."

"There, I knew I was right. How can I help keeping
it back? And don't, Frank lad. I say, how strong you
are. You're ragging my collar about. I shan't be fit to
be seen."

"Then why don't you speak? It's .cruel, horrible,"
cried Frank hoarsely.

"Because it comes so hard, old lad. I feel just as you

told me you felt when you had to go and tell Lady Gowan that morning."

"Yes, yes, I know; but do—do speak! You've tortured me enough."

"I've just seen Captain Murray."

"Ah!"

"He was coming out of the colonel's quarters."

"Well? Be quick—oh, do be quick!"

"I ran to him, and he took me into his room and told me."

"Yes—told you—what?"

"He said he was very sorry for you and Lady Gowan, but the King was as hard as a rock. The Prince had been at him, and the Princess too; but he would hardly listen to them, and the most he would do was—— It seems that Steinberg is a very old favourite."

"Oh, I knew all that long ago! Why do you break off in that tantalising way?"

"There is to be no regular court-martial, such as was to have been as soon as the doctor said Sir Robert could bear it."

"Yes, yes."

"Oh, it's no, no, Frank. He's to be dismissed from his regiment."

"I was afraid so," cried Frank. "But to exchange into another. What regiment is he to go in?"

Andrew was silent.

"Well, go on! Why don't you speak?" cried Frank wildly. "I asked you what regiment he was to go in."

"No regiment at all. He's dismissed from the King's service, and he is to leave the country. If he comes back, he is to be severely punished."

"Oh, they could not punish him more severely," cried Frank, with an angry stamp of the foot.

"Yes, they could. His Majesty"—Andrew Forbes said the two last words with bitter irony in his tones—"might order his execution."

"Then we are all to go away," said Frank, frowning.

"I don't know about that," replied Andrew. "But it's a good thing for your father."

"What! A good thing?"

"Yes; to get out of the service of such a miserable usurper. If it were not for the terrible upset to Lady Gowan, I should be ready to congratulate her."

"That will do," said Frank sharply. "Don't get introducing your principles here."

"Our principles," whispered Andrew, with a meaning look.

"Your principles," continued Frank, with emphasis. "I'm in no temper for that, and I don't want to quarrel. I must go and tell her as soon as I'm off duty. She'll be ready to hate the sight of me for always bringing her bad news."

But before the boy was relieved from his daily duties in the anteroom, a note was brought to him from Lady Gowan confirming Andrew's words. In fact, Frank's mother had known the worst over-night. But there was other news in the letter which told the lad that his father was to leave London that evening, that he was to accompany his mother to see him for a farewell interview, and that she wished him to be ready to go with her at seven o'clock.

Frank read the letter twice, and felt puzzled. He read it again, and sought out his friend.

"Been to see Lady Gowan?" Andrew asked.

"No; read this."

The lad took the letter, shrugged his shoulders as he read it, and handed it back.

"That's plain enough," he said bitterly.

"Do you think so? I don't. I can't make out the end."

"You are to call for Lady Gowan, and take her to Sir Robert's quarters."

"No, no, I mean about a farewell visit."

" Well, isn't that plain ? "

" But we shall go too."

" I don't think so. Your mother is the Princess's friend, and she does not wish to lose her. You will both have to stay."

" Impossible ! " cried Frank excitedly.

" Well, we shall see," said Andrew meaningly.

That evening Frank took his mother, closely veiled, to Sir Robert's quarters, where he had been ever since the duel, with a sentry beneath his window, another stationed at his door.

The pass Lady Gowan bore admitted them at once, and the next minute they were in Sir Robert's room, to find him looking pale and stern, busily finishing with his servant the preparations for an immediate start.

The man was dismissed, and father, mother, and son were alone.

Lady Gowan was the first to speak.

" You know the orders that have been given, Robert ? " she said.

" Yes ; I travel with a strong escort to Harwich, where I am to take ship and cross."

" Of course we are going with you, Robert," said Lady Gowan.

Sir Robert was silent for a few moments, and Frank stood watching him anxiously, eager to hear his reply.

" No," he said at last. " I am driven out of the country, and it would not be right to take you with me now."

" Robert ! " cried Lady Gowan.

" Hush ! " he said appealingly. " I have much to bear now ; don't add to my burden. At present I have no plans. I do not even know where I shall direct my steps. I am to be shipped off to Ostend. It would be madness to take you from here yet. The Princess is your friend, and I understand that the Prince is well-disposed toward me. You must stay here for the present."

"But I am sure that her Royal Highness will wish me to leave her service now."

"And I am not," said Sir Robert. "For the present I wish you to stay."

Lady Gowan bent down and kissed his hand in obedience to her husband's wishes.

"But you will take me with you, father?" cried Frank.

"You, my boy? No. You cannot leave your mother. She and I both look to you to fill my place till the happier days come, when I can return to England. You hear me, Frank?"

A protest was on the lad's lips; but there was a stern decision in Sir Robert's eyes and tones which silenced it, and with quivering lip he stood listening to his father's instructions, till there was a tap at the door, and an officer appeared to announce that the visitors must leave.

"Very well," said Sir Robert quietly, and the officer withdrew.

"Oh, father!" cried Frank, "let me go and ask for another hour."

"No, my boy," said Sir Robert, firmly. "It is better so. Why should we try to prolong pain? Good-bye, Frank, till we meet again. You must be a man now, young as you are. I leave your mother in your care."

His farewell to Lady Gowan was very brief, and then at his wish she tore herself away, and with her veil drawn down to hide her emotion, she hurried out, resting on Frank's arm; while he, in spite of his father's recent words, was half choked as he felt how his mother was sobbing.

"Don't speak to me, dear," she whispered, as they reached her apartments. "I cannot bear it. I feel as if we were forsaking your father in the time of his greatest need."

It was painful to leave her suffering; but there was a feeling of desire urging the lad away, and he hurried out, finding Andrew faithfully waiting at the door, and ready to press his hand in sympathy.

"It's terribly hard, lad," he said. "Oh, dear; what a wicked world it is! But you are coming to see him go?"

Frank nodded—he could not trust himself to speak—and they started back for Sir Robert's quarters.

They were none too soon; for already a couple of coaches were at the door, and a military guard was drawn up, keeping back a little crowd, the wind of the approaching departure having got abroad.

The lads noticed that fully half were soldiers; but they had little time for making observations, for already Sir Robert was at the door, and the next minute he had stepped into the first coach, the second, standing back, being filled with guards, one being beside the coachman on the box, and two others standing behind. An officer and two soldiers followed Sir Robert. The door was banged to as Frank and Andrew dashed forward, and forced their way past the sentries who kept back the crowd.

It required little effort, for as soon as the Guards recognised them they gave place, and enabled them to run beside the coach for a little way, waving their hands to the banished man.

Sir Robert saw them, and leaned forward, and his face appeared at the window, when, as if influenced by one spirit, the soldiers uttered a tremendous cheer, the rest joined in, and the next minute the boys stood panting outside in front of the clock tower, with the carriages disappearing on their way east.

"Oh, Frank, Frank!" cried Andrew excitedly, "is this free England? If we had only known—if we had only known."

Frank's heart was too full for speech, and, hardly heeding his companion's words, he stood gazing after the two coaches, feeling lower in spirits than he ever had before in his life.

"We ought to have known that the soldiers and the people were all upon his side. A little brave effort, with some one to lead them, and we could have rescued him. The men would have carried everything before them."

"Rather curious expressions of opinion for one of the royal pages, young gentleman," said a stern voice.

"Captain Murray!" cried Andrew, who was thoroughly startled to find his words taken up so promptly by some one behind him.

"Yes, my lad, Captain Murray. I am glad, Gowan, that such words did not fall from you, though in your case they would have been more excusable."

"Perhaps, sir," cried Frank, in his loyalty to his friend, though truthfully enough, "it was because I could not speak. I wish I had helped to do it, though."

"Hah! Yes, brave and manly, but weak and foolish, my boy. Recollect what and where you are, and that whispers spoken in the precincts of the Palace often have echoes which magnify them and cause those who uttered them much harm."

"I'm not sorry I spoke," said Andrew hotly. "It has been horribly unjust to Sir Robert Gowan."

"Suppose we discuss that shut in between four walls which have no ears, my lad. But let me ask you this, my hot-blooded young friend—suppose you had roused the soldiers into rising and rescuing Sir Robert Gowan, what then?"

"It would have been a very gallant thing, sir," said Andrew haughtily.

"Of course, very brave and dashing, but a recklessly impulsive act. What would have followed?"

Captain Murray turned from Andrew to Frank, and the latter saw by the dim lamplight that the words were addressed more particularly to him.

" We should have set him free."

" No. You might have rescued him from his guards; but he would have been no more free than he is now. He could not have stayed in England, but would have had to make for the coast, and escape to France or Holland in some smuggler's boat. You see he would have been just where he is now. But it is more probable that you would not have secured him, for the guard would at the first attempt have been called upon to fire, and many lives would have been sacrificed for nothing."

" I thought you were Sir Robert Gowan's friend, sir," said Andrew bitterly.

" So I am, boy; but I am the King's servant, sworn to obey and defend him. His Majesty's commands were that Sir Robert should leave his service, and seek a home out of England. It is our duty to obey. And now listen to me, Mr. Andrew Forbes, and you too, Frank Gowan; and if I speak sternly, remember it is from a desire to advise my old comrade's son and his companion for the best. A still tongue maketh a wise head. But I am not going to preach at you; and it is better that you should take it to heart—you in particular, Andrew Forbes, for you occupy a peculiar position here. Your father is a proscribed rebel."

" You dare to say that of my father!" cried the lad, laying his hand upon his sword.

" Yes, you foolish lad. Let that hilt alone. Keep your sword for your enemies, not for your friends, even if they tell you unpleasant truths. Your tongue, my lad, runs too freely, and will get you sooner or later into trouble. Men have been punished for much less than you have said, even to losing their lives."

" Is this what a King's officer should do?" cried Andrew, who was white with anger,—" play the part of a spy?"

" Silly, hot-headed boy," said Captain Murray. " I saw

you both, and came up to speak to my old friend's son, when
I could not help hearing what your enemies would call
traitorous remarks. Frank, my lad, you are the younger
in years, but you have the older head, and you must not
be led away by this hot-blooded fellow. There, come both
of you to my quarters."

"Frank, I'm going to my room," said Andrew, ignoring
the captain's words.

"No, you are coming with us," said Captain Murray.
"Frank, my lad, your father asked me to give an eye to
you, and bade me tell you that if you were ever in any
difficulty you were to come to me for help. Remember
that please, for I will help Robert Gowan's son in every
way I can."

The friendly feeling he had already had for his father's
companion all came back on the instant, and Frank held
out his hand.

"Hah, that's right, boy. You have your father's eye
for a friend. Come along, and let's have a quiet chat. I
want company to-night, for this business makes one low-
spirited. Come along, Hotspur."

"Do you mean to continue insulting me, sir?" said
Andrew sharply.

"I? No. There, you are put out because I spoke so
plainly. Look here, Forbes, I should not like to see you
arrested and dismissed from your service for uttering
treasonable words, and you will be one of these days. It
is being talked about in the Palace, but fortunately only
by your friends. Come, it is only a few steps, and we
may as well talk sitting down."

The lad was on the point of declining coldly; but the
officer's extended hand and genial smile disarmed him,
and there was something so attractive in his manner that,
unable to resist, he allowed Captain Murray to pass an
arm through his and march both lads to his quarters.

"Hah! this is better," he said, as he placed chairs for

his visitors. " Poor old Gowan ! I wish he were with us. Why, Frank, my lad, what a series of adventures in a short time ! Only the other night, and we were all sitting comfortably at dinner. How soon a storm springs up. Heard the last about our German friend ? "

" Enemy," muttered Andrew.

" Well, enemy if you like. I saw the doctor just before I caught sight of you, and he told me——"

" Not dead ? " said Frank wildly.

" No. He has made a sudden change for the better. The doctor says he has the constitution of an ox, and that has pulled him through."

" Ugh !" ejaculated Andrew ; and Frank spoke hastily to cover his companion's rudeness.

" How long do you think my father will have to be away ? "

" Till his Majesty dies, or, if he is fortunate, till your mother and the Princess have won over his Royal Highness to do battle with his father on your father's behalf."

" But do you think he is likely to succeed ? "

" I hope so, my lad. The King may give way. It will not be from friendly feeling, or a desire to do a kind action—what do you call it ?—an act of clemency."

" He'll never pardon Sir Robert !" cried Andrew, bringing his fist down upon the table heavily.

" I think he will," said Captain Murray ; " for his Majesty is a keen man of the world, a good soldier, and a good judge of soldiers. I think that out of policy, and the knowledge that he is very unpopular, he may think it wise to pardon a gallant officer, and to bring him back into the ranks of the men whom he can trust."

" Yes, yes," cried Frank excitedly ; and his eyes brightened as he treasured up words, every one of which would, he felt sure, gladden his mother's heart.

" Hadn't you better get up and see if any one is

listening at the door, Captain Murray?" said Andrew sarcastically.

"Because my words sound treasonable, my lad?"

"Yes, and may be magnified by the echoes of the Palace walls, sir."

The big, frank officer sank back in his chair, and laughed merrily.

"You're a queer fellow, Forbes—a clever fellow—with a splendid memory; but—there, don't feel insulted—you must have been meant for a woman: you have such a sharp, spiteful tongue. No, no, no—sit still. You must take as well as give. Do you two ever fall out, Frank? He's as hot as pepper."

"Yes, often," said Frank, smiling; "but we soon make it up again, for he's about the bravest and best fellow I ever knew."

As Frank spoke, he reached over and gripped his friend's arm warmly.

"You don't know how good and kind and helpful he has been in all this trouble."

"I believe it," said Captain Murray, smiling. "He's a lucky fellow too, for he has won a good friend. You hear, Hotspur? A good friend in Frank here, who is the very spit of his father, one of the bravest, truest soldiers that ever lived."

These words were said in a way which made Frank feel a little choky, and turned the tide of Andrew Forbes's anger, which now ebbed rapidly away.

"You'll come to me, my lads, both of you, if you want help?" said the captain, at their parting an hour later.

"Yes, of course," cried Frank eagerly; but Andrew Forbes was silent.

"And you, Andrew lad. Gowan asked me to be a friend to you too; for he said that Lady Gowan liked you, and that it was a hard position for a lad like you to be placed in, and he is right."

"Did Sir Robert say that, sir?" said the lad huskily.

"Yes, when we said good-bye."

"Yes, I will come to you, sir—when I can."

The last words were to himself, and he was silent for some time as they walked back to their quarters.

"I wish I hadn't such a sharp temper, Frank," he said at last. "But it is a queer position, and the harness galls me. I can't help it. I ought to go away."

CHAPTER XVIII.

"YOUR mother must be a favourite with the Princess, and no mistake," said Andrew one morning, "or after that business of your father's you would never be allowed to stay."

"If you come to that said Frank in retort, "if one half of what I know about were to get abroad, where would you be?"

"Perhaps in two pieces, with the top bit carefully preserved, as a warning to treasonable people—so called."

"I don't think that," said Frank gravely; "for they would not go to such lengths with a mere boy."

"Who are you calling a mere boy?"

"You," replied Frank coolly. "You are quite as young as I am in some things, though you are so much older in others."

"Perhaps so," said Andrew rather haughtily. "Anyhow, I don't feel in the least afraid of my principles being known. You can't tell tales, being one of us."

"I—am—not—and—never—will—be!" said Frank, dividing his words as if there were a comma between each pair, and speaking with tremendous emphasis.

"Oh, all right," said Andrew, with a merry laugh. "I should like to hear you say that to Mr. George Selby."

"I'd say it plainly to him and the whole of the members of his club," said Frank hotly.

"Not you.   Wouldn't dare.   Come with me on Friday and say it."

"I ?   No.   Let them come to me if they want it said."

"They don't.   They've got you, and they'll keep you."

"Time will prove that, Drew.   I'm very glad, though, that you have given up going."

"Given up what ? "

"Going to those dangerous meetings; and, I say, give up being so fond of staring at yourself in the glass.   I never did see such a vain coxcomb of a fellow."

"H—r—r—r !" growled Andrew, as he swung round fiercely upon his fellow-page.   "Oh, if I had not made up my mind that I wouldn't quarrel with a brother ! Ah! you may laugh; but you'll repent it one of these days."

The lad clenched his fist as he spoke ; but he was met by such a good-tempered smile that he turned away again more angry than ever.

"I can't hit you—I won't hit you !" he gasped.

"I know that," cried Frank.   "You can't hit a fellow who is fighting hard to make you sensible.   I say, who is this Mr. George Selby ? "

"Never you mind."

"But I do mind.   I want to know."

"Well, a great friend of him over the water."

"How came you to get acquainted with him first ? "

"You wait, and you'll know."

"Don't tell me without you like ; but he's a dangerous friend, and I'm very glad you've given up seeing him."

"Are you ? " said Andrew, with a curious smile.   "Why, I've seen him again and again."

"You have !" cried Frank, in astonishment.   "When ?"

"Oh, at different times.   Last evening, for instance, in the Park, while you were with your mother.   He came to feed the ducks."

"You won't be happy till you are sent away in disgrace."

"That's very true, Franky; but I don't think I shall feel the disgrace. What would you say, too, if I told you that I have been three times to the city?"

"Impossible!"

"Oh no; these things are not impossible to one who wants to do them."

"Oh, Drew, Drew!" cried Frank.

"There, don't you pity me. You are the one to be pitied."

"I say, hadn't we better talk about something else?"

"Yes. Has Lady Gowan heard from Sir Robert?"

Frank shook his head gloomily.

"What, not written yet?"

"No."

"Then they're stopping his letters!" cried Andrew.

Frank started violently.

"That's it. Just the mean thing that these people would do. I'm sure your father would not have let all this time pass without sending news."

"Oh, they would not do that!" cried Frank. "He is waiting till he is settled down, and then we shall go and join him."

"You will not," said Andrew. "They'll keep you both here, as you'll see. But, I say, hadn't we better talk about something else?"

"If you like," said Frank coldly.

"Well, then, I haven't heard, for I haven't seen Captain Murray or the doctor. What news have you heard of Steinberg?"

"He's getting better, and going home to Hanover as soon as he can bear to travel."

"That's good news," cried Andrew. "I wish he'd take the King and his court with him."

Frank gave him an angry look, then a sharp glance round to see if his companion's words had been heard, and the latter burst out laughing.

"Poor old Frank!" he said merrily. "There, I won't tease you by saying all these disloyal things. But, I say, your acts give the lie to your words. You're as true to us as steel. Come, don't be cross."

This sort of skirmishing went on often enough, for the two lads were always at work trying to undermine each other's principles; but they dropped into the habit of leaving off at the right time, so as to avoid quarrelling, and the days glided on in the regular routine of the court. But a great change had taken place in one who so short a time before was a mere schoolboy, and Lady Gowan could not help remarking it in the rather rare occasions when she had her son alone, and talked to him and made him the repository of her troubles.

"I could not bear all this, Frank," she said one day, "if it were not for the Princess's kindness. Some day we shall have your father forgiven, and he will be back."

"But some day is so long coming, mother. Why don't we go to him?"

"Because he wishes us to stay here, and he will not expose me to the miseries and uncertainties of the life he is leading."

"But we would not mind," cried Frank.

"No, we would not mind; but we must do that which he wishes, my dear."

This was three months after Sir Robert's enforced departure from the court, and when Andrew Forbes's words respecting the communications sent by Sir Robert being stopped had long proved to be unjust.

"Is he still in France?" asked Frank.

"Yes, still there," said Lady Gowan, with a sigh.

"And we can't join him. Don't you think, if you tried again, the Princess might succeed in getting him recalled?"

"I have tried till I dare try no more, for fear of disgusting one who has proved herself my great friend by my importunity. We must be content with knowing that some day your father will be recalled, and then all will be well again."

Lady Gowan did not explain to her son by what means she had letters from her husband, and once when he asked her point-blank she did not speak out, and he did not dare to press the matter.

And still the time went on.

Baron Steinberg was declared by the doctor well enough to take his journey; and one day, to Frank's relief, Andrew met him with the news that the German noble had taken his departure.

"I saw him go," said Andrew; "and, as he came out to the carriage, looking as thin as a herring, I couldn't help smiling, for all the bounce seemed to be gone out of him, and he was walking with a stick."

"Poor wretch!" said Frank.

"Nonsense! Got what he deserved. Some of these foreign officers seem to think that they wear swords and learn to use them for nothing else but to enable them to play the part of bullies and insult better men, force them to a fight, and then kill them. I'm only too glad one of them has had his lesson."

"But it's very horrible," said Frank thoughtfully.

"Of course it is," said Andrew, purposely misunderstanding him. "He'd have killed your father with as little compunction as he would a rat."

"Yes, I'm afraid so," said Frank, with a shiver.

"But he won't be so ready to insult people next time; and next time will be a long way off, I know. But, I say, it's sickening, that it is."

"What is?"

"The fuss made over a fellow like that. Baron indeed! He's only a foreign mercenary; and here is your poor father sent out of the country, while my lord has apartments set aside for him in the Palace, and he's petted and pampered, and now at last he goes off in one of the King's carriages with an escort."

"Oh, well, as far as he is concerned, it does not matter."

"Oh, but it does.   I say it's shameful that such prefer- ence should be shown to foreigners.   If matters go on like this, there'll be no old England left ; we shall be all living in a bit of Germany."

"Well, he has gone," said Frank ; "so let it rest."

"I can't, I tell you ; it makes my blood boil."

"Go and drink some cold water to cool it."

"Bah ! You'll never make a good outspoken English- man, Frank."

"Perhaps not.   I shall never make a quarrelsome one," said Frank quietly.

"What! Oh, I like that! Why, you're the most quarrel- some fellow I ever met.   I wonder we haven't had our affair in the Park before now.   If it hadn't been for my forbearance we should."

Frank stared at his companion in astonishment, for it was quite evident that he was speaking sincerely.

"Come along," said Andrew.

"Where ?"

"Out in the Park, where we can breathe the fresh air. I feel stifled in these close rooms, breathing the air of a corrupt court."

"No, thank you," said Frank.

"What ? You won't come ?"

"No, thank you."

"Why ? We're quite free this morning."

"I'm afraid."

"What, that I shall challenge you to fight somewhere among the trees ?"

"No ; I don't want to go and feed the ducks."

"There, what did I say ?" cried Andrew.   "You really are about as quarrelsome a fellow as ever lived.   No, no ; I don't mean that.   Come on, Frank, old lad ; I do want a breather this morning. I'll do anything you like—run races if you wish."

"Will Mr. George Selby be out there on the look-out for you?"

"No," said Andrew, with a gloomy look. "Poor fellow! I wish he would. Honour bright, we shan't meet any one I sympathise with there."

"Very well then, I'll come."

"Hurrah!" cried Andrew eagerly.

"It is stuffy and close in here. I did hope that we should have been down at the old house by this time."

"Yes, that holiday got knocked on the head. Has Lady Gowan heard from your father again?"

"Hush!"

"Oh, very well; I'll whisper. But there are no spies here."

"Mother hasn't heard now for some time, and she's growing very uneasy. She has been getting worse and worse. Oh, what a miserable business it is! I wish we were with him."

"Yes, I wish we were; for if matters go on like this much longer, I shall run away. Here, what do you say, Frank? I'm sick of being a palace poodle. Let's go and seek adventures while we're searching for your father."

"Seek nonsense!" said Frank testily. "Life isn't like what we read in books."

"Oh yes, it is—a deal more than you think. Let's go; it would be glorious."

"Nonsense! Even if I wanted to, how could I? You know what my father said—that I was to stay and protect my mother."

"She'd be safe enough where she is, and she'd glory in her son being so brave as to go in search of his father."

"No, she would think it was cowardly of me to forsake her, whatever she might say; and if I went off in that way, after the kind treatment we have received from the

Prince and Princess, it would make my poor mother's position worse than ever."

"I don't believe that the Prince and Princess would mind it a bit. For I will say that for him—he isn't such a bad fellow; and I nearly like her. He isn't so very easy, Frank, I can tell you. He's pretty nearly a prisoner. The King won't let him go and live away, because he's afraid he'd grow popular, and things would be worse than they are. Look how the people are talking, and how daring they are getting."

"Are they?"

"Oh yes. There'll be trouble soon. Come on."

"Mind, I trust to your honour, Drew."

"Of course. Then you won't come off with me?"

"No—I—will not."

Andrew laughed.

"I say, though," he said, as they went past the quarters the baron had occupied, "it was rather comic to see that cripple go. Just before he got into the carriage, he turned to thank the doctor, and he caught sight of me."

"What! did he recognise you?"

"I don't think so; but I was laughing—well no, smiling— and he smiled back, and bowed to me, thinking, I suppose, that I was there to say good-bye to him. He little knew. what I was thinking. Well, good riddance. But the doctor——"

"Eh?" said a sharp voice, and the gentleman named stepped out of one of the dark doorways they were passing in the low colonnade.

"Want to see me, my lads?"

"N—no," stammered Andrew, thoroughly taken aback. "We—were talking about you starting the baron off."

"Oh, I see," said the doctor, smiling. "Of course, I saw you there. Yes, he's gone. Hah! Yes! That was a very peculiar wound, young gentlemen; and I honestly believe that not one in a hundred in my profession could have saved his life. I worked very hard over his case, and he went off without so much as giving me a little souvenir —a pin or a ring, or a trifle of that kind—seal, for instance."

"What could you expect from one of those Germans, sir?" said Andrew contemptuously.

"Yes, what indeed!" said the doctor, taking snuff, and looking curiously at Frank. "Bad habit this, young man. Don't you follow my example. Dirty habit, eh? But, I say, young fellow," he added, turning to Andrew, "a still tongue maketh a wise head. Wise man wouldn't shout under the Palace windows such sentiments as those, holding the German nation up to contempt. There, a nod's as good as a wink to a blind horse. Here, Gowan, what's the last news?"

"I don't know of any, sir."

"Come, come! I'm a friend of his. You needn't be so close with me. I mean about your father."

"I have none, sir."

"Eh? Don't you know where he is?"

"No, sir," said Frank sadly.

"Humph! Pity!" said the doctor, taking a fresh pinch of snuff. "Because, if you had known, you might have written to tell him that I've cured the baron, and sent him away. Yes, I worked very hard over his case. Many's the night I sat up with him, so that he shouldn't slip through my fingers. For it would have been so much worse for your father if he had."

"Yes, horrible," said Frank.

"I say, you ought to get him back now. Have a try."

"But what can I do, sir?" cried Frank eagerly.

"Oh, I don't know. No use to ask me, boy. Politics are not in my way. If you like to come to me with a broken bone, or a cut, or a hole in you anywhere, I'm your man, and I'll try and set you right. Or if you want a dose of good strong physic, I'll mix you up something that will make you smack your lips and shout for sugar. But that other sort of thing is quite out of my way. What do you say to our all signing a round robin, and sending it into the King? for we all want Gowan back."

"Yes, sir—capital!" cried Frank; but Andrew smiled contemptuously.

"Or look here. You're a boy—smart lad too, with plenty of brains," continued the doctor, who had noticed Andrew's sneer; "sensible sort of boy—not a dandy, gilded vane, like Forbes here. Ah! don't you look at me like that, sir, or next time you're sick I'll give you such a dose as shall make you smile the other way."

"Come along, Frank," said the lad angrily.

"You wait a minute. I haven't done with him yet. Look here, boy," he continued, clapping Frank on the shoulder; "there's nothing a man and a father likes better than a good, natural, straightforward, manly sort of boy. I don't mean a fellow who spends half his time scenting himself, brushing his hair to make it curl, and looking at himself in the glass.—Here, hallo! what's the matter with you, Forbes? I didn't say you did. Pavement warm? Cat on hot bricks is nothing to you."

Andrew tightened his lips, and the doctor went on.

"Look here, Gowan; I tell you what I'd do if I were you. I should just wait for my chance—you'll get plenty —and then I should go right in front of the King, dump myself down on one knee, and when he asks you what you want, tell him bluntly, like a manly boy should, to forgive your father, who is as brave an officer as ever cried 'Forward!' to a company of soldiers."

"Bah!" ejaculated Andrew.

"Bo!" cried the doctor. "Good-looking gander! What do you know about it?—You ask him. As the offended king, he may feel ready to say *no*; but as the man and father, he'll very likely be ready to say *yes*."

"Oh, I never thought of that!" cried Frank excitedly.

"Then think about it now, my boy. That's my prescription for a very sore case. You do it and win; and if your mother doesn't think she's got the best son in the world, I'm a Dutchman, and we've got plenty without."

"Oh, thank you, thank you, doctor!" cried Frank.

"Wish you luck, boy. Do that, and you may be as proud as a peacock afterward—proud as Andrew Forbes here, and that's saying a deal."

The doctor nodded to them both, took a fresh pinch of snuff loudly, and went off.

"Bah!" growled Andrew, as he went off at a great rate toward the Park. "Ridiculous! How can an English gentleman advise such a degrading course. Go down on your knees to that Dutchman, and beg!"

"I'd go down on my face to him, Drew," cried Frank excitedly.

"You won't follow out his advice?"

"I will, and when everybody is there," cried Frank. "He's right, and I believe that the King will."

Andrew was silent for some minutes, and they walked on, inadvertently going down by the water-side, and directing their steps to the clump of trees where the duel had taken place.

They passed over the ground in silence, each picturing the scene, and then went slowly on, so as to pass round the end of the canal—for such it was in those days—and return by the other side.

Andrew was the first to break the silence, Frank being plunged in deep thought over the doctor's advice.

"You ought to be very proud of your father, Frank," he said.

"I am," was the laconic reply.

"My father, when I told him, said he behaved most gallantly, but that he ought to have killed his man."

"Your father!" cried Frank, staring. "Why, when did you see your father?"

"Can't people write?" said Andrew hastily; and he looked slightly confused. "I did learn how to read and write," he added, with a forced laugh.

Frank was silent for a few moments.

"I say," he said at last, "doesn't it seem strange that we should be both like this—each with his father obliged to keep abroad?"

"Very," said Andrew drily, and he glanced sidewise at his companion; but Frank was thinking with his brow all in lines, till they came round opposite to the house overlooking the Park, where he stopped to gaze up at the windows.

"Poor old place looks dismal," said Andrew, "with its shutters to and blinds drawn down. I wonder your mother doesn't let it."

"What, our house?" cried Frank, flushing. "Oh, they wouldn't do that."

"Seems a pity for such a nice place to be empty. But there is some one in it of course?"

"Only our old housekeeper and a maid. Come along; it makes me feel miserable to look at the place."

"But doesn't your mother go there now?"

"No; she has not been since—since——"

He did not finish his sentence, for a curious sensation of huskiness affected his throat, and he felt determined now to follow out the doctor's suggestion, so that there might be some one to take interest in the old town house again.

He took a step or two, and then waited, for Andrew appeared to be attracted more than repelled by the gloomy aspect of the blank-looking place, and then, all at once, Frank's heart seemed to stand still, and a stifling sense of suffocation to affect him, so that it was some moments before he could speak, and then it was in a tone of voice that startled his companion.

"Come away!" cried Frank angrily, and with singular

haste. "Don't stop there staring at the windows ; it looks
so absurd."

Andrew made no reply then, but walked sharply off
with his companion till they were some hundred yards
away.

"Don't be cross with me, Franky," he said gently.
"It isn't my fault, and you ought to know. I feel it as
much as you do. I always liked Sir Robert, and you
know how much I care for Lady Gowan."

Frank turned to him warmly.

"Yes, I know you do," he said, with a wild and wistful
look in his eyes ; and his lips parted as if he were eager
to say something particular to his companion.

"There, don't take on about it.   Things seem all out of
joint with us all ; but they'll come right some day.   And
don't you take any notice of me. I feel sometimes as if
I'd turned sour, and as if everything was wrong, and I
was curdled. I can't help it. Perhaps the doctor's right.
You do as he said, and ask the King boldly. For some
things I should like to see Sir Robert back."

Frank made a quick gesture as if to speak out, but
Andrew checked him with a laugh.

"Oh, I mean it," he said.   "I'd rather he joined us."

Frank gave an indignant start.

"There, there !   Don't be cross.   I won't say any
more. You ask the King. He's only a man, if he is a
king ; and if he doesn't grant your petition, I shall hate
him ten times as much as I do now. Why, what a fellow
you are ! You're all of a tremble, and your face is quite
white."

"Is it ?" said Frank, with a strange little gasp.

"Yes ; either thinking about that petition, or the sight
of your poor, dismal old house, or both of them, have
regularly upset you. Come along, and don't think about
them. I must say this, though, for I want to be honest :
if I were placed as you are, with a father who had stood

so high in George's service, I think perhaps I should be
ready to do what the doctor said for the sake of my mother
if she was alive."

Again Frank gave his companion that wistful look, and
his lips parted, but no words came ; and they went on
down by the water-side, without noticing that a shabby-
looking man was slouching along behind them, throwing
himself down upon the grass, as if idling away the time.
And all the while that the two lads were in the Park he
kept them in sight, sometimes close at hand, sometimes
distant, but always ready to follow them when they went on.

Frank noticed it at last, as they were standing by the
water's edge, and whispered his suspicions that they were
being watched.

" Who by ?   That ragged-looking fellow yonder ? "

" Yes ; don't take any notice."

" No, I'm not going to," said Andrew, stooping to pick
up a stone and send it flying over the water. " Spy,
perhaps. Well, we're not feeding the ducks to-day. He's
a spy for a crown. Well, let him spy. The place is full
of them. I've a good mind to lead him a good round, and
disappoint him. No, I will not ; it might lead to our being
arrested for doing nothing, and what would be the good of
doing that ? "

The man did his work well, for he kept them in sight
without seeming to be looking at them once, till they went
back to the Palace, where they parted for a time, and
Andrew said to himself :

" I wish I had not talked as I did about his father and
mother. Poor old fellow ; how he was upset ! "

CHAPTER XIX.

IT WAS NOT FANCY.

ANDREW FORBES would have felt more compunction had he seen Frank when he was alone; for the lad hurried to his room, where he stood trembling with agitation and thinking of what he should do.

His first thought was to go to his mother; but he knew that he could not see her at that hour, and even if it had been possible, he shrank from telling her, partly from dread of the state of agitation in which his news would plunge her, partly from the thought that he might have been mistaken—that fancy had had a great deal to do with it.

" But I'll put that to the test as soon as it's dark, if I can get away unseen," he said to himself; and then he walked up and down his room, wondering whether Andrew had seen anything—coming to the conclusion at last that if he had he would have spoken out at once.

Then came another vein of thought to trouble him, and he was mentally tossed about as to whether he ought not to have confided in his companion. Then again he tortured himself as to whether he ought not to go at once to Captain Murray and confide in him. Question after question arose till his head felt dizzy, and he was so confused that he was afraid to go and join his companion at the evening meal.

But at last his common sense told him that all this worry of thought was due to the cowardly desire to get help, when, under the circumstances, he knew that he ought to have sufficient manliness to act and prove whether what he had seen was fancy or the reality.

If it proved to be real——

He trembled at the thought; but making a brave effort, he well bathed his aching temples with cold water, and went down to the evening meal, made a show of eating, and then excused himself on the plea of a very bad headache, got up, and was leaving the room, when, to his horror, Andrew joined him.

"Here," he said, "I don't like to see you in this way. I helped to give you this headache. Let's go and have a walk up and down the courtyard."

"No, don't you come," said Frank, so earnestly that Andrew gave way and drew back.

"Very well," he said. "Go and lie down for a bit; you'll be better then."

Frank made as if to go to his room, but took his hat and cloak and slipped out, forcing himself to cross the courtyard calmly and walk carelessly by the sentries, turning off directly after in the opposite direction to that in which he wished to go, and without seeming to pay any attention kept his eyes travelling in all directions in search of the man they had seen in the afternoon.

But he was nowhere visible, and to make more sure the lad took off his hat to fan himself, the evening being warm, and in so doing purposely dropped his glove, so that in stooping to recover it he could give a good look to the rear to see whether he was followed.

But there was no one suspicious-looking in sight, and, taking advantage of the darkness of the soft, warm evening, he began to walk more sharply, going through the Park till he was opposite to the house, and after glancing to right and left, to make sure that he was not observed, he began to examine it carefully. Those to right and left had several windows illumined, but his old London home was all in complete darkness, though he felt that if he went round to the street front he would see a light in the housekeeper's room.

Dark, everywhere dark; no gleam showing anywhere, not even at the window upon which his eyes had last rested when he was there that afternoon.

"Fancy," he thought; and he breathed more freely. "Yes, it must have been fancy."

"No, it was not fancy!" and his heart began to throb violently, his breath came short, and he looked wildly to right and left, and then walked across the road to stand beneath the trees to make sure that no one was watching from there.

But he was quite alone as far as he could see, and he ran lightly back to the railings, wild with excitement now, and stood gazing across the little garden at that back window which was heavily curtained; but right up in the left-hand corner there was a faint glow, which he soon proved to himself could not be a reflection on the glass from outside.

Then he was right; and, panting now as if he had been running heavily, he went round into the street, reached the front of the house, where, as he had expected, he could see low down the faintly illumined blind of the housekeeper's room, and then rang gently.

He waited, and there was no response; and he rang again, but the time passed again; minutes—more probably moments—elapsed before he heard a window opened softly overhead.

"What is it?" said a woman's voice.

"Come down and open the door, Berry," said the boy quickly.

"You, Master Frank?"

"Yes; make haste."

"Is—is any one with you?" said the woman in a whisper, "because I don't like opening the door after dark."

"No, I'm quite alone. Make haste."

The woman did not stop to close the window, and the next minute Frank heard the bolts drawn softly back, the key turned, and as the door was being opened he stepped forward, but only to stop short on the step, for the housekeeper had not removed the chain.

"What is it, my dear?" she said.

She had not brought a light, and Frank could dimly see her face at the narrow opening.

"What is it?" cried Frank impatiently. "Take down the chain, and let me in. Don't keep me standing here."

"But her ladyship gave me strict orders, my dear, that I wasn't to admit any one after dark, for there are so many wicked people about."

"Did my father tell you not to admit me?" whispered Frank, with his face close to the narrow slit.

"What! before he went abroad, my dear?" faltered the woman.

"No, no—yesterday, to-day—whenever he came back."

"Sir Robert, my dear?" whispered the woman, with her voice trembling.

"Don't be so stupid. I must—I will see him. I saw his face at the window this afternoon."

"Oh, my dear, my dear!" stammered the woman.

"There, take down the chain, Berry."

"I—I don't think I ought, my dear. Stop a minute, and I'll go and ask him."

"No, no. Let me go up at once. You'll be quite right in letting me."

The woman uttered a gasp, closed the door, and softly unhooked the chain, after which she opened the door just sufficiently for the boy to pass in, and closed and fastened it again.

The hall was dark as could be, save for a faint gleam from the fanlight; but Frank could have gone blindfold,

and dashing over the marble floor to the foot of the staircase, he bounded up two steps at a time, reached the door
of the back room, beneath which shone a line of light, and
turned the handle sharply. As he did so, there was a
dull sound within, and the light was extinguished.

"Open the door, father," whispered the boy, with his
lips to the keyhole. "It is I—Frank."

There was the dull tremor of a heavy step crossing the
floor, the door was unlocked, and the boy sprang forward
in the darkness, the door was closed and relocked, and he
was clasped in a pair of strong arms.

"Oh, dad, dad, dad!" cried the lad, in a panting
whisper.

"My own boy! Then you saw me this afternoon?"

"Yes, just a faint glimpse of you. Oh, father, father, it
wasn't safe for you to come back!"

"No, not very, my boy; but I couldn't stop away any
longer. How is the dear one?"

"Quite well—only she looks thin and pale, father.
She's fretting so because you are away."

"Hah!" ejaculated Sir Robert, in a long-drawn sigh.
"I felt that she must be, and that helped to draw me
back. Heaven bless her!—Frank lad, as you have
found me out—— But stop, did you tell her you had seen
me?"

"I haven't seen her since, father; and if I had, I
shouldn't have dared. What would she think?"

"Bullets and bayonets, or worse, my boy. Quite
right; spoken like the brave, thoughtful lad you are
growing. But it's very hard, Frank. Don't you think
you could manage to bring her over here—say this time
to-morrow evening?"

"Yes, father, easily," said Frank.

"My boy. Oh, if you knew how I long to see her
again!"

"Yes, father," said Frank bitterly, "I could bring her,

but for what ?—to see you arrested for coming back. It would be madness. There are spies everywhere. I had to be so careful to get round here without being followed."

Sir Robert groaned as he stood there in the darkness, holding his son by his arms in a firm grip.

"I can't help it, father. I must tell you the truth," cried the boy passionately.

"Yes, you are quite right, boy, and I'm weak and foolish to have proposed such a thing. But it's hard, my lad— very, very hard."

"Don't I know, father ? "

"Yes, yes, boy. But tell me, does she talk about me to you much ? "

"She talks of nothing else, father. But listen ; I'm going to petition the King myself. I'm going to kneel to him, and beg him to give you leave to return."

"You are, my boy ? "

"Yes, father," cried Frank excitedly, "directly I get a chance."

"No, Frank, don't do that," said Sir Robert, rather sternly.

"You don't wish me to, father ? "

Sir Robert drew a deep breath, and then hoarsely :

"No. I desire that you do not. Your mother has through the Princess prayed and prayed in vain. No, Frank, you shall not do that."

"Very well, father," said the boy drearily.

"Hist ! Some one !" whispered Sir Robert ; and Frank turned sharply to see light gleaming beneath the door, and his father stepped away from him, and something on the table grated softly as it was taken up.

Then a soft voice said :

"Wouldn't you like a light, Sir Robert ? I saw yours was out."

"Yes," came from close to where Frank stood with his

hands turning wet in the darkness, and then he felt his
father brush by him, the door was unlocked, and the
housekeeper's white face was seen lit up by the candle
she carried.

"Thank you, Berry," said Sir Robert; and he took the
candle and relocked the door after the woman.

The light dazzled Frank for a few minutes, and then he
was gazing wonderingly in his father's face, to see that
it was thin and careworn, while the lines in his forehead
were deepened.

His sword and pistols lay upon the table close to some
sheets of paper, the inkstand showing that he had been
writing when he was interrupted by his visitor; and the
boy noticed, too, that there was a heavy cloak over a chair
back, and the curtains were very closely drawn.

"Don't look so smart as in the old days, Frank, eh?"
said Sir Robert, with a sad smile.

"You look like my father," said the boy firmly.

"And you like my son," cried Sir Robert, patting the
boy's head.

"Then you really would not like me to venture to ask
the King, father?"

Sir Robert pointed to a chair close by his own, and
they sat down, the father still retaining his boy's hand.

"No, Frank," he said gravely. "I should not now. It
is too late."

"But it would mean bringing you back, father."

"I am not a clever man, Frank lad," said Sir Robert.
"I am fair as a soldier, and I know my duties pretty
well; but when we get into the maze of politics and social
matters, I am afraid that I am very stupid. Here,
however, I seem to see in a dim sort of way that such
a thing as you propose would be only weak and romantic.
It sounds very nice, but it would only be raising your
hopes and—— Stop. Does your mother know that you
think of doing this?"

"Oh no, father; the doctor only just suggested it—now that Steinberg has recovered."

"Very good of the doctor, and I am deeply in his debt for saving that wretched German baron's life. Not pleasant to have known that you had killed a man in a quarrel, Frank."

"Horrible, father!" said the boy emphatically.

"Yes, horrible, lad. But the doctor is a better man at wounds than he is at giving counsel. No, Frank, under any circumstances it would not have done. King George is too hard and matter-of-fact a man of the world to be stirred by my boy's appeal. His German folk would look upon it as weakness, and would be offended. He cannot afford to offend the German people, for he has no real English friends, and between the two stools he'd be afraid of coming to the ground. No, you shall not humble yourself to do this; and," he said firmly, "it is too late."

There was something so commanding in the way these last words were said that Frank drew a deep sigh of regret, and the hopeful vision faded away behind the cloud his father drew over it. But the minutes were precious, and he could not afford time to regret the dashing of his hopes, when he had him for whose benefit they were designed sitting there holding his hand.

"Then you are going to stay here now, father?" he said.

"Here? No, Frank. It is only a temporary hiding-place. I shall be off to-morrow."

"Where to, father?"

"Humph! Don't know for certain, my boy. As you say, the place swarms with spies, and though I have had to give up my gay uniform, plenty of people know my face, and I don't even feel now that they are not hunting me down."

"But if they did, what would happen?"

"A fight, Frank—don't tell your mother this; she

suffers enough. I can't afford to be captured, and—you know what they do with the poor wretches they take?"

Frank shivered, and glanced at his father's sword and pistols.

"Loaded, father?" he said in a whisper.

"Yes, boy."

"And is your sword sharp?"

"As sharp as the cutler could make it. And I know how to use it, Frank; but a man who carries a sword—if he is a man—is like a bee with its sting; he will not use it save at the last extremity. You must remember that with yours."

"Yes, father. But do think again; we are both so unhappy there at the court."

"What, in the midst of luxury and show!" said Sir Robert banteringly.

"Pah! What is the use of all that when we know that you are driven away and dare not show your face? Oh, do think again. Can't you let us come and join you?"

"It is impossible, my boy. Don't press me. I have too many troubles as it is. Look here, Frank; you are growing fast into a man, and you must try to help me as you did just now when I turned weak and foolish. The intense longing to see your mother was too much for me, but I have mastered it. You two are safe and well-cared for at the Palace, where the Princess is your mother's friend. I am nobody now, and what I do will not count as regards your mother and you. So try and be content, and stay."

"But you, father? Surely the King will forgive you soon."

"Never, boy," said Sir Robert sternly. "So be careful. A hint dropped of my whereabouts would give your mother intense suffering and dread for my life; so she must not know."

"But your friends, father? Captain Murray—the doctor. Every one likes you."

"They must not know, so be cautious. I feel quite a young man, Frank, and don't want to have my life shortened, nor my body neither," he added, with a grim smile.

"Oh, father!" cried the boy, with a shudder.

"We must look the worst in the face, Frank. By my return here my life is forfeit, and the King's people would be justified in shooting me down."

"Oh, but, father, this is horrible."

"Not to a soldier, Frank," said Sir Robert, smiling. "Soldiers get used to being shot at, and they don't mind so much, because they know how hard it is for any one to hit a mark. There, you are warned now, so let's talk of pleasanter things."

"Yes, of course, father; but I may come and see you again often?"

"If you wish to see me taken."

Frank shuddered again.

"No. This must be your only visit. I am glad you have come; but I can't afford to indulge in good things now."

"You are going to stay in England, father?" cried Frank anxiously.

"I don't know."

"What are you going to do?"

"That I cannot tell either, my boy; and if I did know, for your mother's and your peace of mind I would not tell you."

"That isn't trusting me, father," said Frank gloomily.

"And that is not trusting me, Frank—to know what is best."

"Oh, but I do trust you, father. Now tell me," cried the boy eagerly, "what shall I do to help you?"

"Stay where you are patiently, and watch over and help your mother."

"Is that all, father?" said the boy, in a disappointed tone of voice.

"All? Is it not enough to be trusted to keep my secret, the knowledge which means your father's life, boy, and to have the guardianship of the truest and best woman who ever lived—your mother? And you ask 'Is that all?'"

"Don't be angry with me, father. I am very young and stupid. I will be as contented as I can; only it is so hard to know that you are in danger, and to be doing nothing to help you."

"You will be doing a great deal to help me, for you will be giving me rest of mind—and I want it badly enough. There, now you had better go. You may be asked for, and you can't make the excuse that you have been to see your father."

"No," sighed Frank. "But I shall see you again soon?"

"Perhaps. I may come here sometimes. An extra hole is useful to a hunted animal, Frank; but don't question me, my boy, even if I seem mysterious. As your father, I can tell you nothing."

Frank sighed and clung to his father's arm.

"There, I'll run one risk. You may come here some-times. It will not look suspicious for you to visit your mother's empty house."

"My father's empty house," said the boy.

"No, your mother's. Your father is an exile, an outcast, without any rights in England. I am dead in the eyes of the law, Frank, and when you come of age you can reign in my stead. Why, boy, if you liked to make a stand for it, they would, I dare say, tell you that you are now Sir Frank Gowan."

He looked so merrily in his son's face, that the boy joined in his mirth.

"You must go now, my boy. I have work that will

take me all night. But if you do come here in the hope of seeing me——"

"I shall not come," said the boy firmly.

" Why ? "

"Because, to please myself, I will not do anything to make your position dangerous."

"Well said, Frank ; but come now and then for my pleasure, and if I am not here, do this."

He rose and walked to a portrait framed in the wainscotting over a side table, pointed to one little oval nut in the carving, twisted it slightly, and the picture swung forward, showing a shallow closet behind fitted with shelves, and in which were swords and pistols, with flasks of powder and pouches of ball.

"You can look in there ; and if I have been, you will find a letter, written for you and your mother, by a Mr. Cross to apparently nobody. I am Mr. Cross, Frank. There. Try if you can open it."

He closed the picture door, and the boy tried, and opened and shut the panel easily, noting at the same time how ingeniously the carving tallied with portions on the other side of the framing.

"Now, then, sharp and short like a soldier, Frank. Heaven bless and protect you and your mother, who must not know I have been here. Good-bye ! "

"Good-bye, father," cried the boy in a choking voice as he clung to the strong, firm man, who pressed him to his breast, and then snatched himself away, and caught up sword and pistol from the table.

For there was a sharp, impatient knocking on the panel of the door, and Sir Robert whispered :

" We have stayed too long ! "

CHAPTER XX.

OBEYING the impulse of the moment, Frank snatched the remaining pistol from the table, and drew his sword, seeing his father nod approval, as he stretched out his hand to extinguish the light; but before he had dashed it out, the knocking was repeated, and they heard a well-known voice.

"Robert—Robert! Open quickly, dearest. It is I."

"Ah!" cried Frank, with his heart giving a tremendous bound, while Sir Robert unlocked and flung open the door, and clasped his wife to his breast.

Lady Gowan was half swooning and speechless from excitement; but, making a brave effort, she recovered herself, and panted out as she struggled to free herself from her husband's firm arms:

"Quick! Not a moment to lose. Escape for your life."

"What! They know?"

"Yes. The Princess came to my room to warn me. The spies have traced you here; information has been given at the Palace. The King has been told, and the Princess bade me try to save your life before the guard came to arrest you."

"Hah! Sharp work for us, Frank lad. Well, I have seen and kissed you, darling. Now I must try and save your husband's life."

As he spoke he buckled on his sword belt, thrust his pistols in his pockets, Frank handing him the second, and took up his hat and the heavy cloak from where they lay.

"Good-bye, darling. Frank knows how I can get a letter to you through him."

"Yes, yes; but you are killing me, Robert; for pity's sake, fly!"

"My own! Yes," he whispered, as he folded Lady Gowan in his arms again.

"Ah!" cried Frank wildly, for a heavy series of blows from the front-door knocker resounded through the house.

"Too late!" cried Lady Gowan wildly, as Frank dashed out of the door to the front room to peer through the window.

He was back in a few moments, to find his mother clinging to his father, ghastly with the horrible dread which had attacked her.

"Soldiers—a dozen at least in front!" panted Frank.

There was another loud knocking at the street door.

"Quick, father, out by that window. You can drop from the balcony."

"Yes, my boy, easily."

"Then get over the railing and cross the Park. Go straight through by the Palace. No one would think you likely to take that way."

"Good advice, boy. Out with the candle. That's right."

Lady Gowan blew out the light, and Frank quickly drew the heavy curtain aside, and uttered a groan, for the garden was full of armed men, dimly seen in the gloom amid the shrubs.

"Trapped, Frank," said Sir Robert quietly, the danger having made the soldier cool.

Lady Gowan uttered a faint, despairing cry.

"Hush, dear!" said Sir Robert firmly. "Be a woman —my wife. I may escape yet. See Berry, and keep her from opening the door, no matter what they say or do."

"Yes, yes," said Lady Gowan excitedly; "but, Robert, what will you do?"

"Escape, if you help me. Now be calm. Let them break in, and when they do face them. You were alarmed, and did not know what evil was abroad. You need no excuse for refusing to have your house—and it is your house—opened to a riotous party of drunken soldiers for aught you know. Now go down. Do anything you can to gain time for me. Heaven bless you, darling, till we meet again!"

Lady Gowan's answer was to hurry out on the staircase, where the place was echoing to the resounding knocks and orders to open in the King's name. She was just in time to seize the old housekeeper by the arm, while a hysterical crying came from the maid below.

"Oh, my lady, my lady! They're going to break in. I was about to unfasten the door."

"Silence! Touch it at your peril," cried Lady Gowan imperatively. "Let them break in if they dare. Go below to that foolish, sobbing girl, and stay there keeping her quiet."

"But they'll break down the door, my lady."

"Let them," said Lady Gowan coolly.

But she started as one of the narrow side windows was shivered by the butt of a musket, and the fragments of glass fell inside with a tinkling sound.

"That's right; now reach in and shoot back the bolts."

A hand and arm were thrust in through the hammered iron scroll work which covered the glass in the place of iron bars across the narrow window for protection, rendering it impossible for a man to creep past.

But the arm came freely right up to its owner's shoulder, and in the gloom could be seen feeling about, the hand strained here and there to reach bolt, bar, or lock. Vainly enough, for they were far out of reach; and at last, after several more angry orders, it was withdrawn.

"Try the other window!" cried the voice of the officer in command. "Quick, men; don't shilly-shally. Use your butts."

Crash, crash and *tinkle, tinkle* went the broken glass as it fell upon the marble floor beyond the mat; but the hole made was not in the best place, and there was another crash as the butt of a musket was driven through higher up, and simultaneously there was the loud report of the piece used as a battering-ram.

"What are you doing?" roared the officer.

"Went off, sir."

"Went off, idiot! You must have touched the trigger."

"No, sir. Both hands hold of the barrel."

"Silence, sir! How dare you!" roared the officer—"how dare you! Any one hurt, sergeant?"

"No, sir; bullet went too high; but it's gone through a window opposite."

Proof came of the truth of the man's word, for a window on the other side of the street was thrown open, and a voice shouted angrily:

"Hallo there! What are you doing? Want to shoot people?"

"Go in, and shut your window!" cried the officer, in an authoritative tone.

"Yes, that's all very well," cried the voice; "but you've no right to——"

"Silence, sir! in the King's name!" roared the officer. "Here, four rear rank face about, make ready, present!"

There was a shuffling sound, and the ring of muskets being brought up to the shoulder; but before the command *Fire!* could be uttered, even if it had been intended, the window opposite was banged down, and a laugh arose.

"Now then there," said the officer to the man who had thrust in his arm on the other side of the door, "can you reach?"

There was no reply for a time, while the man strained
and reached out up and down, his hand making a peculiar
whispering sound as it passed over the panelled woodwork between the door and window.

"Can't reach, sir."

"Here, let me try."

A faint light appeared at the window for a few moments,
and then there was a chinking sound as it was darkened
again, and Lady Gowan, as she stood panting there,
dimly made out that a sword was thrust through, an
arm followed, and she could hear the blade ring and scrape
as it was used to feel for the fastenings, clicking loudly
against the ironwork and the chain which hung at the
side ready for hanging across the door, to pass over a spiral
hook on the other side.

This went on for a few minutes, when, as with an
angry exclamation the officer who had thrust his arm
through paused to rest, Lady Gowan stepped forward out
of the darkness, went close to the door, bent down, and
caught the ring at the end of the hanging chain, and raised
it to hook it across and fasten it to secure the door.

She hardly made a sound with foot or dress ; but as she
drew the chain tight it chinked against the hook, and the
officer heard her.

"Ha !" he shouted, with his face to the broken glass.
"I see you there.   Open this door, or——"

Click, click went the chain into its place, and, raising
the blade of his sword, the officer made a sweeping blow
at the brave woman, which struck her on the shoulder as
she drew back.

"Now," he roared, "will you open ? "

The answer was a faint rustling, as Lady Gowan drew
back into the dark part of the hall, fortunately unhurt,
for the arm which wielded the sword was the left, and
thoroughly crippled by its owner's position.

"Lucky for you I didn't give point," he muttered.

Then aloud: "Once more, in the King's name, open this door!"

"I'd die first," said Lady Gowan to herself; and she stood close to the foot of the great staircase listening, and hardly daring to breathe, as she strained her ears to catch some sound of what might be going on upstairs, her wildly dilated eyes fixed the while on the slips of windows on either side of the door. But from within the house all she could hear was a low sobbing from the housekeeper's room below, and the murmur of her old servant's voice as she tried to calm the hysterical girl who was nearly crazy with terror.

But her attention was taken up directly by the voices outside, which came plainly to her through the broken windows.

"Well?" said the officer sharply; and she knew by the reply that one of the men must have climbed the iron railings and been down into the area.

"Both windows covered with big iron bars, sir, and the door seems a reg'lar thick 'un."

"How long will they be getting back, sergeant, with the hammer and crowbars?"

"'Nother ten minutes or quarter-hour, sir."

"Bah! Well, run round to the back, and tell them to keep a sharp look-out. See that the men are well awake at the end of the street, and keep two more ready back and front to stop every one who comes out of the houses in case he tries to escape by the roof."

"Yes, sir."

"If any one appears on the roof, and does not surrender, fire."

The sergeant's heavy paces were heard going along the pavement, every step seeming to crush down Lady Gowan's heart, as her head swam, and in imagination she saw the flash of the soldiers' muskets, and then heard the heavy fall of one for whom she would have gladly died.

Her hand went out to catch at the bottom pillar of the balustrade, and she stood swaying to and fro in the darkness, struggling hard to master the terrible sensation of faintness which came over her.

It soon passed off, for the thought came to her that she must be firm. She was doing nothing to help her husband; but he had bidden her keep watch there over that door, and guard it against danger from within, and as a soldier's wife she would have died sooner than neglect the duty with which he had intrusted her. For how did she know what pressure might be brought to bear upon the weak woman below? The soldiery had been into the area, where there were only the glass windows between, and a broken pane would form an easy way for passage of threats. If bidden to open in the King's name, what might they not do? Ah, she must guard against that, and with her nerves newly strung, she stood listening for a few moments to the buzz of voices outside, and then, feeling that it was impossible for danger to assail them without warning from the front door, she went to the head of the stairs which led down into the basement.

"In the King's name!" she said softly. "Robert is my king, and I can obey none other."

She was herself again now—the quick, eager, brave woman, ready to do anything to save her husband's life; and gliding down the stairs she silently passed the open door of the housekeeper's room, where she could hear the servant girl sobbing, and the old housekeeper trying to comfort her and then to comfort herself.

The next minute, quite unheard, she was at the end of the stone passage where the big, heavy door opened into the area, and began passing her hand over bolt, bar, and lock, to find all fast; and with a sigh of relief she was in the act of softly drawing out the big key, when a movement outside told her that a sentry had been placed at that door, and that the man must have heard the movement of the key.

This made her pause, with her heart throbbing wildly ; but in a minute or so she recovered herself, and almost by hairbreadths drew the great key slowly out with scarcely another sound, and crept back along the passage once more, past the open doorway through which the light streamed, and then up the stairs, and back to her former position in the dark hall, feeling confident now that no one could pass into the house from below unheard.

The voices of the soldiers came to her, and an angry inquiry or two from the officer, who was getting out of patience.

"Have they gone to the smith's to get the things made?" he cried angrily.

"Well, sir, you see, it aren't like muskets, or swords, or ammynition," said the sergeant. "We don't want pioneering tools every day."

"But they ought to be ready for use at a moment's notice."

"So they are," grumbled the sergeant to himself ; "but you've got to get to 'em first."

And now it appeared to Lady Gowan that an hour passed slowly away, without news of what was passing upstairs, and her agony seemed to be more than she could bear. Every sense had been on the strain, as she stood in trembling expectancy of hearing a shot fired—a shot that she knew would be at the life of her boy's father ; but the sluggish minutes crawled on, and still all was silent above, while outside she was constantly hearing little things which showed how thoroughly the soldiery were on the alert.

She had not heard the officer speak for some time, and she divined that he must have gone round to the back of the house, where it faced the open Park ; but he would, she was sure, return soon, to give directions to the men

who arrived with the tools for breaking in the door; and
when this was done, if Sir Robert had not found a way to
escape, there would be bloodshed. Her husband would
never surrender while he could grasp a sword, and Frank
would be certain to draw in his father's defence, and
then——

Then Lady Gowan felt, as it were, an icy stab, which
passed with a shock right through her; for the thought
suggested itself how easy it would be for the soldiers to
get a short ladder into the garden front of the house, rear
it against the balcony outside the drawing-room window,
and force their way in there. No bars would trouble
them, and the shutters would give but little resistance.
Why had she not thought of that before?

And as she thoroughly grasped this weakness of their
little fort in the rear she turned cold with horror, for there
was a faint sound on the staircase behind her, and as at
the same moment she heard the loud steps of approaching
men on the pavement outside a hand made a quick clutch
from the darkness behind at her arm.

CHAPTER XXI.

FOR DEAR LIFE.

"NOW, Frank, my boy," said Sir Robert, as the door closed on Lady Gowan, "they have us in front, and they have us in the rear. A fox, they say, always has two holes to the earth. A man is obliged to have a third way of escape if his enemies are too many for him, and I don't want to fight with the King's men for other reasons than that they belong to my old regiment."

"Shall I light the candle again, father?"

"No, it will take too long, and I can do what I want in the dark. I've a rope here."

Frank heard his father unlock a cabinet, and his heart beat hopefully, when the next minute his father bade him "take hold," and he felt a thin, soft coil of rope passed into his hands.

He needed no telling what was to follow, for he grasped the idea at once, and followed his father out of the room without a word.

They paused on the staircase for a few moments, and heard the shivering of the glass and the stern summons for the door to be opened; and then Sir Robert laid his hand upon his son's shoulder.

"Seems cowardly, Frank, to try to escape, and leave a woman to bear the brunt of the encounter; but I must play the fugitive now. I can't afford to surrender; the risks are too great. Come on. Your mother must not be disappointed after what she has done, and have to see me marched off."

Frank was astounded at his father's coolness, but he said nothing, and followed him quickly to the top of the house to where there was a trap-door in the ceiling over the passage leading to one of the attics.

Without telling, Frank bent down and raised the light steps which were on one side of the passage, passed his arm through the coil of rope, went up the steps, and pushed open the trap-door, which fell back, leaving an opening for him to pass through into the false roof.

Sir Robert followed, and a door formed like a dormer window in the slope of the roof was unbolted ready for him to step out on to the narrow leads.

" Now, Frank lad, give me the rope," said Sir Robert in a low voice. " Then follow me along by the parapet. We need not crawl, for it will hide us from the soldiers if we lean inward and keep one hand on the sloping slates."

" Yes, I understand," said Frank ; " you mean to go along the roofs right to the end."

" Yes : right."

" And fasten the rope round a chimney stack ? "

" That's quite right too ; and now listen.   I shall not be able to talk to you out there.   As soon as I am down, don't stop to untie the rope ; it will be too tight from my weight.   Cut it, and draw it up again quickly, then get back as you came, shut the door after you, and take down the steps before you join your mother.   But you must do something with the rope."

" Hide it ? " said Frank.

" It would be found, and I don't want you or your mother to have the credit of helping me to escape."

" Burn it in the kitchen fire ? "

" There will not be time.   They will search the house. I cannot propose a way, only do something with it.   Now good-bye."

" Good-bye ? " faltered Frank.

" Yes, while I can speak to you. Quick ! a soldier's good-bye. That will do ; now out after me."

Sir Robert's "good-bye" was a firm grip of his son's hand, and then he crept out on to the roof ; Frank followed him, his heart throbbing with excitement ; and as he stepped out he could hear voices down below in the garden beneath the drawing-room windows.

Frank shivered a little, for he felt sure that they would be seen against the sky, in spite of their precaution of leaning toward the sloping roof, and he fully expected to hear the report of muskets ; but the shiver was more due to excitement than fear.

" They would not be able to hit us on a night like this, while we are moving," he said to himself ; and with a strange feeling of wild exhilaration, he followed the dark figure before him, climbing across the low walls which separated house from house, and finding it easy enough to walk along in the narrow pathlike space of leaded roof, which extended from the bottom of the slate slope to the low parapet with its stone coping, beyond which nothing was visible but the tops of the trees in the Park.

They must have passed over the roofs of twenty houses before Sir Robert stopped ; and, as Frank crept up close to him, he put his lips to the boy's ear.

" It's a drop of ten feet to the next house," he said. " Must go down from here."

A sensation of dread did now attack Frank, as he thought of the descent of a heavy man by the frail rope. If it had been he who was to go down, it would have been different, and he would have felt no hesitation.

Catching at his father's arm, he whispered :

"Are you sure that it will bear you ? "

" Certain."

" But the chimney stack ? " whispered Frank, as he

could dimly make out that his father was uncoiling the rope, and he could see no place that would be suitable.

"Hist! This is better."

Sir Robert was now kneeling down, and after being puzzled for a few moments, Frank then made out that his father was passing one end of the rope through an opening at the corner of the parapet where the rain-water ran through a leaded shoot into the upright leaden stack-pipe which ran down the house and carried it into the drain.

Frank dimly made out that he knotted the rope carefully, and tried it by pulling hard twice over, before throwing a few yards over the parapet and letting the rest run through his hands till it was all down.

His next movement puzzled the boy, but he grasped the meaning directly after.

They were at an angle now, and Sir Robert was carefully testing the stone coping, to see if it were tight in its place and the pieces held together by the iron clamps kept in their places by the running in of molten lead.

Apparently satisfied, he turned quickly to where Frank stood, now trembling, grasped his hand, and whispered:

"Have you a knife?"

"Yes, father."

"Cut the rope, and get back as soon as you can. Don't wait to listen whether I elude the men."

"No, father."

Sir Robert stood holding his son's hand for a few moments, and listening to the murmur of voices at the back of his house, where the soldiers were talking rather excitedly.

"For liberty and life, Frank!" whispered Sir Robert then; and with the perspiration standing in great drops on the boy's face, he saw his father grasp the rope knotted so tightly from the hole by the lead on which he stood over the stone coping, throw back his cloak, and then lay

"'For liberty and life, Frank!' whispered Sir Robert. [p. 190.

himself flat on the parapet, and carefully lower his feet as he held on by the stone. From that he lowered himself, and, partly supported by the top of the leaden

stack-pipe, he slowly changed his right hand to the loop
of the rope; then softly gliding by the wide-open head
of the pipe, he began to descend with the rope well twined
round his right leg, and held to the calf of his heavy boot
by the edge of his left boot sole.

"If the rope should break or come undone!" thought
the boy, as he turned cold and dropped upon his knees to
reach over and grip the knot with both hands, while his lips
moved as he muttered a prayer, feeling the thin cord
quiver and jerk as if it were a strange nerve which
connected him with his father, who was below there
somewhere in the darkness—jar, thrill, and make a
humming noise like the string of some huge bass instru-
ment, but so faint that it would have been inaudible at
any other time. But he could hear plainly enough, without
any exaltation of his senses, that the soldiers were talking
earnestly not a hundred yards away, their voices rising
clearly to where the boy knelt.

How long was it that he could feel that vibration of the
cord which thrilled through him right to his toes, and
made his hair feel as if it were being lifted from his scalp?
Ten minutes—five minutes—a quarter of an hour? Not
many seconds, and then it stopped; and the horror of
feeling it suddenly slacken and hearing a heavy crashing
fall did not assail the anxious boy, though he had fully
expected it. The vibration ceased, and there was a quick,
warning shake, which Frank interpreted to mean a signal
for him to remember his orders, and hasten back to the
house.

He would have liked to lean over, listening and straining
his sight to follow the further movements of his father;
but Sir Robert had, unconsciously to both, gradually
disciplined his son into a prompt, soldierly way of instantly
obeying orders, and directly that wave had passed up to
him, Frank's knife was out, and the rope, after a good
deal of sawing, was cut through, the knife replaced, and

the cord was rapidly drawn up, and laid down on the leads in a loose coil.

He bent over then for a moment or two and listened, but all was still just below. There was no alarm such as he had dreaded, no shouting and firing of shots; and gathering up the rope, he hurried back along the narrow leads, using the same precaution of leaning inward, passed from house to house quickly, and kept on asking himself what he should do to hide the rope.

No idea came, and he had nearly reached home before it flashed across his brain, and he drew a breath of relief.

There was a hiding-place just before him, at the top of the low ridge of the house two doors away from his own. A low chimney was smoking steadily, and without pausing to think whether it was wise or no he crept up the slates, reached the ridge, grasped the side of the chimney stack, and stood upright, finding that he could just reach the top of the smoking pot.

That was enough. The next minute he had the end of the rope passed in; and resting his wrists on the top of the pot, he drew and drew, rather slowly at first, but more and more rapidly as the descending end gained weight, and at last sufficed to run it down, and then it was gone.

He slid down the slates, and, feeling relieved of an incubus, he reached their own house, glided in at the dormer, shut and bolted the door, descended through the trap, drawing it over him, went down the steps, laid them in their place, and, lastly, wondering whether he had soiled his hands with the black on the top of the house, he ran rapidly downstairs.

As he ran he could hear the heavy tramp of the soldiers in the street at the front, and when he reached the lower flights dimly made out the figure of his mother standing at the bottom step, and stretched out his hand and caught her arm.

Lady Gowan uttered a cry of horror, and sprang

forward into the hall, facing round to meet her invisible enemy; but she uttered a faint sigh of relief as her arm was caught again, and she heard the familiar voice whisper :

"Hush ! hush ! mother."

"Ah !" she whispered back. "Your father ?"

Frank's answer was drowned by a thunderous blow delivered with a sledge-hammer upon the door close to the lock, and this was followed by another and another, which raised echoes up the staircase, and brought a series of hysterical shrieks from the housekeeper's room.

But Lady Gowan paid no heed to either. She caught her son by the arms, and drew him farther from the door, placed her lips to his ear, and whispered in an agonised tone :

"Your father ?—speak !"

"Got down safe, and gone," whispered back Frank ; and as his mother clung to him a strange thrill of elation ran through his nerves, making him feel that he was engaged in an adventure full of delirious joy. He felt that he must shout and cheer to get rid of the intense excitement which made his blood bubble in his veins, and he was ready for any mad display in what was like playing some wonderful game, in which, after a desperate struggle, his side was winning.

"Let them hammer and bang down the door, mother. The idiots ! they are giving him time to get safe away. Oh the fools, the fools ! Shall I go and speak to them ?"

"No, no," whispered Lady Gowan, speaking with her lips once more to her boy's ear, for the noise made was deafening. "Let them take time to break in, and then we must parley with them, and let them suspect us and make a regular search. They will waste nearly an hour, Frank."

"Of course they will," cried the boy joyously ; "but, I say, mother, we're not going to put up with this, you know ; I'm not going to have you insulted by these people breaking into the house. I shall show fight."

"No, no, don't do anything imprudent, Frank. We must assume that we took them for a ruffianly mob who tried to break in."

"But they said, 'In the King's name,' mother," said the boy dubiously.

"And we would not believe them, my boy. Frank, Frank, it is horrible to incite you to prevaricate and dally with the truth, but it is to save your father's life. Be silent. On my head be the sin, and I will speak and bear it."

The crashing of the woodwork went on beneath the blows, and the murmur that rose like a low, deep accompaniment outside told that a crowd had collected, and were being kept back by the soldiery.

"This way, Frank," cried Lady Gowan; and she drew her son after her to the head of the basement steps, where she called aloud to the housekeeper, who came hurrying up, candle in hand, to where mother and son stood.

The old woman looked ghastly, and Frank could hear a strange sobbing from below, in spite of the noise at the front, which was partly deadened from where they stood.

"Master, my lady?" cried the woman wildly.

"Safe—escaped, Berry," said Lady Gowan, in a voice full of exultation.

"Safe—escaped, my lady!" cried the woman, with the light of exultation rising now in her countenance. "Then let them batter the house down, the wretches. I don't care now."

"But, Berry, listen. Sir Robert is out of their reach by now; but they must not know that he has been here."

"Ha, ha, ha!" laughed the woman wildly; "they won't get anything out of me. What! me tell 'em that my dear young master, whom I nursed when he wasn't half the size of Master Frank—tell 'em he has been here! I'd sooner have my tongue cut out."

"But the girl—the girl?"

"What her, my lady?" said the housekeeper contemptuously. "Oh, they'll get nothing out of her to-night but shrieks, and nothing now, for she's shruck herself hoarse and speechless."

"Ah!" sighed Lady Gowan, "then now I can feel at rest. Come up, Frank."

She led the way to the staircase, and hurried on to the drawing-room, with the massive front door being broken piecemeal by the heavy sledge-hammer; but each chain and bolt still held, and there was no way in yet but for light and noise, so that, before they gave way, Frank had time to get a light and ignite the candles in two sets of branches in the drawing-room which they had entered and then fastened the door.

This done, he turned in surprise to see that his mother had thrown back her hood, rearranged her hair, and was standing there before him flushed, but proud and perfectly calm.

"Oh, mother!" he cried, stepping up to her and kissing her. "I can't help it. Drew is right. I am so proud of you."

"Are you?" she said, smiling, as she returned his kiss, and her look said that the pride was reciprocal.

They gazed in each other's eyes for a few moments, as if deaf to the sounds below-stairs, which told that the soldiers had at last gained an entrance.

Then a change came over Lady Gowan's face, her upper lip curled, and a look of haughty scorn shone from her eyes.

"They are coming up, my boy," she cried. "Leave me to speak."

For answer Frank drew his sword, caught up the silver branch with its three candles from the table, and took a couple of strides in front of his mother toward the door, as it was dashed open, when, sword in hand, followed by half a dozen men with fixed bayonets, the officer in command rushed in.

CHAPTER XXII.

SAVED!

"HERE, how dare you!" shouted Frank angrily; and, in utter astonishment, the officer stopped short, and lowered the sword he had fully expected to use, while the men threw up their bayonets and stood fast. "I don't know you, but you belong to the Guards, I suppose, and——"

"Silence, Frank! Let me speak," said Lady Gowan, without a tremor in her voice. "Then you are not an armed mob of rioters. Pray, what does this outrage mean?"

"I ask your pardon, Lady Gowan," said the young officer, recovering himself; "it is a painful act of duty."

"To break into my house, sir!" said Lady Gowan haughtily, while her son felt more than ever that he was engaged in some madly exciting game.

"I was refused entrance, after repeatedly demanding it in the King's name."

"In the King's name!" cried Lady Gowan scornfully. "How were I, my son, or my servants to know that this was not the excuse made by one of the riotous Jacobite bands to obtain entrance and plunder my home?"

"I cannot help fulfilling my duty, Lady Gowan," said the young officer respectfully. "I must proceed to the arrest."

"Arrest?" cried Lady Gowan hurriedly. "Oh, Frank!

But surely—ah, I will speak to the Princess.   Such a
trivial act—a thoughtless boy.   Arrest him for absenting
himself without leave—to meet his mother—at his own
home ? "

"Your ladyship must be trifling with me," said the
officer sternly, "and I cannot be played with.   Information was brought to the Palace that Sir Robert Gowan
is here, and at all costs my orders are to arrest him.   I
beg that you will tell him to surrender at once."

"Go back to those who sent you, sir, and tell them that
Sir Robert Gowan is not here."

"Then where is he, madam ? "

"You have no right to question me, sir," said Lady
Gowan haughtily ; "but, to end this interview, I will
answer your question.   I do not know."

"Your ladyship tells me that ? " cried the officer
quickly.

"I refuse to be questioned by you, sir," said Lady
Gowan with dignity.   "You are in the King's Guards ;
you have a duty to perform.   I am helpless at this
moment.   Pray do it, and go.   But I insist, in the name
of the lady whom I have the honour to serve, that you do
not go without leaving a proper guard to protect this
house from pillage by the mob outside."

The officer looked puzzled and confused for a moment
or two, and then he spoke again sharply.

"I am bound to take your ladyship's word," he said ;
"but you know ! " he cried, turning suddenly upon Frank,
and so fiercely intended as to throw him off his guard.
"Come, sir ; it is of no use to prevaricate.   Where is Sir
Robert ? "

But Frank was as firm as his mother, and he met
the young officer's eyes without flinching.

"Where is my father ? " he said quietly.   "I don't
know, and if I did I wouldn't tell you."

A flush of anger suffused the young Guardsman's face ;

but the boy's manner touched him home, and the anger passed away in a laugh.

"Well," he said, "that's not a bad answer. Unfortunately, young gentleman, I can't be satisfied with it. —Lady Gowan, I regret having this duty placed in my hands to carry out, but I must perform it. I am compelled to disbelieve you and your son, and search the house."

'Do your duty then, sir," said Lady Gowan coldly; "but I cannot stay here to submit to the insult. I insist upon my house being protected."

"My men are at the door, madam, and no one will be allowed to pass. I answer for the place being safe."

"Thank you, sir," said Lady Gowan courteously. "I do not blame you for all this. I presume my son and I can pass your men?"

"Of course, madam," said the officer; and his manner changed, for these words impressed him more than any denial that Sir Robert was there. "I thank you for going, though," he said, recovering his composure. "You relieve me from the painful duty of arresting Sir Robert in your presence."

Lady Gowan smiled, and drew her hood over her head.

"Come, Frank," she said; "see me back to the Palace; you will not need your sword."

The officer took up the silver branch Frank had set down, and as the boy returned his sword to its sheath, and his mother took his arm, the officer preceded them, and lit them down the stairs, where Lady Gowan stopped in the splinter-strewn hall to speak to the housekeeper.

"See, Berry," she said quietly, "that this gentleman and his men have every opportunity for searching the house. A rumour has been carried to the Palace that Sir Robert is here. When they have done, men will be placed as sentries to guard the place. In the morning send for the workmen to see that a new door is placed there, and to do first what is necessary to board this one up."

"Yes, my lady," said the housekeeper quietly.

The next minute Lady Gowan and her son passed out of the house with a corporal and four men to escort them back to the Palace, the crowd making way for the armed men, while the officer returned to the hall, and looked at the sergeant fixedly.

"Gone?" said the officer.

"Yes, sir. Bird's flown," replied the sergeant.

"Well, search from top to bottom, from cellar to leads. That's the way he must have gone."

"If it wasn't a false alarm, sir," said the man respectfully. "I never had much faith in any spies."

"Be on your guard; he may be here," said the officer. "Now search."

The sergeant went off promptly with his men, muttering to himself:

"And nobody's better pleased than me. Nicely we should have been groaned at if we had found him. That is, if we had taken him; but he'd have fought like the man he is. Well, I'm glad he's gone."

"Saved, Frank, saved!" whispered Lady Gowan, as they parted on reaching the Palace.

"Yes, mother, saved. Oh, don't look like that!"

She kissed him hurriedly, and entered her apartment, to hurry thence to the Princess's chamber; while Frank made for his own, with his head feeling as if it were full of buzzing sounds, and ready to ask himself if all that he had gone through was not part of a feverish dream.

CHAPTER XXIII.

MORE ABOUT THE DUCKS.

THE news was all over the Palace the next morning ; but before meeting Andrew Forbes, Frank hurried to his mother's apartments, to find her dressed, but lying down, her maid saying that she was very ill, but that she would see Mr. Gowan.

"I thought you would come, my boy," said Lady Gowan, embracing him. "Oh, my darling, what a horrible night! Tell me again all about your father's escape."

"You're not well enough, mother," said the boy bluntly. "It will only agitate you more. Isn't it enough that I helped him to get safe away without any accident?"

"Yes, yes, you are right," said Lady Gowan. "But how rash, how mad of him to come! Frank, remember that you must not breathe a word about how it was that I was able to warn him."

"I see," said Frank ; "it would make mischief."

"And this has undone all that I was trying to do. He might have been forgiven in time ; now we shall have to wait perhaps for years."

"Then don't let's wait, mother. He says that we should have to suffer terribly if we shared his lot with him. But who cares? I shouldn't a bit, and I'm sure you wouldn't mind."

"I, my boy?" cried Lady Gowan passionately. "I'd gladly lead the humblest life with him, so that we could be at peace."

"Very well, then ; let's go."

Lady Gowan shook her head.

"We must respect your father's wishes, Frank," she said sadly. "No ; we must stay as we are till we are ordered to leave here, or your father bids us come."

"There," said the boy, "I was right. You must not talk about it any more ; it only makes you cry. Never mind what happened last night. He has got safely away."

"But if he should venture again, my boy," sobbed Lady Gowan.

"Never mind about *ifs*, mother. Of course he longed to see us, and he ran the risk, so as to be near. I should have done the same, if I had been like he is. There, now you lie still and read all day. He won't run any more risks, so as not to frighten you. I must go now."

Lady Gowan clung to her son for a few minutes, and then he hurried away, to find Andrew Forbes in the courtyard.

"Ah, I was right !" he said. "I went to your rooms, thinking I should catch you ; but you were up and off. I thought this would be where you had come. But, I say, I thought we were friends."

"Well, so we are."

"Don't seem like it, for you to go and have a jolly night of adventures like that, and leave me out in the cold."

"I couldn't help it, Drew," said Frank apologetically.

"Yes, you could. I smell a rat now. I thought you turned very queer when we were by your house yesterday. Then you saw him at one of the windows ? "

Frank looked at him frowningly, and then nodded his head.

"And never told me ! Well, this is being a friend ! I would have trusted you. But, I say, it was grand. I've just seen Captain Murray and the doctor. They were together in the captain's room. They wouldn't say so, of course, but they were delighted to hear he got away, though they say they wouldn't wonder if you were dismissed."

" I don't care, if my mother has to leave too."

" Ah ! but the Princess wouldn't let her go. I say, how do you feel now ? "

" Very miserable," said Frank sadly.

" Nonsense ! You mean not so precious loyal as you were."

" If you are going to begin about that business again, I am going," said Frank coldly.

" I've done. I'm satisfied. You'll be as eager on the other side some day, Frank ; and I like you all the better for being so staunch as you are. As my father says, it makes you the better worth winning."

" When did your father say that ? " cried Frank sharply.

" Never mind. Perhaps he wrote it to me. You can't expect me to be quite open with you if you're not with me. But, I say," cried the lad enthusiastically, " it's grand ! "

" What is ? "

" For us to be both with our fathers banished. Why, Frank, it's like making heroes of us."

" Making geese of us ! What nonsense ! "

" Just as you like ; but I shall feel what I please. I never did see such a fellow as you are, though. You have no more romance in you than a big drum. But, I say, tell us all about it."

With a little pressing Frank told him all, the narrative being given, in an undertone, and after a faithful promise of secrecy, on one of the benches under a tree in the Park, while Andrew sat with his fingers interlaced and nipped between his knees, flushed of face, his eyes flashing, and his teeth set.

" Oh," he cried at last, " I wish I had been there, and it had come to a fight."

"What good would that have done?" said Frank.

"Oh, I don't know; but what a night! It was glorious! And to think that all the while I was moping alone over a stupid book, while you were enjoying yourself like that."

"Enjoying myself!" cried Frank scornfully.

"Yes, enjoying yourself. There, with your sword out, defending your beautiful mother from the Guards, after saving your father's life, and keeping the castle—house, I mean—against the men who were battering down the gate—door."

"Well," said Frank drily, "if I have no more romance in me than there is in a big drum, you have."

"I should think I have!" cried the lad, whose handsome, effeminate face was scarlet with his excitement. "Why, you cold-blooded, stony-hearted old countryman, can't you see that you were doing man's work, and having glorious adventures?"

"No; only that it was very horrible," said Frank, with his brow all in lines.

"Bah! I don't believe you felt like that. What a chance! What a time to have! All the luck coming to you, and I'm obliged to lead the life of a palace lapdog, when I want to be a soldier fighting for my king."

"Wait till you get older," said Frank. "I wanted to be a man last night."

"Why, you were a man. It was splendid!" cried Andrew enthusiastically.

"I wasn't a man, and it wasn't splendid," said Frank sadly. "I felt all right then; but when I woke this morning, I seemed to see myself standing there in our drawing-room, with my sword in one hand and the big silver candlestick in the other, and I felt that I must have looked very ridiculous, and that the young officer and the men with him must have laughed at me."

"Er—r—rr!" growled Andrew; "I haven't patience

with you, Franky. You're too modest by half—modest
as a great girl. No, you're not; no girl could have
behaved.like you did. I only wish I had had the chance
to be there. Ridiculous indeed! Very ridiculous to help
your father to escape as you did, 'pon my honour. Oh
yes, very ridiculous! I want to be as ridiculous as that
every day of my life; and if it isn't playing the man——"

"Yes, that's it," said Frank gloomily,—"playing the
man, when one's only a boy."

"Bah! Hold your tongue, stupid. You don't know yet
what you did do. But, I say, that was ridiculous, if you
like."

"What was?" said Frank, starting.

"Climbing up the roof to hide the rope, and stuffing it
down the next-door chimney. I say: I wonder what the
people thought."

Frank smiled now.

"Well, that does seem comic."

"It was glorious. But they'll never know. They'll
think the sweeps must have left it when the chimney
was last swept. But I suppose you've heard about
Lieutenant Brayley's report?"

"No, not a word. I went as soon as I was dressed to
see how my mother was."

"Oh, I heard from Murray. He reported that it was a
false alarm, and that Sir Robert could not have been there,
for he had the house well watched back and front, and
all the approaches to the houses adjoining. Oh, I do enjoy
getting the better of the other side. And, I say, every one's
delighted that he escaped, if he was there; but I hope he
won't get taken. Tell him to mind, Franky, for every
place swarms with spies, and that it's next to impossible to
get out of the country. Oh, I wouldn't have him taken for
all the world."

"Thank ye," said Frank warmly; "but how am I to tell
him that?"

Andrew turned and gave his companion a peculiar smiling look.

"Of course," he said merrily, "how can you tell him ? He did not tell you how to write to him—oh, no; nor where to find the letters he sent to you. Oh, no; he wouldn't do that. Not at all likely, is it ? "

Frank turned white.

"How did you know that ? " he said hoarsely.

"Because I'm rowing in the same boat, Franky. Why, of course he did. Now, didn't he ? "

The boy nodded.

"So did my father, of course. There, I'm going to thoroughly trust you, if you don't me. I'd trust you with anything, because I can feel that you couldn't go wrong. I don't want you to tell me where your father told you to write, or what name he is going to take, or how you are to get his letters, for of course he couldn't write to the Palace. But he told you how to communicate with him, I do know, Frank. It was a matter of course with your father like that. I say, what do you think of a tin box in a hollow tree in the Park, where you can bury it in the touchwood when you go to feed the ducks ? "

"That would be a good way of course," said Frank ; " but no, it isn't like that."

"What, for you and your father ? Who said it was ? I meant for me and mine."

"What ! Feed the ducks ! Drew !" cried Frank excitedly.

"Yes ; what's the matter ? "

" Feed the ducks ? "

"Yes, feed the ducks ! "

"You don't mean to tell me that—that——"

" Mr. George Selby is my father ? Of course I do."

" Oh !" ejaculated Frank in astonishment.

"Isn't it fine ? " cried Andrew. "He comes and feeds the ducks—his Majesty King George's ducks—and the precious spies stand and watch him ; and sometimes he has a chance to see me, and sometimes he hasn't, and then he leaves a note for me in the old tree, for he says it's the only pleasure he has in his solitary exiled life."

" Oh, Drew !" cried Frank warmly.

" Yes, poor old chap. I'm not worth thinking about so much, only I suppose I'm something like what poor mother was, and he likes it, or he wouldn't leave all his plots and plans for getting poor James Francis on the throne to come risking arrest. They'd make short work of him, Frank, if they knew—head shorter. I shall tell him I've told you. But I know what he'll say."

" That you were much to blame," said Frank eagerly.

" Not he. He'll trust you, as I do. He likes you, Frank. He told me he liked you all the better for being so true to your principles, and that he was very glad to find that I had made friends with you. There, now you can tell me as much as you like. Nothing at all, if you think proper ; but I shall trust you as much as you'll let me, my lad. There, it's time to go in. I want to hear more about what they're doing. As they know that your father has been seen, they'll be more strict than ever. But let's go round by your old house."

" No, no," said Frank, with a shudder.

" Better go.—Come, don't shiver like that. You were a man last night ; be one now."

" Come along then," said Frank firmly ; and they walked sharply round by the end of the canal, and back along the opposite side toward Westminster, passing several people on the way, early as the hour was.

" Don't seem to notice any one," said Andrew ; " and walk carelessly and openly, just as if you were going —as we are—to look at your old house where the adventure was."

" Why ? "

"Because several of the people we pass will be spies. I don't want to put you all in a fidget; but neither you nor your mother will be able to stir now without being watched."

"Do you think so?" said Frank, who felt startled.

"Sure of it. There, that's doing just what I told you not to do, opening your mouth like a bumpkin for the flies to jump down your throat, and making your eyes look dark all round like two burnt holes in a blanket. Come along. You mustn't mind anything now. I don't: I'm used to it. Let 'em see that you don't care a rush, and that they may watch you as much as they please. Now don't say anything to me, only walk by me, and we'll go by the Park front of your place. I want to have a quiet stare at the tops of the houses and at the corner where your father slipped down the rope."

Frank obeyed his companion, and they walked on, seeing no one in particular, save an elderly man with a very bad cough, who stopped from time to time to rest upon his crutch-handled stick, and indulge in a long burst of coughing, interspersing it with a great many "Oh dears!" and groans. They left him behind, as they passed the last tall house, where Frank shuddered as he saw the upright leaden stack, the hole in the parapet, where the rope was tied, and the garden beneath.

The boy turned hot as he went over the whole adventure again and thought the same thoughts. Then he glanced sharply through the iron railings in search of footmarks, but saw none, for Andrew uttered a warning "Take care," and he looked straight before him again as he went out by the Park gate, and turned back and through the streets till they reached the front of the house, where men were nailing up boards, and a couple of soldiers stood on duty, marching up and down, as if some royal personage were within.

Frank glanced at the workmen, and would have increased

his pace, but Andrew had hold of his arm and kept him back.

"Don't hurry," he said quietly; and then lightly to one of the sentries, "Got some prisoners inside, my man?"

The sentry grinned, and gave his head a sidewise nod toward Frank.

"Ask this young gentleman, sir; he knows."

Frank flushed scarlet, as he turned sharply to the man, whom he now recognised as one of the Guards who entered the drawing-room with the officer.

"Ah, to be sure," said Andrew coolly; and nodding carelessly, he went on and out by the gate into the Park at the end of the street, where the old man they had previously seen was holding on by the railings coughing violently.

"Poor old gentleman!" said Andrew sarcastically, but loud enough for him to hear; "he seems to be suffering a good deal from that cough."

The man bent his head lower till his brow rested on the hand which held on by the railings, and coughed more than ever.

"You needn't have made remarks about him," whispered Frank. "I'm afraid he heard what you said."

"I meant him to hear," said Andrew loudly; and he stopped and looked back directly. "A miserable, contemptible impostor. I could cure his wretched cough in two minutes with that stick he leans on."

The man started as if he had received a blow, and raised his head to glare fiercely at the youth, who was looking him superciliously up and down.

"Look at him, Frank," continued Andrew; "did you ever see such a miserable, hangdog-looking cur?"

Frank felt in agony, and gripped his companion by the arm.

"Did you mean that to insult me, boy?" said the man angrily.

"Done it without the stick," said Andrew, not appearing to notice the man's words. "You see a good lash from the tongue was enough. Now, can you imagine it possible that any one could sink so low as to earn his living by watching his fellow-creatures, spying their every act, and then betraying them for the sake of a few dirty shillings, to send them to prison or to the gibbet? There can be nothing on earth so base as a thing like this. Why, a footpad is a nobleman compared to him."

"You insolent young puppy!" cried the man; and entirely forgetful of his infirmity, he took three or four paces toward them, with his stick raised to strike.

Frank's hand darted to his sword, but Andrew did not stir. He stood with his lids half closed and his lips compressed, staring firmly at his would-be assailant, never flinching for a moment, nor removing his eyes from those which literally glowed with anger.

"The cough's gone, Frank, and the disguise might as well go with it. He is not an invalid, but one of the vile, treacherous ruffians in the pay of the Government. Let your blade alone; he daren't strike, for fear of having a sword through his miserable carcass. He was dressed as a sailor the other day, and he looked as if he had never had a foot at sea. He has been hanging about the Park for the past month. Pah! look at the contemptible worm."

The miserable spy and informer, who had remained with his stick raised, turned white with passion, as he stood listening to the lad's scathing words, and had either of the boys flinched he might have struck at them. As it was, he uttered a fierce imprecation, let the point of his stick drop to the ground, and turned away to hobble for a few steps, and, as if from habit, began to cough; but Andrew burst into a bitter laugh, and with a fierce oath the man turned again and shook his stick at him before ceasing his cough and walking sharply away, erect and vigorous as any.

"Well," said Andrew, "do you think I insulted him too much?"

"Why, he is an impostor!"

"Pah! London swarms with his kind. They have sent many a good, true, and innocent man to Tyburn for the sake of blood-money—men whose only fault was that they believed James Francis to be our rightful king. Frank," cried the lad passionately, "I can't tell you how I loathe the reptiles. I knew that wretch directly; my father pointed him out to me as one to beware of. If he knew what we do, he would send my dear, brave father to the scaffold, and he is trying hard to send yours. Where's your pity for the poor invalid now?"

"Oh!" ejaculated Frank excitedly, "can such things be true?"

"True? Why was he dogging us this morning? I can't be sure, of course; but as likely as not it was upon his information that your poor father was almost taken last night, and your mother nearly broken-hearted this morning. Why, Frank, I never saw you look so fierce before. It's all nonsense about my being two years older than you. You've overtaken and passed me, lad. I'm getting quite afraid of you."

"Oh, don't banter me now, Drew. I can't bear it."

"It's only my spiteful tongue, Frank. I don't banter you at heart. I'm in earnest. Only a short time ago I used to think I was as old as a man, and it was trouble about my father made me so. Now I can't help seeing how trouble is altering you too. Don't mind what I say, but I must say it. Some day you'll begin to think that I am not so much to blame for talking as I do about our royal master."

Frank drew a long, deep breath, and felt as if it might after all be possible.

"There, that's enough for one morning," cried Andrew merrily. "We're only boys after all, even if I am such a

queer fish.   Let's be boys again now.   What do you say ?
I'll race you round the end of the canal, and see who can
get in first to breakfast."

"No," said Frank; "I want to walk back quietly and
think."

"And I don't mean to let you.   There, we've had
trouble enough before breakfast.   Let's put it aside, and
if we can get away go and see the Horse Guards parade,
and then listen to the band and see some of the drilling.
I want to learn all I can about an officer's duty, so as not
to be like a raw recruit when I get my commission, if I
ever do.   I say : hungry ? "

" I ?   No."

"Then you must be.   Make a good breakfast, lad.
Sir Robert's safe enough by now, and he'll be more
cautious in future about coming amongst his Majesty's
springes and mantraps.   Look yonder; there's Captain
Murray.   Who's that with him ? "

"The doctor."

"So it is.   Let's go and talk to them."

"No ; let them go by before we start for the gate.   'I
feel as if every one will be knowing about last night, and
want to question me.   I wish I could go away till it has
all blown over."

"But you can't, Frank ; and you must face it out like
a man.   I say——"

"Well ? "

"You're not likely to see the King, and if you did it's
a chance if he'd know who you are ; but you're sure to see
the Prince, and I am a bit anxious to know whether he'll
take any notice about what his page did last night, and if
he does, what he'll say."

"I'm pretty well sure to see him this afternoon," said
Frank gloomily ; "and if he questions me I can't tell him
a lie.   What shall I say ? "

"I'll tell you," said Andrew merrily.

" Yes ?   What ? "

" Say nothing.   He can't make you speak."

" Then he'll be angry, and it will be fresh trouble for my mother."

" I don't believe he will be," said Andrew.   " Well, don't spoil your breakfast about something which may never happen.   Wait and see.   The worst he could do would be to have you dismissed; and if he does he'll dismiss me too, for I shan't stop here, Frank, unless my father says I must."

CHAPTER XXIV.

WITH PRINCE AND PRINCESS.

FRANK thought over his companion's proposals for spending such time as they could get away from duty, and soon after breakfast said what he thought.

" Every one seems to know about it," he said mournfully. " It's wonderful what an excitement it has caused."

" Not a bit. Every one knows Lady Gowan and her son, and how Sir Robert was sent out of the country on account of that duel in the Park ; so of course they talk about it."

" But wherever we go we shall be meeting people who will want to question me."

" Yes," said Andrew quietly. " I've been thinking the same. It's a great nuisance, for I wanted to go soldiering to-day."

" There's nothing to prevent you going."

" Yes, there is—you. I'm not going without you go too."

" But, Drew——"

" There, don't say any more about it," said the lad warmly. " I know. It wouldn't be pleasant for you to go, so you stay in, and we'll read or talk."

" But I don't like to force you to give up."

" Not going to force me. I'm going to stay because I like it, and keep you company, and stop people from talking to you."

Frank said little, but he thought a great deal, and the

most about how, in spite of his old belief that he should
never thoroughly care for his fellow-page, the tie of
sympathy between them from the similarity of their
positions was growing stronger every day.

As it happened they did not lose much, for they found
that they would have to be a good deal on duty, and the
consequence was that much of the early part of the day
was spent in the antechamber to help usher in quite a
long string of gentlemen, who wished for an audience with
the Prince.

In the afternoon, just as Frank was longing for his
freedom so that he might go and inquire how Lady Gowan
was, he received a sharp nudge from Andrew, and turned
quickly, to find that a knot of ladies had entered the room,
and naturally his first glance was to see if his mother was
with them. But he did not see her, his eyes lighting
instead upon the Princess, who was on her way to join
her husband.

The blood rose to Frank's cheeks as he saw that her
Royal Highness was looking at him intently, and his confusion increased as she smiled pleasantly at him in passing. Instead of hurrying forward to open the door for
her as usual, he stood in his place as if frozen, and the
duty fell to Andrew, who joined him as soon as the
last lady had passed through the door and the curtain
was let fall.

" I say, Frank," said the lad merrily, " she didn't seem
very cross with you. Lucky to be you, with your mother
a favourite. You're all right, and I don't suppose you'll
hear another word about the business. It's a good thing
sometimes to be a boy."

But Andrew proved to be wrong, and within the next
hour or so ; for the last of the audience—reckless officers
praying for promotion and gentlemen asking the Prince's
support as they sought for place—had gone, when a
servant entered the anteroom, and took Frank's breath

away by saying that the Prince wished to speak with him directly.

"It's all over with you, Frank," whispered Andrew; "leave me a lock of your hair, and you may as well give me your sword for a keepsake. You'll never want it again."

These bantering words did not quell the boy's alarm, but he had no time for thought; he had to go, and, drawing himself up and trying to put on a firm mien, he went to the door, drew aside the curtain, knocked, and entered.

The Prince was busy at a table covered with papers, the Princess sat near him in the opening of one of the windows, and her ladies were at the other end of the room beyond earshot.

The boy grasped all this as he moved toward the table, and then stood waiting respectfully for his Royal Highness to speak.

But some minutes elapsed, during which the boy's heart beat heavily, and he stood watching the Prince, as he kept on dipping his pen in the ink and signed some of the papers by him, and drew the pen across others.

Frank would have given anything for a look of encouragement from the Princess; but she sat with her face still turned away, reading.

At last !

The Prince looked up sharply, as if he had just become aware of the boy's presence, and said in rather imperfect English :

"Well, my boy !"

Frank, who had felt so manly the previous night and that morning, was the schoolboy again, completely taken aback, and for a few moments stood staring blankly at the inquiring eyes before him. Then, as the Prince raised his brows as if about to say, "Why don't you speak ? " the boy said hurriedly :

" Your Royal Highness sent for me."

" Sent for you ?   No—oh yes, I remember.   Well, sir,
what excuse have you to make for yourself ? "

" None, your Highness," said the boy firmly.

" Humph !   Defiant and obstinate ? "

Frank shook his head.   He could not trust himself to
speak.

" Hah ! that's better," said the Prince.   " Well, what
have you to say in excuse for your conduct, before I order
you to quit my service ? "

" Nothing, your Highness."

" Humph !   Very wise of you, sir.   I hate lying
excuses."

Frank darted a quick glance in the direction of the
Princess, in the hope that she would intercede for him, as
he saw himself sent off in disgrace, separated from the
mother whom his father had bidden him to watch over
and protect.   The idea was horrible, and with his hands
turning moist in the palms, and the dew gathering in fine
drops about his temples, he felt ready to promise anything
to ensure his stay at the Palace.

" I may tell you what I have heard from the officer
in charge of the guard last night—everything which took
place.   What am I to think of one of my servants standing
with his sword drawn to resist his Majesty's officer in
the execution of his duty ? "

" It was to defend my mother, sir," said Frank firmly.

" Oh !   Well, that is what a son should do, and that
is some excuse.   A lady I respect, and whom the Princess
esteems.   But this is very serious at a time like this,
when his Majesty is surrounded by enemies ; and there
must be no more such acts as this, Mr. Gowan.   If
you were a man, I should not have spoken as I do ;
you would have been dealt with by others.   But as
you are a mere thoughtless boy, ready to act on the
impulse of the moment, and as, for your mother's sake,

the Princess has interceded for you, I am disposed to look over it."

"Thank your Royal Highness," cried Frank, drawing a long, deep breath, full of relief.

"Now you may go back to your duties, and remember this : you are very young, and have good prospects before you. You are my servant now you are a boy ; I hope you will be my servant still when you grow up to be a man. I shall want men whom I can trust—men to whom I can say ' Protect me,' and who will do it."

"Yes, your Highness, and I will," cried Frank eagerly, as he took a couple of steps forward. "So would my father, your Highness. He is a fine, brave, true soldier, and——"

"He has a son who believes in him. Well ? " .

"He was forced to fight, your Highness. You would not have believed in him as a soldier if he had refused, and it is so cruel and hard that he should have been sent away. Pray—pray ask the King to forgive him now."

"Humph ! You are a very plain-spoken young gentleman," said the Prince sternly. "You draw your sword to protect your mother, and now I suppose if your father is not pardoned you will turn rebel and draw it again to protect him."

"Your Royal Highness has no right to think such a thing of me," said the boy, flushing warmly. "I was taught that I was to do my duty here."

"And very good teaching too, sir ; but boys are very ready to forget what they are taught ; and princes and kings have a right to think and say what they please."

"I beg your Royal Highness's pardon. You said you wanted faithful servants, and a truer and better man than my father never lived."

"Here, how old are you, young fellow ? "

"Seventeen, your Highness."

"And you are arguing like a man of seven-and-forty.

Well, it is a fine thing for a boy to be able to speak like that of his father, and I will not quarrel with you for being so plain. But look here, my boy: I am not the King."

"But your Royal Highness will be some day," said Frank excitedly, for he had the wild belief that he was going to carry the day.

"Humph! Perhaps, boy; but that is a bad argument to use. There, I will be plain with you. It does not rest with me to pardon your father."

"But his Majesty——" began the boy excitedly.

"I cannot ask his Majesty, boy," said the Prince sternly. "I am very angry to find that one of my attendants was mixed up with last night's troubles; but, as I told you, at the intercession of the Princess, I am disposed to look over it, if you promise me that in future you will be more careful, and do your duty as my servant should."

"I will, your Highness.—But my poor father?"

"Must wait until his Majesty is disposed to pardon his offence. Go."

The Prince waved his hand toward the door, and then for a moment or two he looked startled, for in a quick, impulsive way the boy darted forward and caught the raised hand.

The sudden movement startled the Princess too, and she sprang from her chair; but the look of alarm passed from her eyes as she saw the boy bending down to kiss the Prince's hand, and as he let it fall she held out her own.

Frank saw the movement, and the next instant he was down on one knee, kissing it, and rose to give the Princess a smile full of gratitude.

At that moment he felt his shoulder heavily grasped by the Prince.

"Good lad!" he said. "Go to your duties. I see I shall have in you a servant I can trust."

Frank did not know how he got out of the room, for his head was in a whirl, and he did not thoroughly come to himself till he had been seated for some time by his mother's couch and had told her all that had passed.

But somehow Lady Gowan did not look happy, and when she parted from her son there was a wistful look in her eyes which told of a greater trouble than that of which the boy was aware.

"Of course," said Andrew Forbes, when he had drawn the full account of the boy's experiences from him ; " but you need not be so precious enthusiastic over it. You had done nothing, though plenty of people get hung nowadays for that."

"But he was very kind and nice to me."

"Kind and nice!" said Andrew, with a sneer. "That was his artfulness. He wants to make all the friends he can against a rainy day—his rainy day. He's thinking of being king ; but he won't be. I do know that."

Frank gave him an angry look, and turned away ; but his companion caught his arm.

"Don't go, Frank ; that was only one of my snarls. I'm not so generous and ready to believe in people as you are."

Frank remembered his companion's position and his confidence about his father, and turned back.

"I can't bear to hear you talk like that."

"Slipped out," said Andrew hurriedly. "There, then, it's all right again for you. But there's no mistake about your having a good friend in the Princess."

CHAPTER XXV.

FRANK BOILS OVER.

THERE seemed to be a good deal of excitement about the court one day; people were whispering together, and twice over, as Frank was approaching, he noted that they either ceased talking or turned their backs upon him and walked away. But he took no further notice of it then, for his mind was very full of his father, of whom he had not heard for some time.

His mother had seemed terribly troubled and anxious when he had met her, but he shrank from asking her the cause, feeling that his father's long silence was telling upon her; and in the hope of getting news he went again and again to the house in Queen Anne Street, ascended to the drawing-room, and opened the picture-panelled closet door.

But it was for nothing. The housekeeper had told him that Sir Robert had not been; but thinking that his father could have let himself in unknown to the old servant, Frank clung to the hope that he might have been, deposited a letter, and gone again, possibly in the night. In every visit, though, he was disappointed, but contented himself by thinking that his father had acted wisely, and felt that it was not safe to come for fear that he might be watched.

It was nearly a week since he had been to the house, and he was longing for an opportunity to go again, but opportunity had not served, and he came to the con-

clusion that he would slip off that very afternoon, after
exacting a promise from Andrew Forbes that he would
keep in the anteroom ready to attend to any little duty
which might require the presence of one of the pages.

To his surprise, though, Andrew was nowhere to be
seen.   To have inquired after him would only have
served to draw attention to his absence, so he contented
himself with waiting patiently, but minute by minute he
grew more anxious, feeling convinced that something
must have occurred.

"Whatever has happened?" he said to himself at last,
as he saw officers begin to arrive and be ushered into
the Prince's room ; but why, there was no chance for him
to know, as there was no one to whom he could apply for
information, and at last he sat alone in the great blank
saloon, fidgeting as if he were upon thorns, and inventing
all manner of absurd reasons to account for his companion's absence.

"I know," he said to himself at last ; "he has noticed
that there is something on the way, and gone out to try
and pick up news.   He'll be here directly."

But he was wrong.   Andrew did not come, and several
little things occurred to show him that there was undue
excitement about the place.

At last his suspense came to an end, as he sat alone,
for Andrew appeared looking flushed and excited, glanced
sharply round as soon as he was inside the door, caught
sight of his friend, and half ran to join him.

"Oh, here you are, then, at last !" cried Frank.

"At last," said the lad.

"Yes; where have you been—news-hunting?"

"Yes," he whispered excitedly ; "news-hunting, and I
ran it down."

"What is it ?   There are three officers with the Prince,
and I heard some one say that a messenger was to be
despatched to bring the King back to town."

" Did you hear that ? " cried Andrew excitedly.

" Yes."

" Ah ! " ejaculated Andrew.

" What is it ?   A riot ? "

" Yes, a very big riot, lad ; a very, very big one.   Now we shall see."

" It doesn't seem likely for it to be *we*," said Frank sarcastically.   " Why don't you out with it, and tell me what's the matter ? "

" Oh, two things ; but haven't you heard ? "

" Of course not, or I shouldn't be begging and praying of you to speak."

" I found a letter from the dad, that's one thing, and he told me what I find the place is ringing with."

" Something about bells ? " said Frank, laughing.

" Yes, if you like," said Andrew wildly.   " The tocsin. War, my lad, war ! "

" What ! with France ? "

" No ; England.   At last.   The King has landed."

" I say, are you going mad ? "

" Yes, with excitement.   Frank, the game has begun, and we must throw up everything now, and join hands with the good men and true who are going to save our country."

" Bah ! You've got one of your fits on again," cried Frank contemptuously ; " what a gunpowder fizgig you are ! "

" Look here ! " said Andrew, in an angry whisper ; " this is no time for boyish folly.   We must be men. The crisis has come, and this miserable sham reign is pretty well at an end."

" The Prince is in yonder," said Frank warningly.

" Prince ! " said Drew contemptuously ; " I know no Prince but James Francis Stuart.   Now, listen ; there must be no shilly-shallying on your part ; we want every true patriot to draw the sword for his country."

"Ah well, I'm not what you call a true patriot, and so I shan't draw mine."

"Bah!" ejaculated Drew.

"And bah!" cried Frank. "Don't you play the fool, —unless you want some one to hear you," he continued, in a warning whisper.

"What do I care? I have had great news from my father, and the time has at last come when we must strike for freedom."

"Are you mad? Do you know where you are?" cried Frank, catching him by the arm.

"Not mad, and I know perfectly where I am. Look here, Frank; there must be no more nonsense. I tell you the time has come to strike. Our friends have landed, or are about to land. There is going to be a complete revolution, and before many hours the House of Hanover will be a thing of the past, and the rightful monarch of the House of Stuart will be on the throne."

"Then you are mad," said Frank, with another uneasy glance at the curtained door beyond where they stood, "or you would never talk like this."

"I shall talk how I please now," cried the lad excitedly. "Let them do their worst. I feel ready to wait till the Prince comes out, and then draw my sword and shout, 'God save King James the Third!'"

"No, you are not. You would not so insult one who has always behaved well to you."

"Bah! I am nobody. I don't count. How have he and his behaved to my poor father and to yours? Frank, I know I'm wildly excited, and feel intoxicated by the joyful news; but I know what I am talking about, and I will not have you behave in this miserable, cold-blooded way, when our fathers are just about to receive their freedom and come back to their rights."

"It's no use to argue with you when you're in this state," said Frank coldly; "but I won't sit here and have you say things which may lead to your being punished. I should be a poor sort of friend if I did."

"Pah! Have you no warm blood in you, that you sit there as cool as a frog when I bring you such glorious news?"

"It isn't glorious," said Frank. "It means horrible bloodshed, ruin, and disaster to hundreds or thousands of misguided men."

"Misguided! Do you know what you are talking about?"

"Yes, perfectly."

"Have you no feeling for your father and mother's sufferings?"

"Leave my father and mother out of the question, please."

"I can't. I know you're not a coward, Frank; but you're like a stupid, stubborn bloodhorse that wants the whip or spur to make him go. When he does begin, there's no holding him."

"Then don't you begin to use whip or spur, Drew, in case."

"But I will. I must now. It is for your good. I'm not going to stand by and see you and your mother crushed in the toppling-down ruins of this falling house. Do you hear me? The time has come, and we want every one of our friends, young and old, to strike a good bold blow for liberty."

"Let your friends be as mad as they like," said Frank angrily. "I'm not going to stand by either and see Drew Forbes go to destruction."

"Bah!—to victory. There, no more arguing. You are one of us, and you must come out of your shell now, and take your place."

"I'm not one of you," said Frank sturdily, and too warm now to think of the danger of speaking aloud; "I was tricked into saying something or joining in while others said it, and I am not a Jacobite, and I never will be !"

" I tell you that you are one."

" Have it so if you like ; but it's in name only, and I'll show you that I am not in deed. You talked about crying before the Prince, 'God save King James !' God save King George ! There !"

He spoke out loudly now, but repented the next moment, for fear that he should have dared his companion to execute his threat.

" Coward !" cried Andrew. " The miserable German usurper who has banished your father !"

" You said that you knew I was not a coward."

" Then I retract it. You are if you try to hang back now."

" Call me what you like, I'll have nothing to do with it. They don't want boys."

" They do—every one ; and you must come and fight."

" Indeed !"

" Yes, or be punished as a traitor."

" Let them come and punish me, then," said Frank hotly. " I wear a sword, and I know how to use it."

" Then come and use it like a man. Come, Frank. Don't pretend that you are going to show the white feather."

" I don't."

" It is monstrous !" panted the lad, who was wildly excited by his enthusiasm. " I want you—my friend—to stand by me now at a critical time, and you treat me like this. I can't understand it when you know that your father is a staunch supporter of the royal cause."

" Of course I do. What's that got to do with it ? Do you think because he has been sent away that he would forget his oath to the King ? "

" I said the royal cause, not the usurper's."

"It is false. My father is still in the King's service, waiting for his recall."

"Your father is my father's friend, as I am yours, and he is now holding a high command in King James's army."

"It's not true, Drew; it's one of your tricks to get me to go with you, and do what I faithfully promised I never would do. You know it's false. High in command in King James's army! Why, he has no army, so it can't be true."

"I tell you, it is true. My father and yours are both generals."

"Look here," said Frank, turning and speaking now in an angry whisper, "you're going too far, Drew. I don't want to quarrel—I hate to quarrel. Perhaps I am like a stubborn horse; but I did warn you not to use the whip or spur, and you will keep on doing it. Please let it drop. You're making me feel hot, and when I feel like that my head goes queer, and I hit out and keep on hitting, and feel sorry for it afterwards. I always did at school, and I should feel ten times as sorry if I hit you. Now you sit down, and hold your tongue before you're heard and get into a terrible scrape."

"Sit down! At a time like this!" cried the lad. "Oh, will nothing stir you? Are you such a cowardly cur that you are going to hide yourself among the German petticoats about the Palace? I tell you, it is true: General Sir Robert Gowan throws up his hat for the King."

"Cowardly cur yourself!" cried Frank, whose rage had been bubbling up to boiling-point for the last ten minutes and now burst forth.

"Miserable traitor! I thought better of you!" cried Andrew bitterly. "Pah! Friends! You are not worth the notice of a gentleman. Out of the way, you wretched cur!"

He struck Frank sharply across the face with his glove,

as he stepped forward to pass, and quick as lightning the
boy replied with a blow full in the cheek, which sent him
staggering back, so that he would have fallen had it not
been for the wall.

In an instant court rules and regulations were forgotten.
The boys knew that they wore swords, and these flashed
from their scabbards, ornaments no longer, and the next
moment they crossed, the blades gritted together, thrust
and parry followed, and each showed that the instructions
he had received were not in vain.

What would have been the result cannot be told, save
that it would have been bitter repentance for the one who
had sent his blade home; but before any mischief had
been done in the furious encounter, the doors at either
end of the anteroom were opened, and the Prince and the
officers from the audience chamber with the guards from
the staircase landing rushed in, the former narrowly
escaping a thrust from Andrew's sword, as with his own
weapon he beat down the boys'.

" How dare you !" he cried.

" Now !" cried Andrew defiantly to Frank, as he stood
quivering with rage—" now is your time.   Speak out; tell
the whole truth."

" Yes, the whole truth," said the Prince sternly.   " What
does this brawl mean ? "

Frank did not hesitate for a moment.

" It was my fault, your Royal Highness," he cried,
panting.   " We quarrelled ; I lost my temper and struck
him."

" Who dared to draw ? " thundered the Prince.

" We both drew together, your Royal Highness," cried
Frank hurriedly, for fear that Andrew should be beforehand with him ; " but I think I was almost the first."

" You insolent young dogs !" cried the Prince ; " how
dare you brawl and fight here !—Take away their swords ;
such boys are not fit to be trusted with weapons.—As

for you, sir," he said, turning fiercely on Frank, "like
father like son, as you English people say. And you, sir—
you are older," he cried to Andrew. "There, take them
away, and keep them till I have decided how they shall be
punished.—Come back to my room, gentlemen. Such an
interruption is a disgrace to the court."

He turned and walked toward the door, followed by the
three officers, one of whom on entering looked back at the
lads and smiled, as if he did not think that much harm had
been done.

But neither of the lads saw, for Andrew was whispering maliciously to Frank :

"You dared not speak. You knew how I should be
avenged."

"Yes, I dared ; but I wasn't going to be such a coward,"
cried Frank sharply.

"Ah, stop that !" cried the officer who held the boys'
swords, and had just given orders to his men to take their
places in front and rear of his prisoners. "Do you want
to begin again ? Hang it all ! wait till you get to the
guardroom, if you must fight."

"Don't speak to me like that !" cried Andrew fiercely
"It is not the custom to insult prisoners, I believe."

"Forward ! march !" said the officer ; and then, to
Frank's annoyance, as well as that of Andrew, he saw that
the officer was laughing at them, and that the men were
having hard work to keep their countenances.

Five minutes later they had been marched down the
staircase, across the courtyard, to the entrance of the
guardroom, where, to Frank's great mortification, the first
person he saw was Captain Murray.

"Hallo ! what's this ? " he cried. "Prisoners ? What
have you lads been about ? "

"Fighting," said Frank sullenly, Andrew compressing his
lips and staring haughtily before him, as if he felt proud of
his position.

"Fighting! With fists?" cried Captain Murray.

"Oh no," said the officer of the guard; "quite correctly. Here are their skewers."

"But surely not anywhere here?"

"Oh yes," said the officer mirthfully; "up in the ante-room, right under the Prince's nose."

"Tut—tut—tut!" ejaculated Captain Murray, half angry, half amused.

"The Prince came between them, and the tall cock nearly sent his spur through him," continued the officer. "I s'pose this means the Tower and the block, doesn't it, Murray? or shall we have the job to shoot 'em before breakfast to-morrow morning?"

"If I were only free," cried Andrew, turning fiercely on the officer, "you would not dare to insult me then."

"Then I'm very glad you are not. I say, why in the name of wonder are you not in the service, my young fire-eater? You are not in your right place as a page."

"Because—because——"

"Stop! that will do, young man," said Captain Murray sternly. "Let him be," he continued to his brother-officer. "The lad is beside himself with passion."

"Oh, I've done; but are they to be put together? They'll be at each other's throats again."

"No, they will not," said Captain Murray. "Frank, give me your word as your father's son that this quarrel is quite at an end."

"Oh yes, I've done," said the boy quickly.

"And you, Mr. Forbes?"

"No," cried Andrew fiercely. "I shall make no promises.—And as for you, Frank Gowan, I repeat what I said to you: every word is true."

"You think it is," said Frank quietly, "or you wouldn't have said it. But it isn't true. It couldn't be."

"That will do, young gentlemen," said Captain Murray sternly. "I should have thought you could have cooled down now.—Now, Mr. Forbes, will you give me your word that you will behave to your fellow-prisoner like a gentleman, and save me the unpleasant duty of placing you in the cell."

"Yes. Come, Drew," said Frank appealingly. "We were both wrong. I'll answer for him, Captain Murray."

" Well, one can't quarrel if the other will not. You can both have my room while you are under arrest.—Place a sentry at their door," and turning to his brother-officer, and, giving Frank a nod, as he looked at him sadly and sternly, Captain Murray walked away.

A few minutes later the key of the door was turned upon them, and they heard one of the guard placed on sentry duty outside.

CHAPTER XXVI.

"WHAT DID HE SAY?"

FRANK threw himself into a chair, and Andrew Forbes began to walk up and down like a newly caged wild beast.

Frank thought of the last time he was in that room, and of Captain Murray's advice to him; then of the quarrel, and his companion's mad words against his father. From that, with a bound, his thoughts went to his mother. What would she think when she heard—as she would surely hear in a few minutes—about the encounter?

He felt ready to groan in his misery, for the trouble seemed to have suddenly increased.

Andrew did not speak or even glance at him; and fully a quarter of an hour passed before Frank had decided as to the course he ought to pursue. Once he had made up his mind he acted, and, rising from his chair, he waited until his fellow-prisoner was coming toward him in his wearisome walk, and held out his hand.

"Will you shake hands, Drew?" he said.

The lad stopped on the instant, and his face lit up with eagerness.

"Yes," he cried, "if you'll stand by me like a man."

'What do you mean?"

"Escape with me. Get out of the window as soon as it is dark, and make a dash for it. Let them fire; they would not hit us in the dark, and we could soon reach the friends and be safe."

"Run away and join your friends?" said Frank quietly.

"Yes! We should be placed in the army at once, as soon as they knew who we were. Come, you repent of what you said, and you will be faithful to the cause?"

"Won't you shake hands without that?"

"No, I cannot. I am ready to forgive everything you said or did to me; but I cannot forgive such an act as desertion in the hour of England's great need. Shake hands."

"Can't," said Frank sadly; and he thrust his hands into his pockets, walked to the window, and stood looking out into the courtyard.

No word was spoken for some time, and no sound broke the stillness that seemed to have fallen upon the place, save an occasional weary yawn from the soldier stationed outside the door and the tramp of the nearest sentry, while Andrew very silently still imitated the action of a newly caged wild animal. At last he stopped suddenly.

"Have you thought that over?" he said.

"No," replied Frank. "Doesn't want thinking over. My mind was made up before."

"And you will take the consequences?"

"Hang the consequences!" cried Frank angrily. "What is your rightful monarch, or your pretender, or whatever he is, to me? I don't understand your politics, and I don't want to. I've only one thing to think about. My father told me that, as far as I could, I was to stand by and watch over my mother in his absence, and I wouldn't forsake my post for all the kings and queens in the world; so there!"

"Then I suppose if I try to escape you will give the alarm and betray me?"

"I don't care what you suppose. But I shouldn't be such a sneak. I wish you would go, and not bother me. You've no business here, and it would be better if you were away; but I don't suppose you will do much good if you do go."

"Oh!" ejaculated Andrew, as if letting off so much indignant steam; "and this is friendship!"

"I don't care what you say now. Your ideas are wider and bigger than mine, I suppose. I'm a more common sort of fellow, with only room in my head to think about what I've been taught and told to do. Perhaps you're right, but I don't see it."

"I can't give you up without one more try," said Andrew, standing before him with his brow all in lines. "You say your father told you to stay and watch over your mother?"

"Yes; and I will."

"But since then he has changed his opinions; he is on our side now, and I cannot but think that he would wish you to try and strike one blow for his—— Bah!"

Andrew turned away in bitter contempt and rage, for strong in his determination not to be stung into a fresh quarrel, the boy he addressed, as soon as he heard his companion begin to reiterate his assertion that Sir Robert Gowan had gone over to the Pretender's side, turned slowly away, and, with his elbows once more resting on the window-sill, thrust a finger into each ear, and stopped them tight. So effectually was this done, that he started round angrily on feeling a hand laid upon his shoulder.

"It's of no use, Drew, I won't—— Oh, it's you, Captain Murray!"

"Yes, my lad. Has he been saying things you don't like?"

Frank nodded.

"Well, that's one way of showing you don't want to listen. Your mother wishes to see you, and you can go to her."

"Ah!" cried the boy eagerly.

"Give me your word as a gentleman that you will go

to her and return at once, and I will let you cross to
Lady Gowan's apartments without an escort."

"Escort, sir?" said Frank wonderingly.

" Well, without a corporal and a file of men as guard."

" Oh, of course I'll come back," said the boy, smiling.
" I'm not going to run away."

" Go, then, at once."

Captain Murray walked with him to the door, made
a sign to the sentry, who drew back to stand at attention,
and the boy began to descend.

" How long may I stay, sir?" he asked.

" As long as Lady Gowan wishes; but be back before
dark."

" Poor old Drew!" thought Frank, as he hurried across
to the courtyard upon which his mother's apartments
opened; "it's a deal worse for him than it is for me.   But
he's half mad with his rightful-king ideas, and ready to
say or do anything to help them on.   But to say such
a thing as that about my father!   Oh!"

He was ushered at once into his mother's presence, but
she did not hear the door open or close; and as she lay
on a couch, with her head turned so that her face was
buried in her hands, he thought she was asleep.

" Mother," he said softly, as he bent over her.

Lady Gowan sprang up at once; but instead of holding
out her arms to him as he was about to drop on his knees
before her, her wet eyes flashed angrily, and she spoke
in a voice full of bitter reproach.

" I have just heard from the Princess that my son,
whom I trusted in these troublous times to be my stay
and help, has been brawling disgracefully during his duties
at the court."

" Brawling disgracefully" made the boy wince, and a
curious, stubborn look began to cloud his face.

" Her Royal Highness tells me that you actually so far
forgot yourself as to draw upon young Forbes, that you

were half mad with passion, and that some terrible mischief would have happened if the Prince, who heard the clashing from his room of audience, had not rushed in, and at great risk to himself beaten down the swords. That is what I have been told, and that you are both placed under arrest. Is it all true?"

"Yes, mother," said the lad bluntly; and he set his teeth for the encounter that was to come.

"Is this the conduct I ought to expect from my son, after all my care and teaching—to let his lowest passions get the better of him, so that, but for the interference of the Prince, he might have stained his sword with the blood of the youth he calls his friend?"

"It might have been the other way, mother," said the boy bluntly.

"Yes; and had you so little love, so little respect for your mother's feelings, that you could risk such a thing? I have been prostrated enough by what has happened. Suppose, instead, the news had been brought to me that in a senseless brawl my son had been badly wounded—or slain?"

"Senseless brawl" made the boy wince again.

"It would have been very horrible, mother," he said, in a low voice.

"It would have killed me. Why was it? What was the cause?"

"Oh, it was an affair of honour, mother," said Frank evasively.

"An affair of honour!" cried Lady Gowan scornfully; "a boy like you daring to speak to me like that! Honour, sir! Where is the honour? It comes of boys like you two, little better than children, being allowed to carry weapons. Do you not know that it is an honour to a gentleman to wear a sword, because it is supposed that he would be the last to draw it, save in some terrible emergency for his defence or to preserve another's life, and not at the first hasty word spoken? Had you no consideration for me? Could you not see how painful my position is at the court, that you must give me this fresh trouble to bear?"

"Yes, mother; you know how I think of you. I couldn't help it."

"Shame! Could not help it! Is this the result of your education—you, growing toward manhood—my son to tell me this unblushingly, to give me this pitiful excuse —you could not help it? Why was it, sir?"

"Well, mother, we quarrelled. Drew is so hot-tempered and passionate."

"And you are perfectly innocent, and free from all such attributes, I suppose, sir," cried Lady Gowan sarcastically.

"Oh no, I'm not, mother," said the lad bluntly, as he felt he would give anything to get away. "I've got a nasty, passionate temper; but I'm all right if it isn't roused, and Drew will keep on till he rouses it."

"Pitiful! Worse and worse!" cried Lady Gowan. "All this arose, I suppose, out of some contemptible piece of banter or teasing. He said something to you, then, that you did not like?"

"Yes," said Frank eagerly, "that was it."

"And pray what did he say?"

"Say—oh—er—he said—oh, it was nothing much."

"Speak out—the truth, sir," cried Lady Gowan, fixing her eyes upon her son's.

"Oh, he said—something I did not like, mother."

"What was it, sir? I insist upon knowing."

"Oh, it was nothing much."

"Let me be the judge of that, sir. I, as your mother, would be only too glad to find that you had some little excuse for such conduct."

"And then," continued Frank hurriedly, "I got put out, and—and I called him a liar."

"What was it he said?"

"And then he struck me over the face with his glove, mother, and I couldn't stand that, and I hit out, and sent him staggering against the wall."

"Why?—what for?" insisted Lady Gowan.

"And in a moment he whipped out his sword and attacked me, and of course I had to draw, or he would have run me through."

"Is that true, sir—Andrew Forbes drew on you first?"

"Of course it's true, mother," said the lad proudly. "Did I ever tell you a lie?"

"Never, my boy," said Lady Gowan firmly. "It has been my proud boast to myself that I could trust my son in everything."

"Then why did you ask me in that doubting way if it was true?"

"Because my son is prevaricating with me, and speaking in a strange, evasive way. He never spoke to me like that before. Do you think me blind, Frank? Do you think that I, upon whom your tiny eyes first opened—your mother, who has watched you with all a mother's love from your birth, cannot read every change in your countenance? Do you think I cannot see that you are fighting hard to keep something back?—you, whom I have always been so proud to think were as frank by nature as you are by name? Come, be honest with me. You are hiding something from me?"

"Yes, mother," cried the lad, throwing back his head and speaking defiantly now, "I am."

'Then tell me what it is at once. I am your mother, from whom nothing should be hid. If the matter is one for which you feel shame, if it is some wrong-doing, the more reason that you should come to me, my boy, and confide in me, that I may take you once again to my heart, and kneel with you, that we may together pray for forgiveness and the strength to be given to save you from such another sin."

"Mother," cried the boy passionately, "I have not sinned in this!"

"Ah!—Then what is it?"

"I cannot tell you."

"Frank, if ever there was a time when mother and son should be firmly tied in mutual confidence, it is now. I have no one to cling to but you, and you hold me at a distance like this."

"Yes, yes; but I cannot tell you."

"You think so, my boy; but don't keep it from me."

"Mother," cried Frank wildly, "I must!"

"You shall not, my boy. I will know."

"I cannot tell you."

He held out his hands to her imploringly, but she drew back from him, and her eyes seemed to draw the truth he strove so hard to keep hidden from his unwilling lips.

"There, then!" he cried passionately; "I bore it as long as I could: because he insulted my father—it was to defend his honour that I struck him, and we fought."

"You drew to defend your father's honour," said Lady Gowan hoarsely; and her face looked drawn and her lips white.

"Yes, that was it. Is it so childish of me to say that I could not help that?"

"No," said Lady Gowan, in a painful whisper. "How did he insult your father? What did he say?"

"Must I tell you?"

"Yes."

Frank drew a long, deep, sobbing breath, and his voice sounded broken and strange, as he said in a low, passionate voice:

"He dared to insult my father—he said he was false to the King—that he had broken his oath as a soldier—that he was a miserable rebel and Jacobite, and had gone over to the Pretender's side."

"Oh!" ejaculated Lady Gowan, shrinking back into

the corner of the couch, and covering her face with her hands.

"Mother, forgive me!" cried the lad, throwing himself upon his knees, and trying to draw her hands from her face. "I could not speak. It seemed so horrible to have to tell you such a cruel slander as that. I could not help it. I should have struck at anybody who said it, even if it had been the Prince himself."

Lady Gowan let her son draw her hands from her white, drawn face, and sat back gazing wildly in his eyes.

"Oh, mother!" he cried piteously, "can you think this a sin? Don't look at me like that."

She uttered a passionate cry, clasped him to her breast, and let her face sink upon his shoulder, sobbing painfully the while.

"I knew what pain it would give you, dear," he whispered, with his lips to her ear; "but you made me tell you. I was obliged to fight him. Father would have been ashamed of me, and called me a miserable coward, if I had not stood up for him as I did."

"Then—then—he said that of your father?" faltered Lady Gowan, with her convulsed face still hidden.

"Yes."

"And you denied it, Frank."

"Of course," cried the lad proudly; "and then we fought, and I did not know what was happening till the Prince came and struck down our swords."

Lady Gowan raised her piteous-looking face, pressed her son back from her, and rose from the couch.

"Go now, my boy," she said, in a low, agonised voice.

"Back to prison?" he said. "But tell me first that you are not so angry with me. I can't feel that I was so wrong."

"No, no, my boy—no, I cannot blame you," sighed Lady Gowan.

"And you forgive me, mother?"

"Forgive you? Oh, my own, true, brave lad, it is not your fault, but that of these terrible times. Go now, I can bear no more."

"Say that once again," whispered Frank, clinging to her.

"I cannot speak, my darling. I am suffering more than I can tell you. There, leave me, dearest. I want to be alone, to think and pray for help in this terrible time of affliction. Frank, I am nearly broken-hearted."

"And I have been the cause," he said sadly.

"You? Oh no, no, my own, brave, true boy. I never felt prouder of you than I do now. Go back. I must think. Then I will see the Princess. The Prince is not so very angry with you, and he will forgive you when he knows the truth."

"And you, mother?"

"I?" cried the poor woman passionately. "Heaven help me! I do not feel that I have anything to forgive."

Lady Gowan embraced her son once more, and stood looking after him as he descended the stairs, while Frank walked over to his prison with head erect and a flush of pride in his cheeks.

"There," he muttered, as he passed the sentry, "let them say or do what they like; I don't care now."

CHAPTER XXVII.

THE BREACH WIDENS.

ANDREW started from his seat as Frank entered the room and the door was closed and locked behind him ; but, seeing who it was, he sat down again with his face averted.

"Shall I tell him ? " thought Frank. "No ; it would be like triumphing over him to show him I have found out that he has been trying to cheat me into going off."

The boy felt so satisfied and at ease that he was more and more unwilling to hurt his fellow-prisoner's feelings, and after a while he spoke.

"I suppose they'll give us something to eat," he said.

Andrew looked up at him in astonishment, but only to frown the next moment and turn his head away again.

Frank went to the window and stood looking out, one corner commanding a view of the Park ; and after watching the people come and go for some time, he suddenly turned to his companion :

"Here are the Horse Guards coming, Drew. Want to see them ? "

"No. Will you have the goodness to leave me in peace ? "

"No," said Frank quietly. "How can I ? We're shut up together here perhaps for ever so long, and we can't keep up that miserable quarrel now. Hadn't we better shake hands ? "

"What do you suppose I'm made of?" said Andrew fiercely.

"Same stuff as I am," replied Frank almost as sharply; "and as I've shown myself ready to forgive and forget what has happened, you ought to do the same."

But it was of no use. Try how he would to draw Andrew into conversation, the latter refused to speak; and at last the boy gave up in despair, and began to look about the captain's room for something out of which he could drag some amusement. This last he had to extract from one of the books on a shelf; but it proved dry and uninteresting, though it is doubtful whether one of the most cheery nature would have held his attention long. For he had so much to think about that his mind refused to grasp the meaning of the different sentences, and one minute he was wondering whether his father would venture to the house, the next he was going over the scene of the quarrel in the antechamber. Then he thought sadly about his interview with his mother, but only to feel elated and happy, though it was mingled with sorrow at having given her so much pain.

A little resentment began to spring up, too, against Andrew, as the true cause of it all, but it did not last; he felt far too much at rest for that, and the anger gave way to pity for the high-spirited, excitable lad seated there in the deepest dejection, and he began to wish now that he had not called him a liar and struck him.

"I shall go melancholy mad," muttered Frank at last, "if they keep us shut up long, and Drew goes on like this. But I wonder whether there will really be a rising against the King?"

Curiosity made him try to be communicative, and he turned to his silent companion.

"Think there really will be any fighting?" he said.

Andrew turned to him sharply.

"Why do you ask?" he said.

"Simple reason : because I want to know."

" You have some other reason."

" Because I want to send word to the Prince that you are a rebel, and intend to go and join the Pretender's followers, of course," said Frank sarcastically.   " Don't be so spiteful, Drew.   We can't live here like this.   Why don't you let bygones be bygones ? "

" What interest can it be to you ? " said Andrew, ignoring the latter part of his fellow-prisoner's remark.

" Do you suppose such a rising can take place without its being of interest to every one ?   There, we won't talk about it unless you like.   Look here, I can't sit still doing nothing ; it gives me pins and needles in my hands and feet.   I'll ring and ask Captain Murray to let us have a draught board if you'll play."

" Pish ! " cried Andrew contemptuously ; and Frank sighed and gave up again, to take refuge in staring out of the window for some time.

Then his tongue refused to be quiet, and he cried to his silent companion :

" There is something going on for certain.   I've counted twelve officers go by since I've been standing here."

There was no heed paid to his remark, and at last the boy drew a breath full of relief, for he heard steps on the stairs, the sentry's piece rattled, and then the key turned in the lock, and Captain Murray entered, looking very stern.

" Frank Gowan," he said, " you give me your *parole d'honneur* that you will not do anything foolish in the way of attempting to escape ? "

" Oh yes, of course, sir," said the boy.   " I don't want to escape."

" That's right.   And you, Andrew Forbes ? "

" No ; I shall make no promises," was the reply.

" Don't be foolish, my lad.   You ought to have cooled down by this time.   Give me your word : it will make your position bearable, and mine easy."

" I shall give no promises," said Andrew haughtily. "I have been arrested, and brought here a prisoner, and I shall act as a prisoner would."

" Try to escape ? Don't attempt to do anything so foolish, my lad. I will speak out like a friend to you. There has been some important news brought to the Palace ; the guard has been quadrupled in number, double sentries have been placed, and they would fire at any one attempting to pass the gates without the word to-night. Now, give me your promise."

" I—will—not," said Andrew, speaking firmly, and meeting the captain's eyes without shrinking.

" Don't be so foolish, Drew," whispered Frank.

"I shall do as I think best," was the reply. " You are at liberty to do the same, sir."

" Very well," said Captain Murray, interrupting them. " Perhaps you will be more sensible and manly after a night's rest. I did not expect to find a lad of your years behaving like a spiteful girl."

Andrew's eyes flashed at him ; but the captain paid no heed, and went on :

" I have spoken to the colonel, Frank, and for your father's sake he will be glad to see you at the mess table this evening. You are free of it while you are under arrest. I will come for you in half an hour. By the way, I have told my man to come to you for instructions about getting your kit from your room. You will use him while you are a prisoner."

" Oh, thank you, Captain Murray," cried the boy eagerly.

" Pray make use of my servant, Mr. Forbes, and order him to fetch what you require."

Andrew bowed coldly, and the captain left the room, his servant tapping at the door directly after, and entering to receive his orders from Frank.

" Now, Drew," he said at last, " tell him what to fetch for you."

"I do not require anything," said the youth coldly. "Yes, look here. There is a little desk on the table in my room ; bring me that."

"Hadn't you better give in, and make the best of things?" said Frank, as soon as they were alone.

"Had you not better leave me to myself, Frank Gowan?" said Andrew coldly. "We are no longer friends, but enemies."

"No, we can't be that," cried Frank. "Come ; once more, shake hands."

Andrew looked at him for a few moments fixedly, and then said slowly :

"I will——"

"Come, that's better."

"On the day when your King George is humbled to the dust, and you are, with all here, a helpless prisoner. I'll shake hands and forgive you then."

"Not till then?" cried Frank, flushing.

"Not till then."

"Which means that we are never to be friends again, Drew. Nonsense! You are still angry. Captain Murray is right."

"That I speak like a spiteful girl!" cried the lad sharply.

"No, I did not mean that," said Frank quietly ; "but if I had meant it, I should not have been very far from right. I hope that you will think differently after a night's rest. Come, think differently now, and give up all those mad thoughts which have done nothing but make us fall out. It isn't too late. Captain Murray is trying to make things pleasant for us ; tell him when he comes that you'll dine with him."

Andrew made an angry gesture, and Frank shrugged his shoulders, went into the adjoining room to wash his hands, and came back just as the tramp of soldiers was heard outside, the order was given for them to halt, and then followed their heavy footsteps on the stairs.

The next minute Captain Murray entered the room.

" Ready, bloodthirsty prisoner ? " he said, smiling.

"Yes, sir, quite," replied Frank ; while Andrew sat at the other end of the room with his back to them.

Frank glanced in his fellow-prisoner's direction, and then turned back to the captain, and his lips moved quickly as he made a gesture in Andrew's direction.

The captain read his meaning, nodded, walked up to the lad, and touched him on the shoulder, making him start to his feet.

" Life's very short, Andrew Forbes," he said quietly, " and soldiers are obliged to look upon it as shorter for them than for other men. It isn't long enough to nurse quarrels or bear malice. I think I have heard you say that you hope to be a soldier some day."

" Yes, I do," said the lad, with a meaning which the captain could not grasp.

" Very well, then ; act now like a frank soldier to another who says to you, try and forget this trouble, and help every one to make it easier for you. There's care enough coming, my lad ; and I may tell you that the Prince has enough to think about without troubling himself any more over the mad prank of two high-spirited boys. There, I'll wait for you ; go into my room, and wash your hands and smooth your face. I venture to say that you will both get a wigging to-morrow, and then be told to go back to your duties."

Andrew did not budge, and the captain's face grew more stern.

"Come on, Drew," cried Frank ; but the lad turned away.

" Yes, come along," cried the captain ; " a good dinner will do you both good, and make you ready to laugh at your morning's quarrel. Do you hear ? "

There was no reply.

"You are not acting like a hero, my lad," said the captain, smiling once more.

Still there was no reply.

"Very well, sir; you refuse your parole, and I can say no more. I have my duty to do, and I cannot offer you my hospitality here. You are still under arrest."

He walked to the door, threw it open, made a sign, and a corporal and two Guardsmen marched in.

"Take this gentleman to the guardroom," he said. "Your officer has his instructions concerning him."

"Oh, Drew!" whispered Frank; but the lad drew himself up, and took a few steps forward, placing himself between the Guards, and kept step with them as they marched out and down the stairs.

The next minute their steps were heard on the paving-stones without, and Frank darted to the window, to stand gazing out, feeling half choked with sorrow for his friend.

A touch on the arm made him remember that Captain Murray was waiting.

"It's a pity, Frank," he said; "but I did all I could. He's a bit too high-spirited, my lad. The best thing for him will be the army; the discipline would do him good."

Frank longed to speak, but he felt that his lips were sealed.

"Well, we must not let a bit of hot temper spoil our dinner, my lad. By the way, what news of your father?"

"None, sir," said the boy sadly, though the thought of what Andrew Forbes had said made him wince.

"Humph!" said Captain Murray, looking at the boy curiously. "There, I don't want to pump you. Tell him next time you write that there will be a grand night at the mess when he comes back to his old place. Now, then, we shall be late."

"Would you mind excusing me, sir?" said Frank.

"Yes, very much. Nonsense! You must be quite hungry by now."

"No: I was; but it's all gone."

"Hah!" said the captain, gripping him by the shoulder; "you're your father's own boy, Frank. I like that, but I can't have it. You accepted the invitation, and I want you, my lad. Never mind Andrew Forbes; he only requires time to cool down. He'll be ready to shake hands in the morning. Come, or we shall get in disgrace for being late."

Frank was marched off to the messroom; but he felt as if every mouthful would choke him, and that he would have given anything to have gone and shared Andrew Forbes's confinement, even if he had only received hard words for his pains.

CHAPTER XXVIII.

A NIGHT ALARM.

IT was very plain to Frank that the officers did not look upon his offence in a very serious light, for the younger men received him with a cheer, and the elders with a smile, as they shook hands, while the doctor came and clapped him on the shoulder.

"Hallo, young fire-eater !" he cried; "when are you coming to stay ? "

"To stay, sir ?" said the boy, feeling puzzled.

"Yes, with your commission. We've lost your father. We must have you to take his place."

"No, sir," said Frank, flushing. "I don't want to take my father's place. I want to see him back in it."

"Well said !" cried the colonel; "what we all want. But get to be a bit more of a man, and then coax the Prince to give you a commission. I think we can make room for Robert Gowan's son in the corps, gentlemen ? "

There was a chorus of assent at this; and the colonel went on :

"Come and sit by me, my lad. We can find a chair for you and your guest, Murray, at this end. Why, you're not fit for a page, my lad ; they want soft, smooth, girlish fellows for that sort of thing. A young firebrand like you, ready to whip out his sword and use it, is the stuff for a soldier."

Frank wished the old officer would hold his tongue, and not draw attention to him, for every one at the table was

listening, and Captain Murray sat smiling with grim satisfaction. But the colonel went on:

" Very glad to see you here this evening, my boy.
Why, I hear that you are quite a favourite with the
Prince."

" It does not seem like it, sir," said Frank, who was
beginning to feel irritated. " I am a prisoner."

There was a laugh at this, which ran rippling down the
table.

" Not bad quarters for a prisoner, eh, gentlemen ? " said
the colonel. " Pooh ! my lad, you are only under arrest ;
and we are very glad you are, for it gives us the opportunity of having the company of Robert Gowan's son."

Frank flushed with pleasure to find how warmly his
father's name was received ; and the colonel went on :

" Don't you trouble your head about being under arrest,
boy. The Prince was obliged to have you marched off.
It wouldn't do for him to have every young spark drawing
and getting up a fight in the Palace. By the way, what
was the quarrel about ? You struck young Forbes ? "

" Yes, sir."

" Well, of course he would draw upon you ; but how
came you to strike him ? "

The boy hesitated ; but the colonel's keen eyes were
fixed upon him so steadfastly, that he felt that he must
speak and clear himself of the suspicion of being a mere
quarrelsome schoolboy, and he said firmly :

" He said insulting things about my father, sir."

There was a chorus of approval at this ; and as soon as
there was silence, the colonel looked smilingly round the
table :

" I think we might forgive this desperate young culprit
for committing that heinous offence, gentlemen. What do
you say ? "

There was a merry laugh at this ; and the colonel
turned to the lad :

"We all forgive you, Mr. Gowan. It is unanimous. Now, I think we are a little hard upon you; so pray go on with your dinner."

"I don't think his arrest will last long, sir," said Captain Murray, after a while.

"Pooh! No: I'm afraid not," said the colonel; "and we shall lose our young friend's company. The Prince is a good soldier himself, even if he is a German. Gowan will hear no more of it, I should say; and I don't want to raise his hopes unduly, but on the strength of this rising, when we want all good supporters of his Majesty in their places, I should say that the occasion will be made one for sending word to Captain Sir Robert Gowan to come back to his company."

Frank flushed again, and looked at Captain Murray, who smiled and nodded.

"By the way, Murray," said the colonel, "why did you not bring the other young desperado to dinner?"

The captain shrugged his shoulders.

"A bit sulky," he said. "Feels himself ill-used."

"Oh!" ejaculated the colonel; and seeing Frank's troubled face, he changed the conversation, beginning to talk about the news of a rising in the north, where certain officers were reported to have landed, and where the Pretender, James Francis, was expected to place himself at their head, and march for London.

"A foolish, mad project, I say, gentlemen," exclaimed the colonel; "and whatever my principles may have been, I am a staunch servant of his Majesty King George I., and the enemy of all who try and disturb the peace of the realm."

A burst of applause followed these words; and the conversation became general, giving Frank the opportunity for thinking over the colonel's words, and of what a triumph it would be for his father to return and take up his old position.

"Poor old Drew!" he said to himself, with a sigh. "What would he think if he heard them talking about its being a mad project?"

Then he went on thinking about how miserable his old companion must be in the guardroom, watched by sentries; and as he kept on eating for form's sake, every mouthful seemed to go against him, and he wished the dinner was over. For, in addition to these thoughts, others terribly painful would keep troubling him, the place being full of sad memories. He recalled that he was sitting in the very seat occupied by the German baron upon that unlucky evening; and the whole scene of the angry encounter came vividly back, even to the words that were spoken. The natural sequence to this was his being called by Andrew Forbes in the dull grey of the early morning to go and witness that terrible sword fight in the Park; and he could hardly repress a shudder as he seemed to see the German's blade flashing and playing about his father's breast, till the two thrusts were delivered, one of which nearly brought the baron's career to a close.

Nothing could have been kinder than the treatment the young guest received from the officers; but nothing could have been more painful to the lad, and again and again he wished himself away as the dinner dragged its slow length along, and he sat there feeling lonely, occupied toward the end almost entirely with thoughts of his father, Andrew's false charge about him being generally uppermost, and raising the indignant colour to his cheeks.

"I wonder where he is now," he thought, "and what he is doing?"

Then once more about what delight his mother would feel if the colonel's ideas came to pass, and Sir Robert came back in triumph.

"Oh, it's too good to be true," thought the boy; but he clung to the hope all the same.

The only time when he was relieved from the pressure of his sad thoughts was when the conversation around grew animated respecting the probabilities of the country being devastated by civil war ; but even then it made his heart ache on Andrew Forbes's account, as he heard the quiet contempt with which the elder officers treated the Pretender's prospects, the colonel especially speaking strongly on the subject.

"No," he said, "England will never rise in favour of such a monarch as that. It is a mad business, that will never win support. The poor fellow had better settle down quietly to his life in France. The reign of the Stuarts is quite at an end."

"Poor old Drew," thought Frank. "I wish he could have heard that ; but he would not have believed if he had."

Then the officers went on talking of the possibility of their regiment being called upon for active service, and the boy could not help a feeling of wonder at the eager hopes they expressed of having to take part in that which would probably result in several of those present losing their lives or being badly wounded.

"I wonder whether I shall be as careless about my life when I am grown-up and a soldier ?" he thought.

The regular dinner had long been over, and the members of the mess had been sitting longer than usual, the probability of the regiment going into active service having supplied them with so much food for discussion that the hour was getting late, and the young guest had several times over felt an intense longing to ask permission to leave the table, his intention being to get Captain Murray to let him join Andrew Forbes. But he felt that as a guest he could not do this, and must wait till the colonel rose.

He was thinking all this impatiently for the last time, feeling wearied out after so terribly exciting a day as he had passed through, when the colonel and all present suddenly sprang to their feet ; for a shot rang out from close at hand, followed by a loud, warning cry, as if from a sentry ; then, before any one could reach the door to run out and see what was wrong, there was another shot, and again another, followed by a faint and distant cry.

CHAPTER XXIX.

A WATCH NIGHT.

"WHAT is it—an attack?"

"Quick, gentlemen!" cried the colonel; "every man to his quarters."

He had hardly spoken before a bugle rang out; and as Frank was hurried out with the rest into the courtyard, it was to see, by the dim light of the clouded moon and the feeble oil lamps, that the guard had turned out, and the tramp of feet announced that the rest of the men gathered for the defence of the Palace and its occupants were rapidly hurrying out of their quarters, to form up in one or other of the yards.

Frank felt that he was out of place; but in his interest and excitement he followed Captain Murray like his shadow, and in very few minutes knew that no attack had been made upon the Palace, but that the cause of the alarm was from within, and his heart sank like lead as the captain said to him:

"Poor lad! He must be half crazy to do such a thing. Come with me."

Frank followed him, and the next minute they met, coming from the gate on the Park side, a group of soldiers, marching with fixed bayonets toward the guardroom, two of the men within bearing a stretcher, on which lay Andrew Forbes, apparently lifeless. For the lad had been mad enough to make a dash for his liberty, in spite of knowing what would follow, the result being that the sentry by

the guardroom had challenged him to stop, and as he ran on fired. This spread the alarm, and the second sentry toward the gate had followed his comrade's example as he caught a glimpse of the flying figure, while the third sentry outside the gate, standing in full readiness, also caught sight of the lad as he dashed out and was running to reach the trees of the Park.

This shot was either better aimed, or the unfortunate youth literally leaped into the line of fire, for as the sentry drew trigger, just as the lad passed between two of the trees, Drew uttered a sharp cry of agony and fell headlong to the earth.

"Poor lad! poor lad!" muttered Captain Murray; and he made a sign to the soldiers not to interfere, as Frank pressed forward to catch his friend's hand. Then aloud, "Where is the doctor?"

"Here, of course," said that gentleman sharply from just behind them. "Always am where I'm wanted, eh? Look sharp, and take him to the guardroom."

"No, no—to my quarters," said Captain Murray quickly. "Tut—tut—tut! What were they about to let him go?"

In a few minutes the wounded lad was lying on Captain Murray's bed, with the colonel, Captain Murray, and two or three more of the officers present, and Frank by the bedside, for when the colonel said to the lad, "You had better go," the doctor interfered, giving Frank a peculiar cock of the eye as he said, "No, don't send him away; he can help."

Frank darted a grateful look at the surgeon, and prepared to busy himself in undressing the sufferer.

"No, no; don't do that now—only worry him. I can see what's wrong, and get at it."

The position of the injury was plain enough to see from the blood on the lad's sleeve, and the doctor did not hesitate for a moment; but, taking out a keen knife from a little case in his pocket, he slit the sleeve from cuff to shoulder, and then served the deeply stained shirt sleeve the same.

"Dangerous?" said the colonel anxiously.

"Pooh! no," said the doctor contemptuously. "Nice clean cut.—Just as if it had been done with a knife," as he examined the boy's thin, white left arm. "You ought to give that sentry a stripe, colonel, for his clever shooting. Hah! yes, clean cut for two inches, and then buried itself below the skin. Not enough powder, or it would have gone through instead of stopping in here. No need for any probing or searching. Here we are."

As he spoke he made a slight cut with his keen knife through the white skin, where a little lump of a bluish tint could be seen, pressed with his thumbs on either side, and the bullet came out like a round button through a button-hole, and rolled on to the bed.

"Better save that for him, Gowan," said the doctor cheerfully. "He'll like to keep it as a curiosity. Stopped its chance of festering and worrying him and making him feverish. Now we'll have just a stitch here and a stitch there, and keep the lips of the wound together."

As he spoke he took a needle and silk from his case, just as if he had brought them expecting that they would be wanted, took some lint from one pocket, a roll of bandage from another, and in an incredibly short time had the wound bound up.

"Likely to be serious?" said Captain Murray.

"What, this, sir? Pooh! not much worse than a cut finger. Smart a bit. Poor, weak, girlish sort of a fellow; feeble pulse. Good thing he had fainted, and didn't know what I was doing.—Well, squire, how are you?"

Andrew Forbes lay perfectly still, ghastly pale, and with his eyes closely shut, till the doctor pressed up first one lid and then the other, frowning slightly the while.

"Can I get anything for you, doctor?" said Captain Murray.

" Eh ? Oh no ! He'll be all right. Feels sick, and in a bit of pain. Let him lie there and go to sleep."

" But he is fainting. Oughtn't you to give him something, or to bathe his face ? "

" Look here ! " cried the doctor testily, " I don't come interfering and crying ' Fours about,' or ' By your right,' or anything of that kind, when you are at the head of your company, do I ? "

" Of course not."

" Then don't you interfere when I'm in command over one of my gang. I've told you he's all right. I ought to know."

" Oh yes ; let the doctor alone, Murray," said the colonel. " There, I'm heartily glad that matters are no worse. Foolish fellow to attempt such a wild trick. You will want a nurse for him, doctor."

" Nurse ! for that ? Pooh ! nonsense ! I'm very glad he was so considerate as not to disturb me over my dinner. I shouldn't have liked that, Squire Gowan. Didn't do it out of spite because he was not asked to dinner, did he ? "

" Pish ! no ; he was asked," said Captain Murray. " Yes ; you wanted to say something, Gowan ? "

" Only that I will have a mattress on the floor, sir, and stay with him."

" Not necessary, boy," said the doctor sharply.

" Let him be with his friend, doctor," said Captain Murray.

" Friend, sir ? I thought they were deadly enemies, trying hard to give me a job this morning to fit their pieces together again. I don't want to stop him from spoiling his night's rest if he likes ; but if he stays, won't they begin barking and biting again ? "

" Not much fear of that—eh, Frank ? There, stay with your friend. I'm in hopes that you will do him more good than the doctor."

"Oh, very well," said that gentleman.

"Then you don't think there is anything to be alarmed about ? " said Frank anxiously.

"Pooh! no; not a bit more than if you had cut your finger with a sharp knife. Now, if the bullet had gone in there, or there, or there, or into his thick young head," said the doctor, making pokes at the lad's body as he lay on the bed, "we should have some excuse for being anxious ; but a boy who has had his arm scratched by a bullet ! The idea is absurd. I say, colonel, are boys of any good whatever in the world ? "

"Oh yes, some of them," said the colonel, smiling and giving Frank a kindly nod. "Good night, my lad. There will be no need for you to sit up, I think."

" Not a bit, Gowan," said the doctor quietly. " Don't fidget, boy. He'll be all right."

Frank looked at him dubiously.

"I mean it, my lad," he said, in quite a different tone of voice. "You may trust me. Good night."

He shook hands warmly with the boy, and all but Captain Murray left the chamber, talking about the scare that the shots had created in the Palace.

" I hear they thought the Pretender had dropped in," said the doctor jocosely. Then the door was shut, and the sound cut off.

" I'll leave you now, Frank, my lad," said Captain Murray. "Take one of the pillows, and lie down in the next room on the couch. There's an extra blanket at the foot of the bed. I will speak to my servant to be on the alert, and to come if you ring. Don't scruple to do so, if you think there is the slightest need, and he will fetch the doctor at once. You will lie down ? "

" If you think I may," said Frank, as he walked with him to the door of the sitting-room, beyond earshot of the occupant of the bed.

"I am sure you may, my boy. The doctor only

confirmed my own impression, and I feel sure he would know at a glance."

"But Drew seems quite insensible, sir."

"Yes—seems," said Captain Murray. "There, trust the doctor. I do implicitly. I think he proved his knowledge in the way he saved Baron Steinberg's life. Good night. You will have to be locked in ; but the sentry will have the key, and you can communicate with him as well as ring, so you need not feel lonely. There, once more, good night."

The captain passed out, and Frank caught sight of a tall sentinel on the landing before the door was closed and locked, the boy standing pale and thoughtful for some moments, listening to the retiring steps of his father's old friend, before crossing the room, and entering the chamber, which looked dim and solemn by the light of the two candles upon the dressing table. He took up one of these, and went to the bedside, to stand gazing down at Andrew's drawn face and bandaged arm, his brown hair lying loose upon the pillow, and making his face look the whiter by contrast.

"In much pain, Drew ? " he said softly ; but there was no reply.

"Can I do anything for you ? "

Still no reply, and the impression gathered strength in the boy's mind that his companion could hear what he said but felt too bitter to reply.

This idea grew so strong, that at last he said gently :

"Don't be angry with me, Drew. It is very sad and unfortunate, and I want to try and help you bear it patiently. Would you like me to do anything for you ? Talk to you—read to you ; or would you like me to write to your father, and tell him of what has happened ? "

But, say what he would, Andrew Forbes made no sign, and lay perfectly still—so still, that in his anxiety Frank

stretched out his hand to touch the boy's forehead and
hands, which were of a pleasant temperature.

"He is too much put out to speak," thought Frank;
"and I don't wonder. He must feel cruelly disappointed at
his failure to escape; but I'm glad he has not got away; for
it would have been horrible for him to have gone and
joined the poor foolish enthusiasts who have landed in
the north."

He stood gazing sadly down at the wounded lad for
some minutes, and then softly took the extra pillow and
blanket from the bed, carried them to the little couch in
the next room, returned for the candles, and, after holding
them over the patient for a few minutes, he went back
quietly to the sitting-room, placed them on the table, took
a book, and sat down to read.

He sat down to read, but he hardly read a line, for the
scenes of the past twenty-four hours came between his
eyes and the print, and at the end of a quarter of an hour
he wearily pushed the book aside, took up one of the
candles, and looked in the chamber to see how Andrew
appeared to be.

Apparently he had not moved; but now, as the boy was
going to ask him again if he could do anything for him, he
heard the breath coming and going as if he were sleeping
calmly; and feeling that this was the very best thing that
could happen to him, he went softly back to his seat, and
once more drew the book to his side.

But no; the most interesting work ever written would
not have taken his attention, and he sat listening for
the breathing in the next room, then to the movements
of the sentry outside as he moved from time to time,
changing feet, or taking a step or two up and down as
far as the size of the landing would allow. Then came
a weary yawn, and the clock chimed and struck twelve,
while, before it had finished, the sounds of other clocks
striking became mingled with it, and Frank listened to the

strange jangle, one which he might have heard hundreds of times, but which had never impressed him so before.

At last silence, broken only by the pacings of other sentries; and once more came from the landing a weary yawn, which was infectious, for in spite of his troubles Frank yawned too, and felt startled.

"I can't be sleepy," he said to himself; "who could at such a time?" And to prove to himself that such a thing was impossible, and show his thorough wakefulness, he rose, and once more walked into the chamber, looked at the wounded lad, apparently sleeping calmly, and returned to his seat to read.

And now it suddenly dawned upon him that, in spite of his desire to be thoroughly wakeful, nature was showing him that he could not go through all the past excitement without feeling the effects, for, as he bent firmly over his book to read, he found himself suddenly reading something else—some strange, confused matter about the house in Queen Anne Street, and the broken door.

Then he started up perfectly wakeful, after nodding so low that his face touched the book.

"How absurd!" he muttered; and he rose and walked up and down the room. The sentry heard him, and began to pace the landing.

Frank returned to his seat, looked at the book, and went off instantly fast asleep, and almost immediately woke up again with a start.

"Oh, this won't do," he muttered. "I can't—I won't sleep."

- The next minute he was fast, but again he woke up with a start.

"It's of no use," he muttered; "I must give way to it for a few minutes. I'll lie down, and perhaps that will take it off, and I shall be quite right for the rest of the night."

Very unwillingly, but of necessity, for he felt that he

was almost asleep as he moved about, he rose, took up the blanket from the couch, threw it round him like a cloak, punched up the pillow, and lay down.

"There!" he said to himself; "that's it. I don't feel so sleepy this way; it's resting oneself by lying down. I believe I could read now, and know what I am reading. How ridiculous it makes one feel to be so horribly sleepy! Some people, they say, can lie down and determine to wake up in an hour, or two hours, or just when they like. Well, I'd do that—I mean I'd try to do that—if I were going to sleep; but I won't sleep. I'll lie here resting for a bit, and then get up again, and go and see how Drew is. It would be brutal to go off soundly, with him lying in that state.—How quiet it all seems when one is lying down! It's as if one could hear better. Yes, I can hear Drew breathing quite plain; and how that sentry does keep on yawning! Sentries must get very sleepy sometimes when on duty in the night, and it's a terribly severe punishment for one who does sleep at his post. Well, I'm a sentry at my post to watch over poor Drew, and I should deserve to be very severely punished if I slept; not that I should be punished, except by my own conscience."

He lay perfectly wakeful now, looking at the candles, which both wanted snuffing badly, and making up his mind to snuff them; but he began thinking of his father, then wondering once more where he could be, and feeling proud of the way in which the officers talked about him.

"If the King would only pardon him!" he thought, "how—— I must get up and snuff those candles; if I don't, that great black, mushroom-like bit of burnt wick will be tumbling off and burning in the grease, and be what they call a thief in the candle. How it does grow bigger and bigger!"

And it did grow bigger and bigger, and fell into the tiny cup of molten grease—for in those days the King's officers were not supplied with wax candles for their rooms—and it did form a thief, and made the candle gutter down, while the other slowly burned away into the socket, and made a very unpleasant odour in the room, as first one and then the other rose and fell with a wanton-looking, dancing flame, which finally dropped down and rose no more, sending up a tiny column of smoke instead.

Then the sentry was relieved, and so was Frank, for, utterly worn out, he was sleeping heavily, with nature hard at work repairing the waste of the day, and so soundly that he did not know of the reverse of circumstances, and that Andrew Forbes had risen to enter the outer room, and look in, even coming close to his side, as if to see why it was he did not keep watch over him and come and see him from time to time.

History perhaps was repeating itself: the mountain would not go to Mahomet, so Mahomet had to go to the mountain.

CHAPTER XXX.

A STRANGE AWAKENING.

THERE is not much room in a bird's head for brains;
but it has plenty of thinking power all the
same, and one of the first things a bird thinks out is
when he is safe or when he is in danger. As a consequence of this, we have at the present day quite a colony
of that shyest of wild birds, the one which will puzzle the
owner of a gun to get within range—the wood-pigeon,
calmly settled down in St. James's Park, and feeding upon
the grass, not many yards away from the thousands of
busy or loitering Londoners going to and fro across the
enclosure, which the birds have found out is sacred to
birddom, a place where no gun is ever fired save on
festival days, and though the guns then are big and
manipulated by artillerymen, the charges fired are only
blank.

But St. James's Park from its earliest enclosure was
always a place for birds—even the name survives on one
side of the walk devoted by Charles II. to his birdcages,
where choice specimens were kept; so that a hundred and
eighty years ago, when the country was much closer to the
old Palace than it is now, there was nothing surprising in
the *chink, chink* of the blackbird and the loud musical song
of thrush and lark awakening a sleeper there somewhere
about sunrise. And to a boy who loved the country
sights and sounds, and whose happiest days had been spent
in sunny Hampshire, it was very pleasant to lie there in

a half-roused, half-dreamy state listening to the bird
notes floating in upon the cool air through an open
window, even if the lark's note did come from a cage
whose occupant fluttered its wings and pretended to fly
as it gazed upward from where it rested upon a freshly
cut turf.

The sweet notes set Frank Gowan thinking of the broad
marshy fields down by the river, bordered with sedge, reed,
and butter-bur, where the clear waters raced along, and
the trout could be seen waiting for the breakfast swept
down by the stream—where the marsh marigolds studded
the banks with their golden chalices, the purple loose-
strife grew in brilliant beds of colour, and the creamy
meadow-sweet perfumed the morning air. Far more
delightful to him than any palace, more musical than the
choicest military band, it all sent a restful sense of joy
through his frame, the more invigorating that the window
was wide, and the odour of the burned-down candles had
passed away.

He lay imbibing the sweet sounds and freshness
through ear and nostril; but for a time his eyes remained
fast closed. Then, at a loud thrilling burst from the
lark's cage in the courtyard, both eyes opened, and he
lay staring up at the whitewashed ceiling, covered with
cracks, and looking like the map of Nowhere in Wonder-
land. For the lark sang very sweetly to charm the wished-
for mate, which never came, and Frank smiled and gradually
lowered his eyes so that they were fixed upon the un-
curtained window till the lark finished its lay.

Then, and then only, did he begin to think in the way
a boy muses when his senses grow more and more awake.
First of all he began to wonder why it was that the
window was wide open—not that it mattered, for the
air was very cool and sweet; then why it was his bedroom looked so strange; then why it was that the
blanket was close up to his face without the sheet; and,

lastly, he sat up feeling that horrible sense of depression which comes over us like a cloud when there has been trouble on the previous day—trouble which has been forgotten.

For a moment or two he felt that he must be dreaming. But no, he was dressed, this was Captain Murray's room, there was the door open leading into the chamber where Andrew Forbes lay, and yes—— Then it all came with crushing force—he lay wounded after that mad attempt to escape, while the friend who had offered to sit with him and watch had calmly lain down and gone to sleep.

"Oh, it is monstrous!" panted the boy, as he threw the blanket aside, and stepped softly, and trembling with excitement, toward the chamber. For now the dread came that something might have happened during the night, in despite of the doctor's calm way of treating the injury.

The idea was so terrible that, as he reached the door, he stopped short, and turned a ghastly white, not daring to look in. But recalling now that he had heard his friend's breathing quite plainly over-night, he listened with every nerve on the strain. Not a sound, till the lark burst forth again.

He hesitated no longer, but, full of shame and self-reproach for that which he could not help, he stepped softly into the room, and then stood still, staring hard at the bed, and at a blood-stained handkerchief lying where it had been thrown upon the floor.

For a few moments the lad did not stir—he was perfectly stunned ; and then he began to look slowly round the room for an explanation.

The bed was without tenant. Had Captain Murray, or some other officer, come with a guard while he slept and taken the prisoner away ?

Then the truth came like a flash :—

The window in the next room—it was open !

He darted back, and ran to the window to thrust out

his head and look down. Yes, it was easy enough; he
could himself have got out, hung by his hands, and
dropped upon the pavement, which would not have been
above eight feet from the soles of his boots as he
hung.

But the wound! How could a lad who was badly
wounded in the arm manage to perform such a feat?

He must have been half wild, delirious from fever, to
have done such a thing. No.

Fresh thoughts came fast now. It stood to reason that
if Drew had been half wild with delirium he must have
been roused; and he now recalled how coolly the doctor
had taken the injury, and Captain Murray's half contemptuous manner, which he had thought unfeeling. Then,
too, it was strange that Drew should have lain as he did,
with his eyes tightly closed, just as if he were perfectly
insensible, and never making the slightest sign when he
had spoken to him.

For a few minutes Frank battled with the notion; but
it grew stronger and stronger, and at last he was convinced.

"Then he was shamming," he muttered indignantly,
"pretending to be worse than he really was, so as to
throw people off their guard, and then try again to
escape."

Once more he tried to prove himself to be in the wrong
and thoroughly unjust to the wounded lad; but facts are
stubborn things, and one after the other they rose up,
trifles in themselves, but gaining strength as the array
increased, and at last a bitter feeling of anger filled the
boy's breast, as he felt perfectly convinced of the truth
that Drew had lain there waiting till he was asleep, and
then, in spite of his wound, had crept out of the window,
dropped, and gone.

But how could he? The sentries had stopped him
before; why did they not do so at the second attempt?

And besides, there was the sentry just outside the door. Why had not he heard?

Frank went to the window again, and looked out, to find that it was not deemed necessary to place a guard over the guardroom and the officers' quarters, save that there was one man at the main doorway, and this was beyond an angle from where he stood, while the next sentries were in the courtyard to his left, and the stable-yard, to his right. So that, covered by the darkness, it was comparatively an easy task to drop down unnoticed, though afterwards it was quite a different thing.

"Then he has gone!" said Frank softly; and he shrank away from the window, to stand thinking about how the lad could have managed to get away unseen by the sentries.

Thoughts came faster than ever; and he, as it were, put himself in his companion's position, and unconsciously enacted almost exactly what had taken place. For Frank mentally went through what he would have done under the circumstances if he had been a prisoner who wished to get away.

He would have waited till all was still, and when the sentry at the door was pacing up and down, and his footsteps on the stone landing would help to dull any noise he made, he would slip out of the window, drop on to his toes, and then go down on all fours, and creep along close to the wall beneath the windows, right for the piazza-like place, and along beneath the arches, making not for either of the entrance gates, but for the private garden. There he would be stopped by the wall; but there was a corner there with a set of iron spikes pointing downward to keep people from climbing over, but which to an active lad offered good foot- and hand-hold, by means of which he felt that he could easily get to the top. From there he could drop down, go right across the garden to the outer wall, which divided it from the Park, and get on that somewhere by the help of one of the trees. Once on the top, he could choose his place, and crawl to it like a cat. Then all he had to do was to lower himself by his hands, and drop down, to be free to walk straight away, and take refuge with his friends.

"Oh, I could get out as easily as possible, if I wanted to," muttered Frank. "Poor Drew! what's to become of him now?"

Frank stood thinking still, and saw it all more and more plainly. Drew would know where his father was, and go and join him. And then?

Frank shuddered, for he seemed to see ruin and misery, and the destruction of all prospects for his friend; and, in spite of the indignation he felt against him for his deceit, his heart softened, and he muttered, as he turned to go once more into the bedchamber:

"Poor old Drew! I did like him so much, after all."

As the boy entered the bedroom something caught his eye on the dressing table, and he looked at it wonderingly. It was the book he had been reading in the other room; the book, he knew, was there on the table when he lay down. Could he have taken it into the bed-chamber? No, he was sure he had not. Besides, there was a pen laid upon it, and it was open at the fly-leaf. Frank panted with excitement, for there, written in his friend's hand, were the words:

"*Good-bye, old Frank. We'll shake hands some day, when I come back in triumph. I can't forget you, though we did fall out so much. You'll be wiser some day. I can't write more; my wound hurts so much. I'm going to escape. If they shoot me, never mind; I shall have died like a man, crying, 'God save King James!'*

"*DREW F.*"

The tears rose to Frank's eyes, and he did not feel ashamed of them, as he closed the book and thrust it into his pocket.

" Poor old Drew !" he said softly ; "he believes he is doing right, and it is, after all, what his father taught him.   My father taught me differently, so we can't agree."

What should he do ?   He must speak out, and it could make no difference now, for Drew must be safe away. He did not like to summon the sentry, and he shrank too, for he felt that he might be accused of aiding in the escape ; but while he was thinking he heard steps crossing the open space in front, and glancing through the chamber window, he saw Captain Murray and the doctor coming toward the place.

The next minute their steps were on the stairs, the sentry challenged, the key rattled in the door, and the doctor entered first, to say jocularly as Frank advanced from the chamber :

" Morning, Gowan.   Wounded man's not dead, I hope."

CHAPTER XXXI.

FRANK gazed sharply at the doctor, but remained silent, his countenance being so fixed and strange that Captain Murray took alarm.

"Hang it, Frank lad, what's the matter? Why don't you speak?"

He did not wait to hear the boy's answer, but rushed at once into his bedchamber and returned directly.

"Here, what is the meaning of this?" he cried. "Where is young Forbes?"

"Gone, sir," said Frank, finding his voice.

"Gone? What do you mean?"

"I sat up watching him till I could not keep my eyes open. Then I lay down, and when I awoke this morning the window was open, and he had escaped."

"Impossible!" cried Captain Murray angrily.

"Humph! I don't know so much about that, Murray," said the doctor, after indulging in a grunt. "The young rascal was gammoning us last night, pretending to be so bad."

"But there was no deceit about the wound."

"Not a bit, man; but he was making far more fuss about it than was real. It was only a clean cut, especially where I divided the skin and let out the ball. By George! though, the young rascal could bear a bit of pain."

"But do you mean to tell me that he could escape alone with a wound like that to disable his arm?"

"Oh yes. It would hurt him terribly ; but a lad with plenty of courage would grin and bear that, and get away all the same. I'm glad of it."

"What ! Glad the prisoner has escaped ?"

"Oh, I don't mean that," said the doctor. "I mean glad he had so much stuff in him. It was a clever bit of acting, and shows that he must have the nerve of a strong man. I beg his pardon, for last night I thought him as weak as a girl for making so much fuss over a mere scratch. It was all sham, that insensibility. I knew in a moment—you remember I said so to you when we went away."

The captain nodded.

"But I thought it was the weak, vain, young coxcomb making believe so as to pose as a hero who was suffering horribly."

"But once more," cried Captain Murray warmly, "do you mean to tell me that, with one arm disabled, that boy could have managed to escape from the window without help ?"

"To be sure I do. Give him a pretty good sharp, cutting pain while he was using his arm.—Did you hear him cry out, Gowan ?"

"No, sir," said Frank sharply ; and he turned angrily upon the captain : "You said something very harsh about Drew Forbes not being able to get away without help. You don't think I helped him to get away ?"

"Yes, I do, boy," said the captain, with soldierly bluntness. "I think you must have known he wanted to escape, and that you helped him to get out of the window ; and I consider it a miserably contemptible return for the kindness of your father's old friend."

"It is not true, Captain Murray," cried Frank hotly. "You have no right to doubt my word.—Doctor, I assure you I did not know till I woke this morning, when I was utterly astonished."

"And ran to the door, and gave notice to the sentry," said Captain Murray coldly.

"No, I did not do that. I see now that I ought to have done so, and I was hesitating about it when you both came. But I had only just found it out then."

"And I suppose I shall be called to account for letting him go," said the captain bitterly. "Why didn't you go with him? Were you afraid?"

"Oh, come, come, Murray," cried the doctor reproachfully; "don't talk so to the boy. He's speaking the truth, I'll vouch for it. Afraid? Rob Gowan's boy afraid? Pooh! he's made of the wrong sort of stuff."

"Yes, sir," cried the boy, in a voice hoarse with emotion, "I was afraid,—not last night, for I did not know he was going; but when he begged and prayed of me to run away with him, and join the people rising for the Pretender, I was afraid to go and disgrace my mother and father—and myself."

"Well done! well said, Frank, my lad!" cried the doctor, taking him by one hand to begin patting him on the back. "That's a knock down for you, Murray. Now, sir, you've got to apologise to our young friend here—beg his pardon like a man."

"If I have misjudged him, I beg his pardon humbly—like a man," said Captain Murray coldly. "I hope I have; but I cannot help thinking that he must have been aware of his companion's flight.—Mr. Gowan, your parole is at an end, sir. You will keep closely to these rooms."

"Bah!" cried the doctor; "why don't you say you are going to have him locked up in the black hole. Murray, I'm ashamed of you. It's bile, sir, bile, and I must give you a dose."

"I am going now, doctor," said the captain coldly.

"Which means I am to come away, if I don't want to be locked up too. Very well, I have nothing to do here.— There, shake hands, Frank. Don't you mind all this. He believes this now; but he'll soon see that he is wrong, and come back and shake hands. Your father knew how to choose his friends when he chose Captain Murray. He's angry, and, more than that, he's hurt, because he thinks you have deceived him; but you have not, my lad. Doctors can see much farther into a fellow than a soldier can, and both of your windows are as wide open and clear as crystal. There, it will be all right."

He gave the boy's shoulder a good, warm, friendly grip, and followed the captain out of the room. The door was locked, some orders were given to the sentry, Frank heard the descending steps, and after standing gazing hard at the closed door for some minutes he dropped into the chair by the table, the one in which he had had such a struggle to keep awake. Then he placed his arms before him, and let his head go down upon them, feeling hot, bitter, and indignant against Captain Murray, and as if he were the most unhappy personage in the whole world.

A quarter of an hour must have passed before he started up again with a proud look in his eyes.

"Let him—let everybody think so if they like," he said aloud. "I don't care. She'll believe me, I know she will. Oh! if I could only go to her and tell her; but I can't. No," he cried, in an exultant tone; "she knows me better and I know she'll come to me."

CHAPTER XXXII.

A BIG WIGGING.

"I WON'T show that I mind," thought Frank; and in a matter-of-fact way he went into the bedroom, and made quite a spiteful use of the captain's dressing table and washstand, removing all traces of having passed the night in his clothes, and he had just ended and changed his shoes, which had been brought there, when the outer door was unlocked, and the captain's servant came in to tidy up the place.

The servant was ready to talk; but Frank was in no talking humour, and went and stood looking out of the window till the man had gone, when the boy came away, and began to imitate Andrew Forbes's caged-animal-like walk up and down the room, in which health-giving exercise to a prisoner he was still occupied when there were more steps below—the tramp of soldiers, the guard was changed, and Frank felt a strong desire to look out of the window to see if another sentry was placed there; but he felt too proud. It would be weak and boyish, he thought; so he began walking up and down again, till once more the door was unlocked, and the captain's servant entered, bearing a breakfast tray, and left again.

"Just as if I could eat breakfast after going through all this!" he said sadly. "I'm sure I can't eat a bit." But after a few minutes, when he tried, he found that he could, and became so absorbed in the meal and his thoughts that he blushed like a girl with shame to see what a clearance he had made.

The tray was fetched away, and the morning passed slowly in the expectation that Lady Gowan would come ; but midday had arrived without so much as a message, and Frank's heart was sinking again, when he once more heard steps, and upon the door being opened, Captain Murray appeared.

"He has come to say he believes me," thought the boy, as his heart leapt ; but it sank again upon his meeting his visitor's eyes, for the captain looked more stern and cold than ever, and his manner communicated itself to the boy.

"You will come with me, Gowan," said the captain sternly.

"Where to ?" was upon the boy's lips ; but he bit the words back, and swallowed them. He would not have spoken them and humbled himself then for anything, and rising and taking his hat, he walked out and across the courtyard, wondering where he was being taken, for he had half expected that it was to the guardroom to be imprisoned more closely. But a minute showed him that the growing resentment was unnecessary, for he was not apparently to submit to that indignity ; and now the blood began to flush up into his temples, for he grasped without having had to ask where his destination was to be.

In fact, the captain marched him to the foot of the great staircase, past the guard, and into the long anteroom, where he spoke to one of the attendants, who went straight to the door at the end leading into the Prince's audience chamber.

And now for a few moments the captain's manner changed, and he bent his head down to whisper hastily :

"The Prince has sent for you, boy, to question you himself. For Heaven's sake speak out frankly the simple truth. I cannot tell you how much depends upon it. Recollect this : your mother's future is at stake, and——"

The attendant reappeared, came to him, and said respectfully:

"His Royal Highness will see you at once."

There was no time for the captain to say more—no opportunity offered for Frank to make any indignant retort concerning the truth. For the curtain was held back, the door opened, and Captain Murray led the way in, slowly followed by his prisoner, who advanced firmly enough toward where the Prince sat, his Royal Highness turning his eyes upon him at once with a most portentous frown.

"Well, sir," he said at once, "so I find that I have fresh bad news of you. You are beginning early in life. Not content with what has passed, you have now turned traitor."

The Prince's looks, if correctly read, seemed to intimate that he expected the boy to drop on his knees and piteously cry for pardon; but to the surprise of both present he cried indignantly:

"It is not true, your Royal Highness."

"Eh? What, sir? How dare you speak to me like this?" cried the Prince. "I have heard everything about this morning's and last night's business, and I find that I have been showing kindness to a young viper of a traitor, who is in direct communication with the enemy, and playing the spy on all my movements so as to send news."

"It is not true, your Highness!" cried the boy warmly. "You have been deceived. Just as if I would do such a thing as that!"

"Do you mean to pretend that this young Forbes, your friend and companion, is not in correspondence with the enemy?"

"No, your Royal Highness," said the lad sadly.

"You knew it?"

"Yes."

"Then, as my servant, why did you not inform me, sir?"

"Because I was your servant, sir, and not a spy," said the boy proudly.

"Very fine language, upon my honour!" cried the Prince. "But you are friends with him; and last night, after his first failure, you helped him to escape."

"I did not, sir!" cried the boy passionately.

"Words, words, sir," said the Prince; "even your friend here, Captain Murray, feels that you did."

"And it is most unjust of him, sir!" cried the boy.

"Don't speak so bluntly to me," said the Prince sternly. "Now attend. You say you did not help him?"

"Yes, your Royal Highness."

"Mind this. I know all the circumstances. Give me some proof that you knew nothing of his escape."

"I can't, sir," cried the boy passionately. "I was asleep, and when I woke he was gone."

"Weak, weak, sir. Now look here; you say you are my servant, and want me to believe in you. Be quite open with me; tell me all you know, and for your mother's sake I will deal leniently with you. What do you know about this rising and the enemy's plans?"

"Nothing, your Highness."

"What! and you were hand and glove with these people. That wretched boy must have escaped to go straight to his father and acquaint him with everything he knows. What reason have I to think you would not do the same?"

"I!" cried the boy indignantly; "I could not do such a thing. Ah!" he cried, with a look of joy, making his white face flush and grow animated. "Your Royal Highness asked me for some proof;" and he lugged at something in his pocket, with which, as he let his hands fall, one had come in contact.

"What have you there, sir?"

"A book, your Highness," panted the boy; "but it won't come out.—Hah! that's it.—Look, look! I found that on the table when I woke this morning. See what he has written here."

Frank was thinking nothing about royalty or court etiquette in his excitement. He dragged out the book, opened the cover, went close up to the Prince, and banged it down before him, pointing to the words, which the Prince took and read before turning his fierce gaze upon the lad's glowing face.

"There!" cried the boy, "that proves it. You must see now, sir. He cheated me. I thought he was very bad. But you see he was well enough to go. That shows how he wanted me to join him, and I wouldn't. Oh, don't say you can't see!"

"Yes, I can see," said the Prince, without taking his eyes off him. "Did you know of this, Captain Murray?"

"I? No, your Royal Highness. It is fresh to me."

"Read."

Captain Murray took the book, read the scrap of writing, and, forgetting the Prince's presence, he held out his hands to his brother-officer's son.

"Oh, Frank, my boy!" he cried, "forgive me for doubting your word."

"Oh yes, I forgive you!" cried the lad, seizing and clinging to his hands. "I knew you'd find out the truth. I don't mind now."

"Humph!" ejaculated the Prince, looking on gravely, but with his face softening a little. "The boy's honest enough, sir. But you occupy a very curious position, young gentleman, a very curious position, and everything naturally looked very black against you."

"Did it, your Highness? Yes, I suppose so."

"Then you had been quarrelling with that wretched young traitor about joining the—the enemy?" said the Prince.

Frank winced at "wretched young traitor"; but he answered firmly:

"Yes, sir; we were always quarrelling about it, but I hoped to get him to think right at last."

"And failed, eh?" said the Prince, with a smile.

"Yes, sir."

"And pray, was it about this business that you fought out yonder?"

"It had something to do with it, sir," said Frank, flushing up. "He said——"

Frank stopped short, looking sadly confused, and grew more so as he found the questioner had fixed his eyes, full now of suspicion, upon him.

"Well, what did he say, sir?"

Frank was silent, and hung his head.

"Do you hear me, sir?"

"Must I speak, Captain Murray?" said the boy appealingly.

"Yes, the simple truth."

"He said, your Royal Highness, that my father had joined the enemy, and was a general in the rebel army, and I struck him for daring to utter such a lie—and then we fought."

"Why?" said the Prince sternly, "for telling you the truth?"

"The truth, sir!" cried the boy indignantly. "Don't say you believe that of my father, sir. There is not a more faithful officer in the King's service."

"Your father is not in the King's service, but holds a high command with the rebels, boy."

"No, sir, no!" cried the lad passionately; "it is not true."

At that moment, when he had not heard the rustling of a dress, a soft hand was laid upon Frank's shoulder, and, turning sharply, he saw that it was the Princess who had approached and now looked pityingly in his face, and then turned to the Prince.

"Don't be angry with him," she said gently; "it is very brave of him to speak like this, and terrible for him, poor boy, to know the truth."

"No, no, your Highness, it is not true!" cried Frank wildly; and he caught and kissed, and then clung to the Princess's hand.

"My poor boy!" she said tenderly.

"No, no; don't you believe it, madam!" he cried. "It is not—it can't be true. Some enemy has told you this."

"No," said the Princess gently, "no enemy, my boy. It was told me by one who knows too well. I had it from your mother's lips."

Frank gazed at her blankly, and his eyes then grew full of reproach, as they seemed to say, "How can you, who are her friend, believe such a thing?"

"There boy," said the Prince, interposing; "come here."

Frank turned to him, and his eyes flashed.

"Don't look like that," continued the Prince. "I am not angry with you now. I believe you, and I like your brave, honest way in defending your father. But you see how all this is true."

"No!" cried the boy firmly. "Your Royal Highness and the Princess have been deceived. Some one has brought a lying report to my poor mother, who ought to have been the last to believe it. I cannot and will not think it is true."

"Very well," said the Prince quietly. "You can go on believing that it is not. I wish, my boy, I could. There, you can go back to your duties. You will not go over to the enemy, I see."

The boy looked at the speaker as if about to make some angry speech; but his emotions strangled him, and, forgetting all etiquette, he turned and hurried from the room.

"Look after him, Captain Murray," said the Prince quietly; "true gold is too valuable to be lost."

The captain bowed, and hurried into the antechamber; but Frank had gone, one of the gentlemen in attendance saying that he had rushed through the chamber as if he had been half mad, and leaped down the stairs three or four at a time.

"Gone straight to his mother," thought the captain; and he went on down the staircase, frowning and sad, for he was sick at heart about the news he had that morning learned of his old friend.

CHAPTER XXXIII.

FRANK'S FAITH.

FRANK went straight to his mother's apartments.

"I don't think my lady is well enough to see you to-day, sir," said her woman.

"Tell her I must see her," cried the boy passionately; and a few minutes after, looking very white and strange, Lady Gowan entered the room.

She looked inquiringly in the boy's eyes, and a faint sob escaped her lips as she caught him in her arms, kissed him passionately, and then laid her head upon his shoulder, while for some minutes she sobbed so violently that the boy dared not speak, but tried to caress her into calmness once more.

"Oh, Frank, Frank!" she sighed at last; and he held her more tightly to his breast.

"I was obliged to come, mother," he said; "and now that I have come I dare not speak."

"Yes, speak, dear, speak; say anything to me now," she sighed.

"But it seems so cruel, mother, while you are ill like this!"

"Speak, dear, speak. I ought to have sent to you before; but I was so heart-broken, so cowardly and weak, that I dared not confess it even to my own child."

"Mother," cried the boy passionately, "it is not true."

Lady Gowan heaved a piteous sigh.

"The Prince sent for me, thinking I helped Drew Forbes to escape."

"Ah! He has escaped?"

"Yes, gone to join his father with the rebels; but the Prince believes me now. He asked me first if I were going to join my father with the rebels too."

"And—and—what did you say?" faltered Lady Gowan.

"I?" cried the boy proudly. "I told him that he had no more faithful servant living than my father, though he was dismissed from the Guards."

Lady Gowan uttered a weary sigh once more.

"Oh, mother!" cried Frank, "shame on you to believe this miserable lie! How can you be so weak!"

"Ah, Frank, Frank, Frank!" she sighed wearily.

"It seems too horrible to imagine that you could so readily think such a thing. The Prince believes it, and the Princess too, and she said the news came from you."

"Yes, dear, I was obliged to tell her. Frank, my boy, I knew it when I saw you last—when I was in such trouble, and spoke so angrily to you. I could not, oh, I could not tell you then."

"No. I am very glad you could not, mother," said the boy firmly. "You cannot, and you shall not, believe it. Can't you see that it is impossible? There, don't speak to me; don't think about it any more. You are weak and ill, and that makes you ready to think things which you would laugh at as absurd at another time. Oh, I wish I had said what I ought to have said to the Prince," he cried excitedly. "I did not think of it then."

"What—what would you have said?" cried Lady Gowan, raising her pale, drawn face to gaze in her son's eyes.

"That he could soon prove my father's truth by sending him orders to come back and take his place in the regiment."

"Ah!" sighed Lady Gowan; and she let her head fall once more upon her son's shoulder.

Frank started impatiently.

"Oh!" he cried, "and you will go on believing it. There, I can't be angry with you now, you are so ill; but try and believe the truth, mother. Father is the King's servant, and he would not—he could not break his oaths. There, you will see the truth when you get better; and you must, you must get better now. It was this news which made you so ill?"

"Yes, my boy, yes," she said, in a faint whisper; "and I blame myself for not going with him. If I had been by his side, he would not have changed."

"He has not changed, mother," said the lad firmly. "But how did you get the news?"

"It came through Andrew Forbes's father—Mr. George Selby, as he calls himself now. He sent it to—to one of the gentlemen in the Palace. I must not mention names."

"Ha—ha—ha!" laughed Frank scornfully. "I thought it was some miserable, hatched-up lie. Mr. George Selby has been playing a contemptible, spylike part, trying to gain over people in the Palace. He and his party tried to get me to join them."

"You, my boy?" cried Lady Gowan, in wonder; "and you did not tell me."

"No; conspiracies are not for women to know anything about," said the boy, talking grandly. "But I did tell my father."

"Yes; and what did he say?"

"Almost nothing. I forget now, mother. Treated it with contempt. There, I must go now."

"Back under arrest?"

"Arrest? No, dear. I am the Prince's page, and he knows now that I am no rebel. I am to go back to my duties as if nothing had happened."

Lady Gowan uttered a sigh full of relief.

" But I'm going to prove first of all how terribly wrong
you have been, mother, in believing this miserable scandal.
It is because my poor father is down, and everybody is
ready to trample upon him. But we'll show them yet.
You must be brave, mother, and look and speak as if now
you did not believe a word about the story. Do as I will
do : go back to your place with the Princess, and hold up
your head proudly."

" No, no, no, my boy ; I have been praying the Princess
to let us both go away from the court, for that our position
here was horrible."

" Ah ! and what did she say ? " cried Frank excitedly.

" That it was impossible ; that we were not to blame,
and that I was more her friend than ever."

" Oh, I do love the Princess ! " cried the boy enthusiastically. " There, you see, she does not at heart believe the
miserable tale. No, you shall not go away, mother ; it
would be like owning that it was true. Be brave and
good and full of faith. Father said I was to defend you
while he was away, and I'm going to—against yourself while
you are weak and ill. Oh, what lots of things you've taught
me about trying to be brave and upright and true ; now
I'm going to try and show you that I will. We cannot
leave the court ; it would be dishonouring father. Good-
bye till to-morrow. Oh, mother, how old all this makes
me feel."

" My own boy ! "

" Yes, but I don't feel a bit like a boy now, mother.
It's just as if I had been here for years. There, once
more kiss me—good-bye ! "

" My darling ! But what are you going to do ? "

" Something to show you that father has been slandered.
Good-bye ! To-morrow I shall make you laugh for joy."

And tearing himself away from his mother's clinging
arms, the boy hurried out, down the stairs, and out into
the courtyard, full of the plan now in his mind.

CHAPTER XXXIV.

MORE sentries were about the Palace, and the guard-room was full of soldiers; but no one interfered with the Prince's page, who went straight to the gates, and without the slightest attempt at concealment walked across to the banks of the canal, along by its edge to the end, passed round, and made for his father's house.

Twice over he saw men whom his ready imagination suggested as belonging to the corps of spies who kept the comers and goers from the Palace under observation, but he would not notice them.

"Let them watch if they like. I'm doing something I'm proud of, and not ashamed."

In this spirit he made for the house, and reached it, to find that the battered door had been replaced by a new one, which looked bright and glistening in its coats of fresh paint.

He knocked and rang boldly, and as he waited he glanced carelessly to right and left, to see that one of the men he had passed in the Park had followed, and was sauntering slowly along in his direction.

"How miserably ashamed of himself a fellow like that must feel!" he thought.

At that moment there was the rattling of a chain inside, and the door was opened as far as the links would allow.

"Oh, it's you, Master Francis," said the housekeeper, whose scared and troubled face began to beam with a smile; and directly after he was admitted, and the door closed and fastened once more.

Frank confined his words to friendly inquiries as to the old servant's health, and she hesitated after replying, as if expecting that he would begin to question her; but he went on upstairs, and shut himself in the gloomy-looking room overlooking the Park. Then, obeying his first impulse, he walked to the window to throw back the shutters.

"No. Wouldn't do," he said to himself. "There is sure to be some one watching the house from the back, and it would show them that I came straight here for some particular reason. I can manage in the dark."

It was not quite dark to one who well knew the place; and with beating heart he went across to the picture, and, familiar now with the ingenious mechanism, he pressed the fastening, and then stood still, with the picture turned so that the closet stood open before him.

He hesitated, for though he was so full of hope that he felt quite certain that there would be some communication from his father, he did not like to put it to the test for fear of disappointment. That he felt—after his brave defence of his father, and his belief that he would be able to find a letter which would sweep away all doubt and prove to his mother that she was wrong—would be almost unbearable, and so he waited for quite two minutes.

"Oh, what a coward I am," he muttered at last; and running his hand along the bottom shelf, he felt for the letter he hoped to find.

His heart sank, for there was nothing there, and he hesitated once more, feeling that half his chance was gone. But there was the upper shelf, and once more with beating heart he began to pass his hand over it very slowly, and the next moment he touched a packet, which began to glide along the shelf. Then he started back, thrust to the canvas-covered panel and fastened it almost in one movement, turning as he did so to face the door,

which was slowly opened, and a dimly seen figure stepped
forward, to stand gazing in.

"Why didn't I lock the door after me?" thought the

The spy interrupts Frank in his search for the packet.

boy, who was half wild now with excitement and dread,
as he tried to make out by the few rays which struck
across from the shutters who the man could be.

That was too hard ; but it seemed from the attitude
that his back was half turned to him, and that he was
trying to see what was going on in the room.

The next moment he had proof that he was right, for
the dimly seen figure softly turned and gazed straight at
where he stood.

" He must see me," thought the boy ; and in his excitement he felt that he must take the aggressive, and began
the attack.

" Who are you ? What are you doing here ? " he cried
sharply.   " A thief ? "

" Oh no, young gentleman," said a voice.   " What are
you doing here ? "

For answer Frank stepped quickly to the window and
threw open one of the shutters, the light flashing in and
showing him the face of the man he had passed in the
Park, the man who had followed him into the street, and
seen him enter the house.

" Oh, I see," said Frank contemptuously,—" a spy."

" A gentleman in the King's service, boy, holding his
Majesty's warrant, and doing his duty. Why have you
come here ? "

" Why have I come to my own house ? Go back out of
here directly.   How came the housekeeper to let you in ? "

" She did not, my good boy," said the man quietly ;
" and she did not put up the chain."

" Then how did you get in, sir ? "

" With my key of course—into *your* house."

" Oh, this is insufferable ! " panted Frank.   " While my
father is away it is my house.   I am his representative,
and I don't believe his Majesty would warrant a miserable
spy to use false keys to get into people's homes."

" You have a sharp tongue for a boy," said the man
coolly ; " but I must know why you have come, all the
same."

" Watch and spy, and find out then, you miserable,

contemptible hound!" cried Frank in a rage—with the man for coming, and with himself for not having taken better precautions. For it was maddening. There was the letter waiting for him; he had touched it; and now he could not get at it for this man, who would not let him quit his sight, and perhaps after he was gone would search until he found it.

The man looked hard at him for a few moments, but not menacingly. It was in the fashion of a man who was accustomed to be snubbed, bullied, and otherwise insulted, but did not mind these things in the least, so long as he could achieve his ends. He made Frank turn cold, though, with dread, for he began to look round the room, noticing everything in turn in search of the reason for the boy's visit, for naturally he felt certain that there was some special reason, and he meant to find it out.

Frank stood watching him for a while, and then, as the man did not walk straight at the picture, and begin to try if he could find anything behind, the boy began to pluck up courage, and, drawing a long breath by way of preparation, he said, as he stepped forward:

"Now, sir, I don't feel disposed to leave you here while I go upstairs to my old room, so have the goodness to leave."

"When you do, Mr. Gowan—not before."

"What!" cried Frank fiercely; and he clapped his hand to where his sword should hang, but it had not been returned to him by the officer who arrested him, and he coloured with rage and annoyance.

"Ah, you have no sword," said the man coolly. "Just as well, for you would not be able to use it. At the least attempt at violence, one call from this whistle would bring help to the back and front of the house, and you would be arrested. I presume you do not want to be in prison again?"

"What do you know about my being arrested?"

" There is not much that I do not know," said the man, with a laugh. " It is of no use to kick, my good sir. I only wish you to understand that violence will do no good."

" Bah!" ejaculated Frank angrily; and he walked straight out of the room on to the landing, trying to bang the door behind him; but the man caught it, and came out quickly and quietly after him.

" What shall I do?" thought Frank; and for a moment he was disposed to descend and leave the house, but he felt that he could not without first gaining possession of the letter. It would be impossible to bear the strain, especially with the accompaniment of the dread of its being discovered and placing information which might prove disastrous to his father in the hands of a spy.

The next minute his mind was made up. He determined to weary out the man if he could, while he on his part went up to his own old bedroom, which he used to occupy when he came home from school while his father and mother were in town. He would go up to it, and sit down and read if he could. The man should not come in there, of that he was determined; and he felt that he must risk the fellow's searching the place they had left.

" For if he has a key, he could come in at any time, and hunt about the place. But how did he get a key to fit the door?"

Frank thought for a few moments, and then it was plain enough: he had obtained it from the people who made the new door to the house.

" I must get the letter before I go," thought the boy now, " so as to send word to father that he must not venture to come again, because the place is so closely watched; and I must tell him of this piece of miserable intrusion."

He took a few steps down, and the man followed; but before the landing was reached, he turned sharply round, and began to ascend rapidly,

The man still followed close to his elbow, and in this way the second floor was reached, where the door of Frank's bedroom lay a little to the right.

The last time he was up there he was in company with his father in the dark, on the night of the escape, and a faint thrill of excitement ran through him as he recalled all that had passed.

He turned sharply to the spy, and said indignantly :

" Look here, fellow, this is my bedroom ; " and he pointed to the door.

" Yes, I know," said the man coolly ; " but it's a long time since you slept there."

" And what's that to you ? Go down. You are not coming in there."

" I have the warrant of his Majesty's Minister to go where I please on secret service, sir," said the man blandly ; " and you, as one of the Prince's household, dare not try to stop me."

" Oh ! " ejaculated the boy fiercely ; and seizing the door knob he turned it quickly, meaning to rush in, bang the door in the fellow's face, and lock him out.

" Let him do his worst," thought Frank, who was now beside himself with rage ; but he did not carry out his plan, for the door did not yield. It was locked, and as he rattled the knob his fingers rubbed against the handle of the key.

Perhaps it was the friction against the steel which sent a flash of intelligence to his brain ; but whether or no the flash darted there, and lit up that which the moment before was very dark with something akin to despair.

He rattled the handle to and fro several times ; and uttering an ejaculation full of anger, he threw himself heavily against the door, but it did not of course yield.

" Pooh ! " he cried ; and letting go of the door knob, he seized the handle of the key, and dragged and dragged at it, making it grate and rattle among the wards, each moment growing more excited, and ended by snatching his hand away, and stamping furiously on the floor.

"Don't stand staring there, idiot!" he cried, with a flash of anger. "Can't you see that key won't turn?"

"Not if you drag at it like that," said the man, smiling blandly. "That is good for locksmiths, not for locks;" and stepping calmly forward, he took hold of the key, turned it slowly so that the bolt shot back with a sharp snap; then, turning the knob, he opened the door, walked into the little bedroom, and stood back a little, holding it so that there was room for Frank to pass in.

"Bah!" ejaculated Frank savagely; and he stepped in, raising his right hand, and making a quick menacing gesture, as if to strike the man a heavy blow across the face.

Taken thoroughly by surprise by Frank's feint, the spy made a step back, when, quick as thought, the boy seized the handle, drew it to him, banging the door and turning the key, and stood panting outside, his enemy shut safely within.

"Here, open this door!" cried the man; and he began to thump heavily upon the panels. "Quick! before I break it down."

"Break it down," cried the boy tauntingly. "How clever for a spy to walk into a trap like that."

There was a moment's silence, and then—as if long coming—something which resembled the echo of Frank's angry stamp on the floor was heard, followed by a heavy bump. The man had thrown himself against the door.

"He won't break out in a hurry," muttered the boy; and he ran to the staircase, and in familiar old fashion seized the rail, threw himself half over, and let himself slide down the polished mahogany to the first floor, where he rushed in, closed and locked the door of the room, hurried excitedly to the picture door of the closet, the portrait of his ancestor seeming to his excited fancy to smile approval, and, as he applied his hand to the fastening, he heard faintly a noise overhead. The next moment a chill ran through him, for the window of his bedroom had evidently been thrown open, and a clear, shrill whistle twice repeated rang out.

"That means help," thought Frank, and he hesitated; but it was now or never, he felt, and opening the closet, he snatched the desired letter from the shelf, thrust it into his breast, and closed the closet once more.

The whistle was sounded again, and a fresh thought assailed the boy.

"They'll seize me, search me, and take the letter away. What shall I do?"

He ran to the window in time to see a strange man climb the rails, and drop into the garden, run toward the house, stoop down, and pick up something.

"The key that opens the front door," cried Frank in despair. "He must have thrown it out."

For a moment or two he stood helpless, unable to move; then, recalling the fact that the man would have to run round to the front door, he darted out of the room, bounded down the staircase, reached the hall door, and with hands trembling from the great excitement in which he was, he slipped the top and bottom bolts.

"Hah!" he ejaculated; "the key won't open them."

Then, darting to the top of the stairs leading down to the housekeeper's room, he ran almost into the old servant's arms.

"Oh, Master Frank, was that you whistling, sir?" she cried.

"No; that man upstairs."

"What man upstairs, my dear?"

"Hush! Don't stop me. Have you a fire there?"

"Yes, my dear; it is very chilly down in that stone-floored room, that I am obliged to have one lit."

"That's right. Go away; I want to be there alone. And listen, Berry; I have bolted the front door. If any one knocks, don't go."

" Oh, my dear, don't say people are coming to break it down again ! "

" Never you mind if they are. Get out of my way."

There was the rattling of a key faintly heard, and then *bang, bang, bang,* and the ringing of the bell.

" They've come," said Frank. " But never mind ; I'll let them in before they break it."

There was a faint squeal from the kitchen just then.

" Oh ! " cried the housekeeper wildly, " that girl will be going into fits again."

" Let her," said Frank. " Stop ! Is the area door fastened ? "

" Oh yes, my dear. I always keep that locked."

Frank stopped to hear no more, but ran into the housekeeper's room, whose window, well-barred, looked up a green slope toward the Park.

There was a folding screen standing near the fire, a luxury affected by the old housekeeper, who used it to ward off draughts, which came through the window sashes, and the boy opened this a little to make sure that he was not seen by any one who might come and stare in. Then, standing in its shelter, he tore the letter from his breast pocket, broke the seal, opened it with trembling fingers, and began to read, with eyes beginning to dilate and a choking sensation rising in his breast.

For it was true, then—the charge was correct. Andrew Forbes's words had not been an insult, the Prince had told the simple fact.

" Oh, the shame of it ! " panted the boy, as he read and re-read the words couched in the most affectionate strain, telling him not to think ill of the father who loved him dearly, and begged of him to remember that father's position, hopeless of being able to return from his exile, knowing that his life was forfeit, treated as if he were an enemy. So that in despair he had yielded to the pressure put upon him by old friends, and joined them in the bold attempt to place the crown upon the head of the rightful heir.

"Whatever happens, my boy, I leave your mother to you as your care."

Frank's hands were cold and his forehead wet as he read these last words, and the affectionate, loving way in which his father concluded his letter, the last information being that he was in England, and had gone north to join friends who would shortly be marching on London.

"Burn this, the last letter I shall be able to leave for you, unless we triumph. Then we shall meet again."

"'Burn this,'" said Frank, in a strange, husky whisper. "Yes, I meant to burn this;" and in a curious, unemotional way, looking white and wan the while, he dropped the letter in the fire, and stood watching it as it blazed up till the flame drew near the great red wax seal bearing his father's crest. This melted till the crest was blurred out, the wax ran and blazed, and in a few moments there was only a black, crumpled patch of tinder, over and about which a host of tiny sparks seemed to be chasing each other till all was soft and grey.

"I needn't have burned it," said the boy, in a low, pained voice. "What does it matter now?"

He stood looking old and strange as he spoke. It did not seem a boy's face turned to the fire, but that of an effeminate young man in some great suffering, as he said again, in a voice which startled him and made him shiver:

"What does it matter now?"

He turned his head and listened then, before stooping to take up the poker and scatter the grey patch of ashes that still showed letters and words; for he appeared to have suddenly awakened to the fact that the thundering of the knocker was still going on and the bell pealing.

"Hah!" he sighed; "I must go back and tell her I was wrong. Poor mother, what she must feel!"

He moved slowly toward the door of the room, and

then encountered the housekeeper standing at the foot of the stairs.

"Oh, my dear, my dear!" she moaned; "what shall we do? I heard them send for hammers to break in again."

"They will not, Berry," he said quietly. "I will go up and let them in."

"Oh, my dear!" cried the woman, forgetting the noise at the front door. "Don't speak like that. What is the matter? You're white as ashes."

"Matter?" he said, looking at the old woman wistfully. "Matter—ashes—yes, ashes. I can't tell you, Berry. I'm ill. I feel as if—as if——"

He did not finish the sentence aloud, but to himself, and he said:

"As if my father I loved so were dead."

He walked quietly upstairs now into the hall, where there was the buzzing of voices coming in from the street, where people were collecting, and he distinctly heard some one say:

"Here they come."

It did not seem to him to matter who was coming; and he walked quietly to the door, shot back the bolts, and threw it open, for half a dozen men to make a dash forward to enter; but the boy stood firmly in the opening, with his face flushing once more, and looking more like his old self.

"Well," he cried haughtily. "What is it?"

"Mr. Bagot—Mr. Bagot! Where is he?"

"Bagot? Do you mean the spy who insulted me?"

At the word "spy" there was an angry groan from the gathering crowd, and the men began to press forward.

"The fellow insulted me," said Frank loudly, "and I locked him in one of the upstairs rooms."

"Hooray!" came from the crowd. "Well done, youngster!" And then there was a menacing hooting.

"Go and fetch him down," continued Frank.

"Yah! Spies!" came from the mob, and the men on

the step gladly obeyed the order to go upstairs, and rushed
into the house.

"Shall we fetch 'em out, sir," cried a big, burly-looking
fellow, "and take and pitch 'em in the river?"

"No; leave the miserable wretches alone," said the boy
haughtily. "Don't touch them, if they go quietly away."

"Hooray!" shouted the crowd; and then all waited till
Bagot came hurriedly down, white with anger, followed
by his men, and seized Frank by the shoulder.

"You're my prisoner, sir."

"Stand off!" cried the lad fiercely; and he wrenched
himself free, just as the mob, headed by the burly man,
dashed forward.

"You put a finger on him again, and we'll hang the lot
of you to the nearest lamps!" roared the man fiercely;
and the party crowded together, while Frank seized the
opportunity to close the door.

"Look here, fellow," he said haughtily. "I am going
back to the Palace. You can follow, and ask if you are to
arrest me there." Then turning to the crowd:

"Thank you, all of you; but they will not dare to
touch me, and if you wish me well don't hurt these men."

"Ur-r-r!" growled the crowd.

"Look here, you," cried Frank, turning to the leader of
the little riot. "I ask you to see that no harm is done
to them."

"Then they had better run for it, squire," cried the man.
"If they're here in a minute, I won't answer for what
happens."

"Then let your lads see me safely back to my quarters,"
said the boy, as a happy thought; and starting off, the
crowd followed him cheering to the Palace gates, where
they were stopped by the sentries; and they cheered him
loudly once more as he walked slowly by the soldiery.

"Arrested again!" said Frank softly. "Well, if I can
only go and see her first, it does not matter now."

"YES," said Lady Gowan sadly, after her meeting with her son, " it is terrible; but after all my teaching, telling you of your duty to be loyal to those whom we serve and who have been such friends to us, I could not nerve myself to tell you the dreadful truth. You are right, my boy. More than ever now we are out of place here; we must go."

" Yes, mother," said the boy gravely, " we must go."

" Let me read the letter, Frank."

" Read it, mother? I have repeated every word. It wanted no learning. I knew it when I had read it once."

" Yes; but I must read your father's letter to you myself."

" How could I keep it ? " he said, almost fiercely. " I expected to be arrested and searched. It is burned."

Lady Gowan uttered a weary sigh, and clung to her boy's hand.

" Going, dear ? " she said; " so soon ? "

" Yes, mother; I have so much to do. I can't stay now. Perhaps I shall be a prisoner again after this business, and coming back here protected by a riotous crowd."

" No, no, dear; the Prince, however stern his father may be, is just, and he will not punish you."

" I don't know," said the boy drearily. " I want to do something before I am stopped; " and he hurried away,

looking older and more careworn than ever, to go at once
to the officers' quarters, intending to see Captain Murray ;
but the first person he met was the doctor, who caught
him by the arm, and almost dragged him into his room.

"Sit down there," he cried sharply, as he scanned the
boy with his searching gaze.

"Don't stop me, sir, please," said Frank appealingly.
"I am very busy. Do you want me ?"

"No ; but you look as if you want me."

"No, sir—no."

"But I say you do. Don't contradict me. Think I
don't know what I'm saying ? You do want me. A boy
of your years has no business to look like that. What
have you been doing ? Why, your pulse is galloping
nineteen to the dozen, and your head's as hot as fire.
You've been eating too much, you voracious young wolf.
It's liver and bile. All right, my fine fellow ! Pill
hydrarg., to-night, and to-morrow morning a delicious
goblet before breakfast—sulph. mag., tinct. sennæ, ditto
calumba. That will set you right."

Frank looked at him for a moment piteously, and then
burst into a strange laugh.

"Eh, hallo !" cried the doctor ; "don't laugh in that
maniacal way, boy. Have I got hold of the pig by the
wrong tail ? Bah ! I mean the wrong tail by the pig.
Nonsense ! nonsense ! I mean the wrong pig by—— Oh,
I see now. Why, Frank, my boy, of course. Ah, poor
lad ! poor lad ! Murray has been telling me. Well, it's
a bad job, and I shouldn't have thought it of Rob Gowan.
But there, I don't know : *humanum est errare*. Not so
much erroring in it either. Circumstances alter cases, and
I dare say that if I were kicked out of the army, and I
had a chance to be made chief surgeon to the forces of
you know whom, I should accept the post."

The boy's head sank down upon his hands, and he did
not seem to hear the doctor's words.

"Poor lad!" he continued; "it's a very sad affair, and I'm very sorry for you. I always liked your father, and I never disliked you, which is saying a deal, for I hate boys as a rule. Confounded young monkeys, and no good whatever, except to get into mischief. There, I see now —ought to have seen it with half an eye. There, there, there, my lad; don't take on about it. Cheer up! You're amongst friends who like you, and the sun will come out again, even if it does get behind the black clouds sometimes."

He patted the boy's shoulder, and stroked his back, meaning, old bachelor as he was, to be very tender and fatherly; but it was clumsily done, for the doctor had never served his time to playing at being father, and begun by practising on babies. Hence he only irritated the boy.

"He talks to me and pats me as if I were a dog," said Frank to himself; and he would have manifested his annoyance in some way to one who was doing his best, when fortunately there was a sharp rap at the door, and a familiar voice cried:

"May I come in, doctor?"

"No, sir, no. I'm particularly engaged. Oh, it's you, Murray!—Mind his coming in, Gowan?"

"Oh no; I want to see him!" cried the boy, springing up.

"Come in!" shouted the doctor.

"You here, Frank?" said the captain, holding out his hands, in which the boy sadly placed his own, but withdrew them quickly.

"Yes, of course he is," said the doctor testily. "Came to see his friends. In trouble, and wants comforting."

"Yes," said Captain Murray quietly, as he laid his hand upon the boy's shoulder. "Then you know the truth now, Frank?"

"Yes, sir," said the boy humbly. "I was coming to

apologise to you, when the doctor met me and drew me in here."

"Yes; looked so ill. Thought I'd got a job to tinker him up; but he only wants a bit of comforting, to show him he's amongst friends."

"You were coming to do what, boy?" said the captain, as soon as he could get in a word,—"apologise?"

"Yes, sir; I was very obstinate and rude to you."

"Yes, thank goodness, my lad!" cried the captain, holding the boy by both shoulders now, as he hung his head. "Look up. Apologise! Why, Frank, you made me feel very proud of my old friend's son. I always liked you, boy; but never half so well as when you spoke out as you did to the Prince. So you know all now?"

"Yes," said the boy·bitterly.

"How?"

"My father has written to me telling me it is true."

"Hah! Well, it's a bad job, my lad; but we will not judge him. Robert Gowan must have suffered bitterly, and been in despair of ever coming back, before he changed his colours. But we can't see why, and how things are. I want no apology, Frank, only for you to come to me as your father's old friend."

Frank looked at him wonderingly.

"Come with me, boy."

Frank looked at him still, but his eyes were wistful now and full of question.

"I want you to come with me to the Prince."

"Yes, sir," said Frank gravely. "I want to beg for an audience before I go."

"Before you go, Frank?"

"Yes, sir. Of course we cannot stay here now."

"Humph! Ah, yes, I see what you mean," said the captain quietly. "Well, come. You are half a soldier, Frank, and the Prince is a soldier. I want you to come

and speak out to him, and apologise as you did to me—
like a man."

"Yes, sir," replied Frank, "that is what I wished
to do."

"Then forward!" cried the captain. "Let's make our
charge, even if we are repulsed."

"Good-bye, and thank you, doctor," said Frank. .

"What for? Pooh! nonsense, my lad; that's all right.
And, I say, people generally come and see me when they
want something, physic or plasters, or to have bullet
holes stopped up, or arms and legs sewn on again.   Don't
you wait for anything of that sort, boy; you come sometimes for a friendly bit of chat."

Frank smiled gratefully, but shook his head as he
followed Captain Murray out into the stable-yard.

"Come along, Frank; there's nothing like making a
bold advance, and getting a trouble over.   We may not be
able to get an audience with so many officers coming and
going; but I'll send in my name."

Frank followed him into the anteroom, the place looking
strange to him, and seeming as if it were a year since he
had been there last, a fancy assisted by the fact that some
five-and-twenty officers, whose faces were strange, stood
waiting their turns when Captain Murray sent in his
name by a gentleman in attendance.

But, bad as the prospect looked, they did not have long
to wait, for, at the end of about a quarter of an hour, the
attendant came out, passing over all those who looked up
eagerly ready to answer to their names, and walked to
where Captain Murray was seated talking in a low voice
to Frank.

"His Royal Highness will see you at once, gentlemen."

Frank did not feel in the slightest degree nervous as he
entered, but followed the captain with his head erect,
ready to speak out and say that for which he had come,

when the Prince condescended to hear; but he took no
notice of the boy at first, raising his head at last from his
writing, and saying:

"Well, Captain Murray, what news?"

"None, your Royal Highness," said the soldier bluffly.
"I have only come to bring Frank Gowan, your page,
before you."

"Eh? Oh yes. The boy who was so impudent, and
told me I was no speaker of the truth."

"I beg your Royal Highness's pardon."

"And you ought, boy. What more have you to
say?"

"That I was wrong, sir. I believed it could not
be true. I have found out since that it was as you
said."

"Hah! You ought always to believe what a royal
personage says—eh, Murray?"

The captain bowed, and smiled grimly.

"Don't agree with me," said the Prince sharply.
"Well, boy, you are very sorry, eh?"

"Yes, your Royal Highness, I am very sorry," said
Frank firmly. "I know better now, and I apologise to
you."

The Prince, moving himself round in his chair, frowning
to hide a feeling of amusement, stared hard at the lad as
if to look him down, and frowned in all seriousness as he
found the boy looked him full in the eyes without a quiver
of the lid.

"Humph! So you, my page, consider it your duty
to come and apologise to me for doubting my
word?"

"Yes, your Highness, and to ask your forgiveness."

"And suppose I refuse to give it to so bold and
impudent a boy, what then?" and he gazed hard once
more in the lad's flushing face.

"I should be very, very sorry, sir; for you and the

Princess have been very good and kind to my poor mother and me."

"Yes, yes," said the Prince, "too kind, perhaps, to have such a return as——"

He stopped short as he saw a spasm contract the boy's features.

"But there," he continued, "you are not to blame, and I do forgive you, boy. I liked the bold, brave way in which you showed your belief in your father."

Captain Murray darted a quick glance at his young companion, as much as to say, "I told you so."

"Go on, my boy, as you have begun, and you will make a firm, strong, trustworthy man; and, goodness knows, we want them badly enough. There, I will not say any more —yes, I will one word, my boy. I am sorry that your father was not recalled some time back. He was a brave soldier, for whom I felt respect."

Frank could bear no more, and he bent his head to conceal the workings of his face.

"There, take him away, Murray, and keep him under your eye. There's good stuff in the boy, and we must get him a commission as soon as he is old enough."

"No, your Highness," said Frank, recovering himself.

"Eh? What?"

"I came to beg your Royal Highness's pardon, and to ask your permission for my mother and me to leave the royal service at once. We both feel that it is not the place for us now."

"Humph!" ejaculated the Prince, frowning; "and I think differently. Take him away, Murray; the boy is hurt—wounded now.—That will do, Gowan; go. No: I refuse absolutely. The Princess does not wish Lady Gowan to leave; and *I* want *you*."

"There!" cried Captain Murray, as they crossed the courtyard on their way back to the officers' quarters; "it is what I expected of the Prince. You can't leave us unless you run away, Frank ; and you've proved yourself too much of a gentleman for that. You see, everybody wants you here."

Frank could not trust himself to speak, for he was, in spite of his troubles, some years short of manhood and manhood's strength.

CHAPTER XXXVI.

THE WORST NEWS.

NEXT morning Frank rose in his old quarters, firmly determined to keep to his decision. It was very kind and generous of the Prince, he felt; but his position would be intolerable, and his mother would not be able to bear an existence fraught with so much misery; and, full of the intention to see her and beg her to prevail on the Princess to let them leave, he waited his time.

But it did not come that day. He had to return to his duties in the Prince's anteroom, and at such times as he was free he found that his mother was engaged with her royal mistress.

The next day found him more determined than ever; but another, a greater, and more unexpected obstacle was in the way. He went to his mother's apartments, to find that, worn out with sorrow and anxiety, she had taken to her bed, and the Princess's physician had seen her and ordered complete rest, and that she should be kept free from every anxiety.

"How can I go now!" thought the boy; "and how can she be kept free from anxiety!"

It was impossible in both cases, while with the latter every scrap of news would certainly be brought to her, for the Palace hummed with the excitement of the troubles in the north; and as the day glided by there came the news that the Earl of Mar had set up the standard of the Stuarts in Scotland, and proclaimed Prince James King of Great

Britain; but the Pretender himself remained in France, waiting for the promised assistance of the French Government, which was slow in coming.

Still the Scottish nobles worked hard in the Prince's cause, and by degrees the Earl of Mar collected an army of ten thousand fighting men, including the staunch Highlanders, who readily assumed claymore and target at the gathering of the clans.

It was over the English rising that Frank was the more deeply interested, and he eagerly hungered for every scrap of news which was brought to the Palace, Captain Murray hearing nearly everything, and readily responding to the boy's questions, though he always shook his head and protested that it would do harm and unsettle him.

"You'd better shut up your ears, Frank lad, and go on with your duties," he said one day. "But tell me first, what is the last news about Lady Gowan?"

"Ill, very ill," said the boy wearily. "All this is killing her."

"Then the bad news ought to be kept from her."

"Bad news!" gasped Frank. "Is it then so bad?"

"Of course; isn't it all bad?"

"Oh!" ejaculated the boy; "I thought there was something fresh—something terrible. But how can the news be kept from her? The Princess goes and sits with her every day, and then tells her everything. She learns more than I do, and gets it sooner; but I can't go and ask her, for I always feel as if it were cruel and torturing her to make her speak about our great trouble while she is so ill. Now, tell me all you know."

"It is not much, boy. The Duke of Argyle is busy; he is now appointed to the command of the King's forces in Scotland, and some troops are being landed from Ireland to join his clans."

"Yes, yes; but in England?" cried the boy. "My

father is not in Scotland. It is about what is going on in England that I want to know."

It was always the same, and by degrees, as the days went by, Frank learned that his father had, with other gentlemen, joined the Earl of Derwentwater, and that they were threatening Newcastle.

It seemed an age before the next tidings came, and Frank's heart sank, while those in the Palace were holding high festival, for the Pretender's little army there had been beaten off, and was in retreat through Cumberland on the way to Lancashire.

A little later came news that in the boy's secret heart made him rejoice and brought gloom into the Palace. For it soon leaked out that the county militias had been assembled hastily to check the Pretender's forces, but only to be put to flight and scattered in all directions.

Then despatch after despatch reached the Palace from the north, all containing bad news. The rebels had marched on, carrying everything before them till they neared Preston in triumph.

"Then they'll go on increasing in strength," whispered Frank, as he sat with Captain Murray on the evening of the receipt of that news, "and march right on to London!"

"Want them to?" said the captain drily.

"Yes—no—no—yes—I don't know."

"Nice loyal sort of a servant the Prince has got," said the captain.

"Don't talk to me like that, Captain Murray," said the boy passionately. "I feel that I hate for the rebels to succeed; but how can I help wishing my father success?"

"No, you cannot," said the captain quietly. "But he will not succeed, my lad. He and the others are in command of a mere rabble of undisciplined men, and before long on their march they will be met by some of the King's forces sent to intercept them."

" Yes, yes," cried the boy, with his cheeks flushing, " and then ? "

" What is likely to happen in spite of the training of the leaders ? The undrilled men cannot stand against regular troops, even if they are enthusiastic. No : disaster must come sooner or later, and then there is only one chance for us, Frank."

"For us ? I thought you said that the King's troops would win."

" Yes, and they will. I as a soldier feel that it must be so. We shall win ; but I say there is only one chance for us as friends—a quick escape for your father to the coast and taking refuge in France. We must not have him taken, Frank, come what may."

" Thank you, Captain Murray," said the boy, laying his hand on his friend's sleeve. " You have made me happier than I have felt for days."

" And it sounds very disloyal, my boy ; but I can't help my heart turning to my old friend to wish him safe out of the rout."

" Then you think it will be a rout ? " panted Frank.

" It must be sooner or later. They may gain a few little advantages by surprise, or the cowardice of the troops ; but those successes can't last, and when the defeat comes it will be the greater, and mean a complete end to a mad scheme."

" But the Prince must be with them by this time, sir."

" The Pretender ? No ; he is still in France without coming forward, and leaving the misguided men who would place him on the throne to be slaughtered for aught he seems to care."

Captain Murray proved to be a true prophet, for he had spoken on the basis of his experience of what properly trained men could do against troops hastily collected, and badly armed men whose discipline was of the rudest description.

Sooner even than the captain had anticipated the news came in a despatch brought from the north of England. The Pretender's forces, under Lords Derwentwater, Kenmuir, and Nithsdale, were encountered by the King's troops ; and before the two bodies joined battle a summons was sent to the rebel army calling upon the men to lay down their arms or be attacked without mercy.

The Pretender's generals tried to treat the summons to surrender with contempt, laughed at it, and bade their followers to stand fast and the victory would be theirs. But, in spite of the exhortations of their officers, the sight of the King's regular troops drawn up in battle array proved too much for the raw forces. Probably they were wearied with marching and the many difficulties they had had to encounter. Their enthusiasm leaked out, life seemed far preferable to death, and they surrendered at discretion.

There was feasting and rejoicing at St. James's that night, when the news came of the bloodless victory ; while in one of the apartments mother and son were shut up alone in the agony of their misery and despair, for whatever might be the fate of the common people of the Pretender's army, the action of the King toward all who opposed him was known to be of merciless severity. The leaders of the rebellion could expect but one fate—death by the executioner.

"But, mother, mother ! oh, don't give way to despair like that," cried Frank. "We have heard so little yet. Father would fight to the last before he would fly ; but when all was over he would be too clever for the enemy, and escape in safety to the coast."

"No," said Lady Gowan, in tones which startled her son. "Your father, Frank, would never desert the men he had led. It would be to victory or death. It was not to victory they marched that day."

"But his name is not mentioned in the despatch."

"No," said Lady Gowan sadly. "Nor is that of Colonel Forbes."

"Ah!" cried Frank; "and poor Drew, he would be there."

At last he was compelled to quit the poor, suffering woman; but before going to his own chamber, he went over to the officers' quarters, to try and see Captain Murray.

There was a light in his room, and the sound of voices in earnest conversation; and Frank was turning back, to go and sit alone in his despair, when he recognised the doctor's tones, and he knocked and entered.

The eager conversation stopped on the instant, as the two occupants of the room saw the boy's anxious, white face looking inquiringly from one to the other.

"Come in and sit down," said Captain Murray, in a voice which told of his emotion; "sit down, my boy."

Frank obeyed in silence, trying hard to read the captain's thoughts.

"You have come from your mother?"

"Yes; she is very ill."

"She has heard of the disaster, then?"

"Yes. The Princess went and broke it to her as gently as she could."

"And she told you?"

"Yes; she sent for me as soon as she heard."

"Poor lady!" said the captain.

"Amen to that," said the doctor huskily; and he pulled out his snuff-box, and took three pinches in succession, making himself sneeze violently as an excuse for taking out his great red-and-yellow silk handkerchief and using it to a great extent.

"Hah!" he said at last, as he looked across at Frank, with his eyes quite wet; "and poor old Robert Gowan! Rebel, they call him; but we here, Frank, can only look upon him more as brother than friend."

"But," cried the boy passionately, "there is hope for him yet. He is not taken, in spite of what my mother said. He would have escaped to the coast, and made again for France."

"What did your mother say?" asked Captain Murray, looking at the boy fixedly.

"My mother say? That my father would never forsake the men whom he was leading to victory or death."

"Yes; she was right, Frank, my lad. He would never turn his back on his men to save himself."

"Of course not, till the day was hopelessly lost."

"Not when the day was hopelessly lost," said Captain Murray, so sternly that Frank took alarm.

"Why do you speak to me like that?" he cried, rising from his seat. "His name was not in the despatch. Ah! you have heard. There is something worse behind. Oh, Captain Murray, don't say that he was killed."

"I say," said that officer sadly, "it were better that he had been killed—that he had died leading his men, as a brave officer should die."

"Then he did not," cried Frank, with a hoarse sigh of relief.

"No, he escaped that."

"And to liberty?"

"No, my boy, no," said the doctor, uttering a groan.

"But I tell you that his name was not in the despatch. He couldn't have been taken prisoner."

There was silence in the room, and the candles for want of snuffing were very dim.

"Why don't you speak to me?" cried Frank passionately. "Am I such a boy that you treat me as a child?"

"My poor lad! You must know the truth," said Captain Murray gently. "Your father's and Colonel Forbes's names are both in the despatch as prisoners."

"No, no, no!" cried Frank wildly. "The Princess——"

" Kept the worst news back, to try and spare your poor mother pain. It is as I always feared."

" Then you are right," moaned Frank ; and he uttered a piteous cry. " Yes, it would have been better if he had died."

For the headsman's axe seemed to be glimmering in the black darkness ahead, and he shuddered as he recalled once more what he had seen on Temple Bar.

CHAPTER XXXVII.

UNDER THE DARK CLOUD.

THERE was no waiting for news now. Despatch succeeded despatch rapidly, and the occupants of the Palace were made familiar with the proceedings in the north; and as Frank heard more and more of the disastrous tidings he was in agony, and at last announced to Captain Murray that he could bear it all no longer.

"I must go and join my father," he said one day. "It is cruel and cowardly to stay here in the midst of all this luxury and rejoicing, while he is being dragged up to London like a criminal."

"Have you told Lady Gowan of your intentions?" said the captain quietly.

"Told her? No!" cried Frank excitedly. "Why, in her state it would half kill her."

"And if you break away from here and go to join your father, it would quite kill her."

Frank looked at him aghast, and the captain went on:

"We must practise common sense, Frank, and not act madly at a time like this."

"Is it to act madly to go and help one's father in his great trouble?"

"No; you must help him, but in the best way."

"That is the best way," said the boy hotly.

"No. What would you do?"

"Go straight to him and try and make his lot more bearable. Think how glad he would be to see me."

"Of course he would, and then he would blame you for leaving your mother's side when she is sick and suffering."

"But this is such a terrible time of need. I must go to him ; but I wanted to be straightforward and tell you first."

"Good lad."

"Think what a terrible position mine is, Captain Murray."

"I do, boy, constantly ; but I must, as your friend and your father's, look at the position sensibly."

"Oh, you are so cold and calculating, when my father's life is at stake."

"Yes. I don't want you to do anything that would injure him."

"I—injure him !"

"Yes, boy."

"But I only want to be by his side."

"Well, to do that you would run away from here, for the Prince would not let you go."

"No, he will not. I asked him."

"You did ?"

"Yes, two days ago."

"Then if you go without leave, you will make a good friend angry."

"Perhaps so ; but I cannot stay away."

"You must, boy, for it would be injuring your father ; and, look here, if you went, you could not get near the prisoners. Those who have them in charge would not let you pass."

"But I would get a permission from the King."

"Rubbish, boy ! He would not listen to you. He might as a man be ready to pardon your father ; but as King he would feel that he could not. No ; I must speak plainly to you : his Majesty will deal sternly with the prisoners, to make an example for his enemies, and show them the folly of attempting to shake his position on the throne."

"Oh, Captain Murray! Captain Murray!" cried the boy.

"Look here, Frank lad. Your journey to meet the prisoners would be an utter waste of energy, and you would most likely miss them, for to avoid the possibility of attempts at rescue their escort would probably take all kinds of byways and be constantly changing their route."

"But I should have tried to help my father, even if I failed."

"Don't run the risk of failure, boy," said the captain earnestly. "Our only hopes lie in the Prince and Princess. The Prince would, I feel sure, spare your father's life if he could, for the sake of his wife's friend. But he is not king, only a subject like ourselves, and he will be governed by his father and his father's Ministers. Now you see that you must not alienate our only hope by doing rash things."

Frank looked at him in despair.

"Now do you see why I oppose you?"

"Yes, yes," said the boy despondently. "Oh, how I wish I were wise!"

"There is only one way to grow wise, Frank: learn— think and calculate before you make a step. Now, look here, my boy. The Prince has plenty of good points in his character. He likes you; and he shall be appealed to through your mother and the Princess. Now, promise me that you will do nothing rashly, and that you will give up this project."

"Should I be right in giving it up?"

"Yes," said the captain emphatically.

"But what will my father think? I shall seem to be forsaking him in his great trouble."

"He will think you are doing your duty, and are trying hard to save his life. Come, don't be down-hearted, for we are all at work. There is our regiment to count upon yet—the King's own Guards, who will, to a man, join in a prayer to his Majesty to spare the life of the most popular officer in the corps."

"Ah! yes," cried Frank.

"I don't want even to hint at mutiny; but the King at a time like this would think twice before refusing the prayer of the best regiment in his service."

"Oh, Captain Murray!" cried the lad excitedly. "I will promise everything. I will go by your advice."

"That's right, my lad; my head is a little older than yours, you know. Now, go back to your duties, and let the Prince see that his page is waiting hopefully and patiently to see how he will help him. Go to your mother, too, all you can, and tell her, to cheer her up, that we are all hard at work, and that no stone shall be left unturned to save Sir Robert's life."

Frank caught the captain's hands in his, and stood holding them for a few moments before hurrying out of the room.

Then more news came of each day's march, and of the slow approach of the prisoners—the leaders only, the rest being imprisoned in Cheshire and Lancashire to await their fate.

It was hard work, but Frank kept his word, trying to be more energetic than ever over his duties, and finding that he was not passing unnoticed, for every morning the Prince gave him a quiet look of recognition, or a friendly nod, but never once spoke.

The most painful part of his life in those days was in his visits to his mother. These were agony to him, feeling as he did more and more how utterly insignificant and helpless he was; but he had one satisfaction to keep him going and make him look forward longingly for the next meeting—paradoxical as it may sound—so as to suffer more agony and despair, for he could plainly see that his mother clung to him now as her only stay, and that she was happiest when he was with her, and begged and prayed of him to come back to her as soon as he possibly could, now that she was so weak and ill.

"I believe, my darling," she whispered one evening, "that I should have died if you had not been here."

"Yes, my lad," said the Princess's physician to him as well; "you must be with Lady Gowan as much as you can. Her illness is mental, and you can do more for her now than I can. Ha—ha! I shall have to resign my post to you."

"Yes," said the boy to himself, "Captain Murray is quite right;" and he went straight to his friend's quarters, as he often did, to give him an account of his mother's state.

"Yes, sir," he said; "you were quite right: it would have killed her if I had gone away."

"Come, you are beginning to believe in me, Frank. Now I have some news for you."

"About Drew Forbes?" cried Frank eagerly.

"No; I have made all the inquiries I can, but I can hear nothing of the poor fellow. His father is with yours; but the lad seems to have dropped out of sight, and I have my fears."

"Oh, don't say that," cried Frank excitedly; "he was so young."

"Yes," said the captain grimly; "but in a fight young and old run equal chances, while in the exposure and suffering of forced marches the young and untried fare worse than the old and seasoned. Drew Forbes was a weak, girlish fellow, all brain and no muscle. I am in hopes, though, that he may have broken down, and be lying sick at some cottage or farmhouse."

"Hopes!" cried Frank.

"Yes, he may get well with rest. Better than being well and strong, and on his way to suffer by the rope or axe."

Frank shuddered.

" Now then," cried the captain sharply, to change the conversation ; " you found my advice good ? "

" Yes, yes," said Frank.

" Then take some more.   Look here, Frank ; the doctor and I were talking about you last night, and he is growing very anxious.   He said the blade was wearing out the scabbard, and that you were making an old man of yourself."

" Not a young one yet," said the boy, smiling sadly.

" Never mind that.   You'll grow old soon enough.   He says what I think, that you never go out, and that you will break down."

" Oh, absurd !   I don't want exercise."

For answer the captain clapped him on the shoulder, and twisted him round.

" Look at your white face in the glass, my boy.   Don't risk illness.   You will want all your strength directly in the fight for life to come.   Your father will, in all probability, reach London to-morrow."

" Ah !" cried Frank excitedly.

" Yes ; we had news this morning by the messenger who brought the royal despatches.   The colonel had a brief letter.   Get leave to go out to-morrow, and come with me."

" Yes, where ? "

" We'll try and meet the escort, and see your father, even if we cannot speak."

" Oh !" ejaculated Frank ; and, utterly worn out with anxiety and want of proper food, he reeled, a deathly feeling of sickness seized him, and his eyes closed.

When he opened them again he was lying upon the captain's couch, with his temples and hair wet, and he looked wonderingly in the face of his father's friend.

" Better ? "

" Yes; what is it ? Oh my head! the room's going round."

" Drink," said the captain. " That's better. It will soon go off."

" But why did I turn like that ? "

" From weakness, lad. Shall I send for the doctor ? "

" No, no," cried Frank, struggling up into a sitting position. " I'm better now. How stupid of me ! "

" Nature telling you she has been neglected, my lad. You have not eaten much lately ? "

" I couldn't."

" Nor slept well ? "

" Horribly. I could only lie and think."

" And you have not been outside the walls ? "

" No ; I have felt ashamed to be seen, and as if people would look at me and say, ' His father is one of the prisoners.' "

" All signs of weakness, as the doctor would say. Now you want to be strong enough to go with me to-morrow—mounted ? "

" Of course."

" Then try and do something to make yourself fit. I shouldn't perhaps be able to catch you as I did just now if you fainted on horseback, and in a London crowd ; for we should be under the wing of the troops sent to meet the prisoners coming in."

" I shall be all right, sir," said the boy firmly.

" Go and have a walk in the fresh air, then, now."

" Must I ? " said Frank dismally.

" If you wish to go with me."

" Where shall I go, then ? "

" Anywhere ; go and have a turn in the Park."

" What, go and walk up and down there, where people may know me ! "

"Yes, let them. Don't take any notice. Try and amuse yourself. Be a boy again, or a man if you like, and do as Charles II. used to do: go and feed the ducks. Well, what's the matter? there's no harm in feeding ducks, is there?"

"Oh no," said the boy confusedly; "I'll go;" and he hurried out.

CHAPTER XXXVIII.

FEEDING THE DUCKS AGAIN.

"GO and feed the ducks," said Frank to himself, as he obtained some biscuits, and, in his readiness to obey his elder's wishes, went slowly toward the water-side; "how little he knows what a deal that means;" and, almost unconsciously, he strolled on down to the side of the canal, thinking of Mr. George Selby and Drew, and of the various incidents connected with his walks out there, which, with the duel, seemed in his disturbed state of mind to have taken place years—instead of months—ago, when he was a boy.

He went slowly on, forgetting all about the biscuits, till he noticed that several of the water-fowl were swimming along, a few feet from the bank, and watching him with inquiring eyes.

He stopped short, turned to face the water, which was sparkling brightly in the sunshine, and taking a biscuit out of his capacious "saltbox pocket," he began to break it in little bits and throw them to the birds.

"Ah, what a deal has happened since we were here doing this that day," thought the boy; and his mind went back to his first meeting with Drew's father, the invitation to the dinner, and the scene that evening in the tavern.

"Please give me a bit, good gentleman," said a whining voice at his elbow. "I'm so hungry, please, sir. Arn't had nothing since yes'day morning, sir."

Frank turned sharply, to see that a ragged-looking

street boy, whom he had passed lying apparently asleep on the grass a few minutes before, was standing close by, hugging himself with his arms, and holding his rags as if to keep them from slipping off his shoulders. He wore a dismally battered cocked hat which was a size too large for him, and came down to his ears over his closely cropped hair. His shirt was dirty and ragged, and his breeches and shoes were of the most dilapidated character, the latter showing, through the gaping orifices in front, his dirty, mud-encrusted toes.

Frank saw all this at a glance; but the poor fellow's face took his attention most, for it was pitiable, thin, and care-worn, and would have been white but for the dirt with which it was smudged.

Frank looked at him with sovereign contempt.

"So hungry that you can't stoop down by the water's edge to wash your filthy face and hands, eh?"

"Wash, sir?" said the lad piteously; "what's the good? Don't matter for such as me. You don't know."

"Miserable wretch!" thought Frank; "what a horribly degraded state for a poor fellow to be in." Then aloud: "Here, which will you have—the biscuit or this?"

He held out a coin that would have bought many biscuits in one hand, the broken piece in the other.

"Biscuit, please, gentleman," whined the lad. "I am so hungry, you don't know."

"Take both," said Frank; and they were snatched from his hands.

"Oh, thank you, gentleman," whined the lad, as some one passed. "You don't know what trouble is;" and he began to devour the biscuit ravenously.

"Not know what trouble is!" cried Frank scornfully. "Do you think fine clothes will keep that out? Oh, I don't know that I wouldn't change places with you, after all."

"Poor old laddie!" said the youth, looking at him in a peculiar way, and with his voice seeming changed by the biscuit in his mouth; "and I thought he was enjoying himself, and feeding the ducks, and not caring a bit."

"What!" exclaimed Frank wildly.

"Don't you know me, Frank ?"

"Drew !"

"Then the disguise is as right as can be. Keep still. Nonsense! Don't try to shake hands. Stand at a distance. There's no knowing who may be watching you. Give me another biscuit. I am hungry, really. There, go on feeding the ducks. How useful they are. Sort of co-conspirators, innocent as they look. I'll sit down behind you as if watching you, and I can talk when there's no one near."

Frank obeyed with his face working, and Drew Forbes threw himself on the grass once more.

"Drew, old fellow, you make me feel sick."

"What, because I look such a dirty wretch ?"

"No, no. I'm ill and faint, and it's horrible to see you like this."

"Yes ; not much of a maccaroni now."

"We—we were afraid you were dead."

"No ; but I had a narrow squeak for my life. I and two more officers escaped and rode for London. I only got here yesterday, dressed like this, hoping to see you ; but you did not come out."

"No ; this is the first time I have been here since you left. How is the wound ?"

"Oh, pooh! that's well enough. Bit stiff, that's all. I say, is it all real ?"

"What ?"

"Me being here dressed like this."

"Oh, it's horrible."

"Not it. Better than being chopped short, or hung. I am glad you've come. I want to talk to you about your father and mine. They'll be in town to-morrow, I should say."

"Yes, I know. Tell me, what are you going to do?"

"Do? We're going to raise the mob, have a big riot, and rescue them. I want to know what you can do to help."

"We are trying to help in another way," said Frank excitedly.

"How?"

"Petitioning the King through the Prince."

"No good," said Drew shortly. "There's no mercy to be had. Our way is the best."

"But tell me: you are in a terrible state—you want money."

"No. We've plenty, and plenty of friends in town here. Don't think we're beaten, my good fellow."

Frank's supply of biscuit came to an end, and to keep up appearances he began to delude the ducks by throwing in pebbles.

"There's one of those spy fellows coming, Frank," said Drew suddenly. "Don't look round, or take any notice."

Frank's heart began to beat, as he thrust his hand into his pocket, for his fingers to come in contact with one little fragment of biscuit passed over before, and, waiting till he heard steps close behind him, he threw the piece out some distance, and stood watching the rush made by the water-fowl, one conveying the bit off in triumph.

Frank searched in vain for more, and he was regretting that he had been so liberal in his use of the provender, and racking his brains for a means of keeping up the conversation without risk to his companion, when about half a biscuit fell at his feet, and he seized it eagerly.

"He's pretty well out of hearing, Frank; but speak low. I don't want to be taken. You'd better move on a bit, and stop again. I'll go off the other way after that spy, and work round and come back. You go and sit down a little way from the bushes yonder, and I'll creep in behind, and lie there, so as to talk to you. Got a book ? "

" No," said Frank sadly.

" Haven't you a pocket-book ? "

" Oh yes."

" Well, that will do. Take it out after you've sat down, and pretend to make a sketch of the trees across the water."

" Ah, I shouldn't have thought of that."

" You would if you had been hunted as I have. There, don't look round. I'm off."

" But if we don't meet again, Drew ? I want to do something to help you."

" Then do as I have told you," said the lad sharply ; and he shuffled away, limping slightly, while, after standing as if watching the water-fowl for about ten minutes, and wondering the while whether he was being watched, Frank strolled on very slowly in the opposite direction, making for a clump of trees and bushes about a couple of hundred yards away, feeling that this must be right, and upon reaching the end, going on about half its length, and then carelessly seating himself on the grass about ten feet from the nearest bush.

After a short time, passed in wondering whether Drew would be able to get hidden behind him unseen, he took out his pocket-book and pencil, and with trembling fingers began to sketch. Fortunately he had taken lessons at the big Hampshire school, and often received help from his mother, who was clever with her pencil, so that to give colour to his position there he went on drawing, a tiny reproduction of the landscape across the water slowly growing up beneath his pencil-point. But it was done almost unconsciously, for he was trembling with dread lest his object there should be divined and result in Andrew being captured, now that a stricter watch than ever was kept about the surroundings of the Palace.

One moment he felt strong in the belief that no one could penetrate his old companion's disguise; the next he was shuddering in dread of what the consequences would be, and wishing that Drew had not come. At the same time he was touched to the heart at the lad running such a risk when he had escaped to safety among his London friends. For Drew had evidently assumed this pitiful disguise on purpose to come and see him. There could be no other object than that of trying to see his friend. Would he be able to speak to him again?

"I say, they're keeping a sharp look-out, Franky," came from behind in a sharp whisper, making him start violently.

"Don't do that. Go on sketching," whispered Drew; and Frank devoted himself at once to his book. "That fellow went on, and began talking to another. I saw him, but I don't think he saw me. I say, I shall have to go soon."

"Yes, yes; I want you to stay, Drew, but pray, pray escape!"

"Why?"

"Because I wouldn't for worlds have you taken."

There was a few moments' pause, and then Drew spoke huskily.

"Thank ye," he said. "I was obliged to come and see you again. I wanted to tell you that I'm sorry I didn't shake hands with you, Frank."

"Ah!—I'll slip back to where you are and shake hands now," cried the boy excitedly.

"No, no; pray don't move. It's too risky; I don't want to be caught. I must be with those who are going to rescue my father and yours to-morrow.—Think that you are shaking hands with me. Now, there's my hand, old lad. That's right. Yes, I can believe we have hold again. Perhaps I shall never see you again, Franky; perhaps I shall be taken. If I am, please think that I

always looked upon you as a brother, and upon Lady
Gowan as if I were her son."

"Yes, Drew, yes, Drew," whispered Frank in a choking
voice, as he bent over his open book.

"Give my love to dear Lady Gowan, and tell her how
I feel for her in her great trouble."

"Yes, yes, I will," whispered Frank, as he shaded
away vigorously at his sketch, but making some curious
hatchings.

"Tell her that there'll be a hundred good, true men
making an effort to save Sir Robert to-morrow, and we'll
do it. I'd like you to come and help, but you mustn't.
It would be too mad."

"No. I'll come," whispered the boy excitedly.

"No, you will not come," said Drew. "You can't, for
you don't know when and where it will be."

"Then tell me," whispered Frank, with his face very
close to his paper.

"I'd die first, old lad," came back. "Lady Gowan has
suffered enough from what has happened. She shan't
have another trouble through me. I tried to get you
away; but I'm sorry now, for her sake. You stop and
take care of her. Your father said——"

"Yes, what did he say?"

"He told me it was his only comfort in his troubles to
feel that his son was at his mother's side."

"Ah!" sighed Frank; and then he uttered a warning
"Hist! Some one coming;" and he gazed across the
water and went on sketching, for he had suddenly become
aware of some one coming from his left over the grass,
and he trembled lest his words should have been heard,
for every one now seemed likely to be a spy.

It was hard work to keep from looking up, and to
appear engrossed with his task; but he mastered the
desire, even when he was conscious of the fresh-comer
being close at hand, his shadow cast over the paper, and

he knew that he was passing between him and the clump of shrubs.

Then whoever it was paused, and Frank felt that he was looking down at the drawing, while the boy's heart went on thumping heavily.

"He must have heard me speaking," he thought; and then he gave a violent start and looked up, for a voice said:

"Well done, young gentleman. Quite an artist, I see."

The speaker's face was strange, and he had keen, searching eyes, which seemed as if they were reading the boy's inmost thoughts as he faltered:

"Oh no, only a little bit of a sketch."

Then he started again, for there was the sound of a blow delivered by a stick, a sharp cry, a scuffle, and Drew bounded out from the bushes, followed by Frank's old enemy whom he had trapped at the house. But Drew would have escaped if it had not been for the stranger, who, acting in collusion with Bagot, caught the lad by the arm and held him.

Frank had sprung to his feet, to stand white and trembling, and drew sword ready to interfere on behalf of his old companion, who, however, began to act his part admirably.

"Don't you hit me," he whined; "don't you hit me."

"You young whelp!" cried Bagot. "What are you doing here?"

"I dunno," whined Drew. "Must go somewheres. Only came to lie down and have a snooze."

"A lie, sir, a lie. I've had my eye upon you for hours. I saw you here last night."

"That you didn't, sir. It was too cold, and I went away 'fore eight o'clock."

"Lucky for you that you did, or you'd have found yourself in the round house."

"Don't you hit me; don't you hit me," cried Drew, writhing.

"I'll cut you to pieces," snarled Bagot. "I watched him," he continued to the man who held the lad in a firm grip in spite of his struggles to get away. "He was sneaking up to this young gentleman, begging and trying to pick his pocket."

"That I wasn't," whined Drew. "I was orfle 'ungry, and he was pitching away cake things to the ducks. I only arksed for a bit because I was so 'ungry—didn't I, sir?"

"Yes," said Frank hoarsely. "I gave him a biscuit."

"Then what's this?" said the man who held him, wrenching open Drew's hand, in spite of a great show of resistance, and seizing a shilling. "You managed to rob him, then."

"No, no," said Frank. "I gave him the money."

That disarmed suspicion.

"But he'd sneaked round behind you. I watched him, and found him here where he had crawled, and lay pretending to be asleep. I wager you had not seen him."

"No," said Frank sharply. "I had not seen him since he came up to beg;" and the boy drew a breath of relief, for he had shivered with the dread that the man was going to ask him if he knew that Drew was there.

"Better take your shilling back, sir," said the man.

"I? No," said Frank proudly. "Let the poor, shivering wretch go. He wants it badly enough."

"Then thank your stars the young gentleman speaks for you," said Bagot sharply. "Off with you, and don't you show your face this way again."

"Don't you hit me then," whimpered Drew. "Don't you hit me;" and he limped off, repeating the words as he went, while Frank stood looking after him, feeling as if he could not stir a step.

"That was a clever trick of your, young gentleman," said Bagot, with a broad grin. "But I don't bear any malice. King's service, sir. You see, I can take care of you as well as watch."

"Yes. Thank you," said Frank coldly; and with a sigh of relief he tore the leaf bearing the sketch out of his pocket-book, and then turned cold, for he felt that he had made a false move. The other man was watching him.

"Spoiled my sketch," he said, with a half laugh. "Made me start so that my pencil went right across it."

Fortunately this was quite true, and it carried conviction.

"Don't tear it up, sir," said the second man respectfully. "I should like to take that home to please my little girl. She'd know the place. She often comes to feed the ducks."

The man was human, then, after all, even if he was a spy, and Frank's heart softened to him a little as he gave him the sketch.

"Thank ye, sir," said the man, who looked pleased; and the lad stopped and listened to him, feeling that it was giving Drew time to get away.

"I can tell her I saw a young gentleman drawing it. She's quite clever with her pencil, sir; but she can't, of course, touch this."

Frank hesitated for a few moments as to which way he should go, inclination drawing him after his friend; but wisdom suggested the other direction, and he strolled off without looking back till he could do so in safety, making the excuse of throwing in the remains of the biscuit Drew had returned to the ducks.

He had been longing intensely to look back before and see if the men were following his friend; but to his great relief he found that they were not very far from where he now stood.

Then he walked quietly back toward the Palace gates with his head beginning to buzz with excitement at the news he had heard.

"They're going to rescue him to-morrow," he thought.

"Ought I to tell Captain Murray? No; impossible. He might feel that it was his duty to warn the King. It would be giving him a task to fight against duty and friendship. I dare not even tell my mother, for fear the excitement might do her harm. No, I must keep it to myself, and I shall be there—I shall be there."

He did not see where he was going, for in his imagination he was on horseback, looking on at a mighty, seething crowd making a bold rush at the cavalry escort round some carriages. But he was brought to himself directly after by a bluff voice saying :

" Don't run over me, Frank, my lad. But that's right ; the walk has brought some colour into your cheeks."

The colour deepened, as the speaker went on :

" I've arranged for a quiet horse to be ready with mine, my lad, and I have a good hint or two as to where we ought to go so as to be in the route. It will not be till close on dusk, though."

" Oh, if I could tell exactly the way they will come, and the time, and let Drew know, it might mean saving my father's life," thought Frank. ." I must tell Captain Murray then.

" No, it would not do," he mused ; " for if I did, he would not move an inch. How to get the news, and go and find Drew ! But where ? Ah ! I might hear of him from some one at the tavern where they have that club."

" Why, Frank lad, what are you thinking about ?" said the captain. " I've been talking to you for ever so long, and you don't answer."

" Oh, Captain Murray," said the boy sadly, " you must know."

" Yes, my lad," said the captain sadly, " of course I know."

CHAPTER XXXIX.

AT THE LAST MOMENT.

THERE was not much sleep for the boy that night, for he was in the horns of a terrible dilemma. What should he do? He turned from side to side of his bed, trying to argue the matter out, till his father's fate, his duty to the King and Prince, the natural desire to help, his love for his mother, Captain Murray and his duty to the King and friendship for his brother-officer and companion, were jumbled up in an inextricable tangle with Drew Forbes and the attempt at rescue.

"Oh!" he groaned, as day broke and found him still tossing restlessly upon his pillow; "I often used to tell poor Drew that he was going mad. I feel as if I were already gone, for my head won't work. I can't think straight, just too when I want to be perfectly clear, and able to make my plans."

It would have prostrated a cleverer and more calculating brain than Frank's—one of those wonderful minds which can see an intricate game of chess right forward, the player's own and his adversary's moves in attack or defence—to have calmly mapped out the proper course for the lad through the rocks, shoals, and quicksands which beset his path. As it happened, all his mental struggles proved to be in vain; for, as is frequently the case in life, the maze of difficulties shaped themselves into a broad, even path, along which the boy travelled till the exciting times were past.

To begin with, nature knew when the brain would bear no more ; and just at sunrise, when Frank had tried to nerve himself for a fresh struggle by plunging face and a good portion of his head into cold water previous to having a good brisk rub, and then lain down to think out his difficulty once more, unconsciously choosing the best attitude for clear thought, a calm and restful sensation stole over him.   One moment he was gazing at the bright light stealing in beside his blind ; the next he was in profound mental darkness, wrapped in a deep, restful slumber, which lasted till nearly ten o'clock, when he was aroused by a knocking at his door, and leaped out of bed, confused and puzzled, unable for a few moments to collect his thoughts into a focus and grasp what it meant.

"Yes," he said at last.   "What is it ?"

"Will you make haste and go across to Lady Gowan's apartments, sir ?" said a voice.   "She has been very ill all night, and wishes to see you."

"Oh!" groaned Frank to himself.   Then aloud: "Yes ; come over directly."

He began to dress rapidly, with all the troubles of the night magnified and made worse by the mental lens of reproach through which he was looking at his conduct.

"How can I be such a miserable, thoughtless wretch!" he thought.   "How could I neglect everything which might have helped to save my poor father for the sake of grovelling here, and all the time my mother ill, perhaps dying, while I slept, not seeming to care a bit!"

He had a few minutes of hard time beneath the unsparing lashes he mentally applied to himself as he was dressing ; and then, ready to sink beneath his load of care, and feeling the while that he ought to have obtained from Captain Murray the route the prisoners would take, and then have found Drew Forbes and told him, so as to render the attempt at rescue easier, he hurried across the first court, and then into the lesser one to his mother's apartments.

"The doctor's with her, sir," whispered the maid.

"How is she now?" asked Frank.

"Dreadfully bad, sir. Pray make haste to her; she asked for you again when the doctor came."

Frank hurried up, to find the quiet physician who attended her and a nurse in the room, while the patient lay with her eyes looking dim, and two hectic spots in her thin cheeks, gazing anxiously at the door.

A faint smile of recognition came upon her lips, and she raised one hand to her son, and laid it upon his head as he sank upon his knees by the bedside.

"Oh, mother darling!" he whispered, in a choking voice, "forgive me for not coming before."

She half closed her eyes, and made a movement of the lips for him to kiss her. Then her eyes closed, as she breathed a weary sigh.

Frank turned in horror to the physician, who bent down and whispered to him.

"Don't be alarmed; it is sleep. She has, I find, been in a terribly excited state, and I have been compelled to administer a strong sedative. She will be calmer when she wakes. Sleep is everything now."

"You are not deceiving me, sir?" whispered Frank.

"No. That is the simple truth," replied the physician, very firmly. "Your mother may wake at any time; but I hope many hours will first elapse. I find that she has expressed an intense longing for you to come to her side, and, as you saw, she recognised you."

"Oh yes, she knew me," said Frank eagerly. "But pray tell me—she is not dying?"

"Lady Gowan is in a very serious condition," replied the doctor; "but I hope she will recover, and——"

"Yes, yes; pray speak out to me, sir," pleaded the boy.

"Her ailment is almost entirely mental; and if the news

can be brought to her that the King will show mercy to her husband, I believe that her recovery would be certain."

"Then you think I ought to go at once and try to save my father?"

"No," said the physician gravely. "I know all the circumstances of the case. You can do no good by going. Leave that to your friends—those high in position. Your place is here. Whenever Lady Gowan wakes, she must find you at her bedside. There, I will leave you now. Absolute quiet, mind. Sleep is the great thing. I will come in again in about three hours. The nurse knows what to do."

The physician went out silently, and Frank seated himself by his mother's pillow, to hold the thin hand which feebly clung to his and watch her, thinking the while of how his difficulties had been solved by these last orders, which bound him there like the endorsement of his father's commands to stay by and watch over his mother.

He could think clearly now, and see that much of that which he had desired to do was impossible. Even if he had set one duty aside, that to the Prince, his master, and let his love for and desire to save his father carry all before them, he could see plainly enough that it was not likely that he would have found Drew Forbes. A visit to the tavern club would certainly have resulted in finding that the occupants were dispersed and the place watched by spies. Then, even if he had found Drew, wherever he and his friends were hiding, it was not likely that they would have altered their plans for any information which he could give them. Everything would have been fixed as they thought best, and no change would have been made.

Clearer still came the thought that he had no information to give them further than that the prisoners would probably be brought into London that evening, which way Captain Murray might know, but he would never depart from his duty so far as to supply the information that it might be conveyed to the King's enemies. He was too loyal for that, gladly as he would strive to save his friend.

It was then with a feeling of relief that Frank sat there by his mother's bed, holding her hand, and thinking that he could do no more, while upon the nurse whispering to him that she would be in the next room if wanted, and leaving him alone, he once more sank upon his knees to rest his head against the bed, and prayed long and fervently in no tutored words, but in those which gushed naturally and simply from his breast, that the lives of those he loved might be spared and the terrible tribulation of the present times might pass away.

Hour after hour passed, and the nurse came in and out softly from time to time, nodding to the watcher and smiling her satisfaction at finding her patient still plunged in a sleep, which, as the day went on, grew more and more profound.

Then when alone Frank's thoughts went wandering away along the great north road by which the prisoners must be slowly approaching London, to find their fate. And at such times his thoughts were busy about his mother's friends. What were they doing to try and save his father?

Then his thoughts went like a flash to his meeting with Drew the day before; and his words came full of hope, and sent a feeling of elation through him. The rebels were not beaten, as Drew had said, and there was no doubt about their making a brave effort to rescue the prisoners before they were shut up in gaol.

And in imagination Frank built up what would in all probability be done. Small parties of the Jacobites would form in different places, and with arms hidden gradually converge upon some chosen spot which the prisoners with their escort must pass. Then at a given signal an attack would be made. The escort would be of course very strong ; but the Jacobites would be stronger, and in all probability the mob, always ready for a disturbance, would feel sympathy with the unfortunate prisoners, and help the attacking party, or at least join in checking the Guards, resenting their forcing their horses through the crowd which would have gathered ; so that the prospects looked very bright in that direction, and the boy felt more and more hopeful.

Twice over the servant came to the door to tell the watcher that first breakfast, and then lunch, was waiting for him in the room below ; but he would not leave the bedside, taking from sheer necessity what was brought to him, and then resuming his watch.

The physician came at the end of three hours as he had promised, but stayed only a few minutes.

"Exactly what I wished," he said. "Go on watching and keeping her quiet, and don't be alarmed if she sleeps for many hours yet. I will come in again this afternoon."

Frank resumed his seat by the bed, and then hastily pencilled a few lines to Captain Murray, telling him that it would be impossible to leave the bedside, and sent the note across by the servant, who brought a reply back.

It was very curt and abrupt.

"Of course. I see your position. Sorry, for I should have liked him to see you."

The note stung Frank to the quick.

"He thinks I am trying to excuse myself, when I would give the world to go with him," he muttered.

A glance at the pale face upon the pillow took off some of the bitterness, though, and he resumed his watch while the hours glided by.

At four the physician came again.

"Not awake ?" he said ; and he touched his patient's pulse lightly, and then softly raised one of Lady Gowan's eyelids, and examined the pupil.

" Nature is helping us, Mr. Gowan," he said softly.

" But she ought to have awoke by now, sir ? "

" I expected that she would have done so ; but nothing could be better. She is extremely weak, and if she could sleep like this till to-morrow her brain would be rested from the terrible anxiety from which she is suffering. I will look in once more this evening."

Frank was alone again with his charge, and another hour passed, during which the lad dwelt upon the plans that had been made, and calculated that Captain Murray must be about starting on his mission to meet the escort bringing in the prisoners. And as this idea came to him, Frank sat with his head resting upon his hands, his elbows upon his knees, trying hard to master the bitter sense of disappointment that afflicted him.

" And he will be looking from the carriage window to right and left, trying to make out whether I am there!" he groaned. " Oh, it seems cruel—cruel ! and he will not know why I have not come."

But one gleam of hope came here. Captain Murray might find an opportunity to speak with the prisoner, and he would tell him that his son was watching by his suffering mother.

" He will know why I have not come then," Frank said softly ; and after an impatient glance at the clock, he began again to think of Drew and his plans for the rescue.

But now, in the face of the precautions which would be taken, this seemed to be a wildly chimerical scheme, one which was not likely to succeed, and he shook his head sadly as a feeling of despair began to close him in like a dark cloud.

He was at his worst, feeling more and more hopeless, as he sat there, with his face buried in his fingers, when a hand was lightly placed upon his head, and starting up it was to find that his mother was awake, and gazing wistfully at him.

He bent over her, and her arms clasped his neck.

" My boy! my boy!" she said faintly; and she drew him to her breast, to hold him there for some moments before saying quickly :

"Have I slept long, dear ? "

" Yes, ever since morning, mother."

"What time is it ? "

"About half-past five."

" All that time ? " she said excitedly. " He must be near now. Frank, my boy, the prisoners were to reach London soon after dark."

" Yes, mother, I know," he said, looking at her wistfully, as he held her hand now to his cheek.

" Is there any news ? "

" No, mother, none."

" Oh," she moaned, " this terrible suspense! Frank, my darling, you must not stay here. Have you been with me all the time I have been asleep ? "

"Yes, mother, all. You asked for me."

" Yes, my darling, in my selfishness; but you ought to go and get the latest tidings. Frank, it is your duty to be there when your father reaches this weary city. He ought not to be looking in vain for one of those he loves. You must go at once. Do you hear me ? It is your duty."

" The doctor said it was my duty to watch by you," said Frank, with his heart beating fast, as he wondered whether Captain Murray had gone.

"With me ? Oh, what am I, if your being where he could see you, if only for a moment, would give him comfort in his sore distress ! "

" I was going, mother," whispered the boy excitedly. "Captain Murray was going to let me be with him, and he as an officer would have been able to take me right up to the escort."

"Then why are you here ? Oh, go—go at once ! "

"I was to stay with you, mother, so that you might see me when you awoke," he said huskily, the intense longing to go struggling with the desire to stay.

"Yes, yes, and I have seen you ; but I am nothing if we can contrive to give him rest. Go, then, at once."

" But you are not fit to be left."

" I shall not be left," she said firmly. " Quick, Frank. You are increasing my agony every moment that you stay. Oh, my boy, pray, pray go, and then come back and tell me that you have seen him. Go. Take no refusal ; fight for a position near him if you cannot get there by praying, and tell him how we are suffering for his sake—how we love him, and are striving to save him. Oh, and I keep you while I am talking, and he must be very near ! Quick ! Kiss me once and go, and I will lie here and pray that you may succeed."

"You wish it—you command me to go, mother ? " he panted.

"Yes, yes, my boy," she cried eagerly ; and he bent down over her, pressed his lips to hers, and darted to the door.

" Nurse, nurse ! " he said hoarsely, " come and stay with my mother." Then to himself as he rushed down the stairs : " Too late—too late ! He must have gone."

CHAPTER XL.

THE heavy, leaden feeling of despair and disappointment increased as Frank Gowan ran across the courtyard, feeling that it was useless to expect to find Captain Murray, but making for his quarters in the faint hope that he might have been detained, and cudgelling his brains as he ran, to try and find a means of learning the route that the escort would take, so that he might even then try and intercept the prisoners' carriages.

But no idea, not the faintest gleam of a way out ot his difficulty helped him ; and he felt ready to fling himself down in his misery and despair, as he reached the officers' quarters.

It was like a mockery to him in his agony to see the sentry, who recognised him, draw himself up, and present arms to his old captain's son, and it checked the question he would have asked the man as to when Captain Murray had passed, for he could not speak.

" I must see if he is here," he thought, as he ran up the stairs to the room which had been his prison ; and turning the handle of the door, he rushed in and uttered a groan, for the room was, as he had anticipated, empty. But the bedroom door was closed, and he darted to that and flung it open.

" Gone ! gone ! gone !" he groaned. " What shall I do ? Will they take him to the Tower ? "

He knew that there was no saying what might be the

destination of the prisoners; but he rushed back to the staircase, meaning to go straight to the Tower by some means, and then he stopped short and uttered a half hysterical cry, for there was Captain Murray ascending the stairs.

"Not gone?" he cried.

"No; but I am just off. I wish you could have gone with me, Frank. It would have done your poor father good."

"I am going. She wishes it, and sends me."

"Hah! Quick, then. Back to your room."

"Oh, I'm ready," cried the boy.

"Nonsense! We are going to ride. Your boots and sword, boy. I'll lend you a military cloak."

"But it will be losing time," panted Frank.

"It will be gaining it, my boy. You cannot go through a London mob like that. You are going to ride with soldiers, and you must not look like a page at a levée. Quick!"

"You will wait for me?"

"Of course."

Frank ran to his rooms, drew on his high horseman's boots, buckled on his sword, which had been returned to him, and ran back to where Captain Murray was waiting for him with a cloak over his arm.

"No spurs?" he said. "Never mind. You will have a well-trained horse. I have got passes for two, Frank; and, as it happens, I know the officer of the Horse Guards who is in command of the detachment going to meet the escort, so that we can get close up to the prisoners. Let's see: you do ride?"

"Oh yes; my father taught me long ago, anything— bare-backed often enough."

"Good. I am glad, boy. It was sorry work going without you. But I know why it was. Walk quickly; no time to lose."

He hurried his companion to the stables of the Horse Guards, where a couple of the men were waiting, and a horse was ready saddled.

"Quick!" he said to the men. "I shall want the second charger, after all."

It was rapidly growing dark, and one man lit a lanthorn, while the other clapped the bit between the teeth of a handsome black horse, turned the docile creature in its stall, and then slipped on a heavy military saddle with its high-peak holsters and curb-bit.

Five minutes after they were mounted and making for Charing Cross.

"Which way are we going?" asked Frank, whose excitement increased to a feeling of wild exhilaration, as he felt the beautifully elastic creature between his knees, with a sensation of participating in its strength, and being where he would have a hundred times the chance of getting to speak to his father.

"Up north," said the captain abruptly.

"North? Why not east? They will take him to the Tower."

"No. Steady horse. Walk, walk! Hold yours in, boy. We must go at a slow pace till we get to the top of the lane."

The horses settled down to their walk, almost keeping pace for pace, as the captain said quietly:

"I have got all the information I required. No, they will not take the prisoners to the Tower, but to Newgate."

"Newgate?" cried Frank; "why, that is where the thieves and murderers go."

"Yes," said the captain abruptly. "Look here, Frank. They are not to reach the prison till nine, so we have plenty of time to get some distance out. They will come in by the north road, and I don't think we can miss them."

"Why risk passing them?" said Frank.

"Because, if we intercept the escort on the great north road somewhere beyond Highgate, you will be able to ride back near the carriage in which your father is, and, even if you cannot speak to him, you will see him, and be seen."

"But it will be horrible; I shall look like one of the soldiers guarding him to his cell."

"Never mind what you look like, so long as your father sees that he is not forgotten by those who love him."

The captain ceased speaking, and their horses picked their way over the stones, their hoofs clattering loudly, and making the people they passed turn to stare after the two military-looking cavaliers in cocked hat and horseman's cloak, and with the lower parts of their scabbards seen below to show that they were well armed.

St. Martin's Church clock pointed to seven as they rode by; and then, well acquainted with the way, the captain made for the north-east, breaking into a trot as they reached the open street where the traffic was small, Frank's well-trained horse keeping step with its stable companion; and by the shortest cuts that could be made they reached Islington without seeing a sign of any unusual excitement, so well had the secret been kept of the coming of the prisoners that night.

"Not much sign of a crowd to meet them, Frank," said the captain, as they went now at a steady trot along the upper road. "Pretty good proof that we are in time."

"Why, what is a good sign?" asked Frank.

"So few people about. If the prisoners and their escort had passed, half Islington would have been out gossiping at their doors."

"Suppose they have come some other way?"

"Not likely. This was to be their route, and at half-past eight two troops of Horse Guards will march up the road to meet the escort at Islington. That will bring out the crowd."

Frank winced as if he had suddenly felt the prick of a

knife, so sharp was the spasm which ran through him. For the moment he had quite forgotten the prospect of an attempt at rescue ; now the mention of the soldiery coming to meet the unhappy prisoners and strengthen the escort brought all back, and with it the questioning thought :

" Would Drew's friends make the venture when so strong a force would be there ? "

" No—yes—no—yes," his heart seemed to beat ; then the rattle of the horses' hoofs took it up—no, yes, no, yes ; and now it seemed to be the time to tell Captain Murray of the attempt that was to be made, or rather that was planned.

" And if I tell him he will feel that it is his duty as a soldier to warn the officer in command of the escort, and he will take them at a sharp trot round by some other way. Oh, I can't tell him !   It would be like robbing my father of his last chance."

Frank felt more and more that his lips were sealed ; and as to the danger which Murray would incur—well, he was a soldier well mounted, and he must run the risk.

" As I shall," thought Frank.   " It will be no worse for him than for me.   It is not as if I were going to try and save myself.   I'll stand by him, weak boy as I am.   Or no ; shall I not be escaping with my father ? "

He shook his head the next moment, and felt that he could not be of the rescuing party.   He must still be the Prince's page, and return to the Palace to bear his mother the news of the escape.

" For he will—he must   escape," thought the boy. " Drew's friends will be out in force to-night, and I shall be able to go back and tell her that he is safe."

As they rode on through the pleasant dark night Frank thought more of the peril into which his companion was going, and hesitated about telling him, so that he might be warned ; but again he shrank from speaking, for fear that it might mean disaster to Drew's projects.

"And he has his father to save as well as mine. I can't warn him," he concluded. "I run the risk as well as he."

He felt better satisfied the next minute, as he glanced sidewise at the bold, manly bearing of the captain, mounted on the splendid, well-trained charger.

"Captain Murray can take care of himself," he thought; and the feelings which were shut within his breast grew into a sensation of excitement that was almost pleasurable.

"Quite countrified out here, Frank," said the captain suddenly, as the road began to ascend; and after passing Highbury the houses grew scarce, being for the most part citizens' mansions. "Don't be down-hearted, my lad. The law is very curious. It is a strong castle for our defence, but full of loopholes by which a man may escape."

"Escape?" cried Frank excitedly. "You think he may escape?"

"I hope so, and I'd give something now if my oaths were not taken, and I could do something in the way of striking a blow for your father's liberty."

For a few minutes the boy felt eagerly ready to confess all he knew; but the words which had raised the desire served also to check it. "If my oaths were not taken," Captain Murray had said; and he was the very soul of honour, and would not break his allegiance to his King.

"My father did," thought the boy sadly. Then he brightened. "No," he thought, "the King broke it, and set him free by banishing him from his service."

"How do you get on with your horse, lad?—Walk."

The horses changed their pace at the word. The hill was getting steep.

"Oh, I get on capitally. It's like sitting in an easy-chair. I haven't been on a horse for a year."

"Then you learned to ride well, Frank. Find the advantage of having your boots, though. Fancy a ride like this in silk stockings and shoes !—You ought to go into the cavalry some day."

Frank sighed.

"Bah ! Don't look at the future as being all black, boy. Stick to Hope, the lady who carries the anchor. One never knows what may turn up."

"No, one never knows what may turn up," cried the boy excitedly ; and then he checked himself in dread lest his companion should read his thoughts respecting the rescue. But the captain's next words set him at rest.

"That's right, my lad. Try and keep a stout heart. Steep hill this. Do you know where we are ? "

"Only that we are on the great north road."

"Yes. When we are on the top of this hill, we shall be in the village of Highgate ; and if it was daylight, we could see all London if we looked back, and the country right away if we looked forward. I propose to stop at the top of the hill and wait."

"Yes," said Frank eagerly.

"Perhaps go on for a quarter of a mile, so as to be where we are not observed."

The horses were kept at a walking pace till the village was reached, and here a gate was stretched across, and a man came out to take the toll, Frank noticing that he examined them keenly by the light of a lanthorn.

"Any one passed lately—horsemen and carriages ? " said the captain quietly.

The man chuckled.

"Yes, a couple of your kidney," said the man. "You're too late."

A pang shot through Frank, and he leaned forward.

"Too late ? What do you mean, sir ? " cried the captain sharply ; and, as he spoke, he threw back his horseman's cloak, showing his uniform slightly.

"Oh, I beg your worships' pardon. I took you for gentlemen of the road."

" What, highwaymen ? "

"Yes, sir. A couple of them went by not ten minutes ago. But I don't suppose they'll try to stop you. They don't like catching Tartars. Be as well to have your pistols handy, though."

"Thank you for the hint," said the captain, and they rode on.

" What do you say, Frank ? " said the captain. "Shall we go any farther ? It would be an awkward experience for you if we were stopped by highwaymen. Shall we stop ? "

"Oh, we cannot stop to think about men like that," said Frank excitedly.

"Not afraid, then ? "

" I'm afraid we shall not meet the prisoners," said the boy sadly.

" Forward, then. But unfasten the cover of your holsters. You will find loaded pistols there, and can take one out if we are stopped—I mean if any one tries to stop us. But," he added grimly, " I don't think any one will."

At another time it would have set the boy trembling with excitement ; but his mind was too full of the object of their expedition, and as the horses paced on the warning about the gentlemen who infested the main roads in those days was forgotten, so that a few minutes later it came as a surprise to the boy when a couple of horsemen suddenly appeared from beneath a clump of trees by the roadside, came into the middle of the road, and barred their way.

" Realm ? " said one of the men sharply.

" Keep off, or I fire," cried Captain Murray.

The two mounted men reined back on the instant, and, pistol in hand, the captain and Frank went on at a walk.

" I don't think—nay, I'm sure—that those men are not

on the road, Frank," said the captain quietly. "That was a password. *Realm.* Can they be friends of the prisoners sent forward as scouts?"

"Do you think so?" said Frank.

"Yes," replied the captain thoughtfully; "and if they are, we are quite right. The prisoners have not passed, and I should not wonder if there were an attempt made to rescue them before they reach town."

Frank's head began to buzz, and he nipped his horse so tightly that the animal broke into a trot.

"Steady! Walk," cried the captain; and the next minute he drew rein, to sit peering forward into the darkness, listening for the tramp of horses, which ought to have been heard for a mile or two upon so still a night.

"Can't hear them," he said in a disappointed tone. "But we will not go any farther."

At that moment Frank's horse uttered a loud challenging neigh, which was answered from about a hundred yards off, and this was followed by another, and another farther away still.

"There they are," said the captain, "halting for a rest to the horses before trotting down. Forward!"

They advanced again; but had not gone far before figures were dimly seen in the road, and directly after a stern voice bade them halt.

The captain replied with a few brief words, and they rode forward, to find themselves facing a vedette of dragoons, a couple of whom escorted them to where, upon an open space, in the middle of which was a pond, a strong body of cavalry was halted, the greater part of the men dismounted; but about twenty men were mounted, and sat with drawn swords, surrounding a couple of carriages, each with four horses—artillery teams—and the drivers in their places ready to start at a moment's notice.

CHAPTER XLI

FRANK'S eyes took all this in, and then turned dim with the emotion he felt, and for a few moments everything seemed to swim round him. His horse, however, needed no guiding; it kept pace with its companion, and the lad's emotional feeling passed off as he found himself in presence of the officer in command of the escort and his subordinates, a warm greeting taking place between Captain Murray and the principal officer, an old friend.

"Don't seem regular, Murray; but with this note from the Prince, I suppose I shall be held clear if you have come to help the prisoners escape," said the officer lightly.

"Escape!" said Captain Murray sharply.

"No, no; nonsense, old fellow," said the dragoon officer merrily. "Of course I was bantering you."

"Yes, I know," said Captain Murray quickly; "but we were stopped by a couple of mounted men a quarter of a mile back."

"Highwaymen?"

"I thought so at first; but they challenged us for a password." .

"Well! These fellows work hand and glove."

"No," said Captain Murray, "I feel sure they were scouts, ridden forward to get touch with you, and then go back and give warning."

"What for ? Whom to ? You don't think it means an attempt to rescue ?"

"I do," said Murray firmly.

"Thanks for the warning, old fellow," said the officer through his teeth. "Well, mine are picked men, and my instructions are that a strong detachment will be sent out to meet us, and vedettes planted all along the road, to fall in behind us as we pass. Pity too. What madness !"

Frank's heart sank as he heard every word, while his attention was divided between the two dark carriages with their windows drawn up, and he sat wondering which held his father.

"Yes, madness," said the captain sadly.

"I shall be very glad when my job's at an end," said the dragoon officer. "It's miserable work."

"Horrible !" replied Murray ; and then he turned to Frank. "Hold my rein for a few moments," he said ; and, dismounting, he walked away with the officers, to stand talking for a few minutes, while, as Frank sat holding his companion's horse, and watching the well-guarded carriages, a distant neigh and the stamping of horses told of a strong detachment guarding the rear.

"If I only dared ride up to the carriages," thought the boy ; and he felt that he did dare, only that it would be useless, for without permission the dragoons would not let him pass.

But a light broke through the mental darkness of despair directly, for Murray came back with the officer in command, a stern, severe-looking man, but whose harsh, commanding voice softened a little as he laid one hand on the horse's neck, and held out his other to the rider.

"I did not know who you were, Mr. Gowan. My old friend, Captain Murray, has just told me. Shake hands, my lad. I am glad to know the brave son of a gallant soldier. Don't think hardly of me for doing my duty sternly as a military man should. I ought perhaps to

send you both back," he continued in a low tone; "but
if you and Captain Murray like to ride by the door of the
first carriage, you can, and I will instruct the officer and
men not to hinder any reasonable amount of conversation
that may be held."

"God bless you!" whispered Frank, in a choking
voice.

"Oh, don't say anything, my boy. Only give me your
word, not as a soldier, but as a soldier's son, that you will
do nothing to help either of the prisoners to escape."

"Yes, I give you my word," said Frank quickly. He
would have given anything to be near his father and
speak to him for a few minutes.

"That will do.—Murray, we shall go on at a sharp
trot; but you are both well mounted, I see." Then he
said in an undertone: "I don't believe they will venture
anything when they see how strong we are. If the
rascals do, I shall make a dash, standing at nothing; but
at the first threatenings get the boy away. My instructions are that the prisoners are not to escape—*alive!*"

"I understand," said Captain Murray; and he mounted
his horse.

The next minute an order was given in a low tone; it
was passed on, and the men sprang to their saddles.
Then another order, "Draw swords!" There was a
single note from a trumpet; and as Frank and Captain
Murray sat ready, the officer in command led them
himself, and placed one at each door of the first carriage,
a dragoon easing off to right and left to make place
for them.

Frank's hand was on the glass directly, and the window
was let down.

"Father!" he cried in a low, deep voice, which was
nearly drowned by the trampling, crashing of wheels,
and jingle of accoutrements, but heard within; and it was
answered by a faint cry of astonishment, and the rattle

of fetters, as two hands linked together appeared at the window.

"Frank, my dear boy! you here?"

The boy could not answer, but leaned over toward the carriage with his hand grasped between his father's.

"Hah! this is a welcome home!" cried Sir Robert cheerily. "Gentlemen, my son."

"There's Captain Murray at the other window," gasped out Frank at last.

"Ah! more good news," said Sir Robert. "Murray, my dear old fellow, this is good of you."

The prisoner's voice sounded husky, as he turned his head to the right in the darkness.

"I can't shake hands even if you wished to, for we are doubly fettered now."

"Gowan, I'm glad to meet you again," said the captain hoarsely.

"God bless you, old friend! I know you are. I see now; you brought Frank here to meet me. Like you, old fellow. There, I cannot talk to you. But you know what I feel."

"Yes. Talk to your boy," cried Murray. "Quick, while you can. The order to trot will come directly."

"Yes. Thanks," said Sir Robert; and he turned back to his son, who clung to his hands. "Quick, Frank boy. Your mother—well?"

"Very, very ill. Heart-broken."

"Hah!" groaned Sir Robert.

"But, father, these handcuffs? Surely you are not——"

"Yes, yes. I'm a dangerous fellow now, my boy. We are all chained hand and foot like the worst of criminals, my friends and I."

"Oh!" groaned Frank.

"Bah! Only iron," said Sir Robert bitterly. "Never mind them now. Tell me of your mother. Are you still at the Palace?"

"Yes; the Princess—the Prince—will not hear of our leaving, and——"

Then a note from a trumpet rang out, the horses sprang forward at a sharp trot, and the dragoon on Frank's left changed his sword to his left hand, so as to place his right on the rein of the boy's charger, though it was hardly needed, the well-trained horse bearing off a little to avoid injury from the wheel, but keeping level with the window, so that from time to time, though conversation was impossible, father and son managed to bridge the space between them and touch hands.

It was fortunate for the lad that he was mounted upon a trained cavalry charger, for he had nothing to do but keep his seat, his mount settling down at once to the steady military trot side by side with the horse next to it, and keeping well in its distance behind the horse in front, so that the rider was able to devote all his attention to the occupant of the carriage, who leaned forward with his head framed in the darkness of the window, as if pictured in the sight of his son, possibly for the last time, for in those hours Sir Robert Gowan had not the slightest doubt as to what his fate would be.

On his side, Frank sat in his saddle watching his father's dimly seen face, but ready to start and glance in any direction from which a fresh sound was heard.

The first time was on reaching the turnpike gate, where the toll-taker seemed disposed to hesitate about letting the advance guard pass. The result was an outcry, which sent Frank's heart with a leap toward his lips, for he felt certain that the attack had commenced. But the foremost men dismounted, seized the gate, lifted it off its hook hinges, and cast it aside, the troops and carriages thundered through, and made the people of Highgate village come trooping out in wonder to see what this invasion of their quiet meant.

Then the descent of the hill commenced, with the heavy

old-fashioned carriages swaying on their C-springs; but
no slackening of speed took place, and the artillerymen
hurried their horses along, as if the load they drew were
some heavy gun or a waggon full of ammunition.

Twice over Frank gazed at the foremost carriage in
alarm, so nearly was it upset in one of the ruts of the ill-
kept road; but the rate at which they were going saved it,
and they thundered along without accident to where the
gradient grew less steep.

There was very little traffic on the road at that time of
the night, and not many people about, while before those
who were startled by the noise of the passing troops had
time to come out the prisoners had gone by.

Holloway and Highbury were passed, and Islington
reached, but no sign of an attempt at rescue caught Frank's
anxious eyes; neither was there any appearance of fresh
troops till the head of the escort turned down the road
which entered the city at the west end of Cheapside. But
here the boy started, for they passed between two out-
posts, a couple of dragoons facing them on either side of
the road, sitting like statues till the whole of the escort
had passed, when they turned in after it, four abreast, and
brought up the rear, but some distance in front of the rear
guard.

At the end of another fifty yards two more couples were
seen, and at the end of every similar interval four more
dragoons turned in at the rear, strengthening the escort,
while it was evident that they had previously cleared the
road of all vehicles, turning them into the neighbouring
ways, so that the cortège was enabled to continue its
progress at the same steady military trot as they had
commenced with on leaving Highgate.

Again and again Frank, now growing breathless, had
hoped that the walking pace would once more be renewed,
so as to afford him a chance to speak to his father; but he
wished in vain, for, except at two sharp turnings, the whole

body of dragoons swept along at the sharp trot, and without change, saving that as London was neared the men
flanking the carriages were doubled.

But though no sign of rescue caught Frank's eyes, he
saw that the stationing of the dragoons to keep the way
and the turning of the traffic out of the road had had their
effect ; for at every step the collection of people along the
sides and at the windows increased, till, when the road
changed to a busy London street, there was quite a crowd
lining the sides.

" There will be no rescue," sighed the lad ; and he turned
from sweeping the sides of the street to gaze sadly at his
father, whose face he could now see pretty plainly, as they
passed one of the dismal street lamps which pretended in
those days to light the way.

He could see that, brief as the time had been since he
last saw his father, his countenance had sadly altered.
There was a stern, careworn look in his eyes, and he looked
older, and as if he had been exposed to terrible hardships.
He noted too that he did not seem to have had the opportunity given him of attending to his person, but had been
treated with the greatest of severity.

The lad's gloomy musings on the aspect of the face
which beamed lovingly upon him, the eyes seeming to say,
" Don't be down-hearted, boy ! " were suddenly brought to
an end by a check in their progress, for the advance
guard, from being a hundred yards ahead, had by degrees
shortened the space to fifty, twenty, and ten yards, and
finally was only the front of the column. But still they
had advanced at a trot, and the officer in command sent
orders twice over for the vanguard to increase their
distance.

" Tell him I can't," said the officer in front. " It can
only be done by riding over the people."

And now the men stationed to keep the way had utterly
failed, the people having crowded in from the side streets

north of St. Martin's-le-Grand till the pairs of dragoons were hemmed in, and in spite of several encounters with the crowd they were forced to remain stationary.

The check that came was the announcement that the trot could no longer be continued, and, perforce, the escort advanced at a walk; while, as Frank glanced round for a moment, it suddenly struck him that, save at the windows of the houses, there was not a woman to be seen, the crowd consisting of sturdy-looking men.

The lad had no eyes for the crowd, though. The relapse into a walk had given him the opportunity for grasping his father's hand again, and Sir Robert said to him hurriedly :

"My dearest love to your mother, Frank lad. Tell her, whatever happens, I have but one thought, and that it is for her, that we may meet in happier times."

"Meet in happier times" rang through Frank like a death-knell, for he grasped what his father meant, and tried to speak some words of comfort, but they would not come. Even if they had, they would have been drowned by a tremendous cheer which arose from the crowd and went rolling onward.

"The wretches!" muttered Frank ; and he turned to look round, with his eyes flashing his indignation. Then, as the cheer went rolling away forward, he repeated his words aloud, unconscious that they would be heard.

"The wretches ! It is not a sight."

"They're a-cheering of 'em, sir," said the dragoon at his elbow, "not hooting 'em, poor fellows !"

Frank darted a grateful look in the man's eyes, and his heart leaped with excitement as the light flashed upon him. It was a manœuvre, and there would be an attempt to rescue, after all.

"I believe we're in for a row, sir," continued the man, leaning over to him and speaking in a low voice. Strikes me the best thing for you to do would be to step into the carriage to your friend before the fight begins : I'll hold your horse."

" I ! " said Frank sharply. " I wouldn't be such a cur."

" Well said, youngster. Then you try and stick by me. We shall be in the thick of it, and nobody shall hurt you if I can help it."

" Do—do you think, then, that there will be trouble ? "

" Yes, for some of us, sir," said the man. " They mean to try and get the prisoners, and the attack will be here."

Frank was unconscious of a movement behind him, till a horseman forced his way in between him and the dragoon, and Captain Murray said sharply :

" Try and ease off, my man."

" Not to be done, sir," replied the dragoon.

" There's going to be an attempt at rescue, Frank," whispered the captain. " Shake hands with your father before we are forced away."

At that moment word was passed along from the rear, running from man to man as they still kept on at a slow walk :

" Flats of your swords ; drive them back."

The next minute, just as a fresh cheer was being started, the trumpet rang out behind " Trot ! " and the men put spurs to their horses, and dashed on, driving a road through the crowd ; and, amidst a savage yelling and hooting which took the place of the hearty cheer for the prisoners, the escort literally forced their way for another fifty yards, the men in advance striking to right and left with the flats of their heavy cavalry swords.

But it was soon evident that they were slackening speed, and the trumpet rang out again, but with an uncertain sound, for it was nearly drowned by the angry yelling which arose. The command was *gallop*, but the execution of the order was *walk*, and a minute later the whole escort came to a stand, literally wedged in, with the frightened horses standing shivering and snorting, only one here and there trying to rear and plunge.

" We're caught, Frank lad.   Think of nothing but keeping your seat.   Take out a pistol, and point it at the first man who tries to drag you from your horse.   Ah ! I thought so."

Orders were passed along now to the dragoons to defend themselves, for efforts were being made to drag some of the outside men from their horses.   Blades flashed on high, cut and point were given, and amidst howlings and savage execrations blood began to flow.

And now, as if by magic, sticks and swords appeared among the crowd ; men who had forced their way under the horses' necks, or crept under them, appeared everywhere ; and amidst a deafening roar, as the seething mass swayed here and there, Frank caught sight of two men busy just before him, doing something with knives.   One of the dragoons noticed it too, and he leaned forward to make a thrust at one of the two ; but as he bent over his horse's neck a cudgel was raised, fell heavily across the back of his neck, and he dropped forward, and was only saved from falling by a comrade's help.

" They've cut the traces," said Captain Murray hoarsely. " It's an organised attempt."

As he spoke men were rising amongst them ; and, before Frank could realise how it happened, a dozen filled up the little spaces about the carriage, while moment by moment the dragoons were being rendered more helpless. The blows they rained down were parried with swords ; they were dragged from their horses ; and, in several cases, helped by their fellows, men climbed up behind them, and pinioned their arms.

Organised indeed it seemed to be, for while the greater part of the rioters devoted their attention to rendering the great escort helpless, others kept on forcing their way till they had surrounded the carriages, trusting to their companions to ward off the blows directed at them, but in too many cases in vain.

Frank tried his best to remain near his father, but he was perfectly helpless, and had to go as his horse was slowly forced along, till he was several yards away from the carriage door, at which he could still see the prisoner watching him as if thinking only of the safety of his boy, while the captain was still farther away, using his pistol to keep off attempts made to dismount him.

All attempts at combination were getting useless now for the troops, and it was every man for himself; but the mob did not seem vindictive only when some dragoon struck mercilessly at those who hemmed him in, when the result rapidly followed that he was dragged from his horse and trampled underfoot.

Sir Robert was now shut out from his son's gaze by several men forcing themselves to the carriage door, and Frank was rising in his stirrups to try and catch another glimpse of him, when in the wild swaying about of the crowd his horse was forced nearer to Captain Murray, an eddy sending the captain fortunately back to him, so that their horses made an effort, and came side by side once more, snorting and trembling with fear.

"The men are helpless, Frank lad," said the captain, with his lips to the lad's ear. "They can do nothing more. They are literally wedged in."

"My father?" panted Frank.

"It will be a rescue, my lad."

An exultant roar rose now from the dense mass of people which filled the wide street, and, separated from each other, as well as from their officers, the dragoons ceased to use their swords, while the men round them who held them fast wedged waved their sticks and hats, cheering madly.

"Told you so, sir," shouted some one close behind them; and Frank turned, to see a dragoon, capless and bleeding from a cut on his forehead, sitting calmly enough on his horse.

" Can't do any more, sir," said the man, in answer to a frown from Captain Murray. " They've got my sword. It's the same with all of us. We couldn't move."

The cheering went on, and in the midst of it the carriages began to move, dragged by the crowd, for there was not a soldier within a dozen yards. The clumsy vehicles were being dragged by hand, and the horses led away toward a side street, while the cheering grew more lusty than ever, and then changed into a yell of execration.

" What does that mean ? " said Captain Murray excitedly.

" I don't know," said Frank, having hard work to make himself heard. " Let's try and get to the carriage."

" Impossible, my lad," said Captain Murray. " Great heavens ! what a gehenna ! "

The yelling rose louder than ever from the direction of Cheapside, and directly after the cause was known, for a heavy, ringing volley rang out clear and sharp above the roar of the crowd, and went on reverberating from side to side of the street.

Hardly had it died away when another rattling volley came from the other direction; and in answer to an inquiring look from Frank, Captain Murray placed his lips to the boy's ear.

" The foot guards," he cried ; " the mob is between two fires."

The pressure was now terrible, the crowd yielding to the attack from both directions, and yells, wild cries, and groans rose in one horrible mingling, as for a few minutes the seething mass of people were driven together in the centre formed by the carriages ; and from where he sat, gazing wildly at the chaos of tossing arms and wild faces, whose owners seemed now to be thinking of nothing but struggling for their lives, Frank could see men climbing over their fellows' heads, dashing in windows, and seeking safety by climbing into the houses, whose occupants in many cases reached down to drag people up out of the writhing mass beneath. In half a dozen places streams could be seen setting into the side streets; and mingled with the attacking party, dragoons of the escort, perfectly helpless, were pressed slowly along, and in every instance with one, sometimes with two men mounted behind them.

Frank caught these things at a glance, while his and the captain's mounts were being slowly forced farther away from the carriages, which were once more stationary, jammed in by the densest portion of the crowd.

And now, without a thought of his own safety, the boy's heart began to beat high, for not a single dragoon was near the prisoners, and some strange movement was evidently taking place there, but what, it was some moments before he could see.

It seemed to him that several people there had been injured, and that those between him and the first carriage had been crushed to death, while the crowd were passing the bodies over their heads face upward toward the narrow side street up which an effort had been made to drag the carriages.

As far as he could make out by the lamplight, that was it evidently, and so strangely interested was the lad, so fascinated by the sight, that he paid no heed to a couple more volleys fired to right and left. For the moment he hardly knew why he was watching this. Then it came home to him as he twice over saw a gleam as of metal on one of the bodies which floated as it were over a forest of hands and glided onward toward and up the side street.

"Look, boy! Do you see?" said Captain Murray, with his lips close to the lad's ear. "They have dragged

the prisoners out, and are passing them over the heads of
the crowd."

Frank nodded his head sharply without turning to
the speaker, for he could not remove his eyes from the
scene till the last fettered figure had passed from his
sight.

And now at length the awful pressure began to relax, for
the half-dozen streams were setting steadily out of the
main street, while in several spots where dragoons had
sat wedged in singly two had drifted together. Then
there were threes and fours, and soon after a little body
of about twenty had coalesced, stood in something like
order, and were able to make a stand. Right away
toward Cheapside there was now visible beneath a faint
cloud of smoke, which looked ruddy in the torch- and
lamplight, a glittering line above the heads of the still
dense crowd, and Frank grasped the fact that they were
bayonets. Then turning in the other direction he saw,
far up the street toward Islington, another glittering
line, showing that a second body of infantry barred the
way.

And now once more came the sound of firing, and
Frank's heart resumed its wild beating, for it came rolling
down the side street nearly opposite to him, that up which
he had seen the prisoners passed, and he knew that troops
must be guarding the end.

This was plain enough, for the steady stream passing
up it grew slower, then stopped ; there was a tremendous
shouting and yelling, and the human tide came slowly
rolling back, then faster and faster, till it set right across
the main street, and joined one going off in the opposite
direction.

Soon after, to the boy's horror, he caught sight of one
of the prisoners being borne along over the heads of the
returning crowd ; then of another and another. And
now, as the two lines of dimly seen bayonets drew nearer

in both directions, there was once more the sound of the
trumpet ; and in half a dozen places the dragoons began
to form up, and, minute by minute growing stronger
in the power to move, swords were seen to flash, and
they forced their way through the stream, cutting it right
across, and hemming in the portion of the crowd over
whose heads the perfectly helpless prisoners were being
borne.

This manœuvre having been executed, the rest proved
simple.   Knot after knot of the dragoons forced their way
up to what nad become their rallying-point, the foot
guards were steadily advancing up and down the main
street toward the carriages, and another company was
steadily driving the people back along the side street up
which the prisoners had been borne.

"A brave attempt, Frank," said Captain Murray ; "but
they have failed.   Come along ;" and, dizzy with excitement, the boy felt his horse begin to move beneath him
toward the escort which formed a crescent round the
carriages in double rank, through which they passed slowly
the men of the crowd they had entrapped, till some forty
or fifty only remained, whose retreat was cut off by the
bristling line of bayonets drawn across the side street
down which they had come.

Frank had no eyes for the scene behind him, now
shown by the light of many smoky torches,—the roadway
littered with hats, sticks, and torn garments, trampled
people lying here and there, others who had been borne
and laid down close to the houses, whose occupants were
now coming out to render the assistance badly enough
needed, for even here many were wounded and bleeding
from sword cuts : of the ghastly traces of the firing, of
course, nothing was visible there.   He did not heed either
the state of the dragoons, who had not escaped scot free,
many of them being injured by sword and cudgel ; some
had been dragged from their horses and trampled ; others

stood behind the double line, separated from their mounts, which had gone on with the crowd; most of them were hatless, while several had had their uniforms torn from their backs.

Frank had no eyes for all this; his attention was too fully taken up by the proceedings near the carriages, where the fettered and handcuffed prisoners—five—were being passed in by men of the foot guards, who then formed up round the vehicles, toward which the two teams of horses were now brought back, the men roughly knotting together the cut traces, and fastening them ready for a fresh start toward the prison.

"One of the prisoners has been carried off, Frank," whispered Captain Murray then; and in a weak voice the lad said:

"My father?"

"No, my lad; he is in the second carriage now."

The next minute orders were given, and the dragoons advanced to clear the way for the carriages, now surrounded by the bristling bayonets of half a regiment of foot guards, who refused passage to Captain Murray and the boy, so that they had to be content with riding in front of the rear guard of dragoons.

And now once more the yelling of the crowd arose from the direction of Cheapside, where the mob had again gathered strongly; but no mercy was shown. The heavy mass of dragoons that formed the advance guard had received their orders to clear the way, and, finding a determined opposition, the trumpet rang out once more, and they advanced at a gallop, trampling down all before them for a few minutes till the crowd broke and ran. The way was clear enough as at a double the Grenadiers came up, and passed round the angle at Newgate Street, the escort driving the mob before it; and the wide space at the west end of the Old Bailey was reached.

This was packed with troops, who had preserved an opening for the carriages, and into it the Grenadiers marched, and formed up round the massive prison gates. And now Frank made an effort, with Captain Murray's assistance, to get to the carriage door again for one short farewell. But in the hurry and excitement of the time, the pass from the Palace and the military uniform the captain wore went for nothing, the dense mass of Grenadiers stood firm, and very few minutes sufficed for the prisoners to be passed in and the gates closed. A strong force of infantry was stationed within and without, for the authorities dreaded an attack upon the prison; and the regiment of dragoons that had been detailed to meet the escort and guard the road to Islington patrolled the approaches, while the rest marched off to their quarters amidst the hooting and yelling of the crowd.

Captain Murray turned off at once into a side street, and rode beside Frank for some distance, respecting in silence his young companion's grief, hardly a word passing till they reached the Guards' stables and left their horses, which looked, by the light of the men's lanthorns, as if they had passed through a river. Then the pair hurried across the Park, feeling half-stunned by their adventure, Frank so entirely exhausted that he would have gladly availed himself of his friend's arm.

But he fought hard, and just as the clock was striking twelve he made his way to his mother's room, wondering whether he was to be called upon to face some fresh grief. But he found Lady Gowan lying awake, and ready to stretch out her hands to him.

"You saw him, Frank?" she whispered; and the disorder of his appearance escaped her notice.

"Yes, mother; I rode beside him, and he spoke to me."

"Yes, yes; what did he say?" cried Lady Gowan.

Frank delivered his father's loving message, and his mother's eyes closed.

"Yes," she said softly, "to meet again in happier times." Then, unclosing her eyes again, she moaned out, "Oh, Frank, Frank, my boy, my boy!" and he forgot his own weakness and suffering in his efforts to perform the sacred duty which had fallen to his lot.

CHAPTER XLII.

AFTER THE FAILURE.

THAT next morning, after a long sleep, the result of exhaustion, Frank Gowan awoke with the horrors of the previous night seeming to have grown so that they could no longer be borne. He hurried across to his mother's apartments, to find from the nurse that she was sleeping, and must not of course be disturbed; so he went over to Captain Murray, who received him warmly.

"Better, my lad?" he said.

"Better?" cried Frank reproachfully.

"I mean rested. Frank lad, we had a narrow escape of our lives last night. I hear already that about fifty dragoons were more or less injured."

"And how many of the people?" said Frank bitterly.

"That will never be known, my boy. It is very horrible when orders are given to fire upon a crowd. Many fell, I'm afraid. But there, don't look so down-hearted."

"Have you heard who was the prisoner that escaped?"

"Yes. They have not taken him again yet; but I don't think he will be able to get right away."

"Not if he can reach the coast?" said Frank.

"Ah! he might then. There, Frank lad, I want to be true to my duty—don't tell upon me—but I can't help feeling that we had bad luck last night, or some one we know might have been the lucky man."

Frank caught at his hand and held it.

"If I were the King, I'd pack the prisoners off to France," continued Captain Murray. "I don't like taking revenge on conquered enemies."

"Ah, now you make me feel as if I can speak openly to you," cried Frank. "Tell me, do you think there is still any hope of an escape?"

"There always is, my lad. One thing is very evident, and that is that your father and his companions have plenty of friends in London who are ready to risk their lives to save them. Come, don't be down-hearted; we must hope for the best. They have to be tried yet. A dozen things may happen. Besides, your father was not one of the leaders of the rebellion. What's the matter with your arm?"

"My arm? Oh, I don't know. It's so stiff and painful I can hardly lift it. Yes, I remember now. Some one in the crowd struck me with a heavy stick. I did not feel it so much then; it was only numbed."

"You had better let the doctor see it."

"Oh no," replied Frank. "I have too many other troubles to think about. Captain Murray, what shall I do? I must see my father. Give me your advice, or come with me to ask permission of the Prince."

The captain sat frowning for a few moments, and then rose.

"Yes," he said abruptly; "come."

Frank sprang after him as he moved toward the door, and in a few minutes they were in the antechamber, where a knot of officers were discussing the proceedings of the previous night, but ceased upon their attention being directed to the son of one of the prisoners.

The captain sent in his name as soon as he could; but his efforts to gain an audience were not so successful as upon previous occasions. There were many waiting, and the Prince made no exception in Captain Murray's favour.

The order of precedence was rigidly adhered to, and hours had passed away before the attendant came to where Frank and the captain were seated waiting.

"His Royal Highness will see you, sir," said the gentleman-in-waiting.

Frank sprang to his feet as the captain rose, and moved toward the curtained door.

"I am sorry," said the attendant, with a commiserating look, "but his Royal Highness expressly said that Captain Murray was to come alone."

Frank's lips parted as a look of anguish came into his pale face, and he turned his appealing eyes to the captain, who shook his head sadly.

"I will beg him to see you, my boy," he whispered. "I look to his seeing you to get his consent."

Frank sank back into his seat, and turned his face to the window to hide it from those present, and seemed to them to be gazing out at the gay show of troops under arms and filling the courtyard; but, as he sat, he saw only the interior of the Prince's room, with Captain Murray appealing on his behalf: all else was non-existent.

He had not moved, he had not heard the low buzz of eager conversation that went on, new-comers being unaware of his presence. Fortunate it was that he was deaf to all that was said, for the fate of the prisoners lodged like ordinary malefactors the previous night in Newgate was eagerly discussed, and his father's name was mentioned by several in connection with the axe.

He was still sitting in the same vacant way when, at the end of half an hour, a hand was laid upon his shoulder, and the captain's voice said in a low tone, "Come."

"He will see me?" cried Frank, rising quickly.

"Hush! Keep your sorrow to yourself, as an Englishman should," whispered the captain. "The room is full of people."

"But he will see me?"

"No. Come away," said the captain quietly.

Frank gave him a defiant look; then turned away and walked straight toward the curtained door, which the attendant was about to open to admit another gentleman to the Prince's presence.

Before he was half-way there the captain's strong grasp was upon his shoulder.

"What are you going to do, boy?" he said sternly.

"See the Prince myself. He must—he shall give me leave to go."

"Do you wish to destroy the last chance? Frank, for your mother's sake!"

"No; don't make me struggle before all these people to get free," said the boy firmly; but as he spoke the captain's last words stood out before him in their real significance.

"For your mother's sake!"

He turned back without another word, and walked with his companion out of the room and down into the court-yard without a word.

"Take me somewhere," he said, in a strange, dazed way. "My head feels confused. I hardly know what I am saying."

Captain Murray drew the boy's hand through his arm, and made as if to lead him to his quarters; but it meant passing crowded-together troops, and, altering his mind, he walked with him sharply out into the Park, till they reached a secluded place where there was a seat.

"Sit down, boy."

"Yes," said Frank obediently. "Now tell me, please."

"I was in there long, but there is little to tell you, boy," said the captain, in a harsh, brusque way to conceal the agony of disappointment he felt. "I appealed again and again to the Prince to give me an order to admit us to the prison, but he sternly refused me, and I have angered him terribly by my obstinate return to the assault. Frank boy, it is like this. The Prince told me that, before your father joined the Pretender, he had made a direct appeal, at his wife's wish, for your father's pardon, and been refused. He says that now, after this open act of rebellion, it is impossible for him to appeal again. That the King is furious because one of the most important prisoners has been allowed to escape—there is a rumour that it was Prince James Francis himself—and that it would be madness to ask for any permission. Men who rebel against their lawful sovereign have no wives or children; they are outlaws without rights. That it is sad for those who love them, but that they must suffer, as they have made others suffer by causing so much blood to be shed."

"He said those cruel words?" said Frank, with his eyes flashing.

"Yes," said the captain sadly.

"Knowing what my poor mother suffers, and my despair?"

"He was angry, and spoke more hardly than he meant, my boy. There is another thing too; the Prince and his Majesty are not on friendly terms. I hear that they have quarrelled, and that they parted in great anger. Frank, you must wait and hope."

"Wait and hope—wait and hope!" said Frank bitterly. "Is that the way a son should seek to comfort his father, and try to save his life? Sit still, and do nothing but wait and hope! Oh, it is of no use! I cannot bear it. I will not stay chained up in this dreadful place. I cannot, I will not serve either the prince or king who would hurry my father to the block."

"Stop! Think what you are saying, boy. What rash thing are you going to do?"

"Rash? Nothing can be rash at such a time. I am going to try and save my father."

"Once more, boy—your mother, have you forgotten her ? "

" No," said the lad firmly ; " but I should be forgetting her if I made no effort, but sat still and let things drift."

Captain Murray sighed, and rose from his seat.

" Frank," he said gravely, " I never had a brother, but for years now your father seemed to fill a brother's place with me, and I tell you as a man that there is nothing I would not do to save his life. I am a simple soldier ; I know my duties well, and if the need arose I could go and face death with the rest, feeling that it was the right thing to do ; but I am not clever, I am no statesman—not one of those who can argue and fence—unless," he said bitterly, " it is with my sword. I looked upon you as a mere boy, but over this you are more the man than I. You master me. I cannot do more than defend myself. Still, I think I am advising you rightly when I beg and pray of you to do nothing rash. Don't take any step, I say once more, that will embitter the Prince against you. I will go now. Stay here for a while till you grow calmer, and then come to my quarters. I feel that I only irritate you, and must seem weak and cowardly to you. You will be better alone. I, too, shall be better alone. I want to try and think, and it is hard work this morning, for I am in terrible pain. One of my ribs was broken last night in that crowd, and at times I am sick and faint."

Frank heard his words, but did not seem to grasp them, and sat back in his seat with his chin resting upon his breast as the captain walked slowly away. Had he looked after him, he would have seen that twice over he stopped to lean for a few minutes against a tree.

But the boy neither looked up nor stirred. He sat for some time as if completely stunned, till he heard steps approaching, and then, with an impatient movement, he turned a little in his seat, so as to hide his face from whoever it was coming by.

The next moment a familiar voice said distinctly behind him :

" Don't look up—don't move or speak. Be at your father's house at four this afternoon, holding the door ajar till I slip in."

" Drew !" ejaculated Frank, in a sharp whisper, as he obeyed the order, thrilling the while as if with new life infused through his veins ; and his eyes followed the tall, slight figure of a jaunty-looking young man, dressed in the height of fashion, walking along as if proud of his bearing and the gold-headed, clouded cane he flourished as he promenaded the Park.

Drew Forbes, whose life would probably be forfeit in those wild times if he were recognised by either of the spies who haunted the Palace precincts—Drew, wearing no disguise, though changed in aspect by his hair being so closely cropped behind ! What his appearance might be face to face Frank could not tell.

CHAPTER XLIII.

A MEETING BETWEEN FRIENDS.

"' BE at your father's house at four this afternoon,
holding the door ajar till I slip in,'" said Frank,
repeating his old companion's words, trembling with
excitement the while, as he watched till the figure had
disappeared, when a feeling of resentment sent the hot
blood to his temples. "No. I will not go. It only
means more trouble. Oh, how much of it all is due to
him!"

"No," he said a few minutes later. "That is unjust.
He must have been with the people who attempted the
rescue last night. I will go. He is brave and true, after
all. Yes, it is to help again to save my father, and I will
be there."

It was like a fillip to him, and a few minutes after he
rose, and went back to the Palace, passing several officials
whom he knew, all saluting him in a kindly way, as if full
of sympathy, but not attempting to speak.

His goal was his mother's room, and to his surprise
he found her evidently anxiously expecting him, but very
calm and resigned in her manner.

"Frank dear," she said gently, "I feel as if it is almost
heartless of me to seem so, but I am better. I will not
despair, my own boy, for I feel so restful. It is as if
something told me that our prayers would be heard."

"And with him lying in irons in that dreadful gaol,"
thought Frank, with a momentary feeling of resentment—

momentary, for it passed away, and he sat with her, telling her, at her urgent prayer, of all the proceedings of the past night, as well as of his ill-success that morning.

He had prayed of her not to press him, but she insisted, and it was to find that, in place of sending her into a fit of despondent weeping, she spoke afterwards quite calmly.

"Yes," she said gently, as she raised his hand to her cheek and held it there; "all these things are the plans of men, kings, and princes, with their armies. But how insignificant it all seems compared with the greatness of the Power which rules all. Frank dearest, we cannot—we must not despair."

He looked at her wonderingly, and with his heart very sore; but somehow she seemed to influence him, the future did not look quite so solidly black as it had that morning, and he felt ready to tell her of his encounter with Drew. But fearing to raise her hopes unduly on so slender a basis he refrained, and stayed with her till the time was approaching for his visit to the house across the Park. Then he left her wondering at the feeling of lightness that came over him, and not attributing it to the fact that he had something to do—something which called his faculties into action to scheme and contrive the meeting without being baffled by those who dogged the steps of every one about the place.

Hope was inspiring him too again, and he refrained from going near Captain Murray, setting quite at nought all thought of his duties at the Palace, and waiting in his room watching the clock till he felt that it was time to go.

He sat for a few moments longer, trying to come to a conclusion which would be the better plan—to go carefully to the house after taking every precaution against being seen, or to go boldly without once looking back.

The latter was the plan he determined to adopt; but to throw dust in the eyes of any watcher, he placed a couple of books under one arm, and determined to bring three or four different ones back, so as to make it appear that he had been to change some works in his father's library.

Whether any spy was upon his track or no he could not tell, for, following out his plan, he went straight away to the house, thundered loudly at the door, and dragged at the bell.

The old housekeeper admitted him with her old precautions, and eagerly asked after her ladyship's health. Her next question, whether he had heard from Sir Robert, convinced the lad that, living her quiet, secluded life, she was in perfect ignorance of the stirring events of the past two or three weeks, and he refrained from enlightening her.

"Now, Berry," he said, "go down and stay there till I call you up again."

"Oh, my dear young master!" said the old woman, beginning to sob.

"Why, what's the matter, Berry?" he cried.

"Oh, my dear, my dear!" she sobbed, with her apron to her eyes; "it's glad I am to see you when you come, but I do wish you'd stay away."

"Stay away! Why?"

"Because it only means fresh trouble whenever you come over here. I don't care for myself a bit, my dear; but as soon as I see your bonny face, I begin to quake, for I know it means spies and soldiers coming after you and I expect to see you marched off to the Tower, and brought back with your head chopped off and put up along with the traitors. Don't do it, my dear; don't do it."

"Don't do what?" cried Frank impatiently.

"Don't go running dreadful risks, my dear, and meddling with such matters. Let 'em have which king they like, and quarrel and fight about it; but don't you have anything to do with it at all."

"And don't you try to interfere with matters you can't

understand, you dear old Berry," cried the lad, kissing her affectionately.

"Ah! that's like the dear little curly-headed boy who used to come and kiss me, and ask me to melt lumps of sugar in the wax candle to make him candy drops. I often think now, Master Frank, that you have forgotten your poor old nurse. Ah! I remember when you had the measles so badly, and your poor dear little face was red and dreadful——"

"Yes, yes, Berry; but I am so busy now. I expect some one to come."

"Not the soldiers, my dear?"

"No, no, no!"

"Nor those dreadful spies?"

"I hope not, Berry. You go down, please, at once, and wait till I call you up."

"Yes, my dear, yes," said the woman sadly. "You're master now poor dear Sir Robert is away. I'll go; but pray, pray be careful. It would kill me, my dear."

"Kill you?" cried Frank. "What would?"

"I should—yes, I would do that!—I should crawl somehow as far as the city to have one look at your poor dear head sticking on a spike, and then I should creep down a side street, and lay my head on a doorstep, and die."

"No, you shan't!" cried Frank, laughing in spite of his excitement, as he hurried the weeping old woman to the top of the basement stairs. "I'll come here properly, with my head upon my shoulders. There, there; go down and wait. I don't think anything will happen to-day to frighten you. Never mind; if any one comes I'll open the door."

"Oh, my dear, I can't let you do that," remonstrated the old woman. "What would my lady say?"

"That old Berry was a dear, good, obedient house-keeper, who always did what she was told."

"Ah!" sighed the old lady, with a piteous smile; "you always did coax and get the better of me, Master Frank; and many's the time I've made you ill by indulging you with pudding and cakes that you begged for. Yes, I'll go down, my dear; but I'll come the moment you call or ring."

Frank stood watching her till she reached the foot of the stairs, and then started and ran across the hall in his excitement, for a clock was striking, and he had hardly let down the chain and unfastened the door to hold it ajar, when there was a step outside, it was pushed open, and Drew Forbes glided in, and thrust it to.

"Frank, old lad!" he cried excitedly, as the chain was replaced; and he seized his companion by the shoulders, and shook him. "Oh, I am glad to see you again."

"And I you," cried the lad, as full of excitement.

"Hah! these are queer times. I am fit to touch now. Did you ever see such a miserable, dirty beggar as I was that day in the Park?"

"Don't talk about that, Drew," cried Frank; "come upstairs."

"Yes, we may as well sit down, for I'm nearly run off my legs. I say, did you get hurt in the crowd?"

"A little," said Frank eagerly. "Were you there?"

Drew did not reply till they were in the room on the first floor looking over the Park; and then he threw himself full length on one of the couches, while Frank closed and locked the door.

"Not laziness, old lad—fagged, and must rest when I can. Was I there? Of course I was. But oh, what a mess we made of it! Everything was well thought out; but you were too strong for us. We should have got them all away if they had not trapped us with the foot guards. Some soldier must have planned it all. Our fellows fought like lions till they began firing volleys and drove all before them with fixed bayonets. Poor dear old Frank! I am sorry for you."

"And I'm as sorry for you," said the boy sadly, as he pressed the thin, white, girlish hand which held his.

"Sorry for me ? " said Drew sharply.   "I'm all right."

"Then your father was not one of the prisoners ? " said Frank eagerly.

"Not with them ?   Didn't you see him there ? "

"No ; I only saw that two other gentlemen were in the carriage with my father.   I only had eyes for him."

"That's natural enough," said Drew ; "I hardly saw your father till we got them all out of the carriages, chained hand and foot.   Oh, what miserable, cowardly tyranny !   Gentlemen, prisoners of war, treated like thieves and murderers !   Poor fellows ! they could do nothing to help themselves."

"But you rescued one," said Frank.   "Is he safe ? "

"Safe as safe," cried Drew joyously.

"Ah !" said Frank with a sigh, "you are very loyal to your Prince."

"I don't know so much about that, old lad.   He does not turn out well."

"Not grateful to you all for saving him, while the others were recaptured and cast in gaol ! "

Drew sat up suddenly.

"I say, what are you talking about ? " he cried.

"About your rescuing and carrying off the Prince to safety."

"Nonsense !   He was safe enough before.   Didn't I say he does not turn out well ? "

"Yes ; but you rescued him last night : I heard it at the Palace this morning."

"Stuff !   He kept himself safe enough over the water without showing his face."

"Then who was it you saved ? "

"Who was it ?   Why, my dear old dad, of course.   We nearly lost him, for a great tall Guardsman had got hold of him by the fetter ring round his waist, only I made him let go. I hope I haven't killed him, Frank," added the lad between his teeth; "but I had a sword in my hand—and I used it."

"Oh, I am glad you have saved your father, Drew."

"And I am sorry we did not save yours, Frank. Perhaps if you had been helping us you might have done as I did, and he too might have been where your King's people couldn't touch him.

"There, I did not mean to say that," continued. Drew, after a short pause. "It isn't kind and straight to you. I won't reproach you, Franky; for I can't help feeling that you are, as father says, the soul of honour. He said I was to tell you how proud he felt that you were my best friend—we are friends still, Frank?"

"Of course."

"But I have said some nasty things to you, old lad."

"I can't remember things like that," said Frank sadly; "only that when you did not talk of the other side we were very jolly together."

"And I couldn't help it," said Drew earnestly.

"I know it."

"Well, I didn't come here to talk about that."

"No, it's all past. Let's talk about the future."

"Yes; how's dear Lady Gowan?"

"How can she be, Drew?" said Frank wearily.

The tears started to Drew's eyes, which filled, as he caught his friend's hands in his, and the next moment the big drops began trickling down.

"There," he said quietly, "I'm crying like a great girl. I can't help it when I think about her. I always was a weak, passionate, hysterical sort of fellow, Frank, and I'm worse than ever now with all this strain. But you tell her when you go back that there are some thousands of good men and true now in London who will not stop till they have saved dear Sir Robert, and the other brave leaders who are shut up in that wretched prison."

"Ah!" sighed Frank; "if they only could!"

"But we will," cried Drew excitedly.

"Well, your father is safe," said Frank bitterly. "I suppose he will leave the country now?"

"What, and forsake his friends?" cried Drew proudly. "You don't know my father yet. No; he says he will not stir till your father is safe; and we'll have them out yet, if we have to burn the prison first."

Frank looked at him wildly.

"But there are more ways of killing a cat than hanging it, lad," continued Drew with a laugh, as he dashed away the last of his hysterical tears. "I look a nice sort of a hero, don't I? But I came to tell you not to be down-hearted, for there are plenty of brains at work."

"And I must help!" cried Frank excitedly.

"No; you leave it to the older heads. I should like to help too; but my father says that I am to leave it to him. He has a plan. And now I am coming to what I came principally for."

"Then you have something else to say?"

"Yes. Is your mother still so very ill?"

"Yes, very."

"That is bad; but ill or no, she must make an effort."

"Oh, she is making every effort to get my father spared," cried Frank bitterly.

"I suppose so," said Drew. "But look here; your poor father is suffering horribly."

"As if I did not know that!" cried Frank.

"And my father says that Lady Gowan must get a permit to allow her to go and see him in prison."

"Yes, of course," cried Frank excitedly.

"Go back then now, and tell her to get leave; the Princess will—must get that for her. They can't refuse it."

"No, they dare not!" said Frank, whose pale face was now quivering with emotion.

" When would she go ? "

" As soon as possible—to-day if she could."

" To-morrow would be better," said Drew quietly. " She would go in her carriage, of course."

" Oh no ; she would go in one of the royal carriages— the one used by the ladies of honour."

" Of course. I did not see that."

" I shall go with her," said Frank.

" No ; she must go to him alone. You saw Sir Robert yesterday. My father thought of that. He said it would be better."

" I'll do anything he thinks best."

" Then go back now, and tell her to be calm, and to try all she can to be strong enough to see the Princess and get the permission."

" Yes, I'll go directly," said Frank. " But you ? I don't want you to run any risks."

" And I don't want to. May I stay here' till dark ? "

" Of course."

" Then call up your housekeeper, and tell her that I am to come and go here just as if I belonged to the place."

Frank hesitated for a moment, and then said, " Yes, of course."

" I'll tell you why, Frank, my lad," said Drew quickly. '' When your mother leaves the Palace to go to Newgate, she must call here first."

" Here first ! Why ? "

" To see me. I shall be here with a very important message from my father to yours. Tell Lady Gowan she must come, for it may mean the saving of your father's life."

" But——"

" Don't raise obstacles, lad," cried Drew angrily. " Is there anything so strange in her telling the servants to drive to her own house and calling here first ? "

" Then it is to take files and ropes," whispered Frank.

" It is to do nothing of the sort," said Drew sharply. " Such plans would be childish. Lady Gowan will not be asked to do anything to help her husband to escape. It can't be done that way, Frank. Now, then, you are man enough to think for her in this emergency. Tell her what to do, and she will cling to you and follow your advice. Will you do this ? "

" Will I do it ! " cried the lad. " Is there anything I would not do to spare her pain ? "

" That's good. Come here, and meet her afterwards."

" Yes, of course."

" Give her plenty of time first. Now ring for your old lady, and tell her I am to stay and do as I like. And, I say, Frank, I'm starving. I have eaten nothing to-day."

" Oh ! " ejaculated the lad. " Well, that will please her."

" I must have a key to come and go."

" You shall do what you please, only pray be careful. Don't get yourself arrested."

" Not if I can help it, lad. Now, be of good heart ; we shall save your father yet. It may not be till after his trial."

" His trial ? "

" Of course. They'll all be tried and condemned ; but we will have them away, and perhaps James Francis on the throne even yet."

Frank looked at him searchingly, when Drew lay down again, as if something was on his mind that he could not clearly grasp ; but he said nothing, and rang the bell, which was answered directly by the old housekeeper.

" Mrs. Berry," said Frank, " my friend here——"

" Mr. Andrew Forbes, sir, yes."

" Hi ! Hush ! What are you talking about ? " cried Drew, starting up angrily. " I'm not here, my good woman. Do you want to send me to prison ? "

"Oh dear me, oh dear me!" cried the poor woman excitedly. "What have I done now?"

"Nothing, nothing, Berry," said Frank hastily, "only it must not be known that Mr. Forbes is here. You must not mention his name again."

"Very well, sir," said the woman sadly; and she gave her young master a reproachful look.

"My friend will have the front-door key, and stay here or come and go as often as he likes."

"Very well, sir. You are master now," said the housekeeper sadly.

"He will be here to meet my mother, who will probably come over to-morrow."

"Oh, my dear Master Frank!" cried the woman, brightening up. "That is good news."

"So do all you can for my friend. He wants breakfast or lunch at once. He's faint and hungry."

"Oh, I'll get something ready directly, sir."

"And you will be silent and discreet, Berry."

"You may trust me, sir; and I'll do my best to make your friend comfortable. Will he sleep here to-night?"

"If he wishes, Berry."

"Certainly, sir;" and the housekeeper hurried away.

"That's right," said Drew quietly. "I don't think any one saw me come. Now you be off, and don't fail to send Lady Gowan to comfort your poor father in his distress."

They parted directly after, and Frank hurried back, and went straight to his mother's apartments.

CHAPTER XLIV

THE PRISON PASS.

"OH, my boy!" cried Lady Gowan, "how long you have been without coming to me."

Frank looked at her in surprise, as she rose from the couch on which she had been lying—dressed.

"Yes, yes, dear, I feel stronger now. Have you any news? Where have you been?"

"Home," said Frank, watching her intently. "I have seen Drew Forbes."

"Yes, yes; has he any news?"

"He has seen his father, and says that you are not to lose hope."

"All words, words!" sighed Lady Gowan, wringing her hands.

"And that it is your duty to go and see my father in prison."

"As if we needed to be told that," cried Lady Gowan scornfully. "I am going to him directly I can get permission."

"You are?" cried Frank excitedly.

"Of course. The Princess has been here to see me, and she has promised that if I am well enough I shall have an order to see your father in his prison to-morrow."

"Oh!" cried Frank excitedly, "that is good news. I had come to beg you to appeal to the Princess. Mother dearest, the Forbeses are our friends, but you must not speak about them to a soul."

"I, my boy?" cried Lady Gowan, clinging to him, and speaking passionately; "I can speak of no one—think of no one but your father now."

"But you must, mother. It is important. They have promised to help my father to escape."

"Frank!—no, no; it is impossible. Oh, my dear boy, you must not join in any plot. You must not—yes, yes, it is your duty to try and save his life, come what may," cried Lady Gowan.

"Hush, mother! Pray be calm," whispered Frank. "Now listen. You will not be asked to do anything but this."

"Yes, yes. What, dear?" she said, in a sharp whisper. "No: wait a moment."

She made an effort to regain her composure, and at last succeeded.

"Don't think ill of me, my boy," she said. "I wished to be—I have tried to be—loyal to those who have been our truest friends; but your father's life is at stake, and I can only think now of saving him. Speak out—tell me what they wish."

"I hardly know, mother; but they only ask this: that you convey an important message from Andrew's father to mine."

"Is that all?" sighed Lady Gowan.

"You must drive over to our house when you leave here to-morrow; go in, and you will find Drew waiting there."

"Drew Forbes waiting at our house?" said Lady Gowan in astonishment.

"Yes; he will have the message from his father for you to bear, and you must not fail, for it may mean the ruining of his hopes."

"I—I do not understand, my dear," sighed Lady Gowan; "but I will do anything now. I would die that I might save his life."

"But will you be able to go, mother? You are so weak."

"The thought that I shall see him and bear him news that may save his life will give me strength, Frank. Yes, I will go."

Frank felt astonished at the change which had come over her, and sat answering her questions about his proceedings on the previous night, for, in her thirst to know everything, she made him repeat himself again and again ; but he could not help noticing that all the while she was keenly on the alert, listening to every sound, and at last starting up as her attendant entered the room with a letter.

"Hah!" she cried, snatching it from the woman's hands.

"And the nurse says, my lady, may she come in now ? "

"No, no; I cannot see her. Go!" cried Lady Gowan imperiously ; and she tore open the letter, as the woman left the room. "Hah! See, see, Frank! It is an order signed by the King himself. With the Princess's dear love and condolence. Heaven bless her ! But oh ! Look ! "

Frank took the order and read it quickly.

It was for Lady Gowan, alone and unattended, to be admitted to the prisoner's cell for one hour only on the following day.

"I must write and appeal again, my boy. You must be with me."

"No, mother," said Frank sadly. "I was with my father last night. This visit should be for you alone."

She looked at him half resentfully, and then drew him to her breast.

Before he left her he once more drew from her the promise that she would fulfil the instructions he gave her, and call in Queen Anne Street, go up, see Drew Forbes, and take the message from his father.

"I don't understand it," said the lad to himself, as he left his mother's apartments; "but it must mean something respecting my father's prospects of escape—some instructions perhaps. Oh, everything must give way now to saving his life."

Then thinking and thinking till his brain began to swim, he went to his own room, feeling utterly exhausted, but unable to find rest.

In the morning he ran round, and found that the doctor was with his mother; and as the great physician came out he shook hands with the lad.

"Yes?" he said smiling; "you wish to know whether I think Lady Gowan will be able to go and pay that visit this afternoon? Most certainly. Her illness is principally from anxiety, and I have no hesitation in saying that she would be worse if I forbade her leaving her apartments. I will be here to see her in the evening after her return."

Frank entered his mother's room to find her wonderfully calm, but there was a peculiarly wild look of excitement in her eyes; and as the lad gazed inquiringly at her, she said softly:

"Have no fear, dear. I shall be strong enough to bear it. You will come, and see me start! The carriage will be here at two."

"And you will go round home first?" said Frank softly.

"Yes," she cried, with the excited look in her eyes seeming to grow more intense. "But, my boy, my boy, if I could only have you with me! Frank dear, we must save him. But do you think that these people can and will help him?"

"I feel sure, mother," replied Frank. "Take the message Drew brings to you, and see what my father says."

"Yes," she said thoughtfully. "I feel that they will help, for these people are staunch to each other. They helped the Pretender to escape."

"It was not the Pretender, mother," whispered Frank;

"it was Drew's father. And he has vowed that he will not leave England and seek safety until my father is safe."

"Then Heaven bless him!" cried Lady Gowan, passionately. "I had my doubts as to whether it would be wise to bear his message to your father, but I am contented now. Leave me, my dearest boy. I want strength to bear the interview this afternoon, and the doctor told me that, unless I rested till the last moment, I should not have enough to carry me through. But you will be here?"

"I will be here," he said tenderly; and once more they parted, Frank going across to Captain Murray, and telling him of his mother's visit.

"It is too much for her to bear," he said sadly. "Surely she has not the strength!"

"You don't know my mother's determination," said the boy proudly. "Oh yes, she will go."

"Heaven give her the fortitude to bear the shock!" muttered the captain. "Can I do anything—see her there?" he asked.

"No, no," said Frank hastily. "She must go alone. The carriage will take her and wait. But you; how is the side?"

"Oh, I have no time to think about a little pain, my boy. Frank, we are all trying what we can do by a petition to his Majesty. The colonel will present it when it is ready. He must—he shall show mercy this time; so cheer up, boy. No man in the army has so many friends as your father, and the King will see this by the names attached to our prayer."

But these words gave little encouragement, and Frank felt that in his heart he had more faith in some bold attempt made by his father's friends. He thought, moreover, from Drew's manner, that there must be something more in progress than he divined, and going back to his duties

—which he did or left undone without question now—he waited impatiently for the afternoon.

But never had the hours dragged along so slowly, and it seemed a complete day when, at a few minutes before two, he went round to his mother's apartments, and found one of the private carriages with the servants in plain liveries waiting at the door.

On ascending to his mother's room, he found her seated there, dressed almost wholly in black, and with a thick veil held in her hand. She was very pale and stern; but her face lit up as the boy crossed to her, and took her cold, damp hands in his.

"There," she said tenderly, "you see how calm I am."

"Yes; but if I could only go with you, mother!" he said.

"Yes; if you could only go with me, my boy! But it is impossible. No, not impossible, for you will be with me in spirit all the time. I take your love to your father—and—ah!"

Her eyes closed, and she seemed on the point of fainting, but, struggling desperately against the weakness, she mastered it and rose.

"Take me down to the carriage, Frank," she said firmly. "It is the waiting which makes me weak. Once in action, I shall go on to the end. You will be here to meet me on my return? It will be more than two hours—perhaps three. There, you see I am firm now."

He could not speak, and he felt her press heavily upon his arm, as he led her downstairs and handed her into the carriage.

Then for the first time a thought struck him.

"Mother," he whispered, as he leaned forward into the carriage. "You ought not to go alone. Some lady——"

"Hush! Not a word to weaken me now. I ought to go alone," she said firmly. "I could not take another there.

I could not bear her presence with me. It is better so. Tell the men to drive to Queen Anne Street first."

The door was closed sharply, he gave the servants their instructions, and then stood watching the carriage as it crossed the courtyard. But as it disappeared he felt that the excitement was more than he could bear, and, in place of going back to the Prince's antechamber, he hurried out into the Park, to try and cool his heated brain.

CHAPTER XLV.

THE walk in the cool air beneath the trees seemed to have the opposite effect to that intended, for the boy's head was burning, and his busy imagination kept on forming pictures of what had passed and was passing then. He saw his mother get out of the carriage at their own door, that weak, sorrow-bent form in black, and enter, the carriage waiting for her return. He followed her up the broad staircase into the half-darkened drawing-room, where Drew was waiting to give her the important message from his father.

"Yes," thought the boy; "it will be a letter of instructions what he is to do, for they have, I feel certain now, made some plan for his escape. But what?"

Then, with everything in his waking dream, he saw his mother descend and leave the house again, enter the carriage, the steps were rattled up, the door closed, and he followed it in imagination along the crowded streets to the dismal front of Newgate, where, with vivid clearness, he saw her enter the gloomy door and disappear.

"I can't bear it," he groaned, as he threw himself on the grass; "I can't bear it. I feel as if I shall go mad."

At last the hot, beating sensation in his head grew less painful, for the vivid pictures had ceased to form themselves as he mentally saw his mother enter the prison, and in a dull, heavy, despairing fashion he reclined there, waiting until fully two hours should have passed away before he attempted to return to his mother's apartment to await her return.

The time went slowly now, and he lay thinking of the meeting that must be taking place, till, feeling that if he lay longer there he should excite attention, he rose and walked slowly on, meaning to go right round the Park, carrying out his original intention of trying to grow calm.

He went slowly on, so as to pass the time, for he felt that it would be unbearable to go back to his mother's room, and perhaps have the nurse and maid fidgeting in and out.

The result was that he almost crept along thinking, but in a different strain, for there were no more vivid pictures, his brain from the reaction seeming drowsy and sluggish. Half unconscious now of the progress of time, he sauntered on till the sight of the back of their house roused the desire to go and see if Drew were still there ; and, hurrying now, he made his way round to the front, knocked, heard the chain put up, and as it was opened saw the old housekeeper peering out suspiciously.

The next minute he was in the hall, with the old woman looking at him anxiously.

" Did my mother come ? " he said hoarsely.

" Poor dear lady ! Yes, my dear, looking so bent and strange she could hardly speak to me ; and when she lifted her veil I was shocked to see how thin and pale she was."

" Yes, yes ; but did she go up and see——"

" Mr. Friend ? Yes, my dear, and stayed talking to him for quite half an hour before she came down. She did not ring first ; but I saw her from the window almost tottering, and leaning on the footman's arm. He had quite to help her into the carriage. Oh, my dear, is all this trouble never to have an end ? "

" Don't talk to me, Berry ; but please go down. I am

going up to see my friend. He is in the drawing-room, I suppose ? "

" Oh yes, my dear. He has been in and out when I have not known, and I heard him talking to himself last night. Poor young man ! he seems in trouble too."

" Yes, yes. Go down now," said Frank hastily ; and as the old woman descended, he sprang up the stairs, and turned the handle of the drawing-room door.

But it was locked.

He knocked sharply.

"Open the door," he said, with his lips to the keyhole. " It is I—Frank."

The key was turned, and he stepped in quickly, to stand numbed with surprise ; for Lady Gowan, looking ghastly white, stood before him, without bonnet or cloak.

" Well ? " she cried ; "tell me quick ! " and her voice sounded hoarse and strange.

" You here ! " stammered Frank. " Oh, I see. Oh, mother, mother, and you have been too ill to go."

" No, no. Don't question me," she said wildly. " I can't bear it. Only tell me, boy—the truth—the truth ! "

" You are ill," he cried. " Here, let me help you to the couch. Lie down, dear. The doctor must be fetched."

" Frank ! " she cried, "do you wish to drive me mad ? Don't keep it back. I am not ill. Your father ! Has he escaped ? "

It was some minutes before he could compel his mother to believe that he knew nothing, and grasped from her incoherent explanations that, when she had reached the house two hours before, she had come up to the drawing-room and found Drew impatiently waiting there.

He had then given her his father's message of hope for his dear friend's safety, and his assurance that a couple of thousand friends would save him. Moreover, the lad unfolded the plan they had made.

It was simple enough, and possible from its daring, for at the sight of the King's order the authorities of the prison would be off their guard.

Lady Gowan was to give up dress, bonnet, and cloak, furnish Drew with the royal mandate, leave him to complete the disguise by means of false hair, and thus play the part of the heart-broken, weeping wife.

Thus disguised, he was to go down to the carriage, be helped in, and driven to the prison. There he was to stay the full time, and in the interval to exchange dresses with the prisoner, who, cloaked and veiled, bent with suffering and grief, was to present himself at the door when the steps of the gaolers were heard, and suffer himself to be assisted back to the carriage and driven off.

"Yes, but then—then——" cried Frank wildly. "Oh, it is madness ; it could not succeed ! "

"Don't, don't say that, my boy," wailed Lady Gowan.

"I must, mother, I must," cried the boy passionately. "Why did he not confide in me ? I could have told him what I dared not tell you."

"Yes, yes, what ? " cried Lady Gowan. "Tell me now. I can—I will bear it."

"My poor father was fettered hand and foot. It was impossible for him to escape."

There was a painful silence, which was broken at last by Lady Gowan, who laid her hands with a deprecating gesture upon her son's breast.

"Don't blame me, Frank," she whispered. "I was in despair. I snatched at the proposal, thinking it might do some good, when my heart was yearning to be at your father's side. You cannot think what I suffered."

"Blame you ? " cried Frank. "Oh, how could I, mother ? But I must leave you now."

"Leave me ! At a time like this ? "

"Yes, you must bear it, mother. I will come back as soon as possible ; but Drew—the carriage ? Even if he succeeded in deceiving the gaolers and people, what has happened since?"

"Yes, you must go," said Lady Gowan, as she fought hard to be firm. "Go, get some news, my boy, and come back to me, even if it is to tell me the worst. Remember that I am in an agony of suspense that is killing me."

Frank hurried out, feeling as if it was all some terrible dream, and on reaching the street he directed his steps east, to make his way to the great prison. But he turned back before he had gone many yards.

"No," he thought; "everything must be over there, and I could not get any news. They would not listen to me."

He walked hurriedly along, turning into the Park, and another idea came to him: the royal stables, he would go and see if the carriage had returned. If it had, he could learn from the servants all that had occurred.

He broke into a run, and was three parts of the way back to the stable-yard, seeing nothing before him, when his progress was checked by a strong arm thrown across his chest.

"Don't stop me!" he shouted.—"You, Captain Murray!"

"Yes, I was in search of you. Have you heard?"

"Heard? Heard what?" panted the boy.

"Your father has escaped."

Frank turned sharply to dash off; but Captain Murray's strong hand grasped his arm.

"Stop!" he cried. "I cannot run after you; I'll walk fast. My side is bad."

"Don't stop me," cried Frank piteously.

"I must, boy. It is madness to be running about like this. Don't bring suspicion upon you, and get yourself arrested—and separated from your mother when she wants you most."

Andrew brings Sir Robert a disguise.

"Hah!" ejaculated Frank; and he fell into step with his father's old comrade.

"I will not ask you where you are going; but I suppose in search of your mother."

"Yes; she is at home."

"What? My poor boy! No. The news is now running through the Palace like wildfire. She went to visit your father in Newgate this afternoon, as you know. I don't wish to ask what complicity you had in the plot."

"None," cried Frank excitedly.

"I am glad of it, though anything was excusable for you at such a time. On reaching the prison she was supported in by the servants and gaolers. She stayed there nearly an hour, and, as the people there supposed, she was carried back to the carriage in a chair, half fainting."

"Ah!" ejaculated Frank, who was trembling in every limb.

"The servants say that the carriage was being driven back quickly by the shortest cuts, so as to avoid the main thoroughfares, when in one of the quiet streets by Soho three horsemen stopped the way, and seized the reins as the coachman drew up to avoid an accident. A carriage which had been following came up, and half a dozen men sprang from it—one from the box, two from behind, and the rest from inside. The footmen were hustled away, and threatened with drawn swords by four of the attacking party, while the others opened the door, as one of them says, to abduct Lady Gowan, but the other declares that it was a man in disguise who sprang out and then into the other carriage, which was driven off, all taking place quickly and before any alarm could be given. The startled men then came on to state what had occurred; but almost at the same time the tidings came from the prison that Lady Gowan remained behind, and that it was Sir Robert whom they had helped away."

"Oh!" groaned Frank, giddy with excitement. "Come faster, or I must run. She is dying to know. I must go and tell her he is safe."

"You cannot, you foolish boy," cried the captain, half angrily. "Do you suppose they would admit you to the prison now?"

"Prison!" cried Frank wildly. "Did I not tell you that she was close here—at our own house."

"What! When did you see her?"

"Not a quarter of an hour ago."

Captain Murray uttered a gasp.

"My poor lad!" he groaned. "Poor Rob—poor Lady Gowan! Then it is all a miserable concoction, Frank. He has not escaped."

"Yes, yes," cried the lad wildly. "You don't understand. It was Drew Forbes who went—my mother's cloak and veil."

"What! And your mother is safe at home?"

"Yes, yes," cried Frank. "Don't you see?"

The captain burst into a wild, strange laugh, and stood with his face white from agony and his hand pressed upon his side.

"Run," he whispered; "I am crippled. I can go no farther. Tell her at once. They will get him out of the country safely now. Oh, Frank boy, what glorious news!"

Frank hardly heard the last words, but dashed off to where he found his mother kneeling by the couch in the darkened room, her face buried in her hands.

But she heard his step, and sprang up, her face so ghastly that it frightened him as he shouted aloud:

"Safe, mother!—escaped!"

"Ah!" she cried, in a low, deep sigh full of thankfulness; and she fell upon her knees with her hands clasped together and her head bent low upon her breast, just as the clouds that had been hanging heavily all the day opened out; and where the shutters were partly thrown back a broad band of golden light shot into the room and bathed the kneeling figure offering up her prayer of thankfulness for her husband's life, while Frank knelt there by her side.

It was about an hour later, when mother and son were seated together, calm and pale after the terrible excitement, talking of their future—of what was to happen next, and what would be their punishment and that of the brave, high-spirited lad who was now a prisoner—that Berry tapped softly at the door.

"A letter, my lady," she said, "for Master Frank;" and as she came timidly forward, the old woman's eyes looked red and swollen with weeping.

"For me, Berry?" cried Frank wonderingly. "Why, nurse, you've been crying."

"I'm heart-broken, Master Frank, to see all this trouble."

"Then go and mend it," cried the lad excitedly. "The trouble's over. It's all right now."

"Ah! and may I bring your ladyship a dish of tay?"

"Yes, and quickly," said Frank tearing open the letter. "Mother!" he cried excitedly, "it's from Drew."

It was badly written, and in a wild strain of forced mirth.

"Just a line, countryman," he wrote. "This is to be delivered when all's over, and dear old Sir Robert is safe away. Tell my dear Lady Gowan I'm doing this as I would have done it for my own mother, and did not tell you because you're such a jealous old chap, and would have wanted to go yourself. I say, don't tell her this. I don't believe they'll do anything to me, because they'll look upon me as a boy, and I'm reckoning upon its being the grandest piece of fun I ever had. If they do chop me short off, I leave you my curse if you don't take down my head off the spike they'll stick it on, at the top of Temple Bar, out of spite because they could not get

Sir Robert's. Good-bye, old usurper worshipper. I can't help liking you, all the same. Try and get my sword, and wear it for the sake of crack-brained Drew."

"Poor old Drew!" groaned Frank, in a broken voice. "Oh, mother, I was not to let you see all this."

"Not see it?" said Lady Gowan softly; and her tears fell fast upon the letter, as she pressed it to her lips. "Yes, Frank, you would have done the same. But no; they will not—they dare not punish him. The whole nation would rise against those who took vengeance upon the brave act of the gallant boy."

That evening the problem of their future was partly solved by another letter brought by hand from the Palace. It was from the Princess, and very brief:

"I cannot blame you for what you have done, for my heart has been with you through all your trouble. At present you and your son must remain away. Some day I hope we shall meet again.

'Always your friend."

CHAPTER XLVI.

ABOUT a fortnight after the events related in the last chapter a little scene took place on board a fishing lugger, lying swinging to a buoy in one of the rocky coves of the Cornish coast. A small boat hung behind, in which, dimly seen in the gloom of a soft dark night, sat a sturdy-looking man, four others being seated in the lugger, ready to cast off and hoist the two sails, while, quite aft on the little piece of deck, beneath which there was a cabin, stood four figures in cloaks.

"All ready, master," said one of the men in a sing-song tone. "Tide's just right, and the wind's springing up. We ought to go."

"In one minute," said one of the gentlemen in cloaks; and then he turned to lay his hands upon the shoulders of the figure nearest to him: "Yes, we must get it over, Frank. Good-bye, God bless you, boy! We are thoroughly safe now; but I feel like a coward in escaping."

"No, Gowan," said the gentleman behind him. "We can do no more. If they are to be saved, our friends will do everything that can be done. Remember they wish us gone."

"Yes; but situated as I am it is mad to go. You have your son, thanks to the efforts of the Prince and Princess. I have to leave all behind. Frank boy, will you let me go alone ? will you not come with me, even if it is to be a wanderer in some distant land ?"

The departure of the lugger.

Frank uttered a half-strangled cry, and clung to his father's hands.

"Yes, father," he said, in a broken voice; "I cannot leave you. I'll go with you, and share your lot."

"God bless you, my boy!" cried the captain, folding him in his arms. "There," he said the next minute, in decisive tones, "we must be men. No; I only said that to try if you were my own true lad. Go back; your place is at your mother's side. Your career is marked out. I will not try to drag you from those who are your friends. The happy old days may come for us all again, when this miserable political struggling is at an end. Frank," he whispered, "who knows what is in the future for us all?" Then quite cheerfully: "Good-bye, lad. I'll write soon. Get back as quickly as you can. Say good-bye to Colonel Forbes and Drew."

"Good-bye—good-bye!" cried Frank quickly, as he shook hands, and then was hurried into the little boat, his father leaning over from the lugger to hold his hand till the last.

That last soon came, for the rope was slipped from the ring of the buoy as one of the sails was hoisted, the lugger careened as the canvas caught the wind, and the hands were suddenly snatched apart.

The second sail followed, and the lugger seemed to melt away into the gloom, as the boat softly rose and fell upon the black water fifty yards from the rocky shore.

"Good-bye!" came from out of the darkness, and again "Good-bye!" in the voices of Colonel Forbes and his son Drew.

Lastly, and very faintly heard, Sir Robert Gowan's voice floated over the heaving sea:

"*Au revoir!*"

History tells of the stern punishment meted out to the leaders of the rebellion—saving to Lord Nithsdale, who escaped, as Sir Robert had, in women's clothes—of the disastrous fights in Scotland, and the many condemned to death or sent as little better than slaves to the American colonies. But it does not tell how years after, at the earnest prayer of the gallant young officer in the Prince's favourite regiment, Sir Robert Gowan was recalled from exile to take his place in the army at a time when the old Pretender's cause was dead, and Drew Forbes and his father were distinguished officers in the service of the King of France.

THE END.

Printed by Hazell, Watson, & Viney, Ld., London and Aylesbury.